James C. Strouse

Galt Niederhoffer graduated from Harvard and started her own film production company in her twenties. She has produced ten movies, three of them Sundance Award–winners. She lives in New York City, where she grew up.

A
Taxonomy
of
Barnacles

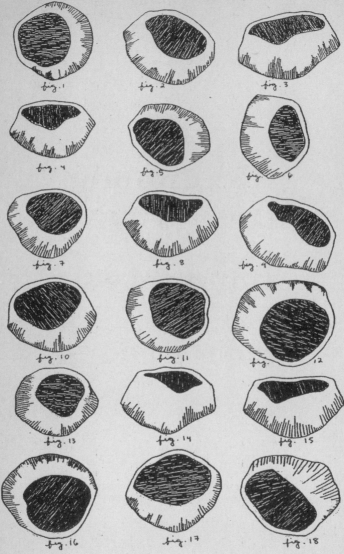

fig. 1   fig. 2   fig. 3

fig. 4   fig. 5   fig. 6

fig. 7   fig. 8   fig. 9

fig. 10   fig. 11   fig. 12

fig. 13   fig. 14   fig. 15

fig. 16   fig. 17   fig. 18

Galt Niederhoffer

A Taxonomy of Barnacles

Picador

St. Martin's Press

New York

www.picadorusa.com

Picador® is a U.S. registered trademark and is used by St. Martin's Press under license from Pan Books Limited.

For information on Picador Reading Group Guides, as well as ordering, please contact Picador.
Phone: 646-307-5629
Fax: 212-253-9627
E-mail: readinggroupguides@picadorusa.com

Design by Kathryn Parise
Illustrations by James C. Strouse

LIBRARY OF CONGRESS CATALOGING-IN-PUBLICATION DATA

Niederhoffer, Galt.
    A taxonomy of Barnacles / Galt Niederhoffer.
        p.   cm.
    ISBN-13: 978-0-312-42651-4
    ISBN-10: 0-312-42651-8
    1. Sisters—Fiction.   2. Apartment houses—Fiction.   3. Evolution (Biology)—Fiction.   4. Children of the rich—Fiction.   5. Fathers and daughters—Fiction.   6. Conflict of generations—Fiction.
    7. Inheritance and succession—Fiction.   8. Eccentrics and eccentricities—Fiction.   9. Fifth Avenue (New York, N.Y.)—Fiction.   I. Title.

PS3614.I355T39 2006
813'.6—dc22   2005050405

First published in the United States by St. Martin's Press

First Picador Edition: January 2007

10   9   8   7   6   5   4   3   2   1

For Mom and Dad

Contents

Part Two: Nurture
179

Acknowledgments

I owe a huge debt to my editor, Elizabeth Beier, and my agent, Joy Harris, for their perfect advice, elegant examples, and life-changing belief in me.

I am grateful to Alexia Paul for her endless patience, and to the following people for their time and encouragement: Dan Chiasson, Rashida Jones, Ben Wilcox, Isabel McDevitt, Daniela Lundbergh, Casey Thinnes, Celine Rattray, Gaella Gottwald, Walker Allen, Dana Wallach, Angela Wilcox, Sarah Bacon, Amy Larocca, Sophie di Sanctis, Alexia Landeau, Sam Lipsyte, Brad Watson, Lan Samantha Chang, Nicola Kraus, Galaxy Craze, Rosemary Mahoney, Claire Danes, and Lucinda Rosenfeld.

I am thankful to my family for their love and inspiration: Mom, Dad, Susan, Elaine, Katie, Rand, Victoria, Artemis, Kira, Magnolia, Rocket, and Lucky.

I could not have written this book without my darling Jim, who drew me a diagram of the outline in that restaurant in Porter Square and has helped me ever since.

Whilst this planet has gone cycling on . . . from so simple a beginning, endless forms most beautiful and most wonderful have . . . evolved.

—CHARLES DARWIN, *On the Origin of Species*

Part One

Nature

PROLOGUE

Heredity

*H*eredity works in mysterious ways but in the case of the Barnacle sisters, it was downright weird. All six of them were perfectly normal girls and their parents were anything but. Parent and child were so unalike as to seem like two different species. The Barnacles were Darwin's case in point, proof there is simply no way to predict how children will turn out.

Miraculously, most of the parents' worst traits had passed over the girls. Both parents had brown eyes. All the girls had blue. Barry was severely nearsighted. The girls had perfect vision. Bella's eyebrows were bushy and brown and furrowed even when she was in a good mood. The girls' were thin and arched in a way that made them look curious even when they were bored. Barry was plagued with insomnia. The girls enjoyed vivid dreams every night. Bella was tormented by depression. The girls were graceful and tall. There was simply no way, friends and neighbors whispered, to credit these parents with their girls' traits. Surely the girls were adopted. Perhaps they had been misplaced. Such drastic divergence took several centuries.

As though to invite still more gossip, the girls varied greatly among themselves. Benita, age ten, was a natural athlete; Beryl, thirteen, had a musical ear; Belinda, sixteen, could transform hand-me-downs into a stylish outfit; Beth, nineteen, was a science nerd; Bridget, twenty-five, boasted the best looks; and Bell, twenty-nine, though competent at many things, at the moment, could not remember a single one at which she was particularly good. Of all the girls, Bell varied most from her parents. Her IQ was higher, her laugh was louder, and, though neither parent boasted this trait, her legs were predisposed to flight. Never was a girl so tall and nimble, so bold and yet so very graceful, so skilled at hoisting herself from her window into the city night.

"Someday," her sister Bridget would warn her, "this window will be locked when you get back."

"Someday is not soon enough," Bell would scoff as she wriggled down the fire escape.

We're not related, Bridget would decide. And nurture would spit in nature's eye.

She was adopted, Bell would resolve. And nature would get the last laugh.

On one such night, Bell found herself in the throes of this age-old fistfight. Unable to sleep, Barry paced the halls. Plagued by anxiety, Bella stirred from bed to pour herself a drink. Unfortunately for Bell, Bella drank in the pantry, the window of which overlooked the fire escape. At the sight of her daughter, Bella raised her glass in a hearty toast. But Barry was far less forgiving. Hearing the creak of the metal grates, he rushed down the hall, rang for the elevator, and intercepted Bell on the sidewalk.

For a time, nurture took the lead in the Barnacle house. Bell adapted quickly to these constraints, selecting a different window and befriending the night doorman. But soon enough, the incumbent rallied against the favorite. The Barnacles' next-door neighbors jumped into the ring and the tussle turned into a fight.

The Finches and the Barnacles lived on the same floor but the two families had diverged drastically. The Finches were not Jewish, did not have six children, did not appreciate being Darwin's family of choice. The Finches' apartment did not have an indoor jungle, did not need whole rooms to display trophies, nor collections of conchs. The Finches' couches were not called "couches"; Mrs. Finch preferred the word "sofa." The Finches were not excluded from membership to New York's prestigious Colony Club; on the contrary, Mrs. Finch was its proud president. Mr. Finch was not known as Brooklyn's Pantyhose Prince; he was known as Dr. Finch. No books could be found in the Finches' kitchen. No forks could be found in their bedrooms. No one in the Finch family shared a room with his sister. And, of course, no girls marred the birth order of the Finches' two handsome sons, who boasted, in addition to their gender and good looks, the shocking perk of being identical twins.

Twins are, of course, heredity's favorite lab rats, unwitting test tubes for variation, walking displays of environment's force. But Billy and Blaine were less malleable than most. Even those who had known them since birth struggled to tell them apart. They often got headaches at the same time, ran fevers of the exact same degree, ordered the same salami-and-swiss sandwich for lunch, finished each other's sentences, honed the same tennis strokes, felt the same sadness when they were apart, even fancied the same girl. By the time they were teenagers, the boys had differed only slightly, Billy falling head over heels for Bridget while Blaine nursed a crush on Bell.

Barry Barnacle, of course, did his best to thwart love's progress. The twins were two large thorns in his side, two jabs at his virility, two monuments to nature's threat. From this moment on, he patrolled the halls with new vigilance. He scrutinized the boys as a scientist, watching for even the most minor distinctions, hopeful of stifling romance. Gradually, Barry's laboratory moved into his apartment. Friendship blossomed between the girls and the twins, the boys delighted by the auspicious boy-girl ratio and the girls happy to experiment with such attractive specimens. Throughout, Barry was resolute: the twins could be teased apart. Divergence need not dally so. Variation could be forced. So, it was with great joy and relief that he discovered his first batch of evidence when, on a routine patrol of the halls, he found Billy clambering up the fire escape without his twin in tow. For the first time, Barry checked his urge and allowed the teenagers their mischief. As far as he was concerned, this was cause to rejoice. Nurture had thrown a new punch.

1

Long Legs

*T*rot had just arrived at the Barnacles' when he was tackled to the ground. A large mass moving at a breakneck speed clipped him at the knees. He lunged to avoid what he thought was a dog, but tripped and landed on his side. Winded, he remained still for a moment, then stood up cautiously. The dog, Trot realized with some surprise, was not a dog but a man. The man was Bridget's father, Barry, rolling rapidly and, it seemed, dangerously into the living room.

"Pardon me," Barry said once he'd come to a full stop. He lay on his back, both arms outstretched, eyes scanning the ceiling as though for cracks. His odd choice of dress, red pants, yellow T-shirt, and a stained seersucker jacket contributed to Trot's confused sense that this was all part of some beloved family joke onto which he would soon be let in.

Trot stared curiously at Bridget's father.

Barry stared curiously at Trot.

"Doctor's orders," Barry said blithely, extending his hand toward the ceiling.

Assuming Barry wanted to shake his hand, Trot offered his in return.

"No," Barry scoffed. "Help me up."

Trot recoiled in embarrassment. Bridget glared at Trot impatiently and, before Trot had time to respond, extended a hand to her father and hoisted him to his feet.

Though his hip had been replaced three years ago in May, Barry still preferred this mode of transportation to more traditional ones. Finding his mobility severely compromised after the surgery, he had taken to rolling around the house whenever he was in a rush. Rolling, Barry found, diminished impact to his hip, enabled him to make dramatic entrances, and when necessary, disoriented guests who were already ill at ease in the Barnacle apartment. Barry rolled into rooms as he did most things in his life, without apology or awareness of its idiosyncrasy, as though rolling were one of many ways to enter a room, as though one might choose to walk, roll, or dance into a room depending on one's mood or the time of day.

No doubt, this willingness to choose an alternate path accounted for Barry's success. One did not get to be New York's Pantyhose Prince without a penchant for innovation. Indeed, Barry Barnacle clung to his business more feverishly than his products did his customers' thighs. (At times, he also seemed to cling to his customers' thighs as feverishly as his products.) But, like all great businessmen, he knew when to hold and when to sell. The same force that projected him across the living room floor propelled his course in life. After changing his name from Baranski to Barnacle, Barry catapulted from Brooklyn's Brighton Beach to Manhattan's garment district, where he quickly made his fortune and proceeded, at a tumble, to the Upper East Side.

Like many sons of immigrants, Barry worshipped at the altar of hard work. He lived in a world ordered only by the invincible logic of cause and effect. Of course to most, Barry's logic seemed quite illogical, compelling him to use socks as gloves, to wear the first two shoes he came across in his closet—even if both belonged on the same foot, to leave the house in clothes that betrayed not only his bad eyesight but perhaps early signs of color blindness, to mix plaids and stripes with such abandon that one could easily mistake his attire for a parody of a certain country club type, to eat so rapidly and with such neglect of his napkin that his daughters refused to dine with him, to retain such a heavy Brooklyn accent that "daughter" came out as "doowater," "mister" as "mistah," and "salt" as "soowalt." And, at the moment, to choose to roll into a room for a reason that made perfect sense to him while it seemed, to everyone in his vicinity, to have been designed for comic effect. All of these behaviors could be expected when Barry adhered to common sense. When he threw common sense out the window, Barry was indisputably eccentric.

"Hello, Bridge," Barry chirped once back on his feet with the jollity of a proper English gentleman.

"Hello, Dad," Bridget said. "You remember Trot."

Trot tried to seem as unfazed as Bridget by Barry's odd entrance.

"Of course," Barry said without making eye contact. "How's your painting going?"

"Not very well," Trot admitted and then, when he was sure Barry wasn't listening, he added, "Because I don't paint. I'm a writer."

Bridget turned to Trot and shrugged a quick apology.

Trot did not return the shrug. He only stared at Barry, smiling politely. Barry's black bushy eyebrows, Trot couldn't help but notice, would benefit from being clipped.

"Very good," Barry barked with more incongruous formality. He surveyed the room, glanced quickly at Trot, then turned to walk out of the living room, beckoning Bridget to follow. Before disappearing, Barry swiveled on his heels and looked expectantly at Trot.

Confused, Trot looked expectantly at Barry.

"Bridget?" Barry's eyebrows raised an inch.

"Christopher," she said, smiling apologetically.

Trot braced himself; Bridget only addressed him by his real name to reprimand him or deliver bad news.

She paused for a moment, as though he had failed to comply with a perfectly reasonable request. "Trot," she whispered, now irritated, "would you mind taking off your shoes?"

"Yes, of course. I mean, no. No, I wouldn't," Trot stammered. "I wouldn't mind one bit."

Bridget smiled gratefully and paused again. Trot stared back, still confused. Finally, realizing Barry required physical proof that his orders had been followed, Trot knelt down, removed his shoes, and displayed them to Barry for inspection while he stood in his socks. Satisfied, Barry nodded with an utter lack of emotion and headed from the living room down the hall with Bridget trailing behind. For the next several moments, Trot stood perfectly still, trying to decide whether standing or sitting was the more appropriate choice. Opting to stand, he noted that the room, due to its size and acoustics, was more a great room than a living room. The nearest hall, Trot decided, was more of a corridor. The nearest door was not a door but a potential for escape.

Early in March, Barry Barnacle had asked all six of his daughters to come home for Passover, which is to say he asked his ex-wife, Bella, to contact them and ominously summon them home. On receipt of this invitation, the girls sensed trouble. Barry was an atheist and never celebrated Passover. He only called all six girls together to inform them of an illness in the family, to dispense with cryptic information about the family's finances, and, once, to showcase a new invention of which he was especially proud. The girls, though they spoke and e-mailed frequently, had scattered across the eastern seaboard like a handful of tossed coins. Still, each one heard and heeded the call and planned her return to the Manhattan apartment, eager to surprise her beloved sisters with the length her hair had grown, the new music she'd acquired, and the number of boys she had kissed since the sisters were together last. The Barnacle sisters, though they pretended to grumble, liked nothing better than to put on ugly pajamas, cram into one of their twin beds, lie together like egg rolls, and stay up until four in the morning discussing the mysteries of life.

Bell, the eldest, was living in Brooklyn. She claimed she preferred to look at Manhattan than live in it. Lately, she'd been feeling strangely disoriented, as though she'd woken up on the wrong side of the bed, when, in point of fact, she had simply woken up in someone else's bed. Though no one had actually spoken to Bell, everyone was hopeful she would attend. Her sisters had left numerous messages on her answering machine. One had even reached a human voice, a room-mate who claimed, with understandable aggravation, that he only saw Bell on those rare occasions when she bothered to pay her share of the rent. Bridget lived in the West Village with Trot, her boyfriend of three years. Though Bridget routinely declined his proposals, her sisters felt it was fair to say Bridget was on a ring watch. Beth was at college in Massachusetts, studying rigorously. Belinda was at boarding school in a town near Beth, rigorously studying boys. Beryl and Benita, the youngest girls, still found boys insufferably boring, a sentiment for which Barry was duly grateful since both girls still lived at home.

Of all the girls, Bell was the most skeptical of her father. Since adolescence, she had filtered him through a sieve of sorts, evaluating his various notions with mixed curiosity and mistrust. Due to the degree to which she had been privy to her parents' divorce (and, as a result, her parents' worst qualities), she was far more irreverent than the others. Accordingly, she was wary of the general opinion that Barry was eccentric, believing instead that her father was borderline insane. She dismissed most of her father's claims out of hand, combating them with wild teenage logic while he, in turn, dismissed everything she held dear. Bridget was simply too busy to be bothered with her father. The most conventional of the bunch, she was instinctively embarrassed by Barry and learned early on that an arm's-length attitude kept him at a healthy distance. Beth, though she understood and, in some way, respected her father's imagination, was too preoccupied by her own peculiar thoughts to bother with her father's.

Belinda, hostile even before adolescence, sometimes seemed to go out of her way to antagonize her father. Even as a toddler, she bristled at her father's demands, rolling her eyes, shaking her head, and holding up her tiny palms defiantly. Beryl's thinking was too abstract to register much from the literal world. When she did, she considered her father with the vague pity of a fortune-teller. Benita, the youngest and, by all accounts, the most promising of the six, enjoyed the majority of her father's attention and aspirations. She was caught between two opposing forces; too impetuous to side with her sisters and way too eager for her father's praise to defy him. As a result, she catered to her father in a way her sisters found quite nauseating. They routinely and fairly singled her out, accusing her of being a goody-goody and a sympathizer.

As in all families with more than one daughter, fighting was a certain by-product of family gatherings, sometimes reaching such hysteria and volume as to cause concerned neighbors to call the police. But usually the girls restrained themselves to hair-pulling and scratching, only hitting and punching in extreme situations, such as when coveted clothes were stolen or important calls were poorly notated. Six girls in such close proximity were liable to sense each other's angst and were painfully susceptible to the same mood cycles, a casualty of science that caused the apartment to experience monthly fluctuations from homicidal rage to harmony. But for the most part, the girls got along, preferring each other's company to others, insulated by their family's size and singularity. In peacetime, the girls were even prone to sympathy pains, whereby one would sense when another was down and rally around the dejected party like a shepherd herding a lost sheep.

Instinctively, the Barnacle girls knew to keep boys from their family. They were wary of two possibilities: that the family would scare off the prospective suitor or that their wealth would entice him. The Barnacles' money and eccentricity made them more and less attractive respectively, causing visitors to experience the odd and improbable sensation of simultaneous repulsion and attraction. Trot's first visit three years ago was not an exception to this rule except for the fact that it was exceptionally bad. Of course, he had not done himself any favors by beating Benita at Ping-Pong. He felt he had no choice but play to win after he dropped the first game and the little brat laughed in his face when he attributed his poor play to a glare. The low point of the visit occurred at dinner when Bridget was caught in a series of lies about her so-called childhood friend and neighbor Billy Finch. As punishment, every time Billy's name was uttered, Trot reduced his contribution to conversation by one syllable. By the time dessert arrived, he had stopped speaking altogether.

At the moment, Trot stood alone in the living room, floundering more than fidgeting. He regretted, as he had suspected he would, his choice to pair a pale blue shirt with a brown corduroy jacket. The chaos of the Barnacle apartment made him wish he had worn white. The great room was literally breathtaking, its size augmented by the color of the walls. The walls were capped with George Washington molding painted a rich navy blue, a color that gave the room an underwater quality, a depth and certain resonating vibration that was reinforced by the odd acoustics of the space. A faint pulsing note filtered in through the walls as though someone were playing a piano nearby and repeatedly hitting middle C. Trot wondered idly if any of the room's bookshelves could be made to spin by pressing a button, perhaps revealing a secret room or an alternate exit.

Both the room's grandeur and its disrepair betrayed family history.

If the style of the room could be classified, it would be called Baroque Eclectic. It contained a hodgepodge of old opulence tempered with Bella's personal flourishes. Its decorator's determination to achieve elegance and individuality required flouting the rules of decor. For the walls, she avoided the forest green striae favored by so many Upper East Side ladies because, she claimed, green evoked the outdoors and made her feel itchy, as though she were at a garden party at twilight being attacked by mosquitoes. Whereas most women might have relegated bold patterns to one or two areas of the room, Bella rebelled against this mandate. She opted for patterns in all areas, coupling a wild swirling Persian rug with an equally dynamic floral chintz for the sofa, even though the two palates did not so much complement each other as challenge the other to a duel.

Paint, fabric, and artifacts in the room had weathered decidedly since their installation, betraying that the room had been assembled in one concerted flourish. The decorator's recent apathy was obvious even to the most amateur detective. A thick layer of dust added height to books already nudging at overhead shelves. Blue paint on the walls peeled sporadically like rivulets on a hiker's map. Patches of pink in the sofa's classic floral chintz put the original fabric to shame as misplaced cushions revealed the discrepancy between this pastel shade and the fabric's original deep red. The style of the room seemed outdated even for the staid Upper East Side, betraying a lack of awareness of trends toward minimalism.

And the books, the endless array of books. In most Upper East Side apartments books functioned as props, tucked neatly on shelves or atop coffee tables as a cumulative emblem of the erudition of the residents. But, in the Barnacles' apartment, books were used for their intended purpose and then several more still. Once familiarity made a book obsolete, it was reincarnated in a second life, finding a new home and raison d'être somewhere in the apartment. In all cases, a book's placement revealed its utility. A stack of Shakespeare's tragedies towered next to the living room sofa, usurping the place of a standing lamp. A pile of textbooks next to the television indicated a favored homework spot. An anthology of poetry tucked under the right foot of the dining room table served to level a slight imbalance in the furniture. In all cases, these books had accrued conveniently over years, taking on, like most things at the Barnacles', odd and unpredictable identities.

The room's topography was a study in time; each layer unveiling a different civilization, a new pile of books, a different stray shoe, another abandoned board game. A glass coffee table occupied an inordinate amount of space in the center of the room, its surface entirely obscured by a pastiche of objects. Clutter is, of course, common enough in a New York City apartment, a place where the needs of family exceed the resources of the metropolis. However, these objects were entirely uncommon. These were not coffee mugs, coasters, and stacked magazines, but rather dirty test tubes and stray conch shells. Though the apartment appeared normal

enough at first glance, upon closer study it betrayed a certain peculiarity. The sheer quantity of things and their incongruous nature
combined collectively to accost Trot with a tangible weight. This
excess and its seeming lack of organizing principle produced a tangible physical effect, a spinning sensation not unlike being trapped
on a broken carousel.

Dizziness turned quickly to disorientation when Trot approached
the mantel. A framed photograph peeked out from behind two
frames as though it had been intentionally hidden. The picture displayed Bridget, just five years younger, smiling gaily and holding
hands with an equally light-hearted boy. The boy was blessed with
the very features one pictured when one heard the word "fop."
Dressed in a blue blazer and a red and white polka-dotted bow tie
and smiling as though he had just been tapped for coronation, he
seemed to be suspended an inch above the ground, floating, Trot
could only imagine, on a cloud of divine entitlement. This was a
boy, Trot decided, who had been reared on a diet of buttercream
cake. This was a boy, Trot knew for sure, who had never worked a
day in his life. Furious, Trot snatched the picture frame and held it
up to his face. He knew the boy's identity without another clue.
The boy was Bridget's neighbor and alleged childhood friend, the
insidious Billy Finch.

The second and prettiest of the Barnacle sisters, Bridget was accustomed to using her eyes, which is to say, batting, rolling, and
lowering them in order to manipulate men. She had the kind of looks
that made gawkers of pedestrians, encouraging passersby to stop and
stare. Blessed with the Barnacles' uniform traits—limousine legs,
20/20 vision, and hearing more sensitive than some wolves'—Bridget was privileged with the knowledge that she could detect trouble
long before it arrived and that, once accosted, she could run, kick, or
dance her way out of it. The most extroverted of the six, Bridget as-
pired to be an actress. She saw New York as the stage of her own
slightly clichéd melodrama in which she was the heroine and everyone else served either to thwart or aid her happiness. Sometimes

Bridget failed to see her two-dimensionality and erred on the side of self-absorbed.

Despite her flaws, Bridget felt, she was far less flawed than her older sister Bell. As the firstborn, Bell was plagued with all the pitfalls of birth order. As the second child, Bridget was appealingly, if reactively, patient. Roommates since birth, the girls' differences were literally mapped in space. While Bell snuck out, Bridget stayed in. While Bell plundered, Bridget perfected. When Bell messed up, Bridget fixed her older sister's mistakes. If the first two Barnacle girls were any proof, siblings, not parents, shape character. Bell and Bridget's differences were reactions to each other, equal, opposite, and therefore alike. As a result, at least until recently, they considered themselves a pair of very dissimilar twins, a sentiment that allowed Bridget to excuse her flaws by claiming she had learned them from Bell.

Now, as Bridget returned to the living room, she prayed her sisters would help her cause. God forbid they betray the occasional lies she told Trot about Billy, such as that she had spent the day with her family when she had actually been with Billy, or that the phone number that appeared the most on her phone bill was not her grandmother's, as she claimed. To this end, Bridget had gone so far as to call ahead to request that her sisters corroborate her claims and hide any photographic evidence that could damage her case.

Trot waited until Bridget returned to his side to smile sarcastically, betraying, as intended, the exact opposite sentiment. Bridget countered with an overly theatrical sigh that Trot, in turn, amplified. Estranged, the two stood in awkward silence but for the sound of Trot's shuffling feet.

"Feet," said Bridget. She eyed Trot instructively.

"Mouth," said Trot.

Bridget inhaled slowly.

"Maybe if I looked more like Billy," Trot said, "you would be happier with me." Trot produced the framed picture and thrust it into Bridget's palm. "You look so happy with him," he said, shuffling his feet more audibly.

Bridget masked her horror with a trivializing shrug and, deciding silence was the best deflection, replaced the photograph on its shelf and tried to change the subject.

"Do you like this skirt? It's new," she said, spinning flirtatiously. The motion, combined with the color of her clothes, a fishtail skirt in a floral print that flared just below the knee and a delicate pale pink blouse, caused her to look like a top and Trot told her so.

"That's not very nice." Bridget pouted.

"You never put on a skirt when we go out," Trot said.

"I'm dressed up for Passover," Bridget barked and, giving up on Trot for the moment, emitted a soft, rueful sigh and deposited herself on the sofa.

Trot continued to stand in his place and scan the room nervously. "Does it look really bad that I didn't bring a gift?"

"No, it's fine." Bridget forced a smile.

"We're the only ones here," Trot pressed. "I told you we had time to buy flowers."

Bridget sighed wearily and closed her eyes as though to conjure the patience of a saint. "I asked you last night to bring a cake from the bakery."

"By the time you told me there were none left."

Bridget fixed her eyes to a spot on the wall just above Trot's head. "You work in a bakery, Trot," she said. "How hard can it be to get a cake?"

"Besides," Trot said, ignoring the dig, "a cake would have been inappropriate. Isn't the whole point of this thing about unleavened bread?"

Bridget said nothing, refusing to concede. She would not succumb to nastiness. At least, not until they got home.

"Are they going to call me Billy this time?" Trot asked, succumbing.

"Benita's known Billy since she was born. It doesn't mean she won't love you, too."

"I'll just keep quiet and let you two reminisce."

"We were teenagers," Bridget snapped.

"First love," Trot teased, "is such a magical time."

"You promised you wouldn't do this," Bridget scolded.

"You're right," said Trot. "Tell you what. I'll just sit and be quiet. When you need me to say something, nudge."

"You better be nice."

"He better be fat."

Bridget winced and composed her next retort, but before she could respond Benita invaded the living room.

"Bridgie!" Benita shouted.

"Benita!" Bridget cried. She braced herself as Benita jumped into her arms. But it was too late; Benita's weight surprised her. And so did the clumps of batter, sliced apples, and walnuts that were attached to Benita's dress before attaching themselves to Bridget's new blouse. Still, somehow, the little beast managed to look pretty. She wore the traditional party attire for girls under thirteen, a floral Liberty-print dress with capped sleeves and intricate smocking, white tights, and shiny black Mary Janes, as though camouflaging herself for warfare in the hopes that she might be underestimated by her enemy and mistaken for a sweet little girl.

The youngest of the Barnacle girls, Benita was the summary of her older sisters' best qualities. Benita, her father liked to brag, floated in a superior gene pool. Encouraged by Barry to excel at all things except for modesty, Benita, even more than most ten-year-olds, was a fire-breathing brat. Built for a roller derby and yet still graceful at ballet, she had an imposing presence. Mercifully, she was still too short to pass the height requirement at most amusement parks. Like her father, she was a disciple of Darwin, a fervent believer in competition who would, as her second-grade teacher had written on her report card, "chew glass to win." Of the six girls, she was both the most talented and the most driven and, as a result, the subject of constant teasing. Her sisters felt this hazing was necessary to counteract Benita's swelled head. A natural athlete and her father's favorite, she functioned as both daughter and a son. Accordingly, she felt it was only honest to abbreviate Benita to "Ben."

"Thank God you're here," Benita gushed. "The caterers canceled at the last minute so Bunny had to cook the entire meal." She stopped in order to simulate the gesture and sound effect of being gagged with a spoon. "Belinda dyed her hair green but we're not to mention it; Dad's been walking around naked again—he claims it helps his insomnia; still no word from Bell; Beryl's been missing for two days and—" Benita stopped speaking abruptly, turning to scrutinize Trot. "Wait a second," she said, "you're not Billy."

Bridget gasped.

Trot's eyes bulged.

Benita smiled demonically.

"You monster," Bridget said. "Apologize right now."

Benita batted her eyes demurely. "I'm sorry," she said. "Bridget's had so many boyfriends. Sometimes, I get them mixed up."

"No problem," Trot said cordially. He smiled and turned to Bridget. "I thought you said the youngest one was smart."

Bridget replaced her sister on the ground. Trot tapped the floor with his foot. His socked foot produced a slightly muffled tap not unlike a low drumroll. Though the sound was softer than the tap of his shoe, it was equally annoying to Bridget. Benita stared at Trot intently like a scientist at a specimen.

"I remember you," Benita announced. "I killed you in Ping-Pong."

"Actually," said Trot, "I believe I beat you."

"Impossible," said Benita.

Trot held his ground. "Three out of five. Twenty-one to ten, twenty-one to twelve, seventeen to twenty-one, nineteen to twenty-one, and twenty-one to eighteen."

"I doubt it," said Benita, squinting. "How do I know you didn't make those up?"

"Why should I trust your memory?" Trot countered. "You can't even remember my name."

Benita regarded Trot for another second, dispensed with her most outraged look, then turned on her heels, and disappeared down a long hallway.

"Benita, come back," Bridget bellowed but only heard angry foot-steps in response. Defeated, she followed after her sister but not before swiveling to glare at Trot.

Every time Trot proposed, Bridget delayed on a new technical-ity. Once, it was on the grounds that he did it wrong. He asked, or rather shouted it, when he was drunk. Once, she disqualified the proposal based on the absence of a ring. Another time, on the grounds that she deserved a better ring. To be fair, Trot had found it in a Cracker Jack box. But in general, when Trot proposed, Bridget referred to a distant deadline that moved at pace with time itself, like an eastbound car with the sun. When it came to proposals, Bridget was behaving a lot like a boy. And why not, she felt? Things had changed since Jane Austen's day. A girl need not rush into a loveless marriage in order to pay the rent. Nowadays, a girl could afford to be picky. Nowadays, Bridget firmly believed, a girl could take her sweet time.

Of course, there were other more emotional issues that under-scored Bridget's views on the institution. It wasn't that she didn't believe in Trot's writing. She loved every weird word he wrote. And she adored the way he looked, still found him devastatingly hand-some, his lanky walk impossibly sexy, his green eyes endearingly melancholy, his unkempt brown hair irresistibly rebellious, his bookish glasses the perfect foil to his cutting wit. She still noticed how his lips made the most adorable pucker whenever he formed the letter "o." But Bridget couldn't help yearning for certain minor luxuries, like a boyfriend who came home from work before two in the morning, or one who didn't need quite as much encouragement, or one who took her out to dinner more than once in a while, or, God forbid, acted slightly poised around her family. She loved the fact that he held the door for her, but did he have to hold it for everyone else? She didn't mind that he worked in a bakery but was it too much to ask, for God's sake, that he produce a cake on re-quest?

Trot took advantage of his solitude and wandered toward the

front door. Finding Trot missing on her return, Bridget guessed his hiding place and rushed to retrieve him, calling his name sharply as though he were a stray puppy. As expected, Trot had not wandered far. He stood in the foyer, organizing the umbrellas in the stand by color and height.

"Expecting rain?" Bridget asked snidely.

"One never knows," said Trot.

"Are you going somewhere?"

"I wish," said Trot.

Bridget shook her head like a put-upon princess, then stamped her foot like a child. "What in God's name are you doing out here?"

"Admiring the wallpaper," Trot tried.

Bridget rolled her eyes and pointed to the wall. The foyer was painted brown. "Don't you want to spend time with my family?" she asked.

"If it's all the same to you," Trot said politely, "I'm having a fine time out here."

"Thanks for being such a good sport," Bridget hissed.

"You're welcome," Trot said. "Believe it or not this is not my idea of a fun Friday night."

For some reason, this insult struck Bridget as previous ones had not. "Trot," she sighed. "It's not Friday yet. It's Thursday."

Humbled, Trot recalibrated, looking to the ground. "God," he sniffed haughtily, "why do you always have to be so technical?"

Bridget regarded her boyfriend with new disillusionment. Rational debate was impossible with Trot, not unlike trying to decide on the exact color of the sky with a color-blind person. Acknowledging its futility, Bridget changed her tack. She forced her voice to resemble sweetness. "Don't you want to see my sisters?" she asked.

Trot paused to consider this in earnest, then seemed to make a decision. "No," he said, "but they can find me out here if they want to challenge me to anything."

Bridget widened her eyes theatrically, then opened the front door.

Trot inhaled deeply, clenched his hands, and reluctantly followed Bridget inside. When they returned, two new sisters, Belinda and Beth, had congregated in the living room. Beth stared at Trot unapologetically, her arms folded across her chest. Still, Trot found her the warmest sister. Beth's scrutiny was, at the very least, evidence of her consideration. Just remain calm, he told himself. Children can smell fear.

Beth, nineteen and already a senior in college, was congratulated for looking impressively old. Born third, she was privy to the family's increasing novelty, her arrival bringing the family one girl closer to eligibility for a sideshow. As a result, Beth was blessed with a wry sense of humor and accordingly fixed her eyebrows into a permanent smirk. Her personality was so unique as to defy traditional adjectives. When called upon to describe her, one was tempted to invent words like "Beth-ism" or "Beth-like." It was Beth's idea, several years ago, to kidnap Benita and hold her ransom. It was Beth's idea to paint her mother's bedroom black when Bella claimed light depressed her. She even dressed for comic effect, wearing black, brown, and blue so as to resemble a bruise; she claimed this was the true state of her inner self. Still, despite Beth's fashion faux pas, her sisters were grateful she'd come. Beth's migraines acted up unless she took frequent naps and one such episode had threatened to preclude her attendance.

At the moment, Beth wore brown leggings, a dark blue sweater, and heavy black eyeliner, choosing Goth attire as an equal and opposite antidote to her sisters' insufferable girliness. All of this dark and baggy clothing functioned much like insect repellant, causing her sisters to shun Beth as a rule and to warn her routinely that she would grow up to be a lesbian. The prophecy had come true but only for a month during her sophomore year at college, when Beth dated a woman. She preferred not to be called a lesbian, deeming it an arcane and arbitrary category. She had fallen in love with a person, she claimed, not a gender. "Sexuality" was an obsolete word, as primitive and extinct as the dodo bird. And anyway, it was now a moot point since she and the girl were no longer speaking. With the phase in her past, Beth had receded back into ostensible asexuality, eschewing both boys and girls in favor of science textbooks.

An odd and introspective child, she had always confounded her sisters with her long silences, her strange attire, and, her sisters felt justified in saying, her more alarming than impressive array of creepy looks. The least social of the bunch, she had few friends throughout elementary school, even fewer in high school, and the ones she did have were, in her sisters' humble opinion, garden-variety geeks. Most of these geeks were female, though one could not always tell their gender by their odd, androgynous dress and their unanimous consensus that makeup was a worldwide conspiracy. But any debate on the subject of Beth's peculiarity was immediately quelled in adolescence when Beth's childhood love of animals turned into an unholy fascination. It was one thing, her sisters claimed, for a child to be attached to dogs, cats, and the odd guinea pig. But Beth's interest was far less innocent than most; it was downright morbid. Indeed, she had little interest in cuddling or cooing at furry animals, but rather in breeding, killing, and collecting the various species of the animal kingdom.

The obsession began as a passing interest in home-reared butterflies. Born in a box, these creatures had little hope of surviving in nature. They fared poorly when Beth tested their ability to fly by hurling them out her bedroom window. Discouraged but not dissuaded, Beth moved on to more mundane subjects, availing herself of Central Park's varied flora and fauna. Hours were spent teasing pollen from stamens, coaxing bees from blossom to bud, inserting tweezers and eyedroppers in anything that bore fruit. At age twelve, during a routine dig in the sandbox at the Seventy-second Street playground, she discovered an odd, unfamiliar worm and removed it from the sandbox to examine it more rigorously. Under the microscope, the worm revealed truly unusual properties, proving to be a new species of earthworm and earning Beth first place at the New York Regional Science Fair as well as the attention of the CIA. This discovery, combined with Beth's history-making ERB scores, gave her the option of attending college as an eighth-grader. But finding her research at home too promising, she deferred admission several years and devoted herself to a more concerted study of evolutionary biology.

But soon this presentable pastime blossomed a mutant leaf as Beth sought new subjects for her microscope. Worms, beetles, even kitchen cockroaches were all fair prey for her lens. All were hoarded and hacked up in a makeshift lab she created in her bedroom to the great distress of her roommate, Belinda. So it was with justified concern that the Barnacle girls witnessed Beth's first major abduction when she returned from a stroll in Central Park with two New York City pigeons. Like all fledgling scientists, Beth was torn between affection and curiosity. Finally, the latter won out, enabling her to stomach the gore required of truly stringent study. By high school, she had perfected the art of skeletonizing insects and mice along with dissection procedures usually reserved for college classrooms. With chilling detachment, she suffocated baby pigeons under large salad bowls, using both hands to contain their struggle, shuddering only slightly during their last seizures of life. Her sisters protested vocally, repulsed by Beth's morbid practices— Belinda in the form of her frequent claim that Beth should be hospitalized for mental illness and Beryl with more than one desperate call to the ASPCA.

The fourth girl, Belinda, was born belligerent. She was convinced her older sisters were guilty of diminishing valuable resources owed to her. Even at the age of sixteen, she resented the three girls born before her for sapping her wedding fund. Luckily, she learned during puberty to redirect her anger toward her father. In turn, she learned at boarding school to redirect this anger toward teenage boys. She also learned how to make bongs out of oranges, how to sneak out of her dormitory window wearing a skirt, how to cheat on exams without getting caught, and how to dress like a hippie while still retaining a timely consciousness of designer labels. Belinda loved to combine filthy-looking Tibetan prints and overpriced accessories bearing designer insignias. Sometimes, she would accent the whole dreadful ensemble with an unfortunate bright red scarf. Her latest egregious fashion faux pas occurred at the hairline. She had finally completed her transformation into the black, or in this case the green sheep of the family by shaving her head to a neat military buzz, then dyeing the remaining spikes a distinctive lime green.

At boarding school, Belinda had become highly evolved. During the fall semester, she had adopted a new language, a hodgepodge of slang and an affectation that resembled the Queen's English. Instead of "yes," Belinda now pursed her lips and said "mmm." She said "mates" instead of "sisters," "carry on" instead of "what's up?" She used "fancy" as a verb and said "quite" all the time, causing bland statements to sound more emphatic than they were and, sometimes, more interesting. She often ended declarations with questions as was the fashion in England, causing her to say, "It's awfully cold, isn't it?" instead of just, "It's awfully cold." This produced the illusion that Belinda had posed a thoughtful question when, in fact, regarding other people's opinions, Belinda could have cared less.

Unfortunately, Belinda had eschewed most of the traditional facets of boarding school life, namely attending class, completing homework, and competing on sports teams. With the exception of a fall semester commitment to the girls' junior varsity field hockey team, a concession made only due to the team uniform, a very attractive plaid skirt, Belinda had made a policy of abstaining from typical activities. She had, however, devoted herself to one pastime throughout: getting to know upperclassmen one dormitory at a time.

"So, what's the body count now?" asked Beth.

"A lady never tells," sniffed Belinda.

"What's his name?" Benita pressed.

"*Their* names, isn't it?" Belinda corrected.

"Their names," Beth said.

"Tom, Dick, Harry . . ." Belinda trailed off carelessly, applying this musing dreamy tone to imply she'd quite forgotten. "Harry," she added, "proposed over dinner. But I told him I would never marry before twenty-five. Besides which and far more importantly, dinner is so cliché. Isn't it?"

"No, it's not," Beth said, mistaking Belinda's rhetorical question for an actual one. "Dinner's not that bad. It's not as contrived as proposing on a ski lift or the banks of the Seine."

"The worst is without a ring," said Benita. "At least, that's what Bridget thinks."

Trot smiled hatefully at Bridget. Bridget, this time, did not so much as offer a shrug of apology.

Everyone disagreed on the merits of proposing in a girl's childhood bedroom.

"I think it's romantic," said Bridget.

"I think it's creepy," said Beth.

"Believe it or not, I agree with Beth," said Belinda. "The point of getting married is to escape your family, not crawl back into the womb."

The symbolic proposal, all the girls agreed, was more trouble than it was worth.

"Why do guys think they're suddenly transformed into poets when they propose?" Belinda said. "If you think you're a poet, write me a sonnet. Don't put a ring in my food."

"Talk about mixed metaphor," Bridget agreed. "If a guy ever tried that on me, I'd swallow it whole just to teach him."

"Ouch," said Beth.

"Ouch," agreed Belinda.

Benita joined her sisters in the act of imagining the digestion of such a snack and snickered knowingly.

"Or you could do what Mom and Dad did. I think that's romantic," said Beryl.

"Yeah," scoffed Belinda. "The perfect way to ensure your marriage ends in a bitter divorce."

Trot looked from sister to sister while the debate gained steam. As he did, he was reminded of the distinct sensation of playing Ping-Pong and losing. Attempting to quell this feeling, he opened his mouth to request further elaboration on the story of Bella and Barry's proposal, but a new and contentious thread of discussion was introduced before he could get in a word.

"I'd take a piece of twine any day to some obnoxious ring," said Beryl.

While Beryl was defied to defend this claim, a final method was introduced.

"The only thing worse," Beth agreed, "is a sporting event. Who wants to share life's most intimate moment with all of Yankee Stadium?"

Finally, the girls reached consensus. Every Barnacle lowered her head and murmured her assent.

"Mmm, quite," said Belinda, though it was anyone's guess to whom or what she was responding.

"If a guy ever asked me at a baseball game," said Bridget, "I'd dump him on the spot. It's tacky to turn something so private into a public spectacle."

"Worse than that," scoffed Beth, "it's totally distracting." She pumped the air with her fist. "Why don't guys understand the stadium is a sacred space?"

Bridget lowered her voice to indicate upcoming sensitive information. "I knew someone whose boyfriend proposed during the 'eighty-six World Series. So the Mets are down at the bottom of the ninth, and this girl is a big Mets fan, when all of the sudden, she looks up at the stadium screen and who should she see staring back but herself and her corny boyfriend."

"I assume she declined," Beth sniffed haughtily.

"Of course." Bridget pursed her lips. "He almost caused her to miss Garcia's game-winning throw."

"Honestly," said Beth. "Can you think of anything worse?"

"Actually, I can," said Belinda. She sealed her mouth mysteriously. "Without a doubt, the single worst way to propose is right after sex."

Bridget turned suddenly to Belinda. "And how would you know?"

Belinda offered Bridget her most innocent look, batting her eyelashes furiously, and effectively ending the debate.

Throughout this exchange, Trot avoided making eye contact with any of the girls and did his best to appear as though he were lost in his own thoughts. And yet he was painfully conscious of his observer. Benita stared unapologetically, leaning gradually closer to him as though honing in on a fly. Finally, a memory jolted her from her trance. "I played you left-handed," she announced. "I remember now. I played you left-handed," she repeated. "That's the only reason you won."

Already unnerved by the proposal debate, Trot prepared to respond to Benita with equal and opposite force. But before another dispute could erupt, Bridget inquired as to the state of their mother's mental health and all four sisters adjourned to a bedroom to discuss the matter in private, leaving Trot blessedly alone.

2

Well-Defined Lips

*A*gain, Trot felt and fought the urge to hide under the sofa. Anxious for some, any ally in this endeavor, he walked to the bookshelf that lined the living room and stared at its odd, incongruous contents: books peppered with large, lustrous seashells. Intrigued, he removed a spiral conch, then held it to his ear as though straining to hear advice. Fortunately, the doorbell rang, triggering both the traditional bell sound and a chorus of screams from deep within the apartment. Trot jumped at the opportunity to serve a purpose and rushed to open the door for arriving guests. For a moment, he feared he was seeing double, but he had no such luck. He quickly realized there were, in fact, two identical boys at the door with two identical, hideous, self-congratulatory grins. Bad qualities in the Finch twins, Trot decided, were not multiplied by two, but squared.

"New butler?" asked Blaine.

"Blaine," Billy scolded. He turned to Trot with disingenuous decorum. "Please forgive my brother," he said. "During his two-year marriage, his wife made all of his small talk for him."

"That's funny," Blaine quipped with a droll nod. "That was the very reason she supplied when she told me she wanted a divorce."

"Pleased to meet you," the boys said in unison. Both extended their hands at the same time, then, when they realized their tandem gesture, turned to one another, rolled their eyes, and dropped their hands to their sides with a unison slap.

"Don't mind us," Billy confided, "we're always doing eerie twin things. We say the same thing at the exact same time, crave the same foods, excel at the same subjects, we even have the same tennis game."

"Except Billy is hopeless to my killer backhand," said Blaine.

"And my serve is superior to Blaine's," said Billy.

"When we were younger," Blaine jumped in, as though to prove they also finished each other's sentences, "we even had crushes on the same girls. Once," Blaine paused to steal a devious glance, "we fell for a pair of sisters—"

"Just last night," Billy interrupted, anxious to silence his brother, "I was on the way to the phone to call Blaine, but it rang before I picked it up." Billy shook his head and shrugged. "It was Blaine calling me, of course."

"Ignore Billy," Blaine whispered. "He's prone to exaggeration. First off, his serve is extremely erratic. I was always the stronger student. And I fare much better with women." He paused and leaned in toward Trot like a football coach cementing a play. "I was born four minutes earlier. That's four minutes of critical oxygen." He flashed a vaudevillian smile. "So though we may look similar, in fact, we're polar opposites. I'm the one you want on your side. Billy's my evil twin."

Even without this glowing introduction, Trot recognized the twins immediately. He had seen Billy's picture on the mantel, was already on high alert, and the two boys were, of course, easily identifiable as identical twins. Out of habit and as a courtesy to confused strangers, the boys sported different baseball hats, Blaine's boasting the blue and white Yankees insignia and Billy's the more audacious white and red of the Sox. Both wore almost the same outfit: faded Levi's jeans dressed up with an oxford shirt—light pink for Blaine and faded gingham for Billy—and a Brooks Brothers blazer. Blaine, as though to distinguish himself from his brother, had completed his ensemble (Trot could barely believe the audacity) with a light yellow bow tie. Both had long, thick eyelashes that made them look impossibly sensitive. Both had full, well-defined, one could almost say womanly, lips. On both, their chipper demeanor registered as chilling smugness. On both, their careless good looks did not seem careless in the least. On both, their skin was translucent in the way that only regular ten-hour sleep affords. Clearly, Trot decided, neither boy had worked a day in his life.

Trot could already tell that he hated Billy. Billy was the reason words like "whiffenpoof" were coined, the type of guy who had both a favorite drink and a favorite toast, the type who could tell, by the spelling of your last name, where you summered and to which country club you belonged, if you belonged at all. Even his smug, anxious smile betrayed his insufferable entitlement. Blaine was equally reprehensible, but at least he came at it honestly. His bone structure, which was slightly sharper than Billy's, belied his clearly insidious intent; his eyes, a darker shade, hinted at the presence of inner plotting. His clothes were far less wrinkled than his brother's, tight in all the right places, and appeared to have been pressed moments before his arrival. Blaine seemed to try concertedly to counteract these subtleties, accenting the boys' shared rosy cheeks with a disingenuous saccharine smile.

"I'm Trot," Trot said. "Pleased to meet you." He extended his hand cautiously as though to allow the twins the choice of which one should shake it first.

"The pleasure is mine." Billy extended a hand. "We've been dying to meet Bridget's boy for a while."

Blaine extended his hand with considerably less enthusiasm and glanced at Trot, it truly seemed, to appraise his clothes. "I'm Billy," he lied and smiled smugly.

"Trot, ignore him," Billy jumped in. "I'm Billy. He's Blaine. If you ever get confused . . ." He tapped his cap with businesslike precision. "Blaine is foolishly a Yankees fan and I stand by the Sox."

Trot nodded and smiled weakly, doing his best to appear amused as opposed to alarmed.

The three young men stood in constipated silence until Billy suggested they adjourn to the living room. Trot was certain this was an aggressive act to assert his superior comfort in the Barnacles' apartment. But, determined not to lose any more footing, Trot attempted to steer the conversation back to familiar territory.

"So, what do you do?" he asked.

Now Billy took the stage, aware due to telepathy, it seemed, that Blaine could not be bothered to reply.

The boys had found a vocation, Billy explained, that provided the perfect arena for their telepathy, pairing up to codirect low-budget movies or, as they preferred to call them, "independent films." Their first collaboration, *Cents and Sensibility,* a modernization of the similarly named Jane Austen novel, earned them praise at a minor film festival, much attention from Hollywood agents, and a distinct low-level celebrity in the world of people who cared about these things. It also earned them brownie points with Bell and Bridget, who, age sixteen and twelve at the time, had played the roles of Marianne and Elinor. Arguably, it was during the filming of Marianne and Brandon's bedside scenes that Billy and Bridget's romance blossomed. But Bridget, when pressed to defend her compelling portrayal of a lovesick teenager, would always claim the experience ignited her passion for acting, not for Billy.

Before he could elaborate, Billy's favorite leading lady entered the room. Seeing the boys, Bridget slowed from a sprint and made a conscious effort to appear nonchalant.

"Hello, boys," she said casually. She turned from the group and inhaled deeply to disguise the act of catching her breath, then proceeded toward the Finch twins and greeted both with a sisterly hug.

Trot watched for evidence of unrequited love as Billy and Bridget embraced.

"Billy, it's been ages," Bridget said stiffly.

"Gosh, when was the last time?" Billy recited.

They hugged, Trot thought, quite familiarly and separated too quickly, as though both were conscious of seeming intimate and had choreographed the move in advance.

"Blaine, I'm so sorry," Bridget began.

"About what?" Blaine asked, genuinely confused.

"Your marriage," said Bridget.

"Oh, don't be," said Blaine. "I, for one, plan to celebrate its completion—that is, if I can still afford a drink." At this, he nodded down the hall as though beckoning a tardy servant. "Bridget, why don't you be a dear and go raid Mummy's cabinet?"

"Yes," said Billy, "I'll take the usual. But make it a little stronger today in honor of your high holy days."

"Here's to sugar on the strawberries," said Blaine.

"Here's to sugar on the strawberries," said Billy.

And both boys raised an imaginary glass in their favorite toast.

Billy chortled and pretended to choke. Blaine pretended to let him. Trot smiled politely as anger choked his veins.

No one knew the exact details of Blaine's divorce. What was known was relayed by Jorge, the senior doorman in the building. Jorge had overheard Mrs. Finch chatting in the elevator. After being kicked out by his wife, Blaine had moved back home in need of a month, or so he told his parents, to find a new apartment and to recover from the trauma of being married. Blaine's bride, Alice Appleton (of the Boston Appletons), was apparently quite relieved. A homely girl with embarrassingly large breasts, Alice Antonia Appleton had always taken great pride in her monogram and had therefore, in some way, dreaded the addition of Blaine's awkward "F." Still, her parents sanctioned the marriage, welcoming the chance for their daughter to shed her associations with the Catholic side of the family by joining forces with a full-blown WASP.

Still, it was unclear whether Alice or Blaine benefited more from the merger. Alice was a haughty society girl who was neither particularly pretty nor smart but managed to make the most of her unfortunate figure by running laps around the Central Park Reservoir as though it was a high school track. Blaine had the better name, but his family's wealth paled in comparison to the Appletons', his own family's fortune suffering the fate of so many, eroding gradually over the years much like the dunes of the beaches on which they summered. Despite her refinements, Alice was somewhat uncouth, partial to a certain obscure French perfume that made her smell slightly pungent. Blaine had managed to suffer through it nonetheless, acquiring an immunity to the scent while he developed an addiction to the life Alice's finances allowed. In a sense, the entire Appleton family filed for divorce from Blaine. They felt they were entitled to all Blaine's earnings not only because they'd paid for the wedding but because they'd paid for everything else since: the honeymoon, the car, the apartment, the weekend home. Accordingly, they encouraged their daughter, in the settlement, to take Blaine for all he was worth.

"So," said Trot, fishing desperately for a new topic of conversation. "I always wished I had a twin. It must have been a lot of fun."

"Pfft." Both boys simultaneously emitted dismissive sighs, then exchanged the same disdainful glance. Blaine bowed, signaling Billy to speak. Billy bowed, signaling Blaine. Again they spoke in unison.

"It ain't all," Blaine said.

"It's cracked up," said Billy.

"To be," they said in unison.

The boys glanced quickly at one another and exhaled large gusts of ennui. Once assured of Billy's silence, Blaine added, "It's overrated. Trust me."

Trot looked from one twin to the other, desperate to discern whether this was a performance. He glanced at Bridget as though for a life raft but she offered him nothing.

"Besides, we were always exempt," said Blaine, "from most of the fun to be had."

"Fun to be had?" asked Trot.

"You know, all the really good tricks . . . convincing people they're seeing double, trading places, switcheroos."

"Switcheroos?" Trot asked.

Blaine ignored the question. "We really were quite tame. Occasionally, we'd order the same thing at lunch just to spook people out."

"Except that's not a good example," Billy conceded, "because we always order the same thing. Salami and swiss."

"On rye," Blaine finished.

Trot looked on helplessly. For the third time, his senses switched into the appropriate mode for a fast-paced game of Ping-Pong.

"If you look closely, it's quite obvious," said Billy. "We really look nothing alike."

"We're as different as two people can be," Blaine said. "Only technically identical."

This last statement, Trot decided, was simply untrue. In fact, as he stared at the twins, he had the distinct impression that the same moment was occurring twice. Even from this distance, the twins were dead ringers, similar to the dot, completely interchangeable were it not for their baseball caps. If they took their caps off, Trot decided, they would be wholly indistinguishable. Indeed, widespread confusion would result. Trot would likely call one by the other's name, perhaps even confide in Billy while actually talking to Blaine. But, Trot considered hopefully, perhaps their hair was slightly different under their caps. Blaine, Trot imagined, had calculated hair, messy in a purposeful way. Billy's was probably more haphazard, his easy curls gently tousled like a plump cherub.

But other than their baseball caps, the boys were ostensibly machine-made clones, except for when they were silent, which, of course, was rare. During lulls in conversation, the twins' mouths fell from their deplorable little smirks to reveal a new discrepancy. Billy's mouth settled into a relaxed grin while Blaine's hardened into a pursed little pout that made him look, at least compared to Billy, decidedly mean-spirited. If you were to make the claim that there was any real difference between the boys, you could only argue that they were related species, one nasty, one nice. Of course, there were those who had no need for such trivial means of distinction. Charles, the dog named for Barry's hero, could tell the twins apart by scent alone. As a result, he treated the boys very differently, greeting Billy with adoring licks and Blaine with a suspicious growl.

Bridget, though she would never admit it, was also availed of such a sixth sense when it came to the twins. She could tell the difference between the two by sheer instinct or, more specifically, by the way she felt in their presence. When Blaine was near, she felt nothing at all, light irritation if anything, as though he were a pesky younger brother or an uncle that no one liked. But when Billy was near, she felt the threat of clumsiness in her feet, a certain quickness in her heart, a distinct tingle somewhere around her heart. She felt younger, lighter, happier, if that was possible, as though the world had just been cleansed of its dust to reveal a new sparkling luster, as though something fun and wonderful could occur at any moment, that adventure was in store even in the most boring places as long as he was near. Indeed, when Billy was in the room, Bridget felt decidedly unnerved, as though a thousand moths had launched inside her stomach. And when Billy touched her hand, Bridget was down for the count. There was no denying she felt a galvanizing thrill.

"Blaine is right about that," Billy insisted. "We're really nothing alike. I love chocolate. He likes vanilla."

"I like the sunrise. He prefers the sunset," said Blaine.

"I like Paris," said Billy. "He loves the south of France."

"I like blondes. He prefers brunettes."

"Blaine could sleep through a tornado," said Billy.

"And a light breeze will wake me up."

Trot eyed the boys skeptically. They grew more inscrutable with every minute. It was impossible to tell if they were being condescending or just plain chipper.

Sensing Trot's discomfort, Bridget finally intervened. She touched his arm in a manner that betrayed more control than intimacy. "Trot, don't listen to a word they say. These two practically share a heartbeat. Sometimes, when we were growing up, we would spend whole weeks in the dark. Billy once took an exam for Blaine. Blaine broke up with a girlfriend for Billy. For a whole month, Billy practiced the piano twice every night. Luckily, Charlie here came to our aid." Bridget patted the invalid dog. "Charlie can tell the difference," she said. "Isn't that right, old boy?"

Charles looked up at Bridget and thumped his tail against the floor.

"Charlie, show them," said Bridget. She smiled proudly like a magician preparing to perform a trick. "Where's Blaine?" she asked the dog.

Charles remained impassive. He placed his head on his paws and sighed dejectedly.

"Okay. Now, where's Billy?" said Bridget.

Suddenly, Charles twitched to attention. He wagged his tail enthusiastically, creating a drumroll on the floor. Then, managing to rise, he hobbled to Billy and nudged him with his snout, proving his understanding of the English language and his undying love for Billy.

"See," said Bridget. She beamed proudly at Charles and leaned down to pat his back. "Had I known this as a child," she said, glaring at Billy, "it would have saved me a lot of trouble."

"Don't listen to Bridget," said Blaine.

"She's full of it," agreed Billy.

"I would take our side," Blaine advised. "There's only one of her."

Bridget regarded the boys skeptically, like a parent deciding on punishment. "In your defense, I will say this: Any girl stupid enough to be fooled by you two probably deserved it."

Billy chortled, then covered his mouth as though Bridget had accidentally stumbled onto a great truth.

Bridget looked quickly from Billy to Blaine.

Blaine shrugged and looked to Billy.

Billy smiled, then pantomimed the act of zippering his mouth.

"Oh, don't you even imply . . ." said Bridget.

Billy narrowed his eyes at Bridget. Bridget narrowed her eyes at Billy. Their intense focus on each other, Trot decided, was not unlike that of lovers.

"I would definitely know," Bridget said, "if you two ever tried that on me."

"Oh really?" asked Billy. "Are you sure about that?"

"Quite," Bridget insisted.

"And how would you know?"

"Because," Bridget said, "there's nothing in the world that can reproduce the way a woman feels in a man's presence. No one can manufacture the turn in her stomach, the dryness in her throat, the heaviness in her feet, or the thrill in her heart."

Bridget held Billy's gaze for a long moment, indicating a personal address. Billy gazed back fondly, acknowledging and doubling the sentiment. Finally, Trot manufactured a cough, breaking their trance. Was it possible he had just witnessed an act of courtship between his girlfriend and another man?

"Anyway," Blaine said, "here's a foolproof tip if you ever get confused. Billy prefers to support underdogs, whereas I wisely put my money on the obvious winner." He paused to tip his Yankees cap.

"If it weren't for these caps," Billy concurred, "no one would even know we were brothers. You and I," he said, gesturing at Trot, "look much more alike."

Trot gave the boys another glance and shifted uncomfortably. Easily, the most insufferable facet of Billy was his taste in baseball. Billy's loyalty to the team was clearly founded in a lingering nostalgia for his Harvard days. Even worse, he used the affiliation to convey a specific persona, as proof of his masculinity, evidence of his compassion for the handicapped, and testament to his camaraderie with the working class. He had perfected this affectation to such an extent that he had come to forget it was an affectation in the first place and now counted himself among the team's most diehard fans.

During college, Billy had little interest in the team. But the day he graduated, he sprouted an obsessive loyalty and began watching or listening to every game during the season and collecting statistics with the rabidity of a bookie during the winter months. When he wasn't appraising team standings, he was engaged in his own analysis of the league, discussing minutiae with anyone who would listen: his brother, cab drivers, even the Barnacle girls. He had come to find sportscasts so comforting he needed them to fall asleep. He had come to consider the opening day of the season a national holiday. He preferred not to bring dates to games lest his companion attempt to distract him too much. Billy might as well have worn the Red Sox white and red uniform instead of his khaki pants and oxford shirt. His affiliation with the team was as much a part of his identity as the fact that he was a twin. The fact that his twin loved the Yankees only cemented the fervor of his love.

In Trot's opinion, Billy's alliance with the Red Sox was clearly a put-on, a blunt attempt to confuse his critics and their wholly justi- fied claim that Billy was an incorrigible snob. To be sure, Yankees fans were repugnant in their own specific way, bankers and blue- bloods who had seen victory too many times to appreciate its sweet- ness. A true Red Sox fan, in Trot's opinion, was an irreproachable soul, tirelessly optimistic, meticulously scientific, and endearingly unflappable. But Billy was a far cry from a true Red Sox fan. Billy's love was so false that Trot had to wonder if Billy himself had cursed the team, causing the long, and recently broken, hex so often attrib- uted to Babe Ruth. Despite his own affection for the Sox, Trot faced a difficult decision. If only out of principle, he had no choice but to root for another team.

Trot looked to the ground in an effort to obscure his growing ha- tred. He was about to inquire further into the nature of a "switcheroo" but Benita reentered before he could, causing him to stiffen the mus- cles in his chest as though bracing for the approach of a hurled object.

His mind shifted gears to fight-or-flight mode. He would need all of his senses.

Benita spotted Billy and shrieked, then ran at him at full speed, tackling him to the ground with the force of her delight.

"Benita." Billy struggled to stand up. When he was back on his feet, he addressed her with, Trot thought, sickening sweetness. "Darling, life has simply been hell without you. Promise me you haven't fallen for another man."

Benita swooned and promised she hadn't and would never in a million years.

Trot waited until he caught Bridget's eye to mouth a statement he'd waited minutes to share. He squinted with all the venom he could muster and whispered, "He isn't fat."

Bridget pretended not to comprehend Trot's import and gestured for him to follow her to the piano. Everyone would benefit, she decided, from a change of scenery.

The grand piano floated in the middle of the living room like a great beached whale. A young teenage boy sat on the bench, sporadically playing and seeming to ponder the sound of middle C. Every few seconds, he leaned over the piano and turned his ear toward the keys as though someone were trapped inside, whispering faintly. The boy's hair had been teased into a matte globe whose surface area easily exceeded his head. His smooth, dark brown skin somehow caused his ample baby fat to appear taut and muscular. His T-shirt bore an intricate replica of the Milky Way, or so Trot thought until closer inspection, when it revealed that its complex network of stars was, in fact, dried whipped cream. The boy's gentle demeanor and disheveled state comforted Trot immensely. Trot was equally relieved to comprehend the source of the apartment's baffling pulsating note. He redoubled his efforts at a positive attitude. Perhaps this world was not unruly, but simply had its own rules.

"Trot, you remember Latrell," Bridget said. She motioned for Trot to sit on the piano bench with a bossy flick of the wrist.

Trot smiled and extended his hand, relieved to be in the presence finally of hospitable male company.

Latrell said nothing, only examined Trot's eyes, and nodded slightly. The salutation was so subtle and begrudging that Trot had trouble discerning whether Latrell had, in fact, nodded or merely shifted to scratch an itch. Lacking further proof of their alliance, Trot stood, staring for a moment. The boy's round face, his beatific smile, his kinky hair, and sizable paunch made him look something like an overweight angel. A thin film of grime on his face further contributed to his beatific glow, bestowing a rugged shine that betrayed his deep aversion to taking showers. His adopted sisters enjoyed teasing Latrell about this; like most teenage boys, he took a secret, perverse pleasure in the scent of his own armpits.

His gaze betrayed kindness and distance at once, a detachment from his surroundings more fitting of an older teen. His eyes, which scanned Trot mechanically, conveyed an odd mixture of wonder and fatigue. Following Latrell's hand to the piano keys, Trot noticed a peculiar birthmark, a long, curling shape with darker pigmentation than the rest of Latrell's hand that resembled, from this angle, the musical notation of a treble cleft. The mark was among Latrell's favorite things about himself. Since he was very young, he had been told that he shared the mark with his biological father. As a result, when they found each other, recognition would be mutual and immediate. The birthmark would function like a broken locket, proving their genetic and emotional bond the moment the two were reunited.

"Latrell, you remember Trot," Bridget said.

Latrell offered a grudging assent and, for perhaps the first time in hours, Bridget relaxed her face to a smile.

Latrell was not technically a Barnacle, but he still used the surname. Bella gave him her married name in part because his adoption papers were completed before her divorce and in part to spite her ex-husband. Sadly, after twenty years, Barry and Bella had parted ways, acknowledging their opposing views on nature and nurture amounted to irreconcilable differences. For years, they divided on these lines, engaging in Barry's favorite debate, fighting for their sides with the same fervor with which other couples discussed politics. Bella was a card-carrying believer in nature while Barry supported nurture to the end. Bella, who had been a beautiful and tempestuous girl, knew nature was a blessing and a curse. Hers arrived like clockwork on the first Thursday of the month. But Barry's moon had no such pull; he had a stronger centrifugal force. Born to immigrants, he was, since birth, subject to the force of hard work. He simply could not imagine an environment in which he could not improve.

Sadly, Barry and Bella parted ways before Barry found his best evidence. By the time they divorced, Barry had succeeded in instilling new traits in Bella. He taught her paranoia by seducing Bunny a month after Beryl was born. He ingrained patience by subjecting Bella to a long covert affair; spite by marrying Bunny less than a week after they divorced; resourcefulness, or so it seemed when Bella demanded, in the settlement, that Barry buy her the apartment upstairs and pay for her renovations. Arguably, Barry even had a hand in Bella's alcoholism and depression. And his tenacity seemed to have rubbed off on Bella when, upon receipt of the title to her real estate, she gutted her new apartment, drilled a hole in her floor, and built a connecting spiral staircase to afford her easy access to her girls. Still, one could never know for sure whether Bella's taste for revenge was innate or learned. The night before Bunny moved in, Bella called her local grocer for a special delivery, then snuck into the apartment and hid twenty-four individual sardines in beds, sofas, and bookshelves, one for every year of her marriage.

And yet, the most striking proof of Barry's influence on Bella was her decision to adopt. Frustrated by her marriage, she turned her attention to the beautification of the Bronx, picking an organization at random to which to devote her time. She found a worthy venue in the yellow pages and took a volunteer position in a shelter for teenage runaways. For a while, this pastime provided the perfect antidote to her torpor. An adopted child, Bella quickly realized, was, after twins, Barry's ultimate subject. An adopted son, she therefore decided, was the perfect revenge. Enthused, Bella chose the runaway whose eyes revealed the most loneliness and, without asking her daughters' opinion, went to volunteer one morning and returned with a ten-year-old boy that night. She parented Latrell fiercely if not perfectly, privileging him with slightly favored treatment. He might as well have been a new Jaguar. To Bella, he was a trophy and a prize.

Trot and Latrell's conversation was interrupted by the return of three Barnacle sisters. As he scanned them, Trot struggled to discern whether these were entirely new sisters or simply the same sisters after a change of clothes. Each girl, Trot noted, caused the air quality in the room to change. It was not unlike being in an airplane and ascending into the atmosphere.

"Lovely, isn't it?" said Belinda.

Confused by Belinda's odd syntax, Trot fumbled for an appropriate response. "Nice hair," he stammered. And he meant it genuinely, but Belinda mistook his sincerity for sarcasm and responded with a chilled smile.

Anxious to spare Trot further discomfort, Bridget struggled to change the subject. "So, what's the word on Bell?" she asked.

At this, all sisters heaved a collective sigh and assumed a look of exhausted expertise.

"She's not coming," said Belinda. "I got an e-mail. She said she loves us but she needs to disown us for a while."

"Wrong," said Beth. "I spoke to her and she said she'd be here."

"She's just in a bad mood because she got fired," Benita suggested.

"Shut up," said Belinda. "She's had it with men so she's boycotting them for a while."

Bridget sighed with genuine concern as a new debate commenced. Her older sister was younger in so many ways.

"Anyway, she's to be ignored. I bet you she'll come," said Beth.

"Wanna bet?" asked Belinda.

"Fine," said Beth.

They cemented the transaction with a hateful sneer.

Bridget looked at Trot and, for the first time all night, imagined things from his perspective. Surveying the room from his vantage point, things seemed uncomfortably bizarre. Why were there so many paintings on the floor? What caused the wallpaper to bubble up in patches? How had the sofas' floral chintz come to resemble a thicket of wild thorns? Finally and more importantly where, in God's name, was Beryl?

"Missing," sighed Beth.

"Seriously?" asked Bridget.

"Ever since Bunny started cooking," Belinda corroborated.

"She feels Bunny's become too Zionist," Beth whispered. "Beryl's a vegetarian now."

"It's blatantly obvious, isn't it?" said Belinda.

"You mean patently obvious," sneered Beth.

Bridget wrinkled her nose in confusion. "What is obvious?"

Belinda sighed. "The disappearing act, the whole 'tortured artist' thing. It's blatantly obvious," she said, glaring at Beth, "that Beryl's trying to be like Bell."

"Maybe she's locked herself in her room," Beth suggested.

"Guys, it's not rocket science," Benita blurted out. "It's probably the same as Trot right here. She just wants to miss the meal."

Bridget did her best to distinguish between good information and bad. "Belinda," she said with forced frivolity, "why don't you take Trot on a tour and on the way you can look for Beryl?"

"We've searched the house," Beth said gravely. "She's definitely not here."

"I'll give him a tour," Benita offered, nudging Belinda conspicuously.

"No thanks," Bridget said, noting the nudge.

"Why not?" asked Belinda. "What harm can it do?"

"No thank you," Bridget repeated, adding spite to her frustrated look.

But the debate was suddenly interrupted as the doorbell rang.

The younger girls raced to evacuate as Bridget hurried toward the door. Benita took advantage of the chaos, grabbing Trot's hand and violently dragging him into the next room.

"Don't worry about Billy," Benita confided once she and Trot were out of Bridget's earshot. "He's not in love with Bridget anymore."

"Good to know," Trot said officiously and released his arm from Benita's grasp.

"Unfortunately, she's still in love with him."

Trot ignored Benita and walked down the hall, noting that it was, in fact, possible to feel hatred for a child.

3

Blue Eyes

The Barnacles' was not a typical apartment. It was more of a manse. Over the years, Barry had bought and conjoined two six-room apartments in order to satisfy the steady expansion of his family. At first, the apartment had grown horizontally, widening at the waist, but due to Bella's addition after the divorce, the property had grown toward the sky as though the Barnacle family needed its very own skyscraper. Each individual apartment boasted the layout known among New Yorkers as a "classic six." As a result, after the purchase of the second apartment and the floor above for Bella, the holdings had essentially tripled into a "classic eighteen." Shaped like a river with tributaries, each apartment emanated from a long, central hall. The rooms themselves were large and airy with high ceilings and wide windows that creaked when you opened them and revealed the age of the apartment with the layers of paint that flaked off when this attempt was made. The hallway itself pulsed with a certain inert noise, causing anyone strolling down to wonder if a wild animal were trapped inside, ready to pounce and leap into the hall should one hazard to open the wrong door.

As Trot passed the kitchen, his senses were overwhelmed by an odd combination of smells. The nutty mist of baking turkey blended with the acrid punch of Passover wine. Baking sweet potatoes added the warmth of butter to the mix. A faint smell of apples offered the most refreshing aspect to the mélange, a reminder of the arduous peeling process required for the Passover charoset. Frying eggs provided the final dissonant note. Trot paused for a moment in the hall, trying to identify the various smells. But he was distracted by new, more pressing sensory demands as Benita yelled at him to hurry while grasping his forearm with an alarmingly tight grip for such a little girl.

"This is Daddy's indoor jungle," she began. "He built it in honor of Charles Darwin. Daddy wanted to build it on the roof, but Mom said he could do it over her dead body or when he married a more submissive woman than her."

"Than she," Trot corrected.

Benita bristled, torn between indignation and respect.

Trot peered cautiously into a room filled with bright petals and leaves and found himself unexpectedly pleased by the faint murmur of animals and birds. The indoor jungle, Benita explained, was initially built as an annex to Barry's aquarium, a passion that began with a single fish tank stowed in a spare room. Like all collections in the house, this one multiplied exponentially as a function of Barry's attention. Quickly, the population of the tank tripled as Barry bought new companions for his garden-variety goldfish, as though providing an only child with siblings. Then came a flood of more exotic fish, neon yellow, fluorescent minnows, a bright red lion fish, an electric eel that actually sparked, and a silver Japanese fighting fish. The latter was safely sequestered in a separate but adjacent tank, allowing the various species to enjoy the appearance of cohabitation without the danger of predation. Unfortunately, Barry's inexperience obscured one critical fact. It was the lion fish, not the Japanese fighting fish, that required such precautions. This realization occurred sadly too late: Barry arrived for a morning feeding and found the entire population of the tank wiped out but for the belligerent victor.

Gradually, the amateur hobbyist yearned for expertise. Refusing to make the same mistake twice, Barry purchased a total of four tanks: one for freshwater species, one for saltwater, one for the pugnacious lion fish, and one for future acquisitions. He had outgrown pink gravel and plastic coral. Soon enough, he commanded a second room in the house for his collection, filling it slowly with animals bought from stores and special catalogs. Thus, he was finally released from his reliance on the local fish store and became the favorite customer of a new pet store. The store sold everything from minnows to macaques and was called, appropriately, "Monkey Business."

Slowly, the indoor jungle blossomed from a modest garden to a small rain forest. The foundations of the room—turn-of-the-century molding, picture panels, and fine, wide planked floors—had long since been obscured by vegetation. Swirling green vines and broad shiny leaves wound their ways up the walls, meeting in the middle of the ceiling to form a canopy. Bamboo trees with delicate trunks stood at every corner, sprouting extravagantly at the top like Corinthian columns. Birds as bright as tropical fruit fluttered in and out of view. A three-toed sloth, a nocturnal animal, allegedly slept in a hidden nook. A low hooting sound in the base register revealed the presence of an owl and provided a stark instrumental contrast to the sporadic high-pitched screeches of what Trot could only assume were bats.

Despite the exotic beauty of this unusual place, there was something disturbing about the room, something decidedly off-putting about seeing this flora and fauna so far from their natural habitats. Once again, high-pitched screeching interrupted Trot's musing.

"Is that a monkey?" he asked casually.

"Of course not," Benita scoffed. "Harry ran away years ago."

"Who?" Trot asked.

"Daddy's macaque," Benita clarified. She rolled her eyes as though elaborating was a horrible inconvenience.

"I see," said Trot, though he did not. He wondered idly if his friends experienced anything like this when visiting their girlfriends' parents.

Benita lowered her voice as though sharing a classified government secret. "Everyone has different theories on the subject. Beryl thinks Mom sold him back to the pet store because she got sick of the mess. Harry used to smash bananas into the wallpaper and throw his feces at guests." Here, she paused to check Trot for her effect and, detecting discomfort, continued her pitch. "I think he got sick of our family and walked across Fifth Avenue to be with his at the Central Park Zoo. Mom insists Harry had enemies in the building. She blames Mr. Finch. Bridget thinks Harry saw Bell sneak out so much he figured it out for himself. Bell claims Mom tied him to the back stairs during a dinner party, and that later, when Dad went to untie him, Harry was hanging from a noose."

"My God," said Trot, wincing noticeably.

"But no one believes that for a second. You can't make a noose without making a slipknot," said Benita. "And, of course, you can't make a slipknot without opposable thumbs."

Despite the contentious nature of this debate, one of Benita's claims was true. The missing macaque bore an uncanny resemblance to a monkey in captivity at the Central Park Zoo. This monkey was endowed with the same gray and black speckled fur, the same deeply inset eyes, the same "nubby" tail, the same pink toes, the same face of a little old man, shrunken perfectly to scale. As a result, Benita could not be dissuaded from her theory of the crime. Harry, she believed, had simply relocated from one side of Fifth Avenue to the other. As a result of this conviction, every Sunday, without fail, she walked across the avenue to the zoo and gazed at the macaques' cage for ten minutes, occasionally whispering promises to Harry—or rather the monkey she had decided was Harry—to bring him back home one day soon.

Trot said nothing. He merely nodded and resolved to ignore Benita. To this end, he focused on a clump of red birds assembled atop a miniature palm tree.

"Those," said Benita, "are Galápagos finches, descendants of Darwin's famous birds. Dad used to call us his little finches, which was often very confusing since the Finches live right next door."

This, unlike most of Benita's claims, was true. According to Barry, barnacles proved Darwin's theory better than the famous finches. No doubt, his sentiment had something to do with science's notorious contest and the barnacle species' not-so-famous eleventh-hour defeat. Barry was haunted by the incongruities in Darwin's biography. In 1839, precisely twenty years before the scientist would publish his famous treatise, his notebooks reveal his theory of evolution was already intact. And yet instead of publishing, he spent the next twenty years dissecting barnacles in his basement. He compiled these findings in a book entitled *A Taxonomy of Barnacles,* a book that was read, despite its merits, by approximately ten people. However, when it came time to write *On the Origin of Species,* a book that changed the course of Western thought, Darwin made nary a mention of barnacles. Instead, he featured the finch.

For obvious reasons, Barry was obsessed by this fact. He simply could not understand why Darwin traded in his old friend for a more photogenic face. Barnacles, Barry claimed, provided just as elegant an example. Barnacles competed for survival. Barnacles adapted. Barnacles diverged. Barnacles proved evolution, too. Thus, Barry felt it simply was not fitting and the pun was most definitely intended, that finches got to prove the survival of the fittest, earning a page in the annals of history while barnacles fell through the cracks. There was some foul play, Barry was sure of it. Why else would Darwin doom the humble barnacle to huddle forever on the bottoms of boats while the finch soared to greater heights? No, history had no accidents. In this situation, someone got screwed. It was prejudice, Barry insisted, discrimination. In his mind, the rivalry between finches and barnacles was nothing less than a war between Christians and Jews.

Everyone in the family espoused a different theory for Darwin's delay, each one revealing more about the theorist than the mystery itself. Bell believed in the feminist argument, that Darwin delayed publication at the request of his religious wife. Bridget believed in the Freudian argument, that Darwin subconsciously repressed his desire to succeed. Beth felt there was good scientific evidence for the delay: Finches simply offered a better example of variation. Belinda abstained from the argument. Did they have to talk about this every night? Beryl was convinced of a conspiracy. Someone, or rather some organization, had impinged on Darwin's freedom of speech. Benita entertained a more Machiavellian approach. Darwin deferred his announcement until he was close to death so as to avoid the wrath of the church during his lifetime. Bella saw it from a Hollywood perspective: Barnacles lacked a clear storyline. Finches had an easy hook, a high-concept plot. But despite the merits of these arguments, Barry was resolute. In his mind, there was no room for doubt. Anti-Semitism was at play. Ultimately though, the Barnacle girls dismissed their father. They felt they understood Darwin's choice: The Finches were a phylum for the masses, a less eccentric family.

"These are Peruvian violets," Benita continued, circling the room with the quick, competent movements of a stewardess. "Daddy wanted to buy more but Mother said it was obscene to buy a plant that costs more than a car."

Trot leaned over, pretending to admire a patch of low-slung lavender flowers that seemed, for all he could tell, to sprout from a hole in the floor. As he looked, he considered Benita's verbiage. As far as he could remember, Bridget called her mother "mom."

"Over there," she said, gesturing grandly in the direction of nothing in particular, "that's where the hollyhock bloom in the summer."

Trot nodded, feigning rapt interest.

"They're terribly pretty," Benita said. "Too bad you won't be around to see them."

Upon delivery of this last insult, Benita glanced quickly at Trot. She stood like this, watching for several moments, waiting for him to digest her meaning. Unfortunately, the full effect of the insult was weakened by a new interruption. As though on cue, a large purple leaf fell from a nearby tree, landing on Trot's head and leaving a sticky adhesive trail. Swatting wildly, Trot managed to detach the leaf. But, patting his hair, he found that the leaf had already left a thick residue.

"Beware," said Benita, "those are poisonous."

Trot patted frantically at his hair. Already unnerved, he jumped and squealed when something grazed his right ear. "What the hell?" he said, swatting wildly. He crouched and braced for another attack.

"Don't be scared." Benita laughed. "It's just a little bat."

"My God," Trot said. "That thing was huge."

Benita stepped into the hall and paused to consider Trot's claim. Then, dismissing his point of view, she sniffed, "I've seen bigger."

Trot made a resolution as his pulse returned to its normal rate: from this moment on, he would consider Benita an adversary and an adult.

Benita did not start the tour in the indoor jungle because it was the best way to intimidate guests. It truly was her favorite room in the entire house. It had not grown out of grand aspirations, but rather grown into them. It was a tribute to a time when indoor jungles were as common as drawing rooms, a time when curiosity was common, when science was approached with wonder. And though the association with the Victorian era was perhaps a strange one for a Jew from Brooklyn, it did make some sense. The era may have been associated with collars and corsets, but it was arguably the moment at which feudal law suffered its fatal blow, when women, though still expected to marry, began the long march to property rights. Bell, of course, had amassed a series of passionate objections to the whole affiliation, armed at college with a host of post-Modern, neo-Feminist meta-revisionist theories. The Victorian novel began with a tour, the author a vendor showing off her wares. The problem was that these wares were usually women.

Trot lingered in the jungle, admiring a rubber plant.

"Hurry up, slowpoke," Benita called down the hall.

And then, for no better reason than to quell his mounting anger, Trot plucked a leaf from the rubber tree and slipped it into his pocket. "Where are you? I think I'm lost," he said, though he knew exactly where he was.

"I'm in Bridget's bedroom," Benita called. "Don't you want to see where she and Billy used to make out?"

Environment maps the geography of the mind. Indeed, the floor plan of the apartment illuminated the psyches of its residents. Despite their vocal protests, the six Barnacle girls were made to pair up, sleeping two to a room in a total of three separate rooms. The apartment, of course, had ample room for each sister to enjoy her own room. But Barry hoped the layout would serve another purpose, encouraging his daughters to engage in constant competition. The arrangement also left three additional rooms available for the storage and display of his collections. In each of the girls' bedrooms, the headboards of two twin beds were adjoined at the top so that the beds formed a stripe across the back of the room, extending parallel to the windows like dominoes laid out back to back. This layout provided a blueprint for the girls' view of the world, creating the sense that the Barnacle sisters formed a balustrade against the world. It also caused each separate pair of roommates to develop either strong emotional bonds or rabid aversions to one another and spurred them to divide into three teams of two in most family disputes.

The decor of each room differed as drastically as the various daughters. For a time, Bella had taunted the girls with promises of wallpaper, accumulating a tantalizing stack of swatches from the best design houses in New York. Each tableau of flowers and ribbons threatened to turn their boudoirs into palaces of femininity. Finally, however, Bella opted for paint, claiming it allowed each girl, or rather each pair of girls, to personalize their living quarters. These choices, which were made when the eldest were still under the age of thirteen, transformed the apartment into a museum, preserving the antiquated tastes of much younger girls and freezing the apartment at the moment in time just before Barry and Bella's marriage had dissolved.

Bell and Bridget chose a bubblegum pink, swayed by an early and overwrought interest in princess narratives. Belinda and Beth failed to come to an agreement and so bisected the room and painted it two different colors. Belinda's side was a lavender hue whose gauzy innocence had long since been obscured by lewd tear-outs from teen magazines and menacing rock posters. Beth's was a deep undulating purple that transformed her side of the room into a tidal pool and caused half of the room to be bathed in black by dusk. Beryl and Benita painted their room an awkward shade of burgundy, a literal compromise between the girls' two preferences. Unable to agree on a single color, they had simply mixed their two favorites, light blue and crimson red, a marriage that resulted in the very same purple shade that graced the walls of their favorite Chinese restaurant. Of all the Barnacle women's rooms, Bella's provided the most apt representation of its inhabitant's interior state. Papered in a busy pale yellow chintz with lavender and green accents, it evoked the very style and mood of a nineteenth-century ladies' sanitarium.

The bathroom situation at the Barnacles' was as telling as the bedrooms. Despite the home's otherwise grand appointments, it was built, like all turn-of-the-century apartments, with six specific rooms in mind, a master bedroom, a living room, three bedrooms for children, and one for a governess or maid. The original apartment had a total of three bathrooms, one adjoining to the master bedroom, one for guests between the living room and kitchen, and one for the children. Of course, doubling the square footage of the apartment should have doubled the amenities therein but the spare space had been put to uses other than practical ones, such as the annex to the indoor jungle, the addendum to Bunny's exercise room, and Beth's lab. As a result, the six sisters had been cursed to share the one facility, a major defect in spatial planning that resulted in long lines, frequent accidents, and an infinite amount of yelling.

As Trot stood at the door of Bridget's bedroom, he struggled to keep these statistics straight. What an odd way to sleep, he thought. No wonder Bridget's an insomniac.

"I'm so glad Billy's moving back," said Benita, interrupting Trot's thoughts once again. She performed what appeared to be a victory dance, twirling several times, jumping up and down, and stamping her feet triumphantly.

"Why'd he decide to do that?" Trot asked, doing his best to simulate a carefree tone.

"He ran out of money," Benita said. She said this as though it was the most common thing in the world, as though boys of all ages ran out of money and then, rather than pound the pavement for a job, simply moved back home.

"Wow," said Trot. "That's nice of his parents . . . to support him at this age."

"I guess," said Benita, "but if you want my opinion, I don't think Billy's broke." She closed her mouth and covered her eyes as though her secret might escape through one of the two orifices.

"What's your opinion?" Trot demanded.

Benita smiled in slow motion, as though Trot had requested that she display the anatomy of a smile. Finally, she answered with another question. "What do you think?"

Bridget sat down on the living room sofa and smiled at Billy carefully. Glancing down, she realized that her hands were folded on her lap, their slightly clenched position betraying an unattractive amount of unease. Consciously taking deeper breaths, she unclasped her hands and rearranged them, ironically, with some force into a more relaxed position. For a moment, she debated rescuing Trot. By now, Benita had likely coerced him to play another game of Ping-Pong or tackled him and pinned him to the ground, demanding he empty his pockets. But, deciding that she craved and deserved a moment alone with Billy, Bridget willfully thrust the thought from her head and left

Trot to fend for himself while she settled into the sofa. I am sinister, Bridget thought. No, she changed her mind quickly. One deserves to be sure.

As was custom, Billy greeted Bridget with a marriage proposal. "Since the first day I met you, I knew you were the one," he began with a solemn look. His speech, for effect, was halting and nervous, as though he were, in fact, a timid suitor.

"Set the scene," Bridget demanded. She made a show of sinking yet deeper into the sofa to make it clear she was finally ready to be entertained.

"Traditional. Dinner. Cipriani's in Rome. Kneeling. Champagne. Et cetera."

It was convention, after delivering the prelude to the proposal, to name and classify its type, to state whether there had been kneeling or none and, of course, to leave the question in question blank. Thus, the two friends slowly compiled a taxonomy of proposals.

"No, no, no," Billy changed his mind. "High Romance. Banks of the Seine. Distant saxophone."

"Kneeling?" Bridget asked.

"Of course," snapped Billy. "Now, please don't interrupt."

"Forgive me," Bridget said with mock seriousness.

Billy closed his eyes like an impassioned conductor and assumed a supercilious smirk, instantly transforming himself into a dumb jock. "Since the first day I met you, I knew you were the one. The way you flipped your hair in my fraternity. The way you kissed me . . . oh my God. And then when you . . . well, you remember . . . I knew I couldn't live without that . . ."

Bridget smiled with due deference, offered Billy a token round of applause, then, after racking her brain for the right opening, launched into her own. "The beach behind the family house. The Vineyard. Sunset."

"Ah," said Billy. "Au naturel."

"Yes," said Bridget, "*très* wholesome." She paused to simulate a gag then lowered her voice to better mimic the boy posing the question.

"As you know, I've wanted to have sex with you for a very long time. But, as you have made clear time and again, you're not comfortable living in sin."

"Of course," Billy cheered. "The Negotiation."

"I've been hedging my bets and dragging my feet for . . . what, is it, already ten years? All of our friends are convinced I'm gay. But ever since your mother showed up at my door and foisted your grandmother's ring on me, I've known I had no choice . . ."

"Not bad," said Billy.

Bridget raised her eyebrow. "Not bad?" she asked, smiling flirtatiously. "Let's see you do better."

It was true that Bridget and Billy were happiest in one another's presence. But the two were never more delighted than when they were proposing to each other. To anyone nearby, they seemed to be enmeshed in a captivating dialogue. But, in truth, they were engaged in a duel of impersonations. For Bridget and Billy, proposing was a reliable thrill. Words, even when they have lost their meaning, somehow manage to retain the power of their vestigial limbs.

"All right," said Billy. "The Jane Austen Special. Height of the Victorian era. An ugly cousin arrives for dinner, willing to take any of six sisters. If none accepts, they lose their fortune and their beloved estate."

"Primogeniture," said Bridget, "is so nineteenth century."

"Milady," Billy sighed, mock-annoyed, "are you going to allow me to propose or not?"

Bridget nodded ceremoniously.

Billy kneeled on the ground.

"Miss Barnacle, I've come in my handsome white carriage driven by my handsome white horse in order to make you, my handsome second cousin, an offer you can't refuse. Bear in mind, of course, that if you reject me your entire family will be penniless, generations of status will go to pot, and you, my dear, will be tarnished and condemned to the life of a lonely spinster." At this, he paused to clear his throat. "As I was saying, ever since the day we met, I knew you were the one . . ." Here, he paused to allow Bridget to air a hearty fit of laughter.

The proposal, though a universal monologue, was something of an inside joke for these two. Billy claimed the marriage proposal was a form with no less variation than the sonnet. (He got away with saying things like this occasionally because he had done two years toward an English Ph.D.) Bridget agreed wholeheartedly, her familiarity with the genre the result of a lifelong study of her social circle, a population obsessed not only with marriage but with every ritual surrounding it. Both friends agreed that the whole wretched tradition degraded everyone involved. Still, it was obvious to those who knew them that their distaste was a mask for their fascination with the institution.

Still, the two friends derived endless amusement from hording the anecdotes of friends and acquaintances and parroting the ridiculous ceremony in private. Over the years, they did this in ever more elaborate language, with ever more vivid description and exacting measurements. Extra points were awarded for number of clichés, original venues, sharp verbiage, and other innovations, while due deference was also paid to well-drawn imagery. The whole pastime had evolved dramatically and suddenly when, during one particularly odd New York nuptial season, no one they knew got engaged, a dry spell that forced Billy and Bridget to invent their own. Thus they began proposing to each other for pure entertainment. It began as a joke, became a compulsion, and was now something of a hobby.

Slowly, the collection had become a running contest. Now, they were experts and aficionados, veritable curators of the marriage proposal. Sometimes Bridget would call Billy from work after hearing of a deliciously feeble attempt. Other times, Billy would call Bridget at home and leave an ornate one on her answering machine. (The practice was, of course, outlawed as soon as Bridget and Trot moved in together, though Billy was often tempted to keep up the ruse just to torture Trot.) They proposed, Billy was sure, by way of substitute, because they were hopelessly in love. In Bridget's opinion, it was purely for amusement. Either way, they did it all the time, during lulls in conversations, on walks in Central Park, when they were drunk over dinner, or over the phone as though they were not exchanging words of love, but rather, barbed insults or hilarious jokes.

And yet, despite the cynicism of the game, the two insisted on one sacred rule: The question itself was not to be uttered. The actual "will you marry me?" part was strictly off-limits. Accordingly, when they were proposing to each other, they always left the end blank, instinctively realizing that voicing the question would serve to weaken the very thing they needed to remain intact. Indeed, a proposal ranks among those few phrases in the English language, what Billy's English professors liked to call "performative words"—among them, "you're fired," "you're out," and "you're under arrest"—whose very utterance enacts the thing they describe. One need only voice such a phrase for it to become a fact, and, in the case of a marriage proposal, to become a binding agreement. Thus, Billy and Bridget never touched the will-you part of the proposal. It was understood, though never discussed, that the question, when spoken, could not be reversed.

"The Walk-Off Home Run," Billy said, wrapping up. "Tie game. Bottom of the ninth. The home team is at the plate."

"How many strikes?" Bridget demanded.

"Three balls and two strikes."

"But which does she love more," Bridget interrupted, "her boyfriend or baseball?"

"My dear," Billy chided, "she's a Sox fan. What do you think?" Billy rolled his eyes in a dramatic show of ennui, then continued. "As you know, a walk-off home run is one of the great events in baseball, not only because one swing ends a tied game but because it is the home team that wins, causing the visitors to *walk off* the field, usually quite dejectedly."

"It's the opposite of hospitality," Bridget elaborated.

"Exactly," Billy smiled. He paused again to allow Bridget to situate herself in a crazed stadium, to imagine the smell of beer and hot dogs, to hear the loudspeaker's manic announcements, the hushed nerves of the crowd. "Sweetheart," he began, assuming the role, "I know you're busy right now, but there's something I've been needing to ask you for a very long time."

"Not now," Bridget quipped, feigning interest in the imagined game. "Can't you ask me later?" she said. "I really need to watch this."

"But darling," Billy said. He paused to eat an imaginary Cracker Jack. "Sweetheart," he said. He paused again for the token shoulder tap, but as he did, his heart swelled with genuine emotion. "I'm truly sorry to bother you but my question is urgent." At this, Billy reached into his pocket and, as far as Bridget could tell, began to fish around frantically as though for a very small object.

This fraught gesture and Billy's odd tone combined to give Bridget pause, causing her to look up suddenly and make direct eye contact. Either Billy had been moved by his mimicry or this was his most convincing performance to date. Bridget's heart lurched from her chest as Billy searched his pocket. Her peripheral vision refined suddenly. Her hearing grew wildly acute. Was this what they called a sixth sense? she wondered. Or was this merely indigestion? Why were her eyes twitching at the corners, watering at the tear ducts? Was this heightened awareness what people meant when they spoke of premonition? Was it possible Billy was brazen enough to propose just like this, with her family roaming around nearby, with her boyfriend just down the hall? And why, more importantly, did this possibility fill her with the certain giddy thrill one experiences in very beautiful cathedrals or due to heavy narcotics?

Finally, Billy removed something from his pocket and hid it behind his back. "This is for you," he said, grinning. He paused a long moment, eyed Bridget sheepishly, then finally extended his hand to reveal a pair of tickets.

"Billy," Bridget said, "you shouldn't have." She smiled unconvincingly.

"It's as much for you as for me," he said. "Tickets to the biggest event of the season, the first game between the Yankees and the Sox."

Embarrassingly, it took Bridget several moments to recover from the shock. In a sense, she had experienced two surprises: first, when she thought Billy was proposing in earnest and second, when she realized she was disappointed he had not. Luckily, at just this moment, Bridget heard Trot's voice down the hall and, dismissing her emotions, smiled a reprimand at Billy and stuffed the tickets into her pocket.

As with most guests, Trot's patience waned as the tour wore on. Benita seemed to seize on this fact by adding new and more extraneous details to her tour. The building in which the Barnacles lived was as remarkable as the family that called it home. From the windows, the residents enjoyed a perfect view of the Central Park Zoo and, from the high floors, Sheep Meadow, the lower loop, and the Reservoir. Turning right, you could see the Seventy-second Street Boat Pond where the children sailed tiny boats in the spring and summer. Turning left, you overlooked the Plaza Hotel, its grand facade perfectly visible even from half a mile away. In every season, the park presented a new and more beautiful vista. It was at its most dramatic in the fall when it looked like a large bouquet and at its prettiest in the spring, when its endless brown was dotted with pink like birthday present ribbon.

The building itself was graced with a charming and well-appointed roof garden whose use was restricted, thanks to Bunny's long campaign, to the Barnacles and the Finches, the families who occupied the top-floor apartments. If all of these flourishes failed to satisfy the discerning tenant, the edifice of the building boasted one last mark of distinction. After much hoopla on the local news, some coverage in national papers, a week of protests on Fifth Avenue, and many thousands of dollars in litigation, Mrs. Finch's aggressive campaign had paid off; a family of endangered red-tailed hawks nested on the roof of the building, evading the serious threat to their perch at Central Park's best address. Despite complaints from many tenants who resented the hawks' tendency to leave carcasses on either side of the awning, the hawks were allowed to stay without paying rent or property tax and did so with seeming aplomb, hatching several new chicks every April like clockwork.

These birds of prey found the building a perfect habitat due to the ample feeding opportunities in nearby Central Park's high population of insects, pigeons, and rats. Furthermore, the hawks enjoyed the affection of the neighborhood. Their nest itself had become the obsession of a local ornithologist who stationed himself at the opposite side of the Boat Pond every Sunday, weather permitting, to monitor the nest with binoculars. Unfortunately, the bird-watcher's gaze only worsened the relationship between the hawks and the tenants, causing them to fear for their privacy. But, thanks to Mrs. Finch, the birds were now safe. They were a hallmark of the neighborhood just like Rumplemeyer's, the Plaza Tea Room, and Bemelmens Bar. They were protected by the nation's preservation of migratory birds and therefore immune to complaints. So they were allowed to enjoy their impressive address, the ample resources of the park, and their unique status as one of the Upper East Side's last stable monogamous marriages.

Benita encouraged Trot to steal a quick glimpse of the roof. But Trot declined, citing fatigue rather than admit to his crippling fear of heights. Typically, Benita took comfort in the roof's panoramic view. Perspective worked its usual magic, encouraging her to imagine herself the princess of New York City and Central Park as her personal playground. The height and beauty of the view did their part to confirm this theory. Her high-powered electron telescope, a gift from her father on her tenth birthday, allowed her to disprove the common misconception that stars were invisible in New York due to the exorbitant electric output of the city's skyscrapers. To the contrary, Benita had spent countless hours peering through her lens in search of evidence to debunk this claim and also in the hopes that a tireless vigil would one day result in the discovery of a new planet.

But, standing firm, Trot refused Benita's entreaty to check out the view and continued down the hall, just ahead of Benita, in search of somewhere to sit. Near the Hall of Collections, Trot experienced sensory shock. Each door in the hall opened onto a different stash. Gold paint announced each new collection on a shiny black plaque.

"That's the portrait gallery," Benita announced. "As you can see, Beryl tried to make me look ugly." Trot scanned the wall for Benita's portrait, expecting a cruel caricature, but found instead a portrait with an almost photographic resemblance. This room was, at least, a good use of space, housing portraits of every member of the family, including a long lineage of pets.

"Our first dog was named after Darwin's grandfather, Erasmus. This is his son, Charles, and his wife, Emma Wedgewood."

The notorious resemblance between dogs and masters was, in this case, more alarming than most. Each dog, Trot noted with some concern, bore a familiar curious look that was expressed most clearly in the eyebrows.

Tiring of this room quickly, Benita continued down the hall. She stopped at another door that was ostensibly the same as the previous one but for a plaque that indicated it as the SHELL COLLECTION.

"These are the conchs," she announced. The walls were lined floor to ceiling with glass shelves, every inch of which was crammed with large lustrous shells. Their long sharp points, at quick glance, caused them to look like severed limbs. Peering into their spiraled cores, Trot was surprised by their colors. Bright pink and purple paved the entrance to their inner depths.

Benita removed a shell from its shelf. "This," she said, "is a barnacle. They have the largest penis of any organism in the animal kingdom. It's called a groping penis because it comes out of its shell and gropes around for mates." As she said the word "grope," she extended her arms and wiggled her fingers menacingly.

Trot nodded and smiled politely, though he found himself suddenly nauseated.

"This is Daddy's prize possession," she went on, straining on her toes to lift one from a higher shelf. "This barnacle lived in prehistoric times. It's the first known specimen on record."

Arguably, the shell collection was the best collection in the house. Painstakingly accumulated over many years, the room was a living catalog of the crustacean kingdom. Each shelf contained one complete set of the thirteen phyla. Every species, extinct or extant, in all of the seven oceans was represented. Like all the collections in the apartment, the shells were the lucky beneficiaries of Barry's obsessive-compulsive disorder, but unlike books or antique toys, rare shells could not always be bought. In some cases, Barry had personally procured his specimens. As a result, the room had a secondary, related collection: the stories of each shell's discovery, intertwining the history of the natural world with that of the Barnacle family. The thorny speckled cowry, for example, was the result of a tussle between Barry and a Gulf Stream jellyfish. The pink-eyed cochina, one of four in the world, was a serendipitous find, uncovered amidst a wedge of sludge on a shelling excursion in Marco Island, Florida. The horseshoe crab had nearly caused Beth to sprain her ankle during a weekend trip to a friend's house in the Hamptons. The dagger-toothed clam was a gift to Barry from the German ambassador. Luckily, no one would ever know that Belinda had glued one of its teeth back together after a particularly violent fight with Beth.

Finally, even Benita seemed ready to conclude the tour. She closed the door to the shell collection and accelerated down the hall. "This is the library," she quipped, abandoning ceremony. "See that Bible over there? It's a first edition."

Trot followed reluctantly and stopped at the next destination. Against his will, he found himself suddenly transfixed. The dampened musk of so many books was completely overwhelming. He felt weak, as in the presence of a new love, painfully aware of his insignificance and inspired to accomplish great things. Leaning against a shelf to steady himself, he wondered if books cast this spell on everyone or just aspiring writers. Either way, the effect was wholly transforming. If he were to be trapped in the apartment, he decided, he would want it to be in this room.

Benita broke into his reverie with a non sequitur. "Bridget is Dad's favorite, after me," she said. "He's not going to let her marry just anyone."

"That's a relief," Trot lied, "since last night she proposed to me."

Frustrated by Trot's quick response, Benita adjourned to the next room. "This is my father's laboratory," she said. The room, cluttered with broken objects, emitted the regular bleep of a broken alarm clock or a detonating bomb. In the corner sat a ten-foot pile of what appeared to be ceramic toilet seats. An oil painting of an ostrich hung above a cluttered desk.

"What are those?" asked Trot, pointing to the toilet seats.

"They're for my father's invention," Benita said. "My stepmother hated it when he left the seat up, so Daddy invented an automatic seat-replacer to save their marriage."

Trot approached the mechanism and pushed an inviting switch, succeeding in administering a small electric shock to his hand. As he recovered, he tried to recall the last half hour of his visit, concerned he'd already committed Bunny's cardinal sin.

"That's Dodo," said Benita, gesturing at the painting. "He's the family mascot."

"That's an odd name for an ostrich," Trot said, adopting a new policy to challenge everything Benita said.

"It's an emu," Benita snorted.

Dodo, she explained, was Barry's proof that Lamarck was not far off the mark, that a species could change its traits over time with enough effort. To this end, Barry cited an example from current zoology. The emu was an endangered species while the ostrich, its close cousin, had managed to outrun this fate. The emu, Barry felt, had only itself to blame for its precarious state. The ostrich, on the other hand, had survived due to sheer perseverance. The ostrich was an emu with a strong work ethic, an emu that struggled and strove. Dodo was the ending to Barry's favorite fable, a warning that, without hard work, any species could go to the birds.

At this point, Benita abbreviated her tour, exhausting even herself. Down the hall was the dance studio that nobody used except Bell for yoga when she came home to visit, which she rarely did anymore, and Belinda, for privacy with boys when she was home from school; a squash court, because nobody wanted a pool; the game room with the hallowed Ping-Pong table; a collection of antique roulette wheels; a second music room with two player pianos; and a variety of rooms devoted to storage and overflow guests. But, even despite this blinding excess, Trot was still charmed by the apartment. There was something about its abundance that was intrinsically different from the offensive hording of the nouveau riche. These collections were way too weird to be public displays of success. These artifacts were not trophies but monuments, statues erected in tribute to Barry's curiosity. Most people, when they toured the house, were blinded by envy or disdain. But those who bothered to look closely found something else: The apartment was an effigy to awe, a museum of marvel. These were the floor plans of a madman's mind.

Finally, Trot gave in to the urge to provoke his guide. During the course of their tour, he had come to think of her as his own younger sister and therefore felt he'd earned the right to razz her a bit. "I'm onto you, Benita," he said.

"No, you're not." She sniffed.

"Yes, I am," Trot said. "You take people on this tour to intimidate them."

Benita smiled with genuine delight. "Why," she asked, "are you intimidated?"

"No, not one bit," Trot said. "In fact, I feel far more comfortable now than when I arrived."

"Oh," said Benita. She smiled cordially. "If I were you, I wouldn't get too attached."

Yet again, Trot detonated Benita's insult with a smile. The charge between them had changed, he decided, in a subtle but striking way. "I'll tell you what else," he went on. He took a step closer, attempting to tower over her. "I think this is how you treat people you like. I think you put people through this test so that you know they won't disappear once you've decided you want them around. In fact," he said, in closing, "I think you like me a lot."

Benita said nothing for several moments, allowing him to punctuate his speech with the fermata he craved. Then once she'd given him, she felt, a more than adequate fighting chance, she rapped the wall with her knuckle. "Actually," she declared, "I like you less than this wall."

With this, Benita continued down the hall with renewed energy. Deflated, Trot opted for silence. Silence, he hoped, would confound the brat more than another duel.

"Last stop," Benita said, "the music room. We're on strike from practicing until Beryl comes back."

Trot paused for a moment, disoriented again. "But what about the piano in the living room?" he asked.

"That one's a Steinway," Benita explained. "This one's a Bösendorfer."

Trot, who had studied piano as a child, admired the fine instrument. It was situated under an arched glass ceiling and bathed in an intricate maze of shadows that made it look almost divine. He stood, transfixed for a moment, then noticed another oddity in the room: a large framed portrait of a young black woman, playing the very same piano.

The portrait's subject was Brandy, the girls' beloved ex-nanny. A plaque underneath the frame bore the span of her stay like the dates on a gravestone. Brandy had lived with the Barnacles for four harmonious years while she combined the duties of a governess with the obligations of a college student. A statuesque Bahamian girl with large devilish eyes, she was one of few teenagers who could enter the Barnacle apartment without feeling intimidated or overwhelmed. In addition to acting as caretaker for the girls, she also served as a live-in music teacher and tutor.

Brandy was uniquely suited to the job, graced by heredity with both musical and rhetorical talent. Her parents, Bertram and Birdie Brown, were the organist and pastor of Coney Island's Lutheran church. Bertram also moonlit in a local piano bar two nights a week. When Brandy answered the ad for the nanny position, her prospective employers were split. Bella felt she was dangerously pretty but Barry ultimately overruled, citing the Brooklyn connection and arguing that Brandy could further the girls' musical education. Within weeks, Brandy was not only teaching piano, but instructing the girls in Caribbean dance, and orchestrating the intra-apartment productions that both cemented the Barnacle girls' love of musical theater and forged the Finch twins' aspirations to direct.

For everyone involved, these performances were fond memories, conjoining the Barnacle and Finch households into one big singing family. So, it was perhaps only natural that conflicting feelings would evolve when the girls asked Barry to round out the orchestra for a production of *Godspell*. While accompanying Brandy on clarinet, he found himself feeling suddenly very much like Captain von Trapp. But who could blame Barry, after such a sonorous partnership, for inviting Brandy to join him for a more extended medley? Who could fault Barry for entreating Brandy back to the shell collection to show her how the clarinet's sound was surpassed by the longing moan of the conch? Who could blame Bella for her response, berating Barry and banishing Brandy when she happened upon this tryst.

"But Dad got his way in the end," Benita concluded.

"How's that?" Trot asked.

"He hung Brandy's portrait over the piano so he could look at her whenever he plays. Then he found a poor replacement in Bunny and left my mom for her."

Trot stared at the piano in a daze, floored by the sheer breadth of information he'd encountered in the last hour. Finally, he roused himself and turned to leave. But as he turned, he stopped again for fear he was hallucinating. The piano bench appeared to have a fifth foot.

"Wait," Trot said. He blinked and looked away as though to make sure his eyes had not fooled him. But, when he looked back, he was even more confused than before. The extra foot under the bench had miraculously disappeared. He stood for a moment, confounded, shaking his head incredulously then, abandoning his pretense at composure, he hit the deck in order to investigate the space under the piano.

Thinking fast, Benita screamed at such a high decibel that Trot was forced to turn his head, if only on reflex. However, just before he turned, he caught another glimpse of the extra foot, or rather an indistinguishable blur that resembled a girl's leg. Desperate now, Benita resorted to bullying tactics, grabbing Trot's wrist and trying in vain to drag him out of the piano room. But, newly confident, Trot held fast and stationed his feet on the ground.

"Would you mind if I played a minute?" he asked.

"We really should get back," Benita said. "Dinner's almost ready."

Trot ignored Benita, wriggling out of her grasp and walking to the piano. He took a seat at the bench, cracked his knuckles theatrically, and competently played the opening chords of Beethoven's madcap, if melodramatic, Fifth symphony.

"How did you know that?" Benita demanded.

"Gosh," said Trot. "I don't know." He paused to play the first four notes again, the opening *da-da-da-dum*. "This is how destiny knocks on the door," he said instructively.

Benita stared at Trot, confused.

"That's how Beethoven described the beginning of his symphony. Those first four notes were meant to sound like someone knocking at a door." Trot played the *da-da-da-dum* again to reaffirm his point. "See," he said. "Doesn't it sound like destiny knocking?"

But before Benita could respond, another point of view made itself known. *"So pocht das schiksel on die forte,"* said the piano bench.

Trot scanned the room with feigned confusion.

The piano bench sighed wearily. "That's German for 'This is how destiny knocks on the door.' The piece is considered Beethoven's masterpiece because he played with both form and time signature. It's considered the quintessential romantic symphony because of its clear narrative arc. Still, the piece is something of a mystery. Some say the music tells the story of a war, the French versus the Germans, fate versus free will, man versus heredity. Others say it's a rhapsody, a love letter to the world written by a deaf man. Others say it's an elegy, a dirge for the funeral of sound."

Trot listened deliberately while the piano bench spoke, one ear tilted toward the ceiling as though he were trying to find the source of a leak.

Finally, Beryl extended her head from under the piano bench. "But, in my father's opinion," she concluded, "musical scholars have got it wrong. The first four notes are the sound of man knocking at destiny's door, not the other way around."

"I see," said Trot. "I stand corrected." He nodded, smiled politely, then stood from the bench and headed for the door as though this last exchange were the most normal thing in the world, as though piano benches conversed with him all the time.

As soon as Trot was gone, Ben dropped to the ground and widened her eyes at Beryl. Beryl acknowledged her deference for Trot with a nod of resignation. Beryl later claimed she had seen Trot and Benita coming, had sensed their approach long before they arrived. She had hidden, Beryl insisted, to test her family's love and intelligence respectively, to see how hard they searched for her and how long the search took. Slowly, she gathered her accumulated belongings—a stockpile of books, snacks, and flashlight—and, using her clothes as a sort of sled, she slid out from under the piano into the room. Without a word to Benita, she stood and departed, leaving her sister to realize, once it was too late to poke fun, that Beryl's black sweater was, in fact, a black cape.

Beryl, the fifth and most sensitive sister, often wondered if she'd been adopted. It was as though she knew she'd been conceived in a test tube in a clinic in Switzerland. After Belinda, Barry had begged Bella to give science a shot. Unfortunately, heredity hates meddlers and, in defiance, produced another girl, a child completely unlike her sisters at the level of the soul. Beryl's angelically sweet disposition and her inherent disdain for her siblings caused many to wonder if she had a different genetic code. The most naturally artistic of the six, Beryl could entertain herself for hours, humming, painting, playing the piano, or rearranging her dolls and acting out elaborate plots with the fervency of a madwoman. As a result, her sisters accused Beryl of being part alien. Beryl only compounded their persecution by making the claim, early in life, that she possessed psychic powers.

Her sisters, of course, dismissed this notion, attributing any correct predictions Beryl made to accident. But Beryl refused to be discouraged, claiming her sensitivity was so acute that she could smell the future like garlic in a frying pan. She could detect a phone call seconds before the phone rang, a cruel sentiment from her sisters before it was expressed, and throbbing pain in her foot before she stubbed her toe. But her powers were most accurate, she argued, in the presence of love. For this reason, when it came to her sisters, Beryl's signals were weak. They were, on the other hand, extremely attuned when it came to her adopted brother. She and Latrell shared a bond that was much stronger than blood. Often, when Latrell ran away, Beryl knew where he was hiding. But this proved nothing to her sisters. Latrell, they explained, simply told Beryl his plans before he left the house. Lacking definitive proof of her talent, Beryl resorted to glancing meaningfully out of windows, saying cryptic, portentous things, and sporadically warning her sisters of their imminent demise.

In addition to this alleged talent, Beryl was a truly gifted musician and so suffered the brunt of her father's vicarious musical aspirations. She spent hours playing the piano on her own and during Barry's regimented hours. The other girls, though relieved to be spared the burden of practicing the piano themselves, were annoyed by the noise Beryl produced nonetheless and urged her to cultivate quieter forms of expression. To this end, she set up an easel in her room and taught herself to paint, using fruit from the kitchen. Gradually, she moved from still lifes to anatomical drawing, and then to portraiture, completing the renderings of the family that hung in the gallery. When she wasn't painting or playing the piano, Beryl could be found sitting in her room, writing poetry, scribbling thoughts in her journal, or just staring into space.

"Wait." Benita ran to catch up with Trot before he reached the end of the hall. When she caught up with him, he was steps away from the living room. "There's something else you should know," she panted. "My father only likes people who are very bizarre."

"Is that right?" Trot asked, humoring her.

"Oh, yes," Benita said, "the weirder the better. But what he really loves is to be insulted."

"Hmm," said Trot, maintaining his pace. "Direct attacks or just gentle barbs?"

"Really nasty stuff," Benita said, narrowing her eyes authoritatively.

"Good to know," Trot said. "Thanks again for the tour. I feel much better equipped."

Eager to return to adult company, Trot hurried into the living room. Benita grabbed his forearm frantically just before he entered.

"Stop," she said. "I owe you an apology. There's something I should have told you."

"What's that?" Trot asked. He was back on his feet. Nothing could throw him now.

"Bridget's been lying to you," Benita announced.

"You are a savage little brat," said Trot.

"Ask her," said Benita. "I'm telling the truth. They had dinner together last week."

Bridget instinctively stiffened at the sound of Trot's voice. But stiffening only made it harder to stand from her position on the floor. As a result, Trot entered the living room in time to find Bridget kneeling in front of Billy. He stood for a moment, looking from Bridget to Benita as though unsure of which one to blame. Wisely, Bridget decided that citing a proposal would do little to explain her compromised position. Instead, she hoisted herself from the ground and assumed a haughty look. As though on cue, Billy stood and walked to the kitchen.

"Reminiscing?" Trot asked. "Something from childhood or dinner last week?"

Without a word or change in expression, Bridget walked to Benita and grabbed her by the back of her neck.

"Monster!" Bridget shouted. "We're not related."

"What?" Benita screeched, wriggling out of Bridget's grasp. "You never said I couldn't mention that."

4

Excellent Peripheral Vision

*T*here is no Jewish holiday on which a girl is more aware of her subordinate status to boys than Passover. The seder is, in essence, a tribute to a generation of Jewish sons. Even at the Barnacles', despite its large female population, the Passover seder was still an ode to boys. The inherent favoritism of the holiday was made all the worse by Bunny, who colonized the occasion when she discovered kabbalah. To her credit, Bunny had not allowed Judaism to eclipse her other passions. She was also devoted to maintaining her hair, torturing Bella, monitoring Barry's finances, and, despite the conflict of interest, spending Barry's money. All of the girls disliked Bunny, except for Belinda; Belinda hated Bunny with all of her heart. If Bunny's demeanor was not enough reason to inspire hatred, her nickname sealed her fate. Every so often, an old friend of hers would call the house asking for Bubbles, the name Bunny had been given during college due to her proclivity for champagne and one infamous night involving the rugby team and a Jacuzzi.

Despite the excesses of her college years, Bunny had grown up in a very religious family that conducted their seder in the ancient language. And though her father had passed away, Bunny insisted that the Barnacle seder be conducted in Hebrew as a memorial to her father. As a result the Barnacle girls, who neither spoke nor read Hebrew, had to smile and make awkward eye contact for the duration of the service, while Bunny belted out her favorite Hebrew songs, enhancing the inherent melancholy of the minor chords with a vibrato learned during singing lessons. Whenever anyone was unfortunate enough to catch her eye, Bunny frowned disdainfully and mouthed the word "sing." She construed any request to skip a song— requests that were motivated both by the desire to quiet her nasal singing voice and by the aching hunger experienced during the third hour of the service—as attacks on her deceased father. Thus, the Passover seder, already a night devoted to sons, evolved into a duel of the dads. The girls liked to joke that their family seder should be renamed the "eleventh plague."

When Barry announced his plans to marry Bunny, the Barnacle girls had done everything in their power to sabotage the union. For the months leading up to the date, the girls lobbied their father to reconsider. At the ceremony, they made one last-ditch effort, creating so much noise that the rabbi had to start the service over three times. When the rabbi surveyed the guests for dissenters, the girls elbowed each other madly. Benita emitted a perfectly timed, if slightly overrehearsed gagging fit at which point, amidst nauseous heaving sounds, Belinda and Beth rushed her down the aisle and out of the synagogue.

"I'm ready," Bunny sang out from the kitchen. "Everyone, please sit down." Everything Bunny said, even the rare pleasantry, was braided with bitterness. This constant confusion of anger and sweetness produced a maddening effect, forcing those around her to brace for attack, particularly when she was nicest. "Girls, Barry, everyone," she called again. And then, as though cordiality had an undertow, she added, shrill and indignant, "I hope you don't expect me to wait for Bell."

Bunny wore a short, black wool sheath that was way too sexy for the occasion, the hemline of which was closer to her waist than her knees.

Grumbling, Belinda and Beth headed toward the table.

"Gross," Belinda said. "I hope she doesn't get her hair in our food."

"Why not?" Beth quipped. "It might make it taste better."

Trot approached the dining room cautiously, tabling his annoyance for the time being. He would put on a good face for the rest of the night, he decided. He would show Bridget, by living comparison, the difference between a gentleman and a buffoon. But as Trot headed toward the table, Barry intercepted again, ushering Trot, by way of an ominous nod, into the nearest bathroom. Trot waited anxiously while Barry cleared his throat. He could only assume Barry was insistent on hearing Trot's intentions with Bridget. Though Trot had planned to ask for Bridget's hand in a more traditional manner and place, he respected Barry's preemptive move and prepared himself for the task.

"See this," Barry said, gesturing toward the commode.

Trot followed Barry's hand to the toilet seat and waited for clarification. Suddenly, Barry clapped loudly. Trot flinched femininely at the sound. The toilet seat dropped from its upright position to snap violently closed.

Barry beamed at his invention.

Trot smiled hesitantly.

"I thought you would like it," Barry said. "Since you're creative."

Trot mumbled an assent and thanked Barry for the compliment. He was pleased by one thing at least. This was already, by leaps and bounds, the longest conversation he and Barry had ever had.

Barry stared at the toilet as though in a reverie, grunted proudly, then, with a quick perfunctory nod, he left Trot alone in the bathroom to contemplate creative solutions to his current plight.

The Barnacle seder always began with the Haggadah's prescribed list of questions and answers. This year, Belinda, sixteen and certain of her convictions, felt these questions raised more important questions that she didn't hesitate to point out. Torah question: Why were Jews encouraged to invite non-Jews to the Passover meal? Torah answer: To share Jewish heritage with others and to work against the religious persecution Jews had historically suffered. Belinda's answer: To torture as many people as possible with the arduous ritual. Torah question: Why did the seder claim to celebrate family when the meal invariably ended with a terrible brawl? Torah answer: Because the seder commemorated the hardship of one loyal family. Belinda's answer: To torture every member of the family, even though most of these people agreed that religion was evil and corrupt.

As Belinda offered her interpretation of the traditional questions, Benita raised her hand and waved it aggressively. "I have a question," she shouted, panting breathlessly.

"Yes," Barry nodded. "What is your question?"

"What is the Jewish mafia?" Benita asked.

"One of many terms," Barry replied, "anti-Semites use to denigrate successful Jews."

"Oops," said Benita, covering her mouth in a manner designed to convey a lack, as opposed to an excess, of remorse.

"Don't ask her why," Beth said.

But it was too late. Barry wanted a detailed explanation of how she'd come to hear the expression and Benita was happy to supply it. Benita's classmate Mary Talbot had told the class that Barry was in the Jewish mafia. Benita suspected that Mary was jealous that she had won the Chapin School talent show last year and would likely win it again. Still, Benita wanted to know if Barry had ever killed a man, put a dead canary on a doorstep, or cut off the head of his enemy's horse.

"Remember when your second-grade teacher said that you would chew glass to win?" Barry asked. At the time, this comment had enraged Barry and caused him, in turn, to chew out the teacher. "Whenever someone tells you you're too competitive," he explained, "they're making an anti-Semitic slur. Ignore all of these people. They're just jealous of you."

Just like this, Benita was encouraged to continue ignoring her teachers and striving to win at any cost. The subject was quickly dropped and the ritual continued.

The table was more crowded than usual this year. The entire Barnacle family was in attendance: Barry, Bunny, Trot, the Finch twins, Bella, though she hadn't arrived yet, and every Barnacle sister with the exception of Bell. The dining room table had been extended with the help of prosthetic desks to accommodate the guests.

"What I don't understand," Beryl said to no one in particular, "is why we have to eat all this terrible food."

"Think of it like reading," Beth said dryly, "except you get to eat the pages."

Beryl and Latrell sat next to each other. Closest in age and preoccupation, they were allies at all such events.

"Billy," Benita whined, "will you sit next to me?"

Trot scanned the table and quickly calculated that this would place Billy next to Bridget. He rushed to intervene while doing his best to maintain an air of nonchalance.

"Benita," Trot said, "sit between Billy and me. That way you can tell me what everything means."

Benita accepted the invitation as a challenge. She was, even at her tender age, a sucker for flattery.

"Thank you, Belinda," Trot said coyly, settling into his seat. Then, feigning horror, he covered his mouth and said, "Sorry, I meant Benita."

The meal began with a commotion of information. Belinda insisted on providing the guests with a glossary to the meal to ensure that everyone was eating from the same translation.

She held up a piece of matzoh like a bored salesclerk. "These tasteless crackers symbolize bread that didn't have time to rise when the Jews had to escape to save their sons. This mush," she went on, scooping up some charoset and dangling a spoonful precariously close to Beth's face, "symbolizes the mortar Jewish sons used to build pyramids."

Beth and Beryl smiled approvingly. Typically, they would have quieted her by now, but it was clear from Belinda's performance that she was attempting something ambitious.

Barry spent Passover intermittently reading and dozing at the head of the table. When he did emerge from his narcoleptic state, startled by singing, squabbling, or Bunny's nudge, he did so to engage in his strange eating ritual, which involved stabbing at his plate, inhaling large chunks of food, hiccupping loudly as he chewed, and thereby rendering digestion impossible for anyone nearby. When he remained conscious long enough to apprehend the service, his boredom spurred him to expedite the meal.

"On Passover," Barry began, interrupting Belinda, "the youngest son asks the four questions. Unfortunately, we have no sons to speak of here, so I will read these myself."

Latrell's heartbreak was imperceptible to everyone at the table but Beryl felt it as though it were her own. His eyes darkened like an overcast sky and he flinched as though he had been punched. Under the table, Beryl touched his hand. Latrell proudly shooed her away.

"Wait," Benita interrupted, "there's a big problem. Trot is sitting in Elijah's place."

"Dad," Bridget snapped, "she's out of control."

Trot stood suddenly from his chair, crimson with embarrassment.

"Ignore her," Bridget said.

"Yes, do," Beth agreed.

"I'll move," Trot insisted.

"Don't you dare," said Bridget.

Trot ignored Bridget and stood up anyway. On instinct, Bridget grabbed for Trot's leg with alarming force.

"I'll move," Billy said gaily. He sprang from his seat with a gallant smile before anyone could protest.

"But, wait," Benita stuttered, her lips trembling. "Now, I can't sit next to Billy." This finally put Benita over the edge, spurring a temper tantrum. She wrinkled her nose, held her breath, and waited for the quivering to spread and then she squeezed every muscle in her face until tears commenced. She heralded her sobbing with one quiet yelp before tears the size of raindrops tumbled down her face.

"That's enough," Barry said, twitching to attention, rejuvenated by another short nap. "Where are my first wife and my eldest daughter?"

"I'm here," Bella called merrily. She stood at the other end of the living room, leaning improbably against a bookshelf as though to balance herself.

Oh God, Bridget cringed. Her mother was wearing a floor-length, red brocade dress, its low neckline a caricature of the letter "V."

"Sorry I'm late," Bella said. She swayed noticeably as she swooped into the apartment, nearly knocking over a large glass vase. Everything about Bella, her tone of voice, her dress, the scent of her perfume registered at a higher volume than most people. Even her once-striking face demanded attention. Her dark-circled eyes betrayed years of sleeplessness. Her thin lips, despite expertly applied lipstick, revealed frequent disappointment. Once at the table, Bella pulled up a chair directly to the left of Barry so that when she sat, she created a Barry sandwich breaded by his first and second wife. Dear God, Bridget thought again, as her mother settled in. Bella was not wearing a red dress. Bella was wearing a red bathrobe.

Once he'd distinguished between the table's offerings of grape juice and kosher wine, Trot poured himself a glass of wine. Unfortunately, Passover wine is quite weak, so Trot waited until the uproar resumed and then took an inappropriately large gulp.

"Where's Latrell?" Barry asked, glancing around the table hastily as though searching for pepper and salt.

"Right here," said Latrell, his voice high and clear.

"Oh," Barry said, squinting irritably. "You ought to wear brighter colors, Latrell. As it is, you tend to blend in."

Bella crossed her fingers behind her back. She prayed Latrell would not take Barry's comment as his exit cue. Latrell, like many adopted children, yearned to find his biological parents and took any opportunity to resume his quest. The mystery of his origin consumed his every fourth thought. As he aged, the mystery evolved from vague curiosity to burning wanderlust. The urge was like a bad case of the mumps; Latrell was infected even if he could cover it up. In its thrall, Latrell ran away from home at least once a month, his desire to find his real parents tempered only by a nagging loyalty to his adopted sisters and mom.

To this end, every time he disappeared, he left conspicuous clues. Usually, he pilfered objects from the house, then left them places he knew his sisters would traverse, such as in the fence of the Chapin School playground or at the stop for the crosstown bus. Sometimes, he hid in obvious places such as the lobby of the building next door, or the shelter in which he'd grown up. Once, he even managed to creep into the periphery of a crime scene, conscious that his sisters' excellent peripheral vision would enable them to pick him out of the crowd while watching the evening news. But lately, his clues had been less obvious and his sojourns longer. Bella dreaded the day Latrell would find his real father and accordingly conjured up a far-fetched myth in an effort to throw him off the scent. Beryl knew Latrell would find him eventually despite her mother's bogus tale. She understood destiny was like a teenage boy: The harder one tried to control it, the more it rebelled.

"Who would like to ask the first question?" Barry asked, his eyebrows arching devilishly. As hunger overwhelmed his boredom, Barry began his campaign to accelerate the meal.

"I will. I will," Benita volunteered.

Beryl and Beth rolled their eyes. Under the table, Bridget took Trot's hand. Trot, newly confident and slightly tipsy, coolly refused Bridget's grasp.

"Why is this night different from all other nights?" Benita began.

"Because," Barry answered, "on this night we pretend we believe in God to lord it over our Protestant friends, whose church is actually a country club and our Catholic friends, who sadly no longer have a religion."

Bunny stared at her husband in shock.

"Here, here," Bella said, lifting a piece of matzoh as though it were a silver chalice. Her predinner drinks mixed surprisingly well with the Passover wine. Bella patted Barry's knee. Bunny dispensed with a pitying look.

"Barry," Bunny reprimanded. "If you're going to mock—"

"You're right, I'm sorry." Barry's eyebrows sank. "Nothing else from me. Beryl, you're up."

Beryl was daydreaming and had to be kicked; Beth was happy to oblige. She flipped frantically through her Haggadah to find the correct page, sighed heavily, handed Beryl the book, and pointed to the correct section.

"Why on this night do we recline when on other nights we sit upright at the table?"

"Because," Barry said, "on this night, we celebrate the fact that Jews have more money than people in other religions thanks to our work ethic and superior intelligence. So we spend a whole night celebrating the fact that we could eat every meal in bed if we so chose."

"That's it," Bunny said, dropping her silverware on her plate. "Why must you make a mockery of everything?"

"Barry," Bella said, laughing flirtatiously, "be nice to your second wife."

Bunny shook her head faintly at Bella as though even this meager effort was too much energy to expend on her behalf.

"Sorry," said Barry, "you won't hear another word from me."

"Thank you," said Bunny.

"Next question," Barry said, arranging his face into the picture of gravity.

"Why on this night do we eat unleavened bread when on other nights we eat bread that has risen?"

"Because," Belinda answered, speed-reading, "the Jews had to hustle to cross the Red Sea and, in their hurry——"

"Good enough," said Barry. "Look alive, Beth. You're next."

"Why on this night do we leave a place empty?" Beth read.

Two hands shot up at either end of the table. Benita ignored protocol and answered, "Because, on this night, we set a place for Elijah. That's why we leave the door open. So Elijah knows he's welcome at the table even if one of our guests is rudely sitting in his seat."

In one graceful movement, Bridget stood up, walked around the table, picked up Benita, swung her over her back, and carried her out of the room. Benita tried every method of weakening Bridget—clawing her back, kicking her stomach, and assaulting her eardrums. But Bridget held fast to her writhing sister until reaching her bedroom, at which point, she dropped Benita with a decisive shove and promptly locked the door. Unfortunately, Benita was also skilled at the art of window escape. Within minutes, the doorbell rang and Bridget, just returning to the living room, opened the front door to welcome Benita back.

The other girls seemed not to notice the entrance.

"I told you Bell wasn't coming," Belinda whispered.

"Just wait," said Beryl, gazing meaningfully at the door.

"I hate to break it to you," said Belinda, "but you're not psychic. I wouldn't trust you with a weather report."

"I see pain in your future," Beryl said. Her eyes glazed over like a storefront gypsy's, and, while smiling innocently, she stomped on Belinda's foot.

"Beth!" cried Belinda.

"What?" screamed Beth.

"You kicked me," said Belinda.

"I did not," said Beth.

Beryl smiled demurely as fighting escalated on either side of her.

At this point, the seder became a lockdown situation. Every time Barry piped in with a story or joke, Bunny recoiled in outrage. She needed only utter the words, "But my father," to shame Barry into submission. The girls mouthed along with the Hebrew to the best of their abilities, having learned that repeating the word "watermelon" made it appear as though they were forming Hebrew words. All guests looked on with aching discomfort, fumbling along with the Haggadah's phonetic spelling while Bunny led the group through an endless series of songs and, for all they knew, nonsensical prayers.

Throughout, Charles presided over the meal from the living room floor. Age had weakened his old bones, preventing him from alighting even the distance from the floor to the living room sofa. When Charles needed food, he hobbled slowly across the floor, his feet making a light skittering sound like a crab on rocks. Now, every time Charles moved, the seder's insufferable music was underscored by the syncopated rhythm of his walk. This sound served as a sadistic reminder to the hungry guests that they must wait patiently for unknowable hours while this barely mobile dog fed himself at will.

Finally, the girls drew on their secret weapon. One by one, they commenced whistling—at first, imperceptibly, then with gusto—a medley of songs they usually reserved for long car trips. Though Charles clued in within the first few bars, the hungry guests only registered an irksome squeak. It was not until the girls cued each other to explode into a chorus that those still intent on reading from the Torah finally admitted defeat. The girls smiled at each other in mutual congratulation. But their smiles faded as they realized their plan had backfired. Bunny, irate at the interruption, began a prayer she'd nearly completed from the beginning.

At nine o'clock, the assembled guests drew dangerously close to diabetic blood-sugar levels. Responding to Bella's pinch under the table, Barry regained sensation in his right leg and awoke from a ten-minute nap.

"Bunny," Barry tried, "here's an idea. Why don't you let Latrell sing a song?"

Belinda glared at her father. She removed a piece of gefilte fish from the seder plate and threw it at her father's head, causing a cross fire of yelling to converge on the table. None of the guests noticed when Trot emptied and refilled his fourth glass, when Bella toasted Trot and winked seductively, or when Latrell excused himself and silently slipped out the front door. Charles, however, saw his chance and slipped out with Latrell.

"I wish Billy was sitting next to me," Benita whined.

"I wish Beth was sitting next to Billy," said Belinda.

"I wish Bell were here," said Beth.

"I wish this service were over," Trot announced, "but that doesn't mean I can eat."

Barry looked up at Trot suddenly and laughed a strange, surprised laugh.

This odd fermata was interrupted by another arrival. Bell stood still at the front door, pale and panic-stricken like a terrified bride. Her clothes, a very worn pair of jeans, ratty sneakers, and an oversized gray sweatshirt, revealed she had forgotten the occasion altogether or else come straight from prison. Two large duffel bags at her feet indicated she planned to stay for a while.

"I told you," said Beryl.

"I knew it," said Belinda.

"Sweetie!" Bella shouted.

"Bell," her other sisters exclaimed in unison.

"Good news," said Barry. "You're just in time. Now, you're still eligible to compete."

Bridget pulled up a chair for her sister and Bell squeezed in between Bridget and Trot. Immediately attuned to Bell's fragile state, Bridget tried to preempt further discomfort by subtly—or so she intended—bringing Bell up to speed. "Psst," she whispered. "Blaine is here." But instead of alerting Bell to his presence, Bridget only succeeded in embarrassing her.

"Bridget," Blaine scolded. "Why are you whispering? I'm getting divorced, not going deaf."

Barry cleared his throat while Bell settled in, at once creating suspense and repulsing those who still harbored hopes of eating. The girls knew their father well enough to distinguish between important announcements and things they could tune out. They sensed, at the moment, that they should remain very alert.

"The approach of my sixtieth birthday has brought up some pressing questions. Age, you will find, is an urgent reminder of youth's tenacity." He paused enigmatically then scanned the room. Finally, pleased with his effect, he launched into his soliloquy. "Girls, I am glad you were born when you were. In feudal times, girls were not so lucky. Land was valuable and families were large. Laws were passed to consolidate property. According to one, the law of primogeniture, the firstborn son was automatically entitled to the family fortune." Barry glanced conspicuously at his daughters to gauge their anxiety. "Because of these terrible laws, the daughters were quite shortchanged. Generations of women were condemned to marry their ugly cousins. Isn't that right?"

The girls nodded at their father.

"Wrong," Barry shouted. "These laws were not terrible. They were quite ingenious. In their absence, land was divided into value-less specks, and, though I mean no offense to Billy and Blaine, a name without money is just a pretty name . . ."

Bell and Bridget exchanged a look of sincere alarm. Both sensed the glimmer of madness in their father's eyes.

"In a matriarchy, one does not have this problem. A queen cannot confer power to her husband nor bestow it upon her younger brother. And yet, while a queen's power matches a king's, it is still no rival to that of her baby boy. A prince—I'm sorry, girls, I didn't write the rules—will always trump a queen."

Barry's rambling had its desired effect, essentially hypnotizing his guests. "Competition," he went on, "is evolution's greatest force. Rivalry between species is the engine of divergence. But competition is at its most forceful when it occurs within one species. Which is why I've designed a contest of sorts . . ."

"I abstain," smirked Belinda.

"I'm going to win," said Benita.

"What is it?" said Beth.

"Now Dad," said Bridget.

Bell avoided her father's gaze. She was suddenly convinced that he was staring directly at her.

Barry smiled then stopped himself, as though to experience such delight in the presence of others was just too cruel. "Due to the shortage of a male heir in your generation, the Barnacle name faces extinction. So, I'm issuing a challenge to you, my six daughters, to remedy this fact. I don't care how you do it, so long as you do. Whoever can figure out a way to immortalize the Barnacle name will be named the sole beneficiary of my estate."

No one spoke for several moments.

Barry luxuriated in the success of his oration by taking several more bites.

"How dare you," whispered Bunny.

"How delightful," cried Bella.

"Sexist bastard," snarled Belinda. "Why don't you just come out and say it? You just want to marry us off."

"Now, Belinda," Barry said. "You're smarter than that. Besides"— he turned to the boys at the table—"I would never allow any daughter of mine to marry a man who had designs on her inheritance."

"I can tell you right now," Beth said, "I'm never getting married so I guess that means I lose."

"Beth," Barry chided, "don't be narrow-minded. Marriage is only one of many ways to perpetuate a name."

"Such as?" Beth asked.

"Getting knocked up," snarled Belinda.

Barry ignored Belinda and answered Beth. "You'll have to figure those out. If I told you there would be no point in competing." He paused to allow his daughters the chance to ponder the thought. "The terms of the contest are simple. I'll accept your proof in any form, any sufficient and credible evidence that you've managed to immortalize your great, challenged name. In exactly one week, we will meet at this table and you will present your achievements to me. After everyone has plead her case, I will name the winner."

Finally, as was custom at the Barnacle seder, the table broke into a brawl.

Bunny stood from the table, flipped her hair violently, and headed for her bedroom.

"You're a sexist and a misogynist," Belinda spat. "God gave you girls to punish you."

"Shut up," Beth whispered. "Both of those words mean the same thing."

Billy and Blaine stood up simultaneously.

Benita jumped up and ran after Billy.

Bridget lunged forward and followed Benita.

Trot toasted the table and downed his glass of wine.

Bell stood still and surveyed the chaos. Perhaps, she decided, this was not the best time to tell her family that she was pregnant. Instead, she took advantage of the lull in conversation. "Dad," she said, "would it be all right if I stayed at home for a while?"

5

Insomnia

*B*ell did not sleep well her first night at home. While she slept, or rather tried to sleep, she found herself repeating the same urgent mantra: You can never go home, you can never go home, you can never go home. It was official, Bell decided. She had become the stuff of romance novels, an aging spinster, a luckless loser, a bona fide burnout, a botched experiment, a big fat letdown. It was not so much that she had fallen behind, but rather that she had dropped out of the race; that, somewhere along the way, she had fallen and couldn't get up. Finally, after hours of torture, Bell gave up on sleep. Perhaps it was her vocation, she decided, to bring the family average down.

Still, she made a mighty effort at optimism. To that end, she switched genres. Her life, she decided, was not a romance, but rather an edge-of-your-seat mystery, the center of which was the paternity of her unborn child. Of course, there were other deep burning questions, such as whether she would ever get out of bed and, of course, how, in God's name, she was going to fix her life. Due to one particularly drunken week three months ago, Bell had finally done irreparable damage. When she looked back on that week, she could neither remember how she'd made it to bed nor with whom. Would that Blaine had been in her bed, she thought, switching genres yet again. Her life would be a raunchy bodice-ripper if Blaine Finch III, the boy next door, were the father of her child. Comforted, Bell drifted back to sleep for a precious minute. But she was jolted awake by a disturbing realization: Her life was a gripping whodunit in which the "it" was sex.

Consciousness came on around ten o'clock. Bell spent her first blurry waking hour staring intently at her bedroom wall as though it hid, in hieroglyphics, the answers to life's mysteries. Within minutes, she felt as she had in sleep, stomped on by worry. The decor of her childhood bedroom did her no favors, its candy pink walls a sneery reminder of her once-rosy outlook. Posters and clippings taped to the walls were in on the joke as well, dating her childhood with the accuracy of an archaeologist. A stack of records she and Bridget had amassed, once coveted, now presented a difficult ethical dilemma, to hock or not to hock. Cluttered trophies, once proud emblems of a shiny future, had transformed into a crowd of spectators cheering her downfall. Her entire bedroom had been preserved as a monument to her early promise. One object in particular stood out.

For ten years straight, a Yankees hat had perched atop her bedpost. It was not a souvenir from a game, but rather a keepsake given to her by Blaine one very memorable night. The night of the twins' sixteenth birthday marked a momentous event, as surprising for the two eldest Barnacle girls as for the history of science. Though the boys had exhibited bizarre twin behavior since the moment they were born, this night they acted in such uncanny synchrony, were graced with such scary telepathy that it truly seemed that the two boys shared the very same brain. Though one would expect environment to whittle them apart by this age, the boys proved to be as linked as ever as they clambered up their neighbors' fire escape without ever discussing such a plan, and crept into Bell and Bridget's window, one ten minutes after the other.

At ten of midnight, Billy climbed in the window and tiptoed across the room, then took a seat on the edge of Bridget's bed and gently shook her shoulder.

"Bridget, will you marry me someday?" he asked. He gripped the comforter nervously as he waited for her response. Lacking a ring, he offered his most valuable possession: his official Red Sox cap.

Unfortunately, Bridget said no and laughed off her hammy friend. Still, she submitted to Billy's request and followed him down the fire escape for a night of underage drinking.

At midnight, Blaine climbed in the same window and tiptoed across the room, and then took a seat on the edge of Bell's bed and gently tapped her arm.

Lacking a ring, he offered his most valuable possession: an official Yankees cap. "Bell, will you marry me someday?" he asked.

But Bell said yes before Blaine said "someday" and she meant it wholeheartedly, too. Even at this tender age, she already understood the nature of this contract. Deciding to hold Blaine to his commitment whenever someday arrived, she placed the cap on her bedpost as a jog to her memory. Guessing that Bridget would be out until morning, she invited Blaine to stay for the night.

Ever since, she cherished her Yankees cap, treating it as collateral of sorts. She used it as a reader would a bookmark, to hold the place of an important chapter, a favorite scene from her life. She wore it all the time, while she studied, at movies, sometimes to sleep. But she was always careful not to wear it in Blaine's vicinity, fearful of betraying her obsession. Instead, Bell packed the cap in a bag whenever she left the house, sometimes walking several blocks before putting it on her head.

Now, Bell decided, the cap had taken on new meaning. It no longer served as a token from a past romance, but rather as a promissory note, a coupon, an IOU. Perhaps, Bell thought hopefully, Blaine had not forgotten his meaningful gift. Perhaps it had been given in expectation of their long separation, in acknowledgment of life's cruel twists and turns, in anticipation of the day when Bell would call on her claim, when her patient love would be rewarded, when she would finally collect. In an instant, Bell revised her life story and hope swirled into her heart. The last ten years had not been a series of delays and missed opportunities. Rather, this time had been a necessary hibernation, just penance for the privilege of perfect love. She had de-evolved, Bell realized now, to another kind of type. First, she was a winner, then she was a quitter, and now, she decided with a deep proud breath, she was . . . well, she wasn't sure yet.

At least it was Saturday, Bell reasoned, that was one comforting fact. On weekdays the city was too quiet; her thoughts, as a result, too loud in her head, each one echoing there for hours like some wild thing, howling. On weekdays, it was impossible to ignore her alienation from the planet. On weekdays, she could not forget the fact that everyone she knew was hard at work, that she could not get a job despite, she thought, her very impressive credentials. It seemed the only task she could accomplish lately was making her bed, and even this was a struggle. Her former boss had seconded this notion when she fired Bell three weeks earlier, suggesting that Bell was perhaps more suited to a job in a creative arena. Did creative arenas, Bell wondered, extend all the way to one's bed? Luckily, on Saturdays, these were not her concerns. On Saturdays, the whole world joined Bell in her day of rest.

"Bell." The voice was high and shrill despite its apparent distance. The voice, Bell noted, as it approached, did not sound entirely unlike a bell, except not the tinkling silvery kind, but rather the kind used to signal the end of class or a five-alarm fire. "Barry said you wanted to wake up early." Bunny was clearly as annoyed as Bell to be enlisted in such distasteful work.

"I never said that," Bell managed to yell, though her vocal cords were not quite up to the task.

"He said you wanted to get an early crack at the want ads," Bunny added.

"It's Saturday," Bell moaned. Then, realizing this statement was not self-explanatory, she added, "It's my day of rest."

A chorus of angels might as well have joined in harmonious reply. Five voices united from their bedrooms to put Bell in her place. "It's Friday," one voice yelled.

"It's Friday."

"It's Friday."

"It's Friday."

Humbled, Bell closed her eyes again and resumed her effort to blot reality out. Unfortunately, closing her eyes brought her yet closer to her muddled thoughts, forcing the searing self-analysis she hoped to avoid. Once, long ago, Bell had been the kind of girl who found life delicious. She had felt and expressed, on a daily basis, delight and wonderment. When it snowed, she was the first to run outside and throw her arms in the air, to gaze up at the sky with real gratitude, cupping her hands and sticking out her tongue so as to catch falling snowflakes. She was the first to call her friends on their birthdays. She coined new holidays all the time and, when she was in a particularly good mood, even invented new drinks. (Her personal favorite was a refreshing winter beverage whose recipe called for fresh New York City snow.)

When it was nice out, she was the first to say what a lovely day it was, to smile instructively at those people who seemed not to have noticed yet. She always watched the weather report, so she knew when to bring an umbrella and when to make alternate plans. She was rarely late, she paid her bills on time, and, on those occasions when she did receive a gift, she wrote long, personal thank-you letters in an impressively prompt amount of time. Indeed, Bell was one of those rare creatures who appreciated life before living much of it, who valued her friends and family before losing any of them. Now, years later, she was truly hard-pressed to remember the girl she used to be and, what's more, found that girl annoyingly earnest and naive.

At least, Bell decided, she could take comfort in the fact that one skill had remained intact: She could still complete the *New York Times* crossword puzzle with a ballpoint pen. On a good day, it took her a couple of hours. On Sunday, it took the whole day. Either way, Bell proudly eschewed pencil and managed, with a few inconspicuous smudges, to complete the puzzle in ink. Encouraged by this fact, Bell did her best to entomb herself in her bed and, within minutes, managed to make serious progress on the puzzle. She knew twelve across immediately: Leda's beaked seducer was Zeus. Twenty-five down came easily, too: Famous brothers in baseball were Don and Joe DiMaggio. At least, Bell decided, the trivia she had accumulated, though essentially worthless in life, was valuable for something.

Indeed, Bell could claim a whole host of useless information at her fingertips. She could recite Yeats's poem "Leda and the Swan" by heart and understood the mythological allusions. She knew that Castor and Pollux, the "Gemini twins," were not actually twins, but half brothers. She knew that the twins abducted a pair of sisters named Phoebe and Hilaria, who were also known, in Greek mythology, as the morning and evening twilight. She knew how the boys were punished for this act, that Pollux was killed by the girls' husbands, and that Castor, bereft without his twin, begged Zeus to let him die, too, so he could rejoin his brother. She knew Zeus took pity on the boys and struck a compromise, allowing the boys to split the duties of the Gemini constellation, one standing guard during the day while the other took his post at night.

Bell knew that the best tennis players in history were also a pair of twins, that the Rinsey brothers only rose to greatness after their competitors, the Doherty brothers, also twins, were killed in World War I. She knew that Joe DiMaggio and Ted Williams were tied for the highest RBI in Yankees history; that the emu had been an endangered species since 1973, two years longer than the manatee. She could tell you the names of all nine muses, the seven colors in the electromagnetic spectrum, the abbreviations for every element on the periodic table. She could tell you how to calculate the volume of a parallelogram, the length of the hypotenuse of an isosceles triangle, the exponential change in a parabolic function and the area underneath. She could recite the dates of Europe's major wars. She could hold her own on Renaissance art. She could recite, in Old English, the first verse of the *Canterbury Tales* and, if pressed, the preamble to the Constitution. She knew where the eustachian tube was found; that the human eye had seven parts, three more than the heart. And yet, despite this wealth of knowledge, Bell still could not tell you, not if her life depended on it, how it felt to love someone and be loved back.

But rather than delay her progress on the puzzle, Bell quickly dismissed these troubling thoughts and, finding herself boxed in on the upper right side, yelled down the hall for some help.

"What do swans and human beings have in common?" she shouted.

"How many letters?" someone replied.

"Eight," Bell yelled then, after counting, "Blank, blank, blank, 'O', 'G', blank, blank, blank."

The voice said nothing for a moment.

Bell tried in vain to fit in "romance," but to no avail.

"Monogamy," said the voice.

Humbled, Bell filled in the letters. Then, setting the paper on her lap, she leaned forward and opened her shutters. And finding even sunlight joined the chorus of her critics, she decided to get out of bed.

Looking down, she was appalled by her appearance. Gone was the leggy and lithe woman of her college days, the swanlike turnout of an unusual, if not technically ugly, duckling. Born nine pounds and seven ounces, she had rivaled the massive Barnacle bird at her first Thanksgiving. But now her once formidable size could be counted as a liability. Her legs now lagged where they had once flown. Her cheeks now drooped instead of smiled. Her eyes, once bright and confident, had flattened to a dull gray. Even her skin had taken on a strange sickly color, as though subject to the same green tint of Belinda's hair. With wind of the right force, her baggy plaid pajamas could have doubled as a hot air balloon. Her T-shirt emitted its own tangy smell. Her unwashed face added further contrast to the dark bags under her eyes. Her teeth felt disturbingly mossy when she ran her tongue across them. Her hair had gone now months without a cut and had reached that alarming length at which split ends and feathered tufts could be confused for a retro haircut. Still, she chose, she thought quite rationally, against changing her clothes. It would be dishonest, a cover-up of sorts. Nice clothes would be an inaccurate representation of her inner state. As though on cue, an old epithet echoed in her head. I'm failing, she thought. I don't work anymore. I can't cope.

Lately, Bell had found even the simplest task challenging: getting through a full day of work, going to the bank or for a run, shopping for groceries, paying her bills, communicating with delivery boys— even the cute one at the local Thai place who clearly had a crush on her. All of these things fatigued her so fully she wondered if she might be terribly ill. She was sure her friends were horribly wrong when they cheerfully insisted that this kind of fatigue was a classic sign of depression and therefore something that could be easily cured by today's myriad drugs. Depression, Bell usually countered, was a euphemism for failure, a way to assuage colossal flame-outs about the magnitude of their flop, a nice name for everyone who had once promised to be a great writer and now had trouble writing a thank-you letter, let alone writing in a straight line.

What, Bell wanted to ask her friends, was the name of the disease she had, a disease whose insidious symptoms included an inability to get through a day of work without crying, to stand up again after sitting down for lunch, to make it through a dinner with friends without yearning to escape to the safety of one's bed? What, Bell wondered, was the name for the disorder that compelled you to throw yourself at random boys in bars, to have sex with total strangers in the bathrooms of those bars, in cabs, in spare bedrooms at parties, and, once, in a subway car. What ailment caused you to cry at the slightest minor chord progression, whether in a favorite Beatles song or a credit card commercial? What sickness allowed you to get dressed for a run only to stop at your own front door; to say things you didn't mean to say, to speak your mind when you really should be polite; to tell the most powerful editor at Gottesman that her biggest book was a flat, self-indulgent piece of crap that was not even fit to be scrap paper in the copy machine at which your time, your mind, and very expensive college education were flagrantly wasted? What sickness then caused you to laugh out loud after losing such ungainful employment, but only long enough to make it to the sidewalk and burst into tears?

Stumped by this onslaught of questions, Bell strained to reach the newspaper on the floor of her bedroom. It didn't matter that it was three days old. Reading the newspaper was an act of rebellion against facts. She had no interest in the news or headlines; it was purely a diversion. She was the first to concede it was an odd and slightly maudlin habit. But in the last few years, she had changed her approach to reading the *New York Times,* replacing her perusal of the wedding announcements with a thorough scan of the obituaries. The two sections, she felt, were oddly similar, both providing snapshots of other lives narrated in euphemistic tones before they headed into eternal bliss. And yet, the change of habit represented a deeper change within Bell, marking the moment at which she realized that her chances of being featured in the former section were slimmer than the latter. So, it was with rapt interest and some measure of bias that she scoured the pithy paragraphs, noting effective prose and moving flourishes as though making a study of the genre.

Finding even this activity failed to lift her mood, she drew on another favorite pastime, removing a magazine from a pile on the floor and turning to the horoscope pages. "Natura non facit saltum." She struggled to remember high-school Latin to interpret the advice of the stars. "Nature does not move in leaps and bounds."

Indeed, Bell thought. Nature is a tortoise. Slow and steady wins the race. Satisfied, she turned to the forecast for Blaine. But before she could indulge in this petty fantasy, she was privy to an unwelcome and wholly unforecasted visit.

An angry rap at Bell's window revealed an intruder. Due to her recent haircut and dye job, Belinda looked something like an alien as she cowered on the fire escape, her face pressed to Bell's windowpane. With the overblown gestures of a silent film actress, Belinda desperately tried to explain through the glass just how cold it was outside and otherwise entreat Bell to grant her reentry. Apartment logistics had forced Belinda to find alternate modes of escape due to the fact that Barry's office looked directly onto her window and Barry was, of course, an insomniac. Luckily, Bell and Bridget had left for college just as Belinda's rebellious streak struck, leaving their bedroom available for use as a launching pad. It was true; rebelliousness was a uniform trait among the Barnacle girls. But Belinda, perhaps because she was born fourth, was four times as wild as the rest.

Too exhausted to protest, Bell opened the window. Belinda squeezed through expertly then proceeded to walk over Bell's bed as though it had been draped with red carpet explicitly for her entry. She jumped to the ground with a small thud, smiled sweetly at Bell then, reaching covertly behind her back, attempted to steal Bell's baseball hat.

"What do you think you're doing?" Bell demanded.

"I need to borrow it," Belinda said, "in order to cover my hair." Belinda's latest boyfriend, a senior at her own prep school, did not approve of Belinda's coif. His argument, however, had more merit than the boy himself.

"What you need," Bell corrected, "is to stop doing stupid things like shaving your head." At this, Bell reached and managed miraculously to snatch back her hat. "How dare you at a time like this? The season starts next week."

It was perhaps the only thing the Barnacle girls agreed on. Every year, from April to October, the Barnacle house was obsessed. The girls spent hours watching and listening to games and, whenever possible, attending them at the stadium. But their agreement ended there. Bell, Belinda, and Beryl were die-hard Yankees fans; Bridget, Beth, and Benita loved the Sox. Both camps were equally vocal in support of their teams and reveled in frequent virulent debates over their respective merits. Nothing could beat the excitement, Bell felt, of Bucky Dent's glorious three-run home run during the one-game play-off in 1978 between the Yanks and the Red Sox. The Sox could beat it, Benita argued. And they finally did in 2004 when, pitches away from elimination, they made the comeback of the century, reversing a three-game losing streak to win the play-offs and then the Series.

Of course, Yankees fans had ample evidence of Red Sox failures with which to combat Benita's bragging. The '86 World Series was one such example. Only a team of misfits and losers could manage to lose with a two-run lead. Moreover, in Bell's opinion, the Red Sox recent victory was but a momentary reprieve from a future of continued failure, an act of mercy from gods embarrassed by their pitiful eighty-six-year losing streak. Of course, the 2004 World Series had fanned the flames of rivalry, giving the Yanks a run for their money and the Red Sox a healthy dose of confidence. The Series, aside from being the most dramatic in recent memory, had turned on a dime in a seven-game play-off when Ortiz hit not one, but two walk-off home runs, saving the Sox from infamy and reversing the fate of his team.

"The hat," Belinda persevered, "is a critical accessory. This guy's not into green spikes."

"The only thing that's critical," Bell countered, "is that you go back to your room. Maybe if you stay in it long enough, your hair will grow back."

Thwarted, Belinda regarded her sister with new antipathy then, changing her tack, she offered her most endearingly desperate look before giving up and resuming her path. She stopped at the door and turned her head with an extravagant swivel. "Also, I'm missing my favorite dress. Strapless. Green. Taffeta. So, if you don't mind," she said, folding her arms, "I'll just wait right here until you return it."

Bell said nothing in response. She only widened her eyes. Then, deciding apathy was her best hope, she allowed her eyelids to droop. Perhaps Belinda was just the narcotic she needed to finally find sleep.

Unfortunately, just before submitting to her drowsiness, Bell was roused by a slight movement in her periphery. She lurched suddenly, intercepting the theft and grabbing her hat from harm's way.

"Get out of my room!" Bell shouted.

"Your room?" Belinda snorted and surveyed it imperiously. Out of habit, she twirled, or rather tried to twirl, a phantom strand of hair much like a person who, after losing his watch, continues to check his wrist. Finding she lacked the hair to twirl, Belinda found a new activity for her free hand and swooped it dangerously close to Bell's face.

"If you're not gone in ten seconds," Bell said calmly, "I'm going to tell Bunny how many times you've had sex in her bed."

"You think you're so much older and wiser," said Belinda.

"I am older and wiser. By about ten years."

"I wouldn't boast," Belinda said. "I hope I don't have as many problems as you by the time I'm your age."

Bell's jaw dropped.

Belinda was silent. Sensing that she had struck a nerve, she smiled and, avoiding eye contact, quietly left the room.

It took Bell a moment to recover. Belinda was right. She was a disgrace. She had achieved the impossible. She, an older sister, had managed to lose her younger sister's respect. Self-pity, however, fueled Bell's temper and, in turn, her vengefulness. She rushed to her door to yell something rude but, finding the hall empty, thought better of it and sheepishly retreated.

Since it was nearing noon, Bell decided to finally start her day. Pulling a blanket around her shoulders, she traipsed across her room and prepared to brave the apartment. As she walked, she whistled Beethoven's Fifth. She was glad Barry had forced her to practice the piece as a child. It was appropriate background music, Bell decided, for her downfall. Hers was the same struggle as Beethoven's, a contest between C major and C minor, a war between nature and nurture, a fight played out, for the moment, on the battlefield of family. Bolstered, Bell skipped to the third movement, to the strange and inscrutable bridge, to the part when the minor theme is usurped by the major one, like a hare by a tortoise, where the minuet becomes a march, when the horn section overwhelms the strings, when ugly ducklings and swans and frogs and princes make their triumphant switch. As she hurried toward the kitchen, Bell decided to make perhaps two cups of coffee.

To Bell's dismay, Benita was already in the kitchen. She was huddled over the kitchen table, working on a complicated art project whose contents threatened, Bell noted, to infest the family's food. At the moment, she was threading string through the two top corners of a long, bannerlike triangle cut from a large sheet of construction paper. The rest of the table was covered with cotton balls that had been stretched and disembodied to resemble a bank of snow.

"Oh no," Bell said at the sight of her sister.

"What's wrong?" asked Benita.

"Oh nothing," said Bell. "It's just that . . . I thought you'd be at school."

"They sent me home," said Benita, "since it's a Jewish holiday. I tried to convince them to let me stay, but they insisted."

"I wonder why," Bell muttered.

Benita looked up. Bell smiled innocently. Benita went back to her work.

As Bell watched, she noted Benita's imperfections. Her eyebrows were slightly too large for her otherwise delicate face. Her eyes crossed slightly when she concentrated. Her legs, though long and lithe like her sisters', were a little bit stockier. There was no denying her mental problems. Barry's emphasis on competition had driven her over the edge. Benita would not stop at chewing glass; the child would kill to win. Luckily, Bell decided with some satisfaction, no one could accuse her of that.

Indeed, Benita had been consumed by the contest since its announcement the night before. At seven o'clock sharp, a half hour earlier than usual, she was practically propelled out of bed, anxious to spend the day finding the perfect strategy. In honor of the occasion, she took some license with her school uniform, eschewing the traditional lower school attire—a pinafore tunic in light yellow or green pinstripes—opting instead to wear her sister's plaid kilt even though the blue and green tartan was reserved for upper school girls. She paired the kilt with a black T-shirt, despite the school's universal mandate for collared white blouses. Wearing black, she felt, afforded an added degree of intimidation, just as flouting the school's strict collar rule suggested her willingness to break rules.

School immediately offered the inspiration Benita craved, with auditions for the Chapin School talent show less than a week away. This marked the recurrence of Benita's favorite school event, the opportunity to remind teachers, family, and classmates of her superiority. She had won it a handful of times with various songs, dances, and orations, and once with a crowd-pleasing performance of Beethoven's Fifth on the glockenspiel. And yet, Benita had never enjoyed a consecutive reign. She had been shortchanged by the school's tacit mandate that excellence be tempered with kindness. As a result of this overly saccharine stance, Benita had been denied the prize several times, suffering several second-place awards so that other, less talented classmates could enjoy their share of the spotlight. Her nemesis Mary Talbot, for example, had benefitted from this affirmative action, led to think she actually deserved first prize for her halting monologues and poor excuse for ballet. As a result, Benita had come to dismiss the talent show as a serious venue. Still, she rose to attention at the sound of the homeroom announcement reminding the girls that tryouts would take place on Monday.

By noon, she had a winning plan. On Monday morning, before the tryouts, she would confront her long-time nemesis, armed with her new information about Mary's anti-Semitism. Then, with Mary sufficiently humbled, Benita would challenge her to a duel. The challenge would amount to their own private battle enacted before the entire school, not only a measure of skill and popularity, but, at its essence, a contest between Christians and Jews. The talent show provided the perfect venue for such a grudge match, enabling Benita to put Mary Talbot in her place, while earning her family's gratitude. Aside from earning brownie points for defending her family name, she would surpass the petty achievements of her sisters, clinching first prize in the talent show, and winning her father's contest by a landslide.

"Want to know how I'm going to win the contest?" Benita demanded. Having successfully threaded the triangle, she began painting glue across its surface area with long leisurely strokes.

"No, not really," Bell responded.

Benita considered this for a moment, then dismissed it with a shrug. "I'm going to win the talent show this year with a scene from *King Lear*. Want to know which part I'm going to play?" she pressed.

"Goneril?" asked Bell.

"Nope," said Benita. "Every single one. I'm going to do different voices and everything."

Turning away, Bell walked to the stove and lit the flame under the teapot. Perhaps, today coffee would serve as an anaesthetic, not a stimulant.

Still smiling as though in response to a piece of very happy news, Benita began pulling stretched cotton over the sticky triangle. Without looking up from her project, she launched into a new line of questioning. "Did you have a nice time with Blaine?" she asked.

"When?" snapped Bell.

"At the seder," said Benita. "Don't even try to deny it. I saw you checking him out."

"Please," scoffed Bell. "He's barely divorced."

"Exactly," said Benita. "So he's looking." She pursed her lips as though to replicate the punctuation of "dot dot dot."

"You don't know what you're talking about," said Bell.

"I saw him looking at you, too," Benita said.

"You did?" Bell asked in spite of herself.

"Oh sure," said Benita. "He couldn't keep his eyes off you."

Bell smiled hopefully and sat down at the table.

"Oh wait," Benita said, tapping her head. "I was thinking of Billy. He was staring at Bridget all night. I had it in reverse."

Stricken, Bell glared at her sister.

Benita shrugged innocently. "You know how it is with those two. Who can tell them apart?"

Eminently pleased with her effect, Benita giggled devilishly. Her pleasure doubled by the simultaneous completion of her art project, she lifted the sticky triangle from the table and, using the string to tie it around the back of her head, held the gauzy mass to her chin and assumed a thespian stance. "Tell me, my daughters, since now we will divest us both of rule, interest of territory, cares of state, which of you shall we say doth love us most? That we our largest bounty may extend where nature doth with merit challenge." For added effect, she threw her voice into the lowest register she could manage and assumed a volume loud enough to project across a large stadium.

Bell stared, transfixed by her sister in spite of herself.

"Pretty good, right?" Benita asked.

But before Bell could muster a response, Benita scurried out of the kitchen, leaving Bell to enjoy a moment of much-deserved solitude. Desperate for any outlet for her irritation, Bell rushed to the refrigerator, removed the most accessible carton of juice and poured it into her mouth.

"How do you spell 'susceptible'?" asked Bunny.

Bell pivoted to find her stepmother standing inches away. Bunny stood, wielding a legal pad like a shield and fiercely clutching a pen.

"S-u-s-c," Bell responded, squinting thoughtfully. Embarrassed by her bad kitchen etiquette, she regarded the carton of juice quizzically as though she had meant to pour it into a glass and only just realized her mistake.

"Thank you," said Bunny. She leaned on the counter and scribbled something on her legal pad, then brushed past Bell impertinently and exited the kitchen.

Once she was alone again, Bell turned back to the refrigerator and emptied the rest of the carton into her mouth. Sated, she replaced the empty carton in the fridge and walked back to the stove. But as she resumed her coffee vigil, she detected something in her periphery. Turning, Bell realized Bunny had taped a note to the refrigerator door.

"WE ARE ALL SUSCEPTIBLE," the note explained in a threatening font, "TO EACH OTHER'S GERMS. SO," it went on, "IF YOU DRINK FROM THE CARTON, DRINK THE WHOLE THING OR THROW IT OUT."

Outraged, Bell surveyed the room and violently tore off the note.

6

Promiscuity

Wary of further contact with her family, Bell resolved to spend the afternoon locked up. No one would bother her in Barry's office. She would spend the rest of the day organizing her life. She opened the top drawer of her father's desk to find a sea of gold: Bunny's lifetime supply of legal pads, Bell remembered, was perhaps the only positive contribution Bunny had made to the family. She had brought it as a dowry of sorts when she moved into the apartment with no more explanation than the ominous claim that her ex-husband was very litigious. Pleased to receive something from Bunny after watching Bunny take freely from her family for so long, Bell availed herself of a brand new legal pad and, despite the association with paperback heroines, commenced writing a list of ways to improve her life.

Number one: Convince Blaine to be the father of her child. Failing this: Find suitable father. Satisfied with these items, Bell progressed to graphs and charts. On one she plotted the progress of her goals, the y-axis demarcating time, the x-axis charting whim. On a bar graph she named each sister and plotted positive and negative traits. On another, she charted the standard deviation of her sisters' IQ. On another, a two-columned "do" and "don't" list, Bell enumerated simple rules for parenting. On the "DON'T" side, she listed her parents' practices; she left the "DO" side empty. Finally, Bell designed a list with real practical value; it was a preventive measure of sorts, a history of her romantic mishaps, a chronicle, she thought, of the miseducation of Miss Bell Barnacle. She drew a line down the middle of the page to create two headings. On the left, she wrote the "UP SIDE" and listed boys before Blaine. On the right, she wrote "THE DOWN SIDE" and listed the boys she'd dated since.

First, there was Bernard, insignificant really, as far as their actual romance, but notable because he had been her first and because Bell had broken his heart. Second, there was Boyd, good-looking for a redhead and sexually voracious even by sixteen-year-old standards. Most of the fun with Boyd, however, was had at his mother's expense (who thought Bell was a bad influence) and, of course, at the sight of Boyd's shock of red hair. Next was Bashar, Indian and intriguing, wholeheartedly committed to Bell's education. Bashar put Bell on a regimen of hard-core heavy metal and underground drugs, or was it underground music and hard-core drugs? There was Brad, a teacher; and Bates, a tennis teacher; and Brant, a thirty-five-year-old tennis teacher; and Ben and Blake and Boris and a few others whose names she couldn't remember.

But Blaine Finch was Bell's first true love. No one else had even come close. Blaine was tall and wildly handsome and sharper than a talk show host. Blaine was talented and terribly cool. Blaine knew how to ballroom dance. Blaine was good at every sport, but his limbs were still long and graceful. And long ago, though Blaine would never admit it, Blaine was in love with Bell. What a terrible curse it was, Bell thought, to experience the best years of your life before turning twenty-one. She was condemned, thanks to Blaine, to the same nostalgia as a faded child star or an injured athlete.

To be sure, Bell's obsession with Blaine had much to do with their breakup. Their love affair ended as it started; in the middle of the night. One week after the double proposal, the twins repeated their trip. Billy and Bridget scampered down the fire escape to roam around the dark city. Bell and Blaine remained in the bedroom to enjoy the dark. Bell, sixteen and certain of nothing, was sure of one thing in life. Someday had finally arrived, she whispered. Someday could be tonight. Terrified, Blaine turned cruel suddenly. The proposal, Blaine claimed, was a joke. The deal was no longer on the table; it was meaningless pillow talk. But Bell was not so easily dissuaded. She was outraged at the injustice. And, already well versed in the law, Bell knew Blaine's proposal remained valid until it was officially retracted. Finally, Blaine lost his patience and fled, offering this as he departed: The proposal was not only null and void, the love behind it had suddenly turned to hatred. From that moment on, both parties rued the day they had allowed themselves to go so far, let alone with someone who lived so close.

Boyfriends after Blaine were decidedly lame. First, there was Bailey, a rebound gone awry. Next was Bobby, a bad actor with a bad cocaine habit. There was Bryan, a singer-songwriter, an Irish boy with an angelic face and the devil's own temper. Biff was a model and a couple years younger and not bad in bed but it was no big deal. Biddle was a blowhard and terrible in bed; Bell suspected, in fact, that Biddle was gay. She had tried hard to forget Bjorn, an obese aspiring poet. Bryce, a fiction professor, had taken Bell back to his office after workshop ostensibly to talk about writers, but actually so she could have sex with one. And let's not forget, though Bell did her best, Bronson, the aging Jewish writer, whom her friends referred to as "the Missing Link" not only because he was so old but because he resembled a chimp.

As her boyfriends grew steadily less promising, Bell's dread and frustration mounted. With every passing day, she grew more acutely aware of her distance from her deadlines. Each day yielded a new theory, a new plan of attack. Often, Bell made a logical error common to many New Yorkers. A New Yorker caught in rush hour traffic believes that some choice, however awful or ancient, could have prevented her current holdup. An alternate route, an earlier departure, a different cab driver, some better decision would have enabled her to end up somewhere other than where she was now. But, Bell, much like every New Yorker, is helpless at the hands of life's traffic jams. There is simply no street, no early enough departure, no kind enough cab driver, no correct decision that will enable you to avoid rush hour in New York.

By one o'clock, Bell had tired of her list and resorted to staring out the window. It was the same position from which she and her sisters had spied on the Finches as children and occasionally done cruel things to pedestrians on the street below. Every time someone passed, Bell leaned farther out the window. Every exhalation brought her closer to death, to a comprehensive view of the Finches' apartment, and to knowledge of the nuances of Blaine Finch's schedule. Blaine's tennis racket leaned on a chair in the Finches' living room. In an instant, Bell knew all she needed to know. Blaine's schedule had not changed in years. In expectation of his return, Bell left her father's office at exactly half past one, rushed down the hall, and positioned herself in the foyer to appear as though she were casually checking her mail.

The elevator arrived, depositing Blaine just as Bell opened the door. She reached for the stack of letters usually resting on the doormat at this hour. But, finding nothing, she stood up and folded her hands into her pockets like a guilty child after stealing a forbidden sweet.

"Bell," Blaine stammered. "Lovely to see you."

"Yes," Bell managed, "you, too."

For a moment, both stood in excruciating silence but for a strange, loud background noise that both deduced simultaneously to be the gurgling of Bell's stomach.

"It's going to be a great season," Blaine said. He smiled, Bell thought, condescendingly, and gestured at her head.

Bell blanched and swatted at her head to find a new source of mortification. In addition to her sagging sweatpants, she was still wearing Blaine's Yankees hat. "Go Yanks," she said, fumbling for something, anything to say. Then finding she had developed a spontaneous stutter, she blurted, "You know, if you're not doing anything, next Thursday is opening day."

"Oh," said Blaine, his smile falling, "unfortunately, I work on weekdays."

"Of course," said Bell. "I totally forgot. It's been so long since I . . ." She trailed off. Better to say nothing than go on like this.

"I'd tell you to ask my brother," Blaine said, "but it would make a traitor of him."

Bell looked at Blaine, confused.

Blaine paused then elaborated, "Billy's a Sox fan, of course."

Bell said nothing for a moment, waiting for inspiration.

"And everyone knows a Sox fan is a fool for life."

Bell smiled appreciatively at Blaine's joke.

Blaine stared at Bell intently as though debating whether she was mentally strong enough to handle his next query. "Bell, can I ask you a question?" he asked.

Bell nodded eagerly.

Blaine paused to torture her, or for effect, it was impossible to know. "Why do you hate me so much?" He asked this question of women often, usually with a smile on his face and at moments in conversation when it was totally apparent to both that he meant "love" not "hate."

"Hmm. I don't know," Bell said, pretending to ponder Blaine's question. Did he expect her to answer in earnest or with a witty remark? Bell considered her options. She could answer sincerely: "Because you broke my heart in a thousand pieces and now expect me to pretend we're mere acquaintances." Or with a joke: "Because of the way you dress." Or with a snide comment: "Because of your obnoxious smirk." Or she could take him by surprise: "The truth, Blaine

Finch, is that I've hated you since the day we met. I was a toddler and you were an infant and I knew even then." And, of course, it would be obvious to both that Bell meant "love" not "hate."

But before Bell could decide on her response, Blaine tired of the suspense. "Well, I'd better go," he said and ducked back into his apartment like a child terrified by a shadow.

Bell stood, paralyzed for a moment, replaying the conversation in her head. Then suddenly, the Finches' door opened again and Blaine stuck his head out, smiling apologetically.

"Hey, Bell," Blaine said, "if you don't mind, can I get that hat back?"

"Of course," Bell said and before she knew it, she reached up and returned her most cherished possession and relinquished the one proverbial thing she still had over Blaine's head.

Blaine took the hat, smiled politely, and disappeared into his apartment.

Bell stood alone in the foyer for a moment, then remembered Jorge. He stood in the elevator, its doors wide open, listening shamelessly to Bell and Blaine's conversation and wearing a pitying cringe. The building was one of the few remaining in New York equipped with a hand-operated elevator. As a result, Jorge had been privy to the high and low points of the Barnacle girls' childhoods. Sometimes, Bell was struck by his complete omniscience. Jorge had met and, in many cases, escorted out every boy Bell had ever allowed to sneak into her house except for, of course, those who took the window route and those who lived next door. In short, Jorge had more intimate knowledge of Bell than anyone in the world; all Bell knew of Jorge was what he chose to disclose.

"Hi, Jorge," Bell said, stepping into the elevator. Until that moment, she'd had no intention of going outside or riding the elevator down, but after her excruciating encounter with Blaine, it seemed like the right thing to do.

"Bell," said Jorge. Jorge claimed, since Bell was first of the Barnacle girls, that she was his first love. Also, Bell was convinced (though she could never be completely sure) that Jorge stared at her backside whenever she left the building.

"I'm glad I don't see you with that boy anymore." Jorge took full advantage of the elevator's forced confinement to make ominous comments like this and otherwise to intimidate his passengers into acquiescence.

"Which one?" Bell asked, distracted.

"All of them," said Jorge.

He had a point, Bell admitted. But the idea of Jorge passing judgment on her romantic history irked her more than usual today. "You shouldn't be so happy," Bell advised. "At this rate, I'm going to die a spinster."

"No way," said Jorge. "How old are you now?"

"Twenty-nine," Bell said.

Jorge's hand slipped from the lever, causing the elevator to stop abruptly. He turned suddenly to face Bell, his eyes bulging as though she'd just informed him she had a life-threatening disease.

"Why are you surprised?" Bell scolded. "You've known me since the day I was born."

Jorge shook his head, befuddled, and applied pressure on the lever again. "I have," he said, stupefied. "I guess I forgot I'd been working here thirty years."

Their stance, Bell noted, two people trapped in a small space, both staring at the same wall, both waiting to make their escape, was an apt, if disturbing metaphor for her family. She decided to keep this to herself and to ignore Jorge's curious stare when she informed him, on arrival in the lobby, that she actually had no intention of leaving the building and could she please ride back up.

When Bell returned to her father's office, Barry was expecting her.

"Perfect timing," he said. "I was just looking for you."

"Don't you mean," Bell said, "you were just spying on me?" She tried to exit her father's office, but he blocked the door and pushed it closed, effectively locking Bell in.

According to her sisters' reports, Barry had finally crossed the line between eccentric and insane. Every day, at six o'clock, Barry walked into his office with the intention of doing an hour of work. Two hours later, he yelled down the hall, more irritated than apologetic, for Bunny to stop pestering him and please start dinner without him. Eight hours later, Barry could still be found refining a new contraption. It was as though his impressive work ethic relied on this feat of self-delusion; he must trick himself into thinking he only had an hour of work in order to sustain concentration for the rest of the night.

If asked to defend this new obsession, Barry drew on his heritage. He threw up his hands, raised his eyebrows, and pursed his lips in the traditional Yiddish gesture for indignation. If pressed, he made stock excuses. Business was no longer challenging, his mind was better utilized in the service of important problems. Among his solutions to these problems were a two-in-one pair of glasses meant to correct both myopia and far-sightedness, colored salt for those who desired a better indication of the amount present on one's plate, a computer rig that allowed writers to type standing up, and a device for hygienic hugging that prevented the exchange of germs.

"A man doesn't want to be pursued," Barry said. "It's in his evolutionary makeup to chase."

Bell delivered a hateful glare and tried to push past again.

"Competition creates value," Barry announced, "in every marketplace." He said this with the volume and pomposity necessary to address a large lecture hall.

"God gave you daughters to punish you," Bell said. "He knew you wanted a son."

"Bell," Barry said, ignoring the attack, "can I ask you a question?"

Bell neither nodded nor acknowledged his request.

"Why do you hate men?" Barry asked. He widened his eyes and tensed his shoulders as though to prepare for physical impact.

"It's said that a woman's relationship with men is a mirror of her relationship with her father."

"Oh," Barry paused to ponder this. "Have you ever considered dyeing your hair blond?"

"Belinda is right. You're a sexist pig."

"I'm simply telling you how men think," said Barry. "It's one thing I happen to know about."

"You know how sexist male chauvinist pigs think." Bell paused for another moment, still registering shock, then plumbed the doorknob violently.

"Oh," Barry said, "one more thing. I want you to meet a friend of mine. I hope you'll cancel your dinner plans." Barry grinned devilishly. "That is, if you have any."

Bell narrowed her eyes hatefully.

"You and Duncan have a lot in common. He's very rich, he's very handsome, and he's an excellent dancer."

"Dad," Bell sighed, "I don't dance anymore."

For some reason, Barry could not be dissuaded of the notion that dancing was Bell's greatest skill. He had been certain of this since Bell's fifth-grade talent show, the very same one in which Benita intended to compete. The event had made an indelible impression on both Barry and Bell. For Bell, who was rejected due, she was told, to the "eccentric" nature of her solo, it was a memory marked by shame. For Barry, who demanded a meeting with the school's headmistress to discuss the meaning of the word "eccentric" and subsequently threatened the school with a lawsuit, it was a very proud day.

"Eccentric" was, in Bell's opinion, a polite way of saying she was a bad dancer. In Barry's opinion, it was overwhelming proof that the Chapin School hated Jews. "Eccentric," Barry informed his daughters, was a disparaging word people used for nonconformists. "Nonconformist," he hastened to add, was a disparaging word people used for individuals. "Individuals," he wrapped up, was simply code for Jews. The world is full of destroyers, Barry would conclude, who wanted to squelch individuality.

Bell knew her relationship with her father was the stuff of psychology textbooks. Freud would have enjoyed hours of amusement parsing out its contradictions. She was at once ashamed and in awe of her father, placing him in the awkward position of idol and idiot. When she was younger, their relationship seemed standard enough; most of her friends were mortified by their parents. And yet, the problem worsened as Bell grew older. Other fathers receded into the background, while Barry loomed larger. Her mortification was justified, Bell felt, despite her deep-seated respect. No one else's father spoke with such a strange accent; no one else's father wore mismatched shoes; no one else's father ate at such fine restaurants and still managed to stain his lapel with soup.

And yet, this deep and abiding shame was accompanied by its polar opposite: Bell was deeply proud and protective of Barry. He was one of the few fathers she knew who had made his things for himself. He had earned, not inherited, the clutter in his house, read all the books on his shelves, could help Bell with her math homework without studying the textbook. Her friends' fathers were, by contrast, wholly incompetent, a pasty race of lazy men who collected children as they did country homes, whose interest in their children matched their interest in their vacations. Even so, Bell couldn't help longing Barry would dress a little more like these men. As Bell aged, these conflicting emotions evolved, morphing, even after years of therapy, into complicated pathologies.

"Bell," Barry tried again, changing his tack. "Duncan Schoenfeld is a very successful doctor. If things don't work out for you in the arts, he could take care of you . . ."

Bell stood still in indignant horror. She had not even mentioned her aspiration to write a novel in several years, wary of her father's token response: She had a greater chance of getting married than getting published and, should she accomplish either goal, neither would afford the lifestyle to which she was accustomed. "Dad, you are all the ways feminism failed. The state should have taken your daughters from you."

"I see," said Barry, grinning slyly. "Do feminists accept monthly checks from their fathers?"

"That's low," Bell hissed.

"I'm genuinely curious," Barry pressed. "Do the fathers of all feminists pay their daughters' phone bills?"

"For your information," Bell announced, "I've been supporting myself since college."

"Since you *dropped out of* college," Barry corrected. " 'Since college' implies that you graduated."

"Dropping out of Harvard," Bell countered, "is like graduating from any other school."

"Bell," Barry said, with a condescending smile, "I just want you to be able to lead the life you are accustomed to."

"To which *you* are accustomed," Bell corrected with a supercilious smirk.

Barry bowed his head in concession.

"If this family is any indication," Bell hissed, "wealth does not ensure happiness."

"I couldn't agree with you more," Barry said then, as though considering the accuracy of this statement, he added, "Besides, I know some poor people who are very happy."

Bell shook her head, trading anger for despair. Her father was beyond reason.

"Anyway, you needn't worry about these things if you take my advice. Just marry a man who's at least fifteen years older than you. That way, relatively speaking, you'll always seem young."

"I am young," sneered Bell.

Barry raised his eyebrows. Bell had to put her hands in her pockets to prevent herself from reaching out and ripping Barry's eyebrows off. Then, as though to preempt such violence, Barry reached into his pocket and produced a wad of cash. "Buy yourself some new clothes," he said. "How can you expect to attract a man when you dress like this?"

Bell was torn between spitting in her father's face and responding intelligently. Garnering all the strength she could muster, she deigned to share what knowledge of women's history she had retained from college. "Spinsters," Bell declared, "were the first businesswomen. They spun cotton in the Middle Ages and, in the opinion of my professor, the chairwoman of the Women's Studies department, they laid the groundwork for European society's transformation from an agrarian to industrial economy. Their American counterparts, several hundred years later, whether manufacturing textiles or preaching temperance, were not only the ancestors of the suffrage movement, but the reason the American economy remained strong during World War II." Satisfied, Bell nodded curtly and decided that she would make an excellent professor. She made a quick mental note: perhaps she should finish college.

"That's amazing," Barry said.

"Isn't it," Bell agreed.

"Women's Studies," he said, nodding. "No wonder your tuition cost so much. They have a department for everyone now."

Bell sighed so forcefully as to exhale bile from her stomach. "Excuse me," she said, reaching again for the door, "I would like to leave now."

Barry stepped back, gesturing magnanimously. Bell inhaled haughtily and passed. But before she had fully departed, Barry voiced an afterthought. "He's still married, you know . . ."

"He's getting a divorce," Bell snapped.

"Did he tell you that or did you hear that from Jorge?"

Bell started to respond then reconsidered. She would not be provoked again.

Barry put his hand on Bell's shoulder with the mildness of a monk. "Trust me," Barry said, "that's not good news, considering your situation." Barry paused and scrutinized Bell thoroughly, as though appraising jewels.

"What is my situation?" Bell asked, pronouncing the "h" in "what" for the first time ever.

Barry raised his eyebrows to new heights.

Bell awaited her father's declaration.

Then, without allowing his eyebrows to drop, Barry pursed his lips and proceeded to whistle, with the musicality of a concert flutist, a tune from *Fiddler on the Roof*. The words, had he chosen to sing them out loud, would have gone as follows: "Matchmaker, matchmaker, make me a match, find me a find, catch me a catch."

Bell rolled her eyes in excruciating detail.

Barry tried to stifle laughter, but succeeded only in transforming his pursed lips from a flute to a trumpet.

"Thank you," Bell said, "that's very kind."

"There's nothing wrong with getting involved with a married man as long as you don't expect anything from him. I, for one, have had several mutually satisfying affairs."

"Who on earth," Bell shrieked, "would have an affair with you?"

"Several people." Barry grinned devilishly. "I can tell you if you want to know."

Bell, of course, did not. She did, however, suddenly need the privacy of her bedroom and rushed back to it in the hopes that a short nap would bolster her for lunch with her mother.

7

Addictive Tendencies

$\mathscr{B}$ell and Bella had grown apart when Bell turned thirteen and had yet to grow back together. They could barely be in the same room for an hour before clenched jaws turned to harsh words, passive-aggressive comments to searing insults. They were angry in all the traditional ways. Bella was hurt by Bell's dismissal and, as a result, demanding. Bell was angered by Bella's demands and, as a result, dismissive. Over the years, mother and daughter had drifted so far apart they barely seemed like family. But now, Bella saw an opportunity. For the first time since Bell was a child, Bella had something her daughter needed: relative peace and quiet. Enthused, Bella invited Bell to come live with her, removed, if only by a spiral staircase, from the madness downstairs. Before making this drastic move, Bell opted for a trial run, suggesting that mother and daughter share a casual luncheon to decide if cohabitation was possible. Before leaving for her mother's apartment, Bell phoned Bella and asked her to agree to avoid a preset list of inflammatory topics.

No expense was spared in the design of Bella's new apartment. In fact, it sometimes seemed to Barry that the expenses had been intentionally increased. For the spiral staircase, Bella had hired an architect, designer, and civil engineer, determined to replicate the central staircase at the Metropolitan Opera House, a plan that combined glass, steel, wood, and marble in a sort of material homage to the four seasons. The marble, pink to signify spring, was cut from a quarry in Madras to which only sacred elephants had access, thus increasing the cost of transporting the already expensive stone. Though the back stairs of the apartment only offered a fraction of the space required to replicate the acclaimed design, Bella persevered with the modest mandate that scale be respected even if proportion could not. So, with blatant disregard of fire codes and building zoning laws, she hung a garland of orange tape over the back stairs, thereby forbidding emergency exit and ironically providing additional encouragement to her daughters to exit via fire escape.

Despite the slow pace of construction on the apartment, the staircase was completed relatively quickly, allowing Bella fluid movement between her previous and future homes. The staircase was draped with an oriental carpet with scarlet and miniver accents meant to invoke royalty, held in place with iron runners, and completed with a twinkling gold banister that squeaked if you held on to it as you walked or, as Benita did despite her mother's scolding, rode it to the lower level. The staircase emptied directly in front of Barry and Bunny's bedroom, allowing Bella to wince at Bunny when she happened on her fussing in front of her mirror and once, when chance and misfortune collided, to pause at the closed door of the bedroom and eavesdrop on a heated lovers' quarrel. And while the staircase afforded Bella obvious amenities, it served as a literal and symbolic pain in Bell's backside. For the duration of her childhood, her mother's bedroom had been right next door, allowing Bella to waltz in and out as though the space was not her daughter's bedroom but merely a dressing boudoir. It was fitting that now, all these years later, her mother was living right directly above.

Due to these negative associations, Bell opted to take the elevator instead of climbing the spiral staircase to her mother's apartment. Perhaps because she'd only woken up two hours earlier, she found it comforting to re-create the sensation of traveling.

Bell greeted Jorge with the usual mixture of fondness and fatigue.

"Good morning, Jorge," Bell said.

"Morning?" he chided. "I've already been working for hours." Over the years, his eyelids had drooped gradually as though due to gravity.

"What's the matter, Jorge?" Bell asked.

"Nothing," Jorge said. He sighed almost imperceptibly.

"What is it?" Bell asked, looking Jorge in the eye.

"Monday," Jorge said with a small proud sniff, "is my seventieth birthday." He pouted slightly to great effect. "And I have to work."

"That's awful," said Bell. "You shouldn't have to work on your birthday. When I turned twenty-nine, I took the day off. Of course, I had just been fired. But I still stand behind it."

Jorge nodded and looked to the floor.

"I know," Bell said suddenly. "I'll run the elevator on Monday."

"That's crazy," said Jorge.

"No," said Bell. "It's the best thing I've thought of in weeks."

"It won't work," said Jorge. "Mr. Finch will tell the management."

"Nonsense," Bell said. "I'll take care of it. You just enjoy your birthday."

And though Jorge offered various reasons why this was a truly terrible plan, Bell insisted. She could be very convincing when she put her mind to it. After promising to speak to Mr. Finch and to show up on Monday at the strike of eight, Bell persuaded Jorge to enjoy his weekend and, for the first time in thirty years, to stay home on his birthday. Pleased, Bell filed the plan in her mental list and alighted at her mother's landing, determined to jot down a reminder before she forgot her promise.

"I'm so glad you're here," Bella said breathlessly before Bell had fully entered. "Peter Finch called the building board again and told them my guys need to stop at five o'clock so he and Anne can eat dinner in peace. Luckily," Bella smiled conspiratorially, "the doormen are on my side. They hate Peter because he scolded them for sitting down during their shift."

The speed of Bella's construction had been delayed by the size of her workforce. The "force" consisted of two guys whom she had hired to do the work of ten, in an effort to cut costs. Also, she had cut a deal whereby they worked off-hours, including evenings and weekends, a decision that further contributed to their slow pace and sizable ruckus. Mrs. Finch's renovation, on the other hand, had only taken six months. This was, of course, an occupational perk. Mrs. Finch was an established interior decorator who was owed favors by all the carpenters, craftsmen, and wallpapers in the city. Mrs. Finch was also an immaculate woman who, in spite of her busy schedule, managed to write all of her Christmas cards, write personal notes to the important recipients, stuff each envelope with photos of the twins and any cocker spaniels in the house at the time, and address every single one by December first.

"I can't stay for long," Bell informed her mother.

"Fine," Bella replied. "We'll eat in a second. But first you must sit and listen to my poem."

Bell felt something like nausea rise and bubble in her throat. Her mother was capable of producing this physical effect. But, too weary for an argument, Bell manufactured a faint smile and looked for somewhere to sit in the wreckage of tarpaulins, paint cans, and ladders in Bella's living room. Finding nowhere, Bell walked to a sawhorse and leaned on it gingerly.

The poem was not entirely bad, but the imagery was too distracting for Bell to appreciate Bella's natural lyricism. Among the images in the first stanza were a "muscular thigh," a "naked groin," and a "shivering crotch."

"Wow," said Bell. "It's wonderful."

"You think?" Bella grinned.

Bell nodded vigorously. "I'm not sure how I feel about the word 'crotch.' Maybe 'pelvis' would work better. It might be more subtle."

Bella considered this suggestion for a moment, then shook her head definitively.

"No, I like 'crotch,'" Bella decided. "It's an onomatopoeia."

Since the divorce, Bella had taken up numerous artistic pursuits and her apartment attested to this fact. Though partially hidden by sawdust, Bella's photographs hung proudly on each wall. One wall displayed a series of New York City skyscrapers, another trees from Central Park, another naked men.

"You're not the only artist in the family," Bella teased.

Bell cringed, nodded, and silently repeated the following mantra: I'm nothing like my mother. I'm nothing like my mother. I'm nothing like my mother. This, after dying a spinster, was Bell's greatest fear. It was, like most fears, at once logical and absurd. Its logic, dictated by the transitive property—if A = B and B = C, then A = C—caused Bell to make the following deduction. A: Her mother's life was tragic. B: She was a lot like her mother. Therefore, C: She, like her mother, would live a tragic life. The easiest way to anger Bell was to tell her she looked like her mother. The easiest way to terrify Bell was to use any of the following clichés: "The apple doesn't fall far from the tree," "From little acorns, great oaks grow," "History repeats itself," and other versions of the notion that life is a repetitive story and family the most predictable one.

Whenever Bell was struck by her similarities to Bella, she immediately retraced her steps. When Bella announced that she loved photography, Bell swore off the visual arts. Since Bella liked vanilla, Bell loved chocolate. Since her mother liked squash, Bell played tennis. Since her mother loved Latrell, Bell was mean to him, and so on. Bell constructed her personality in opposition to her mother, never once stopping to note that her father loved chocolate, too, and also treated

Latrell badly. Still, Bell was comforted by these distinctions, even if it meant ignoring her instincts. Bell, like her father, was too near-sighted to see that due east is eventually and simultaneously due west.

"Please excuse the state of the apartment," Bella said gaily, as though she were an elegant hostess entertaining royalty. She may as well have apologized for the fact that one prized piece of porcelain was missing from her collection of Fabergé eggs. Her arms were full, a tray of food balanced precariously in one, a sheet of plywood in the other. "Bell, we have to eat in the bedroom. You don't mind, do you?" Bella laughed frivolously and turned on her heel.

Bell mumbled that she didn't and followed her mother down the hall. The floor was covered with plastic sheeting and block-aded, every few feet, sawhorses demarcating missing patches of floor. Bell stopped suddenly as her mother leapt expertly over one such chasm.

"Oops. I should have warned you," Bella said. "Say hello to Vlad." Bella said this so loudly and so close to Vlad that Bell had no choice but to comply.

Bell stopped at an open door on the hall and waved reluctantly. Vlad was one of Bella's two workers, a lascivious Russian who leered at Bell unapologetically whenever she visited. Once, while she was house-sitting for her mother, Bell caught him in the act. She had slept late on a Saturday morning in spite of the hammering. Vlad, working in an adjoining room, noticed that Bell's blanket had slipped to reveal a pair of leopard-print underwear and a juicy sliver of thigh. When Bell awoke, she realized her audience, covered herself, and glared. From that day on, there was no love lost. Every time Bell and Vlad made eye contact, they were honest about their intentions: he, to leer in dirty ways and she, to give him dirty looks.

While Vlad's questionable work ethic contributed to the slow pace of the renovation, another man was responsible for prolonging its completion. Don, Bella's other guy, a burly carpenter, con-sciously prolonged the endeavor for no better reason than his finan-

cial gain. When pressed, Bella suggested Don's pace might have
something to do with his feelings for her when clearly, though she
wouldn't admit it, she was quite in love with him. She would only
admit how much fun it was to "make decisions" with him. She loved
calling the lumber people and saying "we" wanted oak planks. She
loved calling the ceramics supplier and saying "we" wanted marble
tile. In her twenty years of marriage, she had never been a "we,"
much less ordered tile with anyone, so could she be blamed for
wanting a competent man with whom to make a home?

Bella's upstairs wing, though the same size as Barry's apartment,
seemed decidedly smaller. Its size was diminished by the shortage of
light in the main hallway and the odd melancholic sounds that
bounced back and forth as though someone were weeping inside each
adjoining room.

Bell continued down the hallway, squinting to better avoid sudden drops. Once in the bedroom, Bella's familiarity turned to fi-
nesse. She maneuvered through the room with the confidence of a
surgeon. In one motion, she placed the plywood plank across two
closely spaced stacks of books and gracefully set the tray of food
upon this new makeshift table. "Not bad, *n'est-ce pas?*" Bella smiled
and allowed herself a devil-may-care laugh.

Who did she think she was? Bell wondered. Why was she acting
like a seasoned baroness, undaunted by the challenge of an unexpected luncheon party? This is insanity, Bell decided; the failure to
notice the difference between your dreams and their decay. Inhaling
deeply, Bell repositioned her chair to face a wall covered with plastic.

"You're hungry," Bella announced, commencing their ritual. First,
Bella scanned her daughter's body. Second, Bell tried to guess the
fluctuation in her weight by the look in her mother's eyes. "Bell,"
Bella said sternly, abandoning formality. "Those baggy pajamas don't
fool me for a second. Why are you starving yourself?"

"Mom," Bell started. "You promised."

"I said no talk of weight," Bella snapped. "I didn't say no matters
of life and death."

In an effort to counteract her anger, Bell focused on her mother's own weight gain. Bella's body would be called a classic "apple" to her daughters' "pear." Accordingly, Bella's legs never suffered much change, but her middle, like the fruit, swelled slowly like an inflating ball.

Luckily, Bella's attention span precluded a continued escalation. "I'm reading a wonderful book," she said, then lowered her voice mischievously. "The writer is a very brilliant man. We had some times." She giggled and looked out the window wistfully. "You know, the south of France is at its best this time of year."

When, Bell wondered, did her mother lose touch? Was it sudden, like a religious awakening? One day, she woke up with a new set of beliefs? Or was it gradual, like standing in mud and realizing you're in quicksand? Had she watched this strange reality dawn at a slow pace? Either way, her mother had undergone a conversion. Was it possible, Bell wondered, that this was an act, that Bella still saw the distance between her dreams and her daily life, that she designed this delusion to draw attention away from that gap?

"I'm sorry," Bella said, taking a seat at the "table." "It's my fault you're drawn to such abusive men."

Bell's chest stung as she inhaled. She wondered idly if she'd inhaled toxic gas. She glanced at the walls but found no wet paint. She looked to the window but found it closed. She searched her mind for some soothing sentiment but found only a stockpile of clichés. "Everything happens for a reason," she tried.

"No," Bella said. "Don't deceive yourself. Reasons are written in retrospect."

"Your daughters are good reasons though, right?" Bell asked. "If you hadn't married Dad, you wouldn't have had us."

Bella's eyes glazed over into a dull stare. She said nothing for several moments. When she spoke, her voice was hoarse, "Who knows what they would have looked like . . ."

"What who would have looked like?" Bell demanded.

Bella ignored the question. "I worry about your sisters," she mused, moving on to a new topic without warning. "But I suppose they'll be all right after their therapy . . ."

Bell looked on, now fully perplexed.

Bella shook her head as though to wring out a thought, then she jumped suddenly from her seat and cried, "Oh no. I've forgotten dessert."

"Here, let me get it," Bell said, standing up.

"No," Bella gasped. "You stay here."

Bella departed, leaving Bell to study the bedroom and to decide, for once and for all, to avoid her mother's fate at all costs. This thought or the temperature in the room, Bell couldn't tell which, caused her to shudder. She wondered idly how it was possible for an indoor room to get so cold. Turning her head, she solved the mystery: The window behind her mother's bed was lacking any glass.

Several minutes passed before Bella returned, empty-handed. She looked around the room nervously, like a child who has just stolen cookies, gave her clothes an optimistic tug, then sunk into her seat.

"What happened to the dessert?" Bell asked.

Bella looked at the floor, ashamed. "Bell," she said, "I have a confession."

"What is it?" Bell said.

Bella paused. "I can't find my forks."

Bell paused, confused, as the news registered. Was her mother speaking in code? But deciding that Bella meant this quite literally, Bell rebounded. "Never fear," she said. She smiled confidently like a camp leader with a broken compass. With new determination, she rifled through objects on the table in search of something that might simulate prongs. But finding only a spoon, she used it to maneuver a piece of chicken to the best of her abilities. "Luckily, it's tender," she said cheerfully. "Who needs forks, anyway?"

Mistaking Bell's efforts at optimism for condescension, Bella squinted, flared her nostrils and hissed, *"Solus detertimus quod ispsum nostrus."* Then, leaning forward as though to share a morsel of gossip, she whispered the transition, "We only hate in others what we hate in ourselves."

Humbled by her mother's telepathy, Bell replaced her spoon on the table like a soldier disarming. Renewed, Bella heaped aggressively large portions on Bell's plate before filling her own with restraint. The elaborate ceremony complete, Bella smiled cordially, said *"Bon appétit"* and promptly burst into tears.

"Mom, what's wrong?" Bell asked, matter-of-fact. Spontaneous weeping no longer elicited her concern.

"Nothing," Bella sniffled. "I'm sorry. I know I promised. It's just that I'm so scared for you."

"Mom," Bell said haughtily. "I'm fine." She stressed the word "I'm" as though to imply that Bella, on the other hand, was not.

"Oh Bell, don't pretend," Bella snorted. "I see what you are . . . how you used to be . . . oh, Bell, it's so awful. You're just like me."

Mothers and daughters fight a war of attrition. This was something Bell had come to understand. Mothers have the advantage of wisdom. Daughters have the advantage of youth. Mothers have the disadvantage of age; daughters, inexperience. Therefore, the two camps are equally matched. But daughters will eventually win, Bell concluded, as long as they fight to the death. Still, for some reason, when Bell and Bella fought, both were incapacitated.

Bella blew her nose with an exaggerated honk.

Bell waited for silence and, assuming a neutral tone, changed the subject. "So," she said, "how is Latrell?"

"Latrell," Bella sneered, "has not been here since yesterday."

"Is he staying with a friend?" Bell asked casually, refusing to acknowledge her mother's loaded look.

"How would I know?" Bella sniffed. "I'm only his mother."

Only a hustler, Bell thought, could couple such vulnerability with such strength. She attempted to prevent her mother from sighing by picking up the conversation's pace. "The apartment looks good," she lied. "You must be almost finished."

"Oh, I don't want them to finish," Bella said. "Then who would I talk to?"

"This food is delicious," Bell tried, inserting a bite in her mouth with her spoon.

Bella sighed, refusing to take Bell's bait.

"Seriously," said Bell. "Where is Latrell?"

"I'm the wrong person to ask," Bella whispered.

"Seriously, Mom. What's the deal? Is he hiding under his bed?"

Bella said nothing. She was too distracted by the task of feeding herself. Awkwardly, she maneuvered an impractically large piece of chicken with her forefinger and her spoon.

Finally, impulse overwhelmed. Bell thrust her hand across the table and snatched the chicken from her mother's hand.

"What on earth has gotten into you?" Bella whispered. "Give that back right now."

But Bell was now quite possessed by her emotions. "How can you live with so much food and not a single fork?"

Bella's eyes narrowed to mere slits. For the first time since sitting down to lunch, she straightened her back. "Every time Latrell runs away," she confessed, "he takes a couple with him. I don't know what he does with them. Either he's having a very civilized picnic or selling them for pocket money."

Bell knew her mother well enough to understand that this was a ploy, but she refused to let pity weaken her resolve. "Maybe if you kept better track of your belongings, you'd know where your son was right now."

"How dare you come into my house," Bella gasped, "and criticize my mothering."

"Am I to blame," Bell asked smugly, "that you can't find my brother?"

"Your brother!" Bella shouted. "Your brother? You didn't even know he was missing."

"Wasn't it enough to lose your own children?" Bell watched her mother's eyes for signs of weakening but they were bright and fierce.

"I am a very good mother," Bella said calmly. "Look how well your sisters turned out."

Bell's pulse accelerated. Her eyes throbbed. Her sense of smell became horribly acute. This must be how it felt, Bell thought, to be trapped in my mother's womb for nine months. "You don't even know where your forks are," Bell scoffed.

"You are a disgrace," Bella said, replacing ferocity with feebleness.

"I give up," Bell said, standing abruptly.

"You gave up a long time ago," Bella mumbled.

"And you," Bell shouted, "what have you done?" She began the treacherous journey down the hall. "Where is your husband?" Bell flailed at a piece of plastic obstructing her path. As she reached the top of the spiral staircase, she paused to administer the fatal blow. "Where are your goddamn forks?"

Bella refused to admit defeat. She rushed down the hall to catch up. "I know where my forks are!" she yelled.

"Oh," Bell said. "Where are they?"

Bella took a long grand pause and then, as though declaring the most obvious truth—that green was composed of yellow and blue, that butter melted in a frying pan, that human beings needed oxygen to breathe—she stopped and announced majestically, "The forks are in the living room."

Finding this precluded most logical responses, Bell proceeded down the spiral staircase. Once downstairs, she rushed down the hall, entered her bedroom, and slammed the door with sufficient force and speed to prevent the flow of remorse.

By the time Bella reached the top of the stairs, both apartments were silent. She stood frozen, leaning over the railing like a dog at an electric fence. She remained like this for a while, one hand raised as though proving a point, the other holding a fistful of forks. Finally, after several moments, she turned back toward her room. But first, she threw her forks at the ground like an impetuous bride disposing of an ugly bouquet. Downstairs, Bell jumped, startled by the sound of metal striking metal.

And so evolution jerked to a start in the Barnacle house. Each girl's response to her father's challenge could be called an adaptation. Benita, the best athlete, was ready and eager to take down anyone in her path. Beryl, the most gifted musician, paired grace with discipline. Beth, the scientist, applied logic, calculating the odds. Belinda clearly intended to aggravate her sisters until they surrendered. Bridget drew on her powers of manipulation. Bell, despite her seeming disadvantage, could still outsmart her younger sisters, if not outrun them.

Day one of competition ended much as it began. Barry anxiously paced the halls, cursed with insomnia.

In Benita and Beryl's room, both girls lay on their beds facing away from each other. Beryl studied a map intently. Benita recited the first scene of *King Lear* from memory.

In Beth and Belinda's room, Beth bolted the window in anticipation of Belinda's return. Belinda slept peacefully, if such snoring could be called peaceful, on the living room sofa.

Bell lay awake in her childhood bed, eyes pinned wide as though with toothpicks.

Several blocks downtown, Bridget tossed fitfully in bed, hitting Trot square in the jaw and, though she didn't succeed in waking him, jolting herself into noisy consciousness so that she, too, much like Bell, lay sleepless and panicked.

8

Hearing Better Than
Some Wolves

espite the warmth he felt for the Barnacles, Latrell was more than slightly relieved to be out of the Barnacle house. Bella, though loving, could be overbearing, the girls were a constant drain on his nerves, and Barry created in Latrell the strange and disconcerting feeling that he had done something wrong even before opening his mouth. Nor did Latrell feel particularly serene at Buckley Boys School. He couldn't help but feel that these boys viewed him as a novelty, seeing him as a curious extension of their parents' interest in philanthropy. As a result, he spent most of the school day haunted by the suspicion that he was being stared at and did his best to catch people in the act by tracking them in his peripheral vision, then whipping his head around to issue a threatening look.

Sometimes, Latrell missed his previous abode. Having spent the first ten years of his life in a family of forty boys, even the raucous Barnacle household sometimes seemed quiet and dull. The Bronx

Boys' Home, a state-funded group residence for orphans and run-aways, was one of the only remaining institutions in the city that provided a viable alternative to foster care. Though it was intermit-tently rough, noisy, and lonely, the Home was ultimately a nurturing place, a progressive shelter that funneled its residents into a nearby charter school, armed with a staff of caretakers who treated their charges like sons. But the noise and squabbling was only one aspect of Latrell's hankering. He missed old friends, even old enemies as anyone misses the fixtures of youth. But more than this, he missed the simple fact of familiarity. His increasing distance from his past created an odd confusion of emotions. He felt equal parts relieved to have moved on and guilty for leaving his past behind. At times, he was unsure which was the greater betrayal, leaving the shelter in the first place or liking the place where he'd ended up.

Luckily, he found respite in one reliable source: Playing or listen-ing to music afforded a momentary reprieve from this constant drift. Accordingly, he sought out any chance to participate in either activ-ity, spending hours in his room staring at his stereo, playing and re-playing songs until he'd deciphered their chord progressions. He exhausted every cent of his allowance on music purchases and then went on to round out his archives with files downloaded off the Web. Over time, he had amassed a respectable collection, impressive both in size and organization. It was laid out in such a way that Latrell could locate files by various reference cues, artist's last name, genre of music, or year of recording. His tastes ran wide and eclectic, from rap to romantic. But his appreciation of music only ignited his desire to participate in its creation. He dreamed, one day, to make the transformation from mere mortal to musician.

As a result, Latrell had found a haven in the most improbable place: Bemelmans, the ritzy piano bar of the nearby Carlyle Hotel, provided an odd and unexpected oasis just ten blocks north of the Barnacles'. The musicians who played at Bemelmans were unique in their aspirations, touring singers and pianists who had chosen it over other local venues, rarely headliners but often virtuosos, backup players or partners to the flashier crooners who played in New York's larger halls. The bartender was a forgiving soul with a soft spot for sad sacks and artists who, recognizing both things in Latrell, allowed him to sit in a booth in the back and enjoy the weekly entertainment without paying the astronomical cover charge required of more moneyed patrons. Provided he remained inconspicuous, Latrell was basically left alone, allowed to enjoy unlimited cashews, and occasionally treated to a complimentary ginger ale.

The environment lived up its musicians, assuming the costume and history of a neighborhood haunt. The space was peppered with small round tables, each one lit with white candles and a tray of delicacies designed, it seemed, to incite an insatiable thirst for martinis. The effect was an ambience of such warmth and intimacy that two complete strangers seated at nearby tables often found themselves in the throes of romance and couples who were trapped in long courtships invariably got engaged by the end of the night. According to legend, the mural on the walls was painted by a patron as an after-the-fact negotiation for an untenable bar bill. Several weeks before a musician began his stint, his picture circulated in the bar, folded atop the tables like name placards at a dinner party. This promotional device was meant to inspire patrons to plan their next trip to the bar and to remind them of the price of a bottle of champagne.

Since his first visit to Bemelmans, Latrell had made a habit of pocketing these folded cards, squirreling them back to the apartment without being blamed for the theft. Over time, he had amassed an impressive collection, a wide assortment of chanteuses and pianists that he displayed on the walls of his bedroom as other boys did baseball cards. The collection was extensive and meticulously archived, each musician's picture mounted with copious amounts of gummy adhesive and arranged on the wall in a manner that only Latrell could decipher. Blossom Dearie, Jackie Martin, Montgomery Brown, Freddie Monk, and Cecilia Jerome were among the glossy portraits that adorned the wall. The latest addition, that of a pianist named Loston

Harris, hung just above Latrell's desk, a position that resulted in frequent viewing, pulling Latrell's gaze easily during study hours.

It was with some curiosity that Latrell examined his latest lift. Loston, dressed in a double-breasted pinstriped suit, looked no older than forty-five despite the fact that his clothes referred to the turn of the century. In the picture, his eyebrows were raised and his head was tipped back with certain unflappable effervescence, as though life was a song composed especially for him. But despite Latrell's unrivaled knowledge of the music scene, Loston was an enigma. He had never seen or heard of Loston Harris, neither on the lists of touring musicians in the local newspapers nor in the endnotes of the albums he stored. And, even more curiously, Latrell was increasingly certain with every moment of staring at the picture that he and Loston looked very much alike. Their eyes were both almond-shaped, widening toward the ears. Their mouths were both weighted by a full lower lip. But Loston's brazen attitude was the final tip-off; Latrell could form the exact same expression when he posed in front of the mirror. He had only to close his eyes halfway, tilt his head back, and form a half-sneer, half-smile. Indeed, within one afternoon, Latrell was completely convinced: The photograph was clear and irrefutable evidence of shared heredity.

In honor of the occasion, Latrell had worn his birthday gift, a navy blue single-breasted Brooks Brothers suit that Bella gave him when he turned thirteen, the purchase of which was made all the more momentous by the unforgettably prickly visit with the tailor in the back of the store. Though Latrell refused to admit it at the time, he agreed with Bella's dewy-eyed claim that he looked impossibly handsome in the outfit, especially when he completed it with the pale blue Liberty print tie Bella slipped into the box. The costume made Latrell look at least five years older, accentuating the shine in his serious eyes and hinting at a fine jawbone still obscured by baby fat. Perhaps, it was a touch serious for an unplanned meeting. But, it was only fitting that he dress formally. A boy had only so many opportunities to meet his biological father.

Spurred by the warm spring air, Latrell headed north on Madison, deeming proximity to the Barnacles worth the risk in this one case. Within seconds of arriving at Bemelmans, his suspicions were confirmed. Loston was already well into his set, luxuriating in the last arpeggio of a Chet Baker standard. As he finished the climb to the top of the keys, he tipped back his head as he did in the photo, ending the song with a rhythmic shaking of his head that made him appear to be affirming a question. As he struck the last note, he closed his eyes and tipped his head farther back, giving the impression that he might soon tip from his chair. He remained like this for several seconds, long after the strings had stopped vibrating, suspending the entire audience in a state of silent reverie. Finally, he opened his eyes, resumed contact with his audience, breaking their trance by excusing himself for a short intermission.

Latrell stiffened immediately, recognizing his moment. He had only been in the bar for ten minutes, not nearly long enough to feel the effects of his first ginger ale. Still, he forced himself to act. Breathing deeply, he stood from his seat and crossed the bar to the piano. But by the time he arrived, Loston was already surrounded. A bevy of Upper East Side women formed a semicircle around him. This traffic placed Latrell so close to Loston as to reveal all the freckles and marks on his face. Several times, he felt and fought the urge to return to his seat. But he ground his teeth and forced his face into a smile. Finally, the crowd let up and Latrell seized his chance.

"Excuse me, sir," said Latrell.

Another woman inched toward Loston. She held up a napkin and pen and gestured for him to sign.

Latrell took another step toward Loston, intercepting the fan. "Excuse me," he said again.

On instinct, Loston shook his sleeve, preparing to sign an autograph.

"Oh no," said Latrell.

Loston stopped, pen poised, and looked at Latrell questioningly.

"I'm Latrell," he clarified. He nodded with strained conviction. "I'm your long-lost son."

Loston tilted his head slightly, now fully perplexed.

Latrell hesitated for a moment, fighting disillusionment. Perhaps, Latrell was not his birth name and this man knew him as something else. "I'm your son," he tried again. He straightened his mouth as though to submit his features for inspection. "Don't you remember me?"

Loston said nothing, only scanned Latrell's face, alternating his gaze from left to right. Finally, he lurched forward and broke into a smile. "Nice one, kid. You had me for a second." He peered past Latrell into the bar. "All right. Joke's over. Who put you up to this?"

"No," Latrell managed. "No one . . . I'm . . ." He trailed off then forced himself to press on. "I'm Latrell. Don't you remember?"

Loston continued to stare at Latrell, scanning his face for the next cue. Finally, he perceived Latrell's desperation and changed his tone mercifully. "I'm sorry, kid," he said, lowering his voice. He placed a hand on Latrell's shoulder. "I'm sure I would remember you. You must be thinking of someone else."

Gravity would have pulled Latrell to the floor had he not fought it so hard. In a moment, all sound faded from the bar but for the clinking of glass. Images drained of color. Weight sapped from his hands. Luckily, pride rushed to his aid. He nodded curtly, apologized for the mistake, then hurried from the bar onto Madison Avenue, hopeful that fresh air would do its part to slow his speeding pulse.

There is no hatred that rivals the loathing the insomniac feels for the person sleeping nearby. Indeed, that hatred is multiplied tenfold when the sleeper is, in any way, responsible for the insomniac's tormented state. And Trot was, in part, responsible for Bridget's restlessness because he had, as he did every night, managed to usurp the better part of the comforter, leaving Bridget with nothing to warm her but a meager sliver of blanket and a cruelly inaccessible mound of tangled sheet. Four such hours of desperate wakefulness had passed by three o'clock in the morning. And now, as Bridget stared at her slumbering boyfriend, she realized that she detested him. "Your ears are huge," she said out loud. "Your nose is pointy," she continued the critique. I do not love you, she thought. And then out loud, "I hate you, Trot."

"We're failing," Bridget added. "We don't work anymore. I can't cope."

Trot rolled over and, as though in assent, offered one forceful grunt.

As Trot snored, his mouth gradually opened wider. Trot's mouth and snoring, Bridget feared, might combine to create a centrifugal force.

"Do you think we've become a two-headed monster?" Bridget asked.

Trot inhaled deeply and sniffed his response.

"We love the West Village but we hate the Corner Bistro. That place is always so crowded—you can't talk. We love the Beatles but hate the Stones. We love New York but could see moving to the country. We don't like going out. We like to stay in and cook. We don't love each other anymore."

Bridget looked to Trot, sincere in her confusion. Insomnia's first blow is common sense.

"Trot and I are getting married," Bridget told her empty room.

She was uncertain as to whether she was talking to herself or simply replaying a conversation she'd had with her mom. Her mother did not approve of their living together, not so much out of principle, but rather due to its threat to Bridget's leverage in future negotiations. Why would anyone buy the cow, Bella asked, when he already lived with the milk? Bridget took offense on feminist grounds and also on the basis of being likened to a cow. In her relationship, she explained, she was definitely the bull. She had the money and the good job. Things had changed a lot, Bridget would point out, since her mother's day.

A woman no longer had to trick a man into marrying her. Gone was the age-old and, Bridget thought, embarrassingly transparent pretense that a woman had religious objections to living together before being engaged. Furthermore, Bridget felt she did a disservice to all women by stowing her grandmother's engagement ring in her Bottega Veneta bag as though the situation were of such dire urgency that Bella might be forced, if Trot didn't pop the question, to hand him the implement of his advantage like a soldier, his reinforcement gun. Often Bridget played out the conversation in which she conceded that her mother had been right and had therefore accepted the first proposal made by a stranger off the street.

As Trot slept, Bridget marveled at the ability of the human face to change at night. Or was it the ability of hatred to change the human face? Oh, how she hated his little nose. It was not the nose of the man she would marry—so pointy and small. She wished his eyes were more widely spaced. Maybe her mother was right; biology was destiny. Trot's narrowed eyes caused an optical illusion, made the world look smaller than it really was. At least when he was sleeping, Trot's eyes didn't bulge as they did when he was making a point. His lips were adequate—not the lips she would want, but adequate— well-shaped, and, from the right angle, full. But why did he insist on licking them the moment before they kissed? This is why poets wrote sonnets, Bridget concluded. When you itemize the facets of beauty, you enhance its sum. She must stop focusing on Trot's worst features. It was her fault. She was making him worse.

Without turning on her light, Bridget climbed out of bed, pulled on her bathrobe and took a seat at her desk. She intended, after alphabetizing her bills, to write a list of all of her friends' birthdays. Luckily, Bridget was spared from this project by her ringing telephone. She was too delirious at this point to wonder who dared call so late.

"Bridge," said the answering machine. "Under the balcony. Urban

Romeo." The speaker laughed, hiccupped, then added, "Wherefore are thou with that deadbeat when you could spend your life with me?"

Bridget lurched from her chair to turn down the volume on the answering machine. She returned to her desk, shaken. But before she recovered her normal pulse, something struck her window-pane. She rushed to the window and lifted it slowly. Billy, even from five flights above, looked wild and debonair.

"I know our families don't really get along," Billy shouted, "but what's a silly feud in the face of love? I've been saving up for a long time now. Of course, I could only afford this rubber band, not that I didn't consider giving you that chalice of hemlock . . ."

"Leave!" Bridget whispered severely though, in truth, she'd never been so happy to see him in her life.

"Bridge," he said, "I've missed you so."

Billy was always so melodramatic. "What are you doing here?" Bridget leaned over the railing. "How dare you come to my house?"

"Come downstairs and go for a walk with me. There's something I need to ask you."

"The answer," Bridget hissed, "is still no." She turned quickly to face the window so he wouldn't see her smile.

Bridget peered quickly into the room to make sure Trot was still asleep. Comforted, she squeezed onto the fire escape and did her best to close the window from outside. Finding her fingertips lacked sufficient force to move the glass, she peered once more into the room and, comforted somewhat by Trot's impenetrable sleep, re-signed herself to leaving the window open.

"Billy," Bridget whispered, shifting her weight in order to hush the metal grates, "you have to leave right now."

"I can't," said Billy.

"Why not?" asked Bridget.

"Because I'm wild with love."

"Come on," Bridget hissed, "you'll wake up Trot."

"Good." Billy flashed a diabolical smile.

"Billy," Bridget said, more forcefully. But it was hard to sound authoritative while whispering from thirty feet above the ground.

"What? It's true." Billy shrugged.

"Billy," Bridget repeated. She raised her eyebrows like a nursery school teacher. "My boyfriend is asleep inside."

"Oh God! Don't say that," Billy squealed.

From five flights up, Bridget angrily noted, Billy's eyes still demanded her full attention. As a child, she had often gazed into their endless green and wished she could trade him for her own boring blue.

"Don't say what?" she hissed. "He's fast asleep."

"Don't say 'your boyfriend.' Have mercy on me."

Though she would never admit it, since she was fourteen Bridget had pictured Billy when she pictured her life. Billy had offered, along with all the obvious attributes of neighbors and twins and neighbors who were twins and also blond twins and, because there were twins, double everything they already were, complete and utter devotion. Billy, ever since he could remember, had been hopelessly in love with Bridget. Billy saw his own house as an airless garden to the Barnacles' burgeoning hothouse, while the Barnacle girls wished, more than anything, that their mother would replicate the Finch apartment in their own. In the Barnacle house, one could enter at any time and find an adventure. In his house, Billy felt like he did at school assemblies, as though he were waiting for something very boring to end.

For Billy, each Barncle offered a different reward. But, Bridget, far and away, was simply the best one. Bell was too mean. She acted as though her year on the twins was actually a decade. She pinched their cheeks routinely and called them the Booby Twins until they were old enough to retaliate. Belinda was too frivolous. She lacked the brainy omniscient aura that surrounded the others like Saturn's rings. Beth was too serious, Beryl was too odd, and Benita was too young. Bridget was the perfect combination of strange and normal, stoic and sassy, sexy and cynical and therefore always just out of reach.

For years, Bridget had handled Billy with the dubiousness of a lion trainer, circling him with a feigned apathy whose fervor betrayed a certain distinct concern. In high school, they were inseparable, confounding their teachers and parents with the threat of their union, Bridget always maintaining a distance motivated by what she could not tell. It's not that she wasn't attracted to Billy, but there was something that prevented her from loving him, some indescribable quality that made her suspicious of his valor and therefore averse to committing.

Accordingly, Bridget appointed Billy her "best friend," and thereby tortured him with every last detail of her early romantic mishaps. Billy listened dutifully as Bridget sampled her high school's store of stocky, insipid athletes, each time considering a bit more seriously if she and Billy should give it a shot. Billy finally seized an opportunity the summer before Bridget left for college. But those heady three months—though blessed with much kissing in the backseats of cars, sneaking into rooms, and one precariously close encounter with sex—were cursed to be a brief and distracted affair that the two would summarize with overblown professions of relief, with phrases like, "Thank God we didn't go all the way" or "It's good we got that out of our systems" or "Let's never jeopardize our friendship again."

But the brief affair did change their friendship. Every boy Bridget dated since, not excluding Trot, had, in some way, undergone comparison with Billy and each one had triggered Billy's increasingly operatic professions of love. Early in these relationships, like clockwork, Billy appeared at a window, on the doorstep of a college dorm, and once, at a rock show to insist that Bridget was the love of his life and he hers, and that she leave whatever guy she was with at the time. Once, Billy was forcibly removed by campus police, when, after staking out her dorm, he tried to jump, piggyback-style, onto the boy who was leaving Bridget's room. Throughout, his line of argument never changed. As he was carried off by campus cops, Billy shouted his call to arms. He could tell, he would say, by the look in the boy's eyes that he didn't love Bridget as much as Billy did. Incidentally, Billy injured himself twice: once, when he attempted to wriggle out of the grasp of campus security and had to be tackled to the ground, and once during the act of surveillance when, intent on watching the boy's departure, he accidentally walked into a tree.

"It's okay, Bridget." Billy changed his tack. "I've seen you together and now I know."

"How dare you," Bridget said at a normal decibel, then lowering her voice, she added, "If you start with this again, I'll do exactly the same thing."

The same thing was, of course, to issue a restraining order. Bridget had done this more for the rhetorical fact than for her actual safety or for Billy's rebuke. For having had to take out a restraining order was one of many status symbols coveted by a certain type of New York City girl, alongside her Hermès Birkin bag or her first Cartier watch.

"Bridge," Billy said, his voice raising an octave, "you're everything to me. Bridget, you're my life." And, as though the simple action would prove the veracity of his statement, Billy fell ceremoniously to his knees. He howled suddenly, surprised by the sharpness of debris digging into his kneecap. Bridget had to look away to keep from laughing. "Bridge," Billy called from his kneeling position. "I've seen the way he looks at you. He doesn't love you the way I do. And, more importantly, how could you love anyone named Trot?"

Bridget's smile abruptly evaporated. "Will you please shut up?!" She rushed back to the window, thrust her head in. Then, calmed by the sight of Trot's oblivious slumber, resumed her post on the fire escape and persisted at the effort of pretending to get Billy to leave. "Billy," she said, affecting a stern tone, "this is not acceptable." Then, softening, she tried a new tack, "Please, don't make this any harder than it is. Will you please be rational and leave without making a scene?"

"No, I will not be rational," Billy said. "Love is irrational. I am in love, therefore I will not leave." He nodded to punctuate this deduction like an ancient philosopher completing a proof.

Bridget felt a nauseating wave of guilt. She had a perfectly adequate boyfriend. She was greedy, she decided, vain and selfish. No, she changed her mind again. It was Trot's fault for depriving her of romance. Every girl in the world deserved to be courted.

"But I will if you come down and go for a walk."

"Billy, this is extortion," Bridget said, a certain coyness creeping into her voice.

"Good idea," said Billy, "because if you don't, I'll simply stay here all night."

Billy released his knees from the strain of kneeling by switching his position again. Something very pointy—a pebble, he hoped, not a shard of glass—jabbed horribly into his skin. First, he slid into a cross-legged position, then, finding this lacked a certain emphatic quality, he uncrossed his feet, extended his legs, put his hands behind his head and reclined luxuriously so that he was staring at the sky like a stargazer set to wait all night for a once-in-a-lifetime comet.

"Billy, you're drunk," Bridget said, noting Billy's tie for the first time.

"How else do you expect me to get through a date with someone else? I have to numb myself to make it bearable, and then it's more excusable when I accidentally call her Bridget."

Bridget could feel her resolve weakening.

"It's true," Billy nodded, and by way of verification, he grabbed one flap of his tie and yanked it to the side of his neck. "Bridget, come down, or I'll kill myself."

From above, Billy looked truly absurd, like a traffic cop halting oncoming cars. Trot, on the contrary, never looked silly. He was always so damn serious.

Noting Bridget's weakening resolve, Billy moved in for the kill. "Bridget," he whispered, "I worship you."

Bridget burst into hearty laughter. "Oh, Billy," she said, "why must you be such a fool?"

"Because," Billy said, "I'm a fool for love." He allowed the menacing noose to fall back onto his lapel.

"Billy," Bridget said, regaining her serious tone. "I don't know what to tell you. Trot and I are very happy."

"If you and Trot are so happy," Billy shot back, "then why are you out here with me?"

Souring, Bridget turned away. She'd had enough of this game. "Sometimes," she whispered, "things are more complicated than they seem."

"So tell me some of those things," Billy pressed.

"Why would I tell you?"

"Because you're standing on your fire escape talking to me, not sleeping next to your boyfriend."

Bridget refused to indulge Billy's impudence. Still, his question struck a chord. She paused, considering whether or not Billy merited her trust. Though she decided that he did not, she confided anyway. "The problem with Trot is," Bridget paused. "The problem is . . ." She looked guiltily at her window. "Oh God, there are so many."

Billy assumed a pious look. "Why don't you start with one."

"Okay," she said. "Just as an example, take what happened on Passover. I asked him to do one simple thing, to get a cake for my parents and, for reasons too boring to recount, he showed up empty-handed."

"So, he's incompetent," Billy said. He managed, while supplying this suggestion, to sound interested as opposed to insidious.

"Well," said Bridget, shifting uncomfortably, "I guess you could say that."

"How hard can it be to produce a cake when you work in a bakery?"

"You wouldn't know," Bridget said, bristling. "You've never worked a day in your life. Besides, it really wasn't his fault. I told him too late."

"Still, I see what you mean," Billy said with an ingratiating nod. He attempted to redirect the conversation. Forcing Bridget to come to Trot's defense was certainly not his intention.

"It's the same way with his writing," Bridget went on. "Trot is incredibly talented, but that's not enough to succeed. You have to be . . ."

"Assertive," Billy suggested.

"Something like that," Bridget sighed. The bile of treachery rose in her throat but she forced herself to ignore it.

"So he's a coward," said Billy.

"Watch it," Bridget snapped. She eyed Billy, now with open misgiving. Clearly, this was the wrong place for a confession and Billy, the wrong confidant.

"Well," said Billy, "there's one thing I can tell you for sure: If you were my girlfriend, I would make sure you had all the cake in the world. If you were my girlfriend, you would eat cake for breakfast, lunch, and dinner."

"Oh, Billy," said Bridget. She shook her head and smiled in spite of herself.

"Come for a walk. I'll do any . . . thing," Billy slurred, pausing in the middle of the word to trip and fall back to the ground.

"Walk ten paces on your knees," Bridget said.

Billy complied eagerly. He completed five steps on his knees then looked up pleadingly. "Bridget, it hurts. Will you come down now?"

And for some odd reason, Bridget agreed. She simply shook her head as a reminder to herself that she was giving in to a vice, gathered her bathrobe around her legs to form more suitable climbing attire, commanded Billy to close his eyes, and proceeded down the five creaky flights to the sidewalk. As she climbed, she muttered reprimands to herself and tried to avoid smiling. Unfortunately, chance had its own rebuke: The squeal of the fire escape's metal grates succeeded where laughter and shouted proposals had failed at interrupting Trot's sleep. And as luck, or rather, bad luck, would have it, declarations of love, shouted or laughed, made by suitors on answering machines, even when only made in jest and even when the proposal part is left out, are simply impossible to explain to one's boyfriend and even more difficult to erase. This bad luck is, of course, all the more apparent when it compels one's boyfriend to throw you out of your own apartment and forces you to return, ashamed and contrite, to your own rapidly crowding childhood home.

9

Killer Instinct

Days after Barry's strange announcement, the apartment was still abuzz. Each girl's approach to the contest differed drastically, her stance on her father a precise function of her specific age. Bell felt the contest was to be ignored, treated as one of the many whims with which Barry expressed his changing moods and in which he eventually lost interest. Bridget, though she and her father enjoyed only the most cursory relationship, heeded the contest as a warning of sorts, but still took it literally. Wary of betraying her competitive nature, she calculated in private, consoled by the knowledge that she had a firm lead. Beth was in agreement with Bell. These were the ravings of a madman. The modern interpretation of *Lear* applied in which the king, possessed by lunacy, divested himself of his kingdom. In Beth's mind, this diagnosis rendered the contest totally dismissible; such a mercurial man would surely change his mind again before the winner was named.

Belinda, though she dismissed her father on reflex, knew the difference between his whims and his serious intentions. Therefore, she saw the contest as a golden opportunity and, though certainly crass and disgustingly nouveau riche, a chance to stage a comeback after the lag of her apathetic teenage years. To this end, she devoted herself to a thorough assessment of the various loopholes and shortcuts with which she might secure a lead. Beryl, torn between her self-proclaimed psychic talents and her pessimism, warned the others of tragic possibilities. Their father was surely using the contest to veil some terrible misfortune such as imminent bankruptcy or a fatal disease. This was his way of preparing the girls for the dismal inevitability so that the real news, when finally conceded, would come as a relief. Benita, however, dismissed her sisters' beliefs, treating the contest as a real and pressing opportunity. She had spent every minute since the announcement of the contest obsessing over the best way to win.

Benita had become completely possessed, frantically running through various schemes as though jolted by an electric surge. Winning consumed her like a poison, quickening her pulse to a drumroll. Her surroundings—dolls, trophies, teddy bears, and roommate—had faded into a blur. Nothing in the world mattered. Every inch of her imagination wrapped itself around this idea. Even a full day later, as she lay in bed she found herself chanting to herself. "Contest. Contest. Contest." This was the new sound of her heartbeat. Plagued by the strange compulsion that affects the very successful and slightly psychotic, she simply could not stand to participate in an activity in which she did not come in first.

To this end, she had spent the better portion of Friday working on her talent show audition, propelled forward by the image of Mary Talbot's face wrinkled into a sour grimace or, better yet, crying. But now that she'd memorized the scene and perfected the voice and costume for each character, she busied herself with other pressing tasks and commenced a brutal assessment of the playing field. Bell could basically be factored out. She lacked the initiative and energy to present any real challenge and she was unlikely to offer her father the deference competing implied. Bridget therefore was the first serious contender. Her self-obsession made her dangerous; she was likely to use the contest as an excuse to focus on herself and to exhibit all sorts of ingenuity for the purposes of self-aggrandizement. Certainly, Bridget's surplus of suitors was a huge cause for concern, threatening to provide Bridget with an accidental victory by way of bended knee.

Beth, too, posed a real threat, her research on evolution already garnering attention from professors at school. Even worse, Beth's subject matter was undeniably close to Barry's heart. And yet, it was possible Belinda presented the more immediate danger. Recklessness made her bold and unpredictable. Luckily, it also made her likely to self-destruct. And so perhaps it was Beryl who was to be watched most closely. She had all the makings of a dark horse, all the stealth and tenacity of a ninth-inning closer. Luckily, proximity was on Benita's side. Because they shared a bedroom, she could keep close tabs on her.

The first order of business was to find the perfect four costumes. It was not enough to perform the lines of every character using feats of ventriloquism. She must fashion the perfect, distinguishing costume for each of the four main characters, rigging the outfits so that all could be worn simultaneously and revealed, through strategic disrobing, at the appointed moment in the scene. For King Lear, she sought a regal brown cape befitting a man of such majesty. For this, she stole a terry cloth bathrobe from her father. Goneril and Regan both required devastatingly beautiful dresses, and yet not so devastating as to overwhelm Cordelia. For these, Benita had no choice but pilfer clothes from her two eldest sisters, singling out a blue gauzy number from Bell and a metallic minidress from Bridget. Cordelia, of course, required the most divine costume of the three and therefore justified a more treacherous act of robbery. Benita knew the very dress, though it would require some alterations.

Undeterred, she waited until Beth and Belinda's room was vacant and hurried in to steal Belinda's beloved green taffeta strapless dress.

Satisfied with her theft, Benita searched the halls for a willing party. She was desperate for someone to read lines with her and help her workshop the scene. Surely, the sign on Bell's door marked KEEP OUT permitted a polite inquiry. Surely Bell would welcome a visit from her. "Bell," Benita shouted.

On sound of Benita, Bell froze and remained very quiet. "Come back later," she finally said. "I'm asleep right now."

"But I have a present for you," Benita lied.

Skeptical, Bell crawled out of bed and opened her door.

Benita stood, obscured by a pile of stolen clothes, decidedly devoid of presents.

"Do I look like him?" Benita asked.

"Like who?" Bell asked.

"King Lear," Benita said.

Bell scrutinized her sister, looked past her into the hall, then forced her mouth into a half-hearted smile, the kind intended to look half-hearted and half-hateful.

"Will you read lines with me?" Benita asked. "I really need to rehearse."

"You said you had a present for me."

"Oh," Benita said. "I was lying." Smiling, she produced a large red book from the bottom of her pile. "You read this," she said, flipping to the correct page. "I already know it by heart."

Deciding that compliance was the quickest way to get rid of her sister, Bell searched the page for the first line and read the part of Lear. " 'Which of you shall we say doth love us most? Goneril, our eldest, speak first.' "

Benita took a loud, deep breath and assumed a pious look. "Sir," she said, "I love you more than words can wield the matter. Dearer than eyesight, space, or liberty, beyond what can be valued rich or rare, no less than life, with grace, health, beauty, honor, as much as child ever loved or father found, a love that makes breath poor and speech unable, beyond all manner of so much I love you."

Bell regarded her sister with unfettered disdain.

"You know," said Benita, indulging in an aside, "I think most people misunderstand this play. King Lear's daughters aren't really evil. The play is told from Lear's point of view. And Lear is an unreliable narrator, delusional, paranoid, and otherwise insane from curtain rise to fall."

Bell paused to consider this in spite of herself. Finally, she dismissed the theory. "I think they're all rotten," she said, slamming her door. "Every single one."

Due to their twinlike telepathy, neither Bell nor Bridget slept much on Friday night. Bell's bed was a cruel parody of a bed, providing the opposite of comfort, reminding her, throughout the night, that she had outgrown it and her surroundings. As a result, she spent most of the night praying for daylight. At six o'clock, she finally gave up, pulled a sweater on over her sweats, and set out to find a phone from which she could call Bridget in private. Knowing Bridget, she would be terribly judgmental about her pregnancy. Still, Bell felt, she had to tell someone. Keeping the secret was too great a burden. And perhaps talking to her sister would lift her spirits. Bridget was sure to find the levity in the situation, or at least the hilarity. Bridget would think of all the fun to be had, all the new stores in which Bell could now shop, the delicious food she could now eat, all the wonderful baby names available when one considered the twenty-five letters in the alphabet other than "B."

But to Bell's great annoyance, no one answered Bridget's phone until well after ten o'clock. Finally, Trot answered, his voice thick with sleep, and offered only the most vague and ominous insight. He had no idea when Bridget would be back, nor did he particularly care. Thwarted again, Bell paced the halls, desperate for a distraction. Luckily, she had only to walk to the living room. In it, she found squadrons of Bridget's luggage and, obscured by the luggage, Bridget sleeping soundly on the sofa, her clothed body draped by a cardigan sweater like a drunken debutante at the end of a wild night. Bell stood above her sister for a moment, attempting to integrate the various clues. Either Bridget had forgotten several critical belongings and returned in the middle of the night to retrieve them or she was in the process, and Bell shuddered at this thought, of moving back into the house.

Bell cleared her throat loudly, anxious to wake her sister. Rousing from sleep, Bridget squinted her eyes and regarded Bell with confusion then, after remembering her surroundings, scowled angrily. Within seconds of encountering Bridget, Bell's mood plummeted, her initial relief to find a companion turning quickly to resentment. Thinking better of smiling, she returned Bridget's scowl with a frown. Bridget simply stared at Bell, her face devoid of emotion as though she were trying to remember the name of an old acquaintance.

After several rounds of this silent exchange, Bridget sat up from her repose and launched into a brief summary of her predicament. Trot had issued an ultimatum: Bridget must marry him or move out and Billy, though he lacked Trot's leverage, ostensibly wanted the same. Cursed with the overwhelming burden of all this love and attention, Bridget was desperate for a reprieve. She felt her childhood home the best place for peaceful contemplation. Despite the inconvenience of the move and the awkwardness of living so close to Billy, she was back indefinitely, she told Bell. And she had every intention of staying in their old bedroom.

"Oh God," Bell said before her inner censor could temper her response. Bridget's return finally ruled out the possibility of a good night's sleep.

Bridget issued a chilly glare.

"Oh good," Bell said, revising. "I'm so glad you're here."

Bridget said nothing. She lifted herself from the sofa with a melodramatic sigh then, shaking her head in response to an invisible oppressive force, she walked across the room to appraise her luggage head-on.

Bell remained still, watching her sister struggle. It was difficult to muster sympathy for Bridget's plight considering her own. Bridget was cursed with a surplus of suitors, while she had a shortage. As she stood, she admired Bridget's matching luggage in spite of herself. Perhaps she should be more like her sister and travel with her very own monogrammed set. But before Bell could consider this fully, she gave in to a pettier notion. She wondered how Bridget had shouldered the cost of all this expensive leather and, deducing their father had paid, nearly exploded with resentment.

"Bridget," Bell called.

Bridget turned her head before exiting the room, as though even uttering the word "what" required more effort than she could spare.

Finally, acknowledging Bridget's distress, Bell walked toward her sister and opened her arms, offering a mandatory embrace. Bridget returned the gesture with minimal effort, opening her arms more to block Bell's affection than hug her back. Once they'd dispensed with these formalities, the girls resumed their previous activities, Bridget whimpering at her luggage and Bell staring at Bridget with open disdain.

With a deep sigh, Bridget began applying herself to the heaviest piece, pursing her lips with determination and emitting, with each new tug, another in a crescendo of indignant grunts.

Begrudgingly, Bell brought herself to lift the smallest bag of the bunch but, finding it heavier than it appeared, she quickly replaced it on the floor.

"If it's too much trouble, don't bother," Bridget sneered.

Bell set herself to the task of testing several other bags until she had found one whose size corresponded to its weight.

"Bell, you've been lying in bed for days. Why are you so fatigued?"

"If you must know," Bell blurted out, "I'm three months pregnant."

"Oh," said Bridget. She stared at Bell for several moments, narrowing her eyes skeptically. "Whose is it?" she demanded, her tone more accusatory than inquisitive.

Bell raised her shoulders in an exaggerated shrug then looked at the floor.

Softening, Bridget dropped her bag on the floor. She rushed toward her sister to offer her first truly affectionate embrace of the day. She remained like this, cooing, shushing, and patting Bell's back for several moments. Then, as though she'd just remembered a critical item on her grocery list, she pulled back, held Bell literally at arm's length, and regarded her with overt suspicion. "So, that means you could win," she said.

Bell stared at her sister with sincere confusion.

"It means you could win Daddy's contest," Bridget clarified. "If you're carrying a boy, you'll be the first to carry on the Barnacle name."

· Bell said nothing, just stared at her sister, immobilized by rage. "That was the first thing that entered your mind? Not 'wow' or 'oh no' or 'congratulations' or 'are you going to keep it?' or 'have you thought of any names?' "

"Sorry," said Bridget in the manner designed to prove that one is not. "I'm just stating fact," she said. "You've got it in the bag."

Bell stared at her sister another moment, weighing her options. She could either engage in this idiotic debate or refuse her sister the respect of such an acknowledgment. Unfortunately, pride tipped the scales. Bell raised her voice to an appropriate fighting volume. "First, let me say, I'm not going to address the particularly disturbing self-absorption you have betrayed with your response. Nor will I bother educating you about the various fallacies of your statement. I will only say that it saddens me to see you say something so inane. It is patently clear to anyone who has lived half a day with our father, not to mention who has half a brain in her head, that his outbursts are to be taken, if at all, with a very large grain of salt. If his absurd little challenge has any meaning, it is surely symbolic. And, more likely, this is simply the first stage of a debilitating mental illness."

Bridget regarded her sister now with her full attention, then shook her head suddenly as though avoiding a fly. "Well, either way," she said, "I plan to be prepared. You never know when he's going to follow through."

Bell searched the room for a potential weapon but, finding nothing, dropped the bag on the floor with all the strength she could muster. Due to its ample cushioning, it landed with only the mildest of thuds. Disappointed, Bell regarded the impotent weapon with the sum of her frustration, then, forgetting they shared the same destination, she pushed past her sister, rushed down the hall, and slammed her, or rather their, bedroom door with terrifying force.

Sadly, Bell had made not one but two tactical errors by confiding in Bridget without conducting a thorough sweep of the apartment for traitors and spies. Benita loitered nearby, sheltered by the crook in the hall, anxious to learn any new curse words or gather incriminating information. At the sound of Bell's angry footsteps, Benita scurried to the end of the hall, disappearing just in time to avoid being sighted. Unfortunately, her new position placed her perilously in between Bell and Bridget's and Beth and Belinda's bedrooms. She crouched in this awkward spot, poised between two hostile territories, praying for a swift resolution. Luckily, a flurry of exhalations and muffled swears indicated a ceasefire. Bridget soon followed Bell to their bedroom and remained that way for the next several hours, pounding on the door, demanding to be let in. This escalation of tension between her elder sisters afforded Benita the opportunity to sneak behind Bridget back to the safety of the first crook in the hall. She remained there for hours, gathering information about her older sisters' fight as well as follow-up details on Bell's astonishing announcement.

Later, when it became clear that Bell had no intention of letting Bridget in, Benita procured a chair from the kitchen so as to spy on the unfolding discord in comfort. For a moment, compassion over-whelmed, compelling her to secure a second chair for Bridget. But deciding the generous act would compromise her camouflage, she decided against it, allowing Bridget to stand while she watched in comfort. For Benita, there was no denying the benefits of Bridget's return. One extra sister multiplied household intrigue exponen-tially; but two extra sisters brought the Barnacle family to the brink of disaster.

10

Predisposition to Flight

*I*t was always difficult to convince the Barnacle girls to separate after spending time together, but this time it was harder than ever. Bell and Bridget's nearly simultaneous return made it almost impossible to convince Beth and Belinda to return to school. Beth, usually restless by her second day of vacation, explained that college had become stifling; even graduate-level courses felt cruelly redundant. Belinda also expressed an uncharacteristic aversion to school. She usually enjoyed it immensely; her enjoyment, as with most things, a direct function of the rules it offered to break. But now she found the apartment offered an excitement of its own. It was simply too rare an occasion; with so many sisters in the house, things were sure to get interesting.

The apartment's high female occupancy endowed it with a decided hum and, due to Bell and Bridget's dangerously close quarters, the promise of fights yet to come. Both Beth and Belinda sensed that they would be missing out and, as a result, campaigned to stay, both girls informing the family, independent of the other, that she planned to boycott school. Belinda employed the odd and ingenious strategy of admitting to transgressions she'd made in the past in the hopes that Barry, newly aware of the school's lenience, would forbid her to return. Beth, in turn, announced her plans to take the rest of the semester off. She would volunteer her services at the family veterinarian and continue her research in her own makeshift lab.

As though in reflection of Beth and Belinda's discord, the standing volume in the house increased. Fights broke out in all corners of the apartment, provoked less by the stated subject than by general malaise. This strife combined with various environmental factors, such as the first prickle of April heat, turning the apartment into a hothouse of female consternation. A walk down the hall that connected the girls' bedrooms revealed the most disparate and peculiar noises. A low murmur accompanied by sporadic sounds of rustling paper emerged from Benita and Beryl's room as Benita rehearsed her lines out loud and Beryl folded and unfolded a large map of Central Park. From Beth and Belinda's room, one could hear the muffled sounds of dueling musical eras, angry punk rock alternating with moody French ballads. Both types of music were punctuated by occasional outbursts of yelling as Beth and Belinda fought over a mutually acceptable soundtrack. Bell and Bridget's room emitted the least audible noise, but inside the silence was deafening. Both girls sat on their beds, facing in opposite directions, seemingly engaged in a contest of who could produce the more meaningful sigh.

Rising tension reached fever pitch as all six girls simultaneously converged on the bathroom. They took the opportunity to compare notes on the events of Thursday evening.

Bell offered the first and most radical perspective on their father's behavior. "Ignore him," she said. "It's obvious what he's trying to do. He has one goal and one alone, to get me and Bridget married."

Bridget, however, had more faith in her father and a slightly para-noid streak. "I wonder if something's wrong," she said, "and this is some sort of cover-up. I really hope he's not in trouble with the IRS."

Beth, however, was blessed with the authority of a scientist. "Don't be hysterical," she cautioned. "After all these years, haven't you learned to ignore Dad's little outbursts? He's having a midlife crisis. Soon they'll have drugs for these things like they do for menopause and PMS."

Belinda paused to consider Beth's assessment but promptly ruled it out. She knew better than to place her trust in Beth. Most likely, Beth was simply trying to throw her sisters off the scent. "Ignore Beth, everybody," she announced. "There's nothing odd about this at all. It's the latest in a long history of grotesque behavior from a man so obsessed with winning that he rates his own you-know-what."

Conversation halted as the others paused to consider Belinda's cryptic and likely crass comment.

"Nope," said Beryl, "you're all wrong."

"Tell us what you see," Beth mocked.

"Yeah," said Benita, "considering your predictions have zero per-cent accuracy."

"I'll tell you this," Beryl said. "Neither one of you is going to win."

"How can you know that?" Benita demanded.

"Because you," she said, turning to Benita, "are too competitive for your own good and you," she said, turning Beth, "well, just look at your losing record."

"Go to hell," said Benita.

"Up and die," said Beth.

"Gladly," snapped Beryl. "It would be a relief. Death would spare me the torture of looking at the two of you."

Inspired by a literal interpretation, Beth took the fight to the next level. She hurried to the kitchen, anxious to realize Beryl's bold claim. She located the phone book above the fridge and found the number for the *New York Times,* then asked a very helpful operator to connect her to the obituary section. As it turned out, next-day announcements cost more than she was willing to spend. Luckily, the standard notice, guaranteed to run within three days, could be ordered free of charge. Beth devoted the next hour to penning the perfect tribute, anxious to find the right balance between praise and honesty. She wrote and rewrote the text several times before submitting a final draft. Ultimately, she was pleased with her effort. She kept it short and sweet.

Beryl Barnacle died at the age of fifteen in her childhood home. She is survived by five sisters, one father, one mother, and various and sundry pets. Though she was, by most accounts, the most eccentric of the Barnacle sisters, Beryl will be missed sorely, if only due to the peace and quiet afforded by her absence. Luckily, she is only dead to her older and much more intelligent sister, Beth.

Wholly unaware of the metaphorical murder being perpetrated in the next room, Belinda returned to her bedroom and dropped to the floor, unable to bring herself to the task of packing for school. Instead, she simply sat and sulked, listening to dirgelike French music and occasionally shifting her position on the floor. On sound of her mother calling out her twenty-, ten-, then five-minute warnings, she assumed the universal pose of teenage angst, lying flat on her stomach with her heels kicking the backs of her knees as though these kicks might enact some minor amount of violence on those who oppressed her. She only deigned to move when the record reached its final, wailing note at which point she lifted herself from the ground, replaced the needle at the beginning of the record, then resumed her prostrate position and the task of tuning her family out.

Despite her well-publicized love of school, Belinda had no interest in going back. Her claim that anything was better than home had always been uttered mostly for effect and now failed to convince even her. During her freshman and sophomore years, she'd been pacified by the change of scenery. The sturdy brick buildings and pristine hedges of the manicured campus had worked its magic on her restlessness, providing a legible and satisfying symbol of captivity and freedom both. Any urge to break free found its ideal opponent in so much impenetrable brick. Any urge to be sheltered found its fulfillment in the form of ubiquitous patrolling guards. So many soccer fields and their store of smiling, sun-kissed, sometimes shirtless boys did their part to ease Belinda's transition from grittier urban landscapes. It was hard to miss the city in the presence of so much well-trimmed grass. It was hard to miss her family in the presence of so many boys.

Nor had she missed the girls she'd left behind at the Chapin School. Even Belinda felt her classmates wore their skirts promiscuously short, permitting other students and utter strangers an effortless glimpse at their thighs. She'd long ago tired of the nightly romp her friends excused for a social life, meeting in clumps at the awnings of their Upper East Side palaces, tramping up and down Park Avenue like a band of well-heeled vagrants. Besides which, she found their hallowed destinations equally laughable; in the winter, the fountain at the Metropolitan Museum of Art, in the spring, Sheep Meadow in Central Park. They trekked to both spots illogically enough so as to imbibe in public the same substances they smuggled into their homes. What was the point of all this traipsing? Belinda often wondered. Why go to such great lengths to find privacy when busy parents offered the same neglect in the comfort of one's own home? She could only conclude the following: It was somehow essential to simulate the act of breaking rules to have fun.

But now, three years later, Belinda had tired of this, too. Just thinking about it exhausted her. She lacked the energy to live up to her ignominious rep. Despite her wise and worldly demeanor, her indisputably impressive wardrobe, and her formidable command of the New York City phone book, she was not, for all her pretense, quite as worldly as she seemed. Truth be told, Belinda had not yet lost her virginity; a confession she would never make in public but of which she was actually quite proud considering the amount of willpower and physical force required to maintain the claim. No, the semblance of wizened cool, her endless supply of drug lore, her mastery of East Village bars were all part of a well-tuned act, all necessary accoutrements of a persona she donned as she might her favorite pair of jeans. This pair incidentally caused further contention, since Bella wished Belinda would throw them away and Bridget wished Belinda would give them back. The perfectly symmetrical rip in the crotch had taken Belinda years to perfect and, Bridget argued, could not have occurred naturally as Belinda claimed.

Indeed, Belinda was locked into a life that wasn't hers. Her friends and family gave her no choice, demanding she uphold her wild-child identity, much like a lawyer forced to defend a dubious witness. Still, Belinda had grown accustomed to living with the burden. She saw it as a duty of sorts. She provided a valuable service to her friends and family. Her alleged rebellion allowed them to find contentment in their uneventful lives. Her contrary behavior offered them a rallying call of sorts, giving them something to oppose, securing their comfortable stasis in lives they would otherwise find too boring to inhabit. It permitted her sisters to deflect their bad behavior, her mother to vent her dissatisfaction, and her father to consolidate the pent-up fury of failing to produce a single male heir. Of course, it was not always easy to play the tortured, sullen teen. Belinda dreaded the screaming matches, the seething looks, the slammed door, as much as everyone else. But she felt she had no choice but play the role in which she'd been cast.

And so it was with no remorse that Belinda prepared for her routine flight, cementing her conviction with the reminder that her rebellion was the fault of those who had typecast her in the first place. With expert speed, she hurried through the ritual's sacred rites, first opening the window a sliver to check the weather outside, tying an extra sweater around her waist so as to be prepared for a change in temperature, firmly closing her bedroom door and locking it from the inside. And despite the fact that she had made this flight at least a hundred times, she was filled with a sudden swell of fear. But, refusing to be slowed, Belinda thrust the window all the way open as though the force with which she shoved might hurry the flight of her conscience.

The thrill of escape came over her as she prepared for descent. First, she wet her index fingers to muffle the squeaks of the window frame. Next, a quick backward glance at the room to make sure she'd remembered everything. Finally, as a last reluctant nod to obligation, she paused in the window's hutch, halfway between freedom and captivity, to consider her mother's feelings on discovering another missing child. But this notion only presented the most fleeting of second thoughts before she continued with the delicate procedure of hurtling herself into space. By the time Bella broke into the room, Belinda was well on her way, already nearing the corner of Sixtieth and Fifth. Heading west, she booked it past the Pierre Hotel just as the evening rush of taxis commenced its daily congestion of Fifth Avenue. She sprinted past the Plaza and its lines of waiting carriages up Central Park South. She slowed down only once she'd reached Eighth Avenue, peering south quickly for a glimpse of Times Square's shimmering red and blue lights. Finally, at Columbus Circle, she ducked into the subway station and hopped the 9 train with no particular plan or itinerary.

All this forward motion should have been liberating. But as Belinda rode downtown, she was plagued by thoughts of her father. Barry provided Belinda an endless source of angry rumination; he was, in her opinion, both the cause and solution to her every single problem. His latest announcement epitomized his deep-seated disorder, revealing with naked transparence his vulgar and, Belinda felt, embarrassingly Jewish obsession with winning and competition. Why could he not be more like the parents of her boarding school friends, discreet in their goals for their children, even charmingly disinterested? Why must his every hope bear the weight of generations of immigrants, as though his daughters, despite their freedom from such concerns, could not live happy, fruitful lives unless they, too, were transported to the squalid streets of the turn-of-the-century shtetl. Of course, Belinda saw the merits of a healthy work ethic. She could agree with her father that the blasé entitlement of the Finches was equally reprehensible. But she still begrudged her father his aching need to win. His overt effort was embarrassing; it reeked of desperation.

Still, she found herself fixating on her father's proposed contest, obsessing over potential strategies with the same vigor as Benita. Nothing would please her more than to mock her father's warped value system by surpassing her crowd-pleasing sisters. Now, as she rode the subway, she recalled the verbiage of Barry's pompous speech and made a concerted and thorough search for possible loopholes and technicalities, scouring his semantics for shortcuts by which she could vault herself to fame and recognition. Luckily, the culture in which she lived was similarly infected by Barry's obsessions and provided a glittering, if questionable, abundance of schemes that enabled one to get rich or at least marginally famous in thirty days or less. She contemplated the alternatives at the exclusion of her surroundings.

A young homeless boy sat across the aisle, gazing intently out the window, his eyes betraying a certain deep and irresistible rage. His hair was dyed blond and dreadlocked, bisected by a bald stripe. His feet were filthy. It seemed two weeks, at the least, since they'd last been washed. His age was hard to determine from his face. He looked at once old and young, blessed with the same translucent skin of spoiled neighborhood boys, but he boasted an attractive weathered quality Belinda had rarely seen, his face revealing the wrinkles and worry of life on the road. She could tell, even from her distance, that he was deeply distracted, surely by a recent criminal offense or the end to a tortured romance.

As she examined this wayward boy, Belinda became increasingly convinced that, after years of bogus leads, she had finally found her soul mate. This boy was twice the man of her fair-faced prep school friends. Even their hairdos proved their kinship. This boy was her long-lost twin. Best of all, this boy would shock and horrify her father. Surely the very sight of him would be the death knell of their relationship. As though propelled by this very thought from her seat into the boy's arms, Belinda crossed the train and seated herself next to him.

"Excuse me," she said.

"Yes," said the boy.

"Will you marry me?" she asked.

The boy said nothing, looked right, then left, then shrugged and said, "Why not?"

"Cool," said Belinda. "Do you promise?"

"Sure," he said, shrugging as though Belinda had only inquired if the seat next to him was free.

"There's one small thing," Belinda added. "You'll have to take my last name."

"That works," he said amiably. "I've never liked mine all that much."

Belinda smiled at the boy. Then, as an afterthought, she asked, "Why, what's wrong with it?"

The boy shook his head and sealed his mouth.

"Come on. It can't be that bad."

"Trust me," he said.

"Come on," said Belinda.

The boy offered a tentative wince. Then, barely in a whisper, he answered, "Goldfarb. What's yours?"

In a moment, Belinda realized the enormity of her mistake. This boy was hardly a ruffian. He was merely a confused teen, a boy bewildered by his privilege, set on the run by the pressure of all that explosive guilt. She knew a hundred just like him. He probably grew up only blocks away. For all she knew, they lived on the very same street. Cringing, she met the boy's eyes and answered his question. "Barnacle," she replied.

"Cool," said the boy.

Belinda mustered a paltry smile, then turned away from the boy. But, determined not to let her father ruin her life even in his absence, she forced herself to wrangle her negative thoughts. Regardless of her error in judgment, she had accomplished one miraculous thing: In all of ten seconds, she had lapped her sisters and taken the lead in her father's contest. Comforted, she imagined her father's face on sight of the new member of the family. She smiled as she pictured her sisters' reactions to the blatant upset. Blessed with the foreclosed possibility of going back to school, she decided to make the most of her vacation. She had only to find somewhere to sleep that night and a way to stomach this boy until they made it official.

Belinda did her best to squelch her conscience as they rode downtown. But against her will, responsible thoughts invaded her head. Finally, based on a mutual consensus made by eye contact alone, the two alighted at Astor Place with the vague intention of killing time in the East Village. Belinda found the first pay phone on the platform and made two strategic calls. First, she called her family to inform them that she had caught an earlier train to school. Then, she called the main number at school and, doing her best impersonation of Bunny, dispensed with any remaining possibility of turning back.

"Due to a family emergency," Belinda said, "Belinda will not be returning to school." And then, as an extra precaution, she added, "Things are tense at the Barnacle apartment, so please do not call them at home."

Very early on Saturday morning or very late on Friday night, Barry was awakened by a faint squeaking sound coming from Bell and Bridget's bedroom. Lately, he had fallen back into the clutches of insomnia, and slept most nights for intervals of less than ten or twenty minutes, often for a total of one or two hours. After several such nights, his investigative powers were less acute than usual and, as a result, caused him incorrectly to attribute the noise in the house to Latrell. Perhaps, he had finally tired of his sojourn and come back of his own volition. But the noise was not Latrell sneaking back in his window; it was the sound of Belinda's shutters, moved by the evening breeze.

Despite his apparent neglect, Barry was very conscious of Bella's adopted son; his apathy, in fact, a conscious rebellion against loving Latrell. In Barry's opinion, the women in the house had coddled Latrell so consistently that they had softened the sharpness of his talents and deprived him the hunger and aspiration a boy needed to become a great man. At the heart of this sentiment was Barry's conviction that Latrell was naturally gifted and that squandering talent was a more flagrant insult than having none in the first place. Still, despite his stated surrender to Bella's policy of indulgence, Barry watched over Latrell from a distance, preferring to keep his affection a secret from the family.

In truth, Barry was fascinated with Latrell, obsessed with the object of his distracted gaze like a mechanic with a machine. He was inherently suspicious of the amount of time Latrell spent staring into space, assuming it meant Latrell was disinterested in him or, worse, disapproving of his transgressions. But rather than acknowledge his own shortcomings, Barry focused on Latrell's, arguing that Bella had spoiled him with liberal administration of television, pizza, and cookies, causing him to swell into a soft mama's boy as opposed to a lean athlete. Latrell is what happens, Barry liked to say, when children play too many video games. Latrell is what happens when children watch too much MTV.

Belinda was the most vocal critic of Barry's treatment of Latrell, perhaps because it mirrored her own relationship with her father. In Belinda's opinion, her father had long since stopped considering her a viable competitor and she had done her best to confirm this theory by abstaining from aspiration. Still, Belinda felt this boycott had not produced its intended result, failing to anger her father in a noticeable way. She felt as she had when she had run away from home as a child, and then returned to find her parents had not yet noticed her absence. Barry's disappointment in Latrell seemed a more active form than his disappointment in her. It betrayed his initial avid interest, whereas his obliviousness to her proved he had never cared in the first place. As a result, Belinda found herself in the odd and illogical position of being jealous of nothing.

She spent an inordinate amount of time engaged in an analysis of Barry's relationship with Latrell. The obvious diagnosis was that Barry's dispassion was displaced anger for never having had a son. But the more subtle interpretation, Belinda claimed, was that Barry was a racist. When pressed, Barry simply defended himself (and revealed that she might be correct) by acknowledging Latrell's numerous talents as though listing the attributes of a racehorse. Latrell, Barry explained, was the most gifted pianist of all the musicians in the house, two years ahead of his class in math, very handsome by all accounts, and coordinated in sports. In keeping with the tactics of their ongoing war, Barry combated Belinda's attack by ignoring it.

In fact, Barry's greatest grievance with Latrell was that he never spoke. Of course, this was to Barry's great advantage because Latrell knew about his affairs and objected to them vehemently. Fearing discovery Barry instituted a system of rewards by which he hoped to keep Latrell in check. He allowed Latrell to accompany him whenever he left the house for his trysts, provided Latrell kept mum about the nature of their forays. As it turned out, this was an ideal trade; Barry provided the perfect antidote to Bella's overprotective mothering and Latrell provided the perfect alibi for Barry's extracurricular activities. And, ironically, these trips improved Barry's reputation, earning him points from his daughters and ex-wife, who felt this time marked a positive change in Barry's treatment of Latrell. In exchange for his silence, Latrell was allowed to roam the city for the duration of Barry's visits provided he arrived on time at the appointed meeting spot. Latrell accepted the privilege with the short-lived guilt of a thief, his conscience bothering him up to the point at which he cashed in.

The arrangement had been particularly beneficial to Barry of late. During the past winter, he had been through a generation of girl-friends, the number of which was only surpassed by their age range.

He liked to think of himself as the kind of man who might one day entertain all these women in the same room while wearing a silk bathrobe and eating strawberries. "Girls," he would say, "I'd like to thank you all for coming over. That is," he would add, "I would like to thank you one at a time. These circumstances," he would continue after laughter subsided, "are incredibly unusual so I do appreciate your congregating on such short notice." At this point, he would allow the assembled women to emit a collective gasp. Some would rush to Barry's side while others jumped to his lap. All would listen with rapt horror while Barry informed them of the news that even his astounding virility had failed to immunize him from a rare terminal disease.

There was, in fact, one shred of truth to Barry's odd fantasy. His mistresses were so unified in one sentiment, they could have started a club; every one of them felt Barry was a bastard and that he should be strung up. Of course, none of these women had real grounds for this complaint since each was guilty of the same crime, not only the betrayal of other women but worse, the folly of thinking that she alone would be the exception to the rule. The only comfort to Barry's jilted lovers was Barry's ineptitude. Despite the frequency of his transgressions, his cover-ups were hopelessly clumsy, providing his lovers with an insurance policy of sorts. Without fail, every time Barry cheated his wife or mistress figured it out within twenty-four hours. Recently, however, the sheer number of these women had produced an interesting effect, rendering Barry's mistresses so shrill and demanding as to seem more like wives.

The line between wife and paramour had blurred to such a great extent that Barry was forced to consider a whole new set of ethical questions. Was it technically adultery, for example, when one cheated on one's mistress with one's own wife? Was it normal to miss one's wife during the act of intercourse with another woman? Was it paranoid to suspect one's mistresses of secretly plotting to litigate? Would it be un-sexy, let alone legal, to ask a woman to sign a release before the naughty act? Was it dangerous, long term, to feel this guilty after having sex? Was guilt a disorder or a revelation brought on by old age? And finally, did it make one less of a man if sometimes, while in the company of even the most beautiful woman, one experienced a craving as intense as a pregnant woman for pickles to flee the lady in one's company and retreat to a dark, quiet room.

If these questions were not enough to incite a nervous breakdown, Barry was also plagued by a slew of minor financial headaches. They included, in addition to the staggering cost of nine dependents (not counting houseguests and pets), the demands of a consortium of spurned female employees whose belligerence was surpassed only by their excellent lawyers. But the problem ran far deeper than mere financial strain. This was something more nebulous, something more cerebral. What if this problem could not be solved? Barry now considered. What if he had finally met his match? Accosted by such overwhelming questions, Barry experienced true desperation. And he learned something new about life. There is nothing more humbling than getting through the better part of one's life without ever having been humbled. Fear, as it turns out, is far scarier at the age of sixty than six.

Of course, this state of existential angst was the exact antithesis to the state of bliss one hopes to attain with adultery. These affairs had served to increase, instead of release, stress. At first, the problem manifested itself subtly, gradually robbing adultery of its previous pleasure. Soon, it became so consuming that Barry stopped seeing women altogether, preferring the solace of his room to the oppressive guilt. But even solitude failed to provide a respite anymore. Lately, he had suffered from such severe insomnia that the world had been drained of color, its contents jaundicing like aging newsprint as the day progressed. It had gotten so bad that the apartment had become a sea of menacing shadows; at times making his daughters indistinguishable from one another, nothing more than six strange blurs.

The affliction caused Barry, for the first time in his life, to feel deeply depressed, a state that was further compounded by the fact that he could not share it with anyone and that it seemed, unlike every other obstacle he had encountered, to be impervious to his will. Having been a stranger to his emotions for sixty years, he now found himself in uncharted territory. If only his ailment were more specific. He would have preferred to be diagnosed with any known disease, even to go bankrupt. But this, this amorphous psychic disorientation was nothing short of torture. And the insomnia, the cruel unceasing sleepless hours cursed Barry to relive his regrets for an additional twelve hours each day.

Finally, just before sunrise on Saturday, Barry gave up on sleep. Inspired by a hallucination or a dream, he couldn't tell which was which anymore, he dressed quickly and crept down the hall, determined to leave the house. As he passed Bell and Bridget's bedroom, he experienced the strangest urge to enter and surprised himself by acting on it without a second thought. Making no particular effort to muffle the sound, he opened the door to the girls' bedroom, crossed the room while they slept, then launched himself out of their window onto their fire escape. Velocity gave Barry new hope, but it caused him to produce far more noise than he'd intended.

As a result, Bella, who was also awake, heard the commotion and stirred. She stopped where she stood in the pantry and held her glass extremely still, waiting for further sound. But, hearing nothing, she assumed the noise came from the usual source. Expectation and inebriation combined to double Bella's surprise when she opened her window to find Barry huddled on the thirteenth-floor fire escape, staring at the city sky as though glimpsing it for the first time. For one brief, deluded moment, she concluded that Barry was en route to her bedroom, that he had finally realized his mistake and now clambered toward her window to beg her to take him back.

"Barry," she whispered.

Barry looked up, shocked by the sound of his name. He stared at Bella as though unsure how he'd arrived at this place.

"Barry," Bella whispered again. "Is everything all right?"

"Oh yes," he mumbled. "Very much so. Just admiring the stars."

Bella followed Barry's gaze to an utterly starless sky.

Barry smiled with nonchalance, then searched for a better excuse. "If you must know, I'm feeling a little haunted."

Bella leaned farther out her window. "Regret is a menacing ghost," she said.

Barry gazed searchingly at Bella, considering her thesis, then dismissing the notion, forced a nervous laugh. "Just ignore me," he announced. "I haven't slept in days."

Bella mistook this for a rejection and shrunk perceptibly. She imagined her face from Barry's perspective and felt a rush of shame. In the five years since their divorce, she had aged at least ten years. Her eyes had frayed at the edges due to constant frowning. Her lips had flattened under the weight of so much disappointment. Even her hair had thinned to resemble dried corn's lusterless silk. The skin on her face displayed her years like rings around a tree. Her pain was perfectly visible in her wide blue eyes. They were still as clear and guileless as a child's.

But Bella's assumption was wrong: Barry was not focused on her flaws. On the contrary, as Barry stared at Bella, he found himself wondering, with the confusion of an amnesiac, why he had ever strayed from her side.

Bella leaned farther out the window, anxious to decipher Barry's look. "Barry," she said. She leaned out farther. "Barry, are you sure you're all right?"

Barry said nothing. He only stood, staring helplessly. "I'm fine," he said. "I was just." He trailed off. "I was just . . . leaving."

"Oh," sighed Bella.

Barry nodded and headed down the fire escape with new determination.

Bella watched Barry descend to the sidewalk, then turned and hurried back to bed, firm in her resolve to remember the exchange as part of a dream the next day.

Barry, too, forced the encounter from his mind as he hurried away from the building and toward Park Avenue. Perhaps, he decided,

this mental anguish signaled a need for repentance. His purpose renewed, he continued east and ducked into the subway station on
Fifty-ninth and Lexington. The D train was Barry's favorite subway
line, not only because it was the fastest route to Coney Island, but
also because, in Barry's opinion, the train circled the city with the intimacy of a lover. First, it clutched the Lower East Side with adoring
thoroughness, next it traced the Manhattan Bridge as though grasping its form. Then, without warning, it swerved, twisting your body
with the tremors of passion itself until suddenly you faced the great
city, its sturdy skyline promising to keep watch no matter how far
you strayed from home.

Barry's senses were accosted even before he got off the train.
Memory performed its usual calculus, subtracting the present from
the past, illuminating details of the world as though to make a case
for the impressive feats of time. The smell of hot dogs and salt air
blended with a sweet, slightly acrid perfume, joining with the
dampness of the ocean to refresh Barry after the train ride. Immediately, his eyes adjusted to the brighter light. Brooklyn's sun
seemed stronger somehow than the one that shone over Manhattan,
its tinge more silvery than gold, its quality unimpeded by the shade
of skyscrapers. Signs and storefronts had submitted to a general fading, red letters bleaching to pink, blacks to gray and blue. It was as
though the area had been victim to a fire and was now covered by a
thin film of soot. Every inch of Coney Island admitted this gradual
decline. But Barry refused to be slowed by nostalgia and continued
down Surf Avenue, hurrying past old memories as though he might
outrun them if he moved fast enough.

In Coney Island, evolution proceeded at a faster rate. The island,
like Galápagos, was galvanized by constant change, colonized by visitors, and propelled forward by adaptation. Sometimes Barry's stories about Coney Island seemed like the stuff of myth, tales of a race
of amphibious men who had risen out of the East River, leaping from
gutters to gold in the span of one lifetime. These men were, of course,
direct descendants of America's first immigrants, vigorous Russians

and Poles who settled in Coney Island, comforted by its resemblance to the coastlines at home.

Like most of the boys in Brighton Beach, Barry was raised a Jew, but his parents had a higher faith, worshipping devoutly at the altar of hard work. Temple, of course, had proven a blessing and a curse for these men, first forcing the flight from their homes, then helping them to build new ones. Their children were witnesses to the divine power of toil, had both heard the tales and seen the proof of relentless effort. Barry's father, Boris Baranski, was high priest of this religion. A professor by training and policeman by necessity, he was a knight of the neighborhood, presiding over his family and the Boardwalk. Soon enough, a seventeen-year-old bride completed his court and a third generation joined the crowded pool. But even a fortified island is vulnerable to attack. Nature paid Boris that most outrageous of insults, cursing him with cancer at the age of sixty-three. Though his struggle lasted many years, Boris told his family about his disease only days before it took his life. Arguably, Barry's hostility to nature hearkened back to this early grudge.

Barry unconsciously picked up his pace, sprinting through the backdrop of his childhood. He turned up Surf Avenue, heading past the amusement park then the Brighton Beach Baths. He hurried past the handball courts and the checker tables, slowing only to avoid collision with the occasional morning jogger. He finally began to slow as he passed Nathan's, turning onto Mermaid Avenue at the old carousel. He stopped at the Mermaid Hotel, a once glamorous seaside resort, now a squatter's haven and home to a population of criminals and vagrants.

Quickly, Barry crossed the lobby and entered the hotel bar, a dank little dive whose lack of light and patrons both contributed to the sense that it was still nighttime inside. He took a seat on a stool and positioned himself with his back to the bar then sat, scanning the bar's patrons for familiar features, as though any one of them might be an old and dear acquaintance. Suddenly, he stood from his stool and ventured deeper into the bar, stopping at a small unoccupied piano. He stared at it for a moment, then seated himself on the bench and caressed the keys with the bemused wistfulness of a man paying last respects.

"Can I help you?" someone called from the bar.

"No," Barry muttered. He remained still, staring at the piano keys. Then, changing his mind, he looked up at the bartender. "Actually, yes," he said though it sounded less like a demand than a plea.

The bartender paused, cocking his head with a mixture of boredom and curiosity.

"Do you know the man who used to work here?" Barry asked.

The bartender waited on more information.

"He used to play the piano here."

"Tuesday nights," he answered.

Barry remained still for another moment, alternating his gaze from the piano to the bar. Then, he stood and rushed back onto the street like a plant desperate for light.

Back on Surf Avenue, Barry held his pace, fueled by the prospect of a new destination. He hurried past all the places that stood in his memories: the Steeplechase, Wonderland, the original Luna Park. Onward past the handball courts, their white cement already shaded by the midday sun, the checkerboard tables, the Brighton Beach Baths, and the aquarium. As he walked, the past and present blurred, reshaping his surroundings. Finally, Barry slowed to a stop at the steps of a small Lutheran church. He stood for a moment as though contemplating the awesome power of God, then pushed the door, crossed the vestibule, and, finding the church empty, took a seat in the last pew.

It was at this moment that something utterly bizarre occurred. Barry, an avid atheist, was overwhelmed with the urge to weep. All at once, his head was filled with a loud and buoyant melody. The opening notes of Beethoven's Fifth symphony resounded with hymn-like grandeur, as though played on this very church organ. To make the experience yet more peculiar, Barry detected another sound just underneath the familiar melody, the notes of which were underscored by the faint sound of knocking. Unfortunately, Barry would never know the source of this beatific noise. Could it possibly be a sign from God or just his mind playing tricks? Either way, he could no longer be sure of anything and questioned, now with new urgency, whether the hand that knocked was that of man or destiny.

Part Two

Nurture

11

Killer Backhand

*J*ust as there are good and bad marriages, there are good and bad proposals. Billy's running contest with Bridget had taught him nothing if not this. But now he faced the ultimate challenge, scripting an authentic one of his own. And for the first time in his life, he was at a loss for words. Whereas before he had been overwhelmed by the sheer abundance of possibilities, he was now completely tongue-tied at the thought. Whereas before he had viewed men in this position as a bunch of leashed puppets, he now found respect, even awe, for those who made it down to one knee. If he was honest with himself, and Billy rarely was, he would have to admit that he did not so much loathe marriage proposals as he loathed the idea of his being rejected. And, lacking insight into Bridget's heart, he mistook her stated antipathy to the proposal for antipathy to him. In thinking about the current task, he employed a process of elimination. If he could not pen the perfect proposal, at least he could decide which to avoid.

First, he ruled out the surprise proposal. Surprise was an overrated state of mind that precluded the flow of necessary emotions such as love and lust. A tear-jerking proposal was not his style. Did it not slightly weaken a woman's credibility to claim it was the happiest day of her life while sobbing into her soup? Next to go were the mid-day proposals, the ones that shocked with their banality. These proposals, rendered on a walk in the park, or while shopping for groceries, had a certain antiquated charm and offered the added financial bene-fit of circumventing the high price of glittery nighttime pomp. But these lacked in force what they gained in spontaneity. By default then, Billy moved on to the numerous nocturnal options, but all of these seemed embarrassingly corny and contrived. A ring dangling from a dinner fork would surely fail to impress. Worse yet, the truly breathtaking proposals, those uttered on the ledge of a canyon or on the hundredth floor of a skyscraper, were too melodramatic to be taken seriously and risked unforeseen contingencies. What if your woman turned green with vertigo just as you hit the deck of the Empire State Building? Surely, this would hurt your chances at acceptance.

No, none of these options would do. Bridget would deem them maudlin musings, labored displays of romance. Billy would rather call on a trained chimp and ask him to perform in his place. Perhaps, he should expand his breadth and consider the truly ornate propos-als. If money was no object, whimsy and imagination were his limits. He could wait for a perfect summer day, hire a skywriter to write the question in the clouds, then take Bridget on a picnic and, at just the right moment, direct her gaze toward the sky. Or, he could rig up a string of lights, spell out the question on a rooftop, then take Bridget on a helicopter ride and direct her eyes to the ground. He could draw on current technology and send the query via text mes-sage. He could encrypt his proposal in an eye chart then submit her to an eye exam. He could wrangle Charles, construct a sign, tie it around the dog's neck, and then lure the dog into her room by way of dangling meat. He could drop the ring into the batter of a cake, bake and present the cake, then wait for Bridget to choke. He could devise an elaborate treasure hunt culminating at their favorite restaurant, then jump out from beneath a table, toppling drinks, terrifying Bridget, and trying the patience of everyone else.

As a last resort, he could always consider the most taboo of options: the postcoital proposal, otherwise known as "popping the question after sex." This proposal had earned a bad reputation for good reason, he supposed. It was manipulative, if not downright mean, to exploit such a vulnerable state. But perhaps, Billy considered, this mode of proposal was so déclassé as to be due for a revival, capable of a comeback like bell-bottoms or the micro-miniskirt. Maybe, he could breathe life into this unseemly tradition, turning raunchy into romantic, salacious into spontaneous. Yes, the more he considered this one, the more inspired he felt. A postcoital proposal allowed the happy couple to ride the coattails of euphoria all the way to the harsh light of sunrise, permitting those with cold feet to warm them on another foot. And yet, Billy had no choice but concede this proposal had its drawbacks. Though dramatic, it risked complete alienation and all but ruled out fireside retelling to posterity. And, more to the point, this proposal required succeeding in the one arena in which Billy had continuously failed. In his twenty-odd years of trying to seduce Bridget, he had never managed to get much farther than first base. Therefore, the postcoital proposal must be ruled out as well; Billy had no right to assume he could even get to the coital part.

Besides, Bridget was far too discerning to approve of these proposals. He would fare better offering her a gift certificate and bidding her to buy her own ring. No, none of these proposals would work. Each one fell too neatly into a category. His proposal must defy genres, must transcend the semantics of love and contracts, must not only sweep Bridget off her feet but sweep up all the competition. And, as though it were not enough pressure to face the poet's empty page, the notorious high standards of his particular princess, and, worse still, the battlefield of those who had tried and failed before him, Billy faced a yet more terrifying challenge: the affection of Bridget herself. For though he suspected that she was warming to him, and there was no denying he had made great strides in the last few days, he still had little reason to believe Bridget loved him back. The task was therefore so monumental and he, so hideously ill-prepared, that he felt he had no choice but call on his brother for help. Feeling particularly disheveled and distraught, Billy arrived at his weekly tennis game with Blaine with the explicit intention of asking his brother for advice.

In tennis, the twins were equally matched, though they both had different strengths. Billy had a superior serve while Blaine had a better net game. Billy's overhead smash was virtually unreturnable but Blaine had a killer backhand. Despite Blaine's tendency toward hyperbole, this backhand was an objective fact, surpassing the speed of some airplanes and, on occasion, causing injury to his opponents. Whenever Blaine had the opportunity to implement this shot, the current rally was sure to end. But unlike typical backhands that lurch due to topspin or halt unexpectedly due to slice, Blaine's coupled delicacy and might, producing on the faces of those at its mercy, a perfect portrait of surprise. Blaine's opponents often took drastic measures to avoid feeding Blaine this shot, hitting to his forehand as a rule and all but giving up on the point when the ball entered Blaine's favored zone.

Still despite this obstacle, Billy loved playing tennis with Blaine. His matching constitution made him uniquely equipped. Billy was blessed with the ultimate opposing weapon to Blaine's backhand; a forehand that possessed, Billy felt, equal and opposite power. Still, according to Blaine, tennis proved their inherent inequity. Their game score, he argued, was indisputable proof of his superiority. He won exactly 51 percent of their matches over the years. When Blaine did win, he usually won by a hair due to a much-debated double-fault or an inaudible bounce on the line. Without fail, on these occasions, Blaine subjected Billy to the most punctilious of victory dances, sending Billy off the court with the heartfelt intention of never playing his brother again. And yet, despite these negatives, the boys still relished their Saturday game and, depending on the score, brunched together afterward. They used their standing date to air out current issues, catch up on pressing gossip, idly bicker, and continue the debate they'd been having since childhood on the subject of the Barnacle girls.

At the moment, Billy and Blaine stood at the net, engaging in their pregame ritual, attempting to intimidate the other with a series of threatening looks. Blaine took the opportunity to remove his sweats, revealing a blinding white tracksuit that made him look debonair in a fastidious sort of way. Billy wore a T-shirt with a rip on the left side of the chest that threatened, with sudden arm extensions, to reveal his left nipple. He wore plaid shorts, hastily grabbed from the top of a soiled laundry pile that, he realized now for the first time, were actually not a pair of shorts but rather a pair of boxers. Tiring of Blaine's intimidating tactics, Billy walked up to the net and tapped it rhythmically with his racket as though he had every intention of chopping it in half. At Blaine's pointed glance, Billy ceased tapping and stared across the court defiantly, then, gripping the net, took a deep, solemn breath and announced, "I think I'm ready."

Despite the vagueness of his announcement, Blaine immediately understood Billy's import. But, rather than respond outright, he opened a new can of balls, miming, in time with their angry pop, the opening of a bottle of champagne. Opposition, Blaine knew, would only strengthen Billy's resolve. Feigned endorsement was the surest way to change Billy's mind. "Well, that's fantastic news," Blaine said. "How are you going to do it?"

"See that's the thing," Billy said. "Bridget and I have that running joke."

"Ah yes," Blaine sighed, "I know it well. Alice and I were the butt of it."

"Blaine, please be serious."

"I'm aware of your game," Blaine sniffed.

"Suffice it to say Bridget is an aficionado of the genre. Proposing to her is like serving wine to a world-class sommelier."

Blaine pursed his lips as though the word itself had conjured up a particularly weak vintage. "An aficionado?" he asked.

"A goddamned connoisseur. So my task is doubly difficult. If I propose . . . when I propose, it needs to be perfect and surprising and romantic, but not pretentious, never pretentious, and above all original."

"That does sound challenging," said Blaine. He paused for a moment as though to give the subject a moment of serious thought. Then, offering his brother an encouraging smile, he said, "Maybe you should ask Trot's advice. He's liable to have some tips."

Billy regarded his brother with overt annoyance.

Blaine rolled a ball to his foot with his racket, and scooped it into his hand. Once he'd palmed it, he began bouncing it intensely as though to replicate for Billy the urgent passing of time. Still bouncing, Blaine turned from Billy and sauntered to the baseline. When he arrived, he looked up to find Billy's back turned, but disregarded this as an inconvenience and hit the ball across the court.

Billy, despite his distracted state, heard and heeded the ball's approach and managed to return with a respectable backhand lob.

It's so like Billy, Blaine decided, to return the ball by accident. Since Billy was a little boy, he'd fallen into his good luck.

Billy relaxed his stance while Blaine set up to return his shot. "Maybe I'll do it on the bus when she's least expecting it."

Shielding his eyes from the sun with his left hand, Blaine prepared to return. He backpedaled to set up for Billy's lob, smacking it back before the bounce with an overhead volley. The force and direction of his shot, Blaine predicted, would preclude Billy's return. But again, though seemingly oblivious to the ball, Billy meandered across the court and managed somehow to return Blaine's volley with a crisp down-the-line forehand.

"No. I suppose I should try for romance," Billy continued. "Central Park at twilight at the Boat Pond . . . or maybe the Museum of Natural History under that great big whale."

Blaine released his mounting annoyance on the tennis ball, returning now with a crosscourt backhand that promised to elude his brother. But again, without the slightest indication of travail, Billy glided across the court and managed, in spite of most laws of physics, to nick the ball back across the court with a deft backhand slice.

Billy hustled to the net to set up for a volley. "To kneel or not to kneel?" he said. "Outdoors or indoors? Do you think Mom will give me Grandmother's ring, or would Bridget prefer something new? Ugh," he moaned. "There are too many choices. It's a wonder people ever get engaged."

Forcing a smile, Blaine took a swing and prepared to throttle the ball, hitting what would have been, under normal circumstances, a picture-perfect passing shot had Billy not managed, at the last second, to jab it back over the net.

"Maybe more pomp and circumstance. Something incorporating fireworks," Billy said.

"Maybe you should wait for Haley's comet," Blaine sneered. He raced to the ball with noticeable effort before dinking it back with a lob.

Billy allowed the ball to bounce while he considered Blaine's last suggestion. He had all but forfeited the point but he changed his mind at the last possible second and funneled his frustration into an overhead smash whose force and power finally ended the rally and officially pissed Blaine off.

Billy bowed his head with excessive largesse as Blaine approached the net.

"Do you want my honest opinion?" Blaine asked.

Billy nodded eagerly.

"All of this crap is beneath you," he said. "Fireworks and roses can't win a girl's heart. Your time and money are better spent. This kind of courtship is out of date. For all intents and purposes, romance is dead."

Billy stared at Blaine indignantly. "I respectfully disagree."

"If I were you, I would wait," said Blaine. "This is not something to rush."

"On the contrary," Billy said. "There's no time to waste. Trot could propose any minute."

Blaine stared blankly at his brother, noting, in spite of himself, the decline in his brother's looks. He tried to appear appropriately concerned while he racked his brain for a credible delay. "Why don't you do it next year at Passover? Or at a baseball game."

"Bridget would hate that," Billy scoffed. "Sporting events are cliché."

Blaine regarded his brother with new irritation. Billy's absurdly furrowed eyebrows, his look of utter helplessness, his melodramatic view of life; he was practically a woman. There was nothing he could say, Blaine now realized, to cure Billy of his ailment. Giving up on sarcasm for the moment, Blaine resorted to a new device and attempted to speak to Billy in his own language. "Remember the 'ninety-two play-offs?" Blaine asked.

"It's time to move on," Billy said. "I know you've tried to block it out, but my team won last year."

"You're absolutely right," Blaine conceded, smiling magnanimously. "You should enjoy that victory. It'll never happen again."

"It must be sad for you," mused Billy. "The end of an era . . ."

"An era," Blaine barked. "How long is that? Oh, I know. Eighty-six years."

Baseball was, to be sure, a particularly hot topic between the twins. Billy had lost many bets on behalf of the Sox, betting on his team for thirty of their eighty-six cursed years. And Blaine had recently suffered the humiliation of watching that very curse broken on his team's home turf. Throughout, Blaine had tortured Billy with incantations of Red Sox defeats, reminding him of their bitter disappointments and near misses in scrupulous detail. Billy took comfort in championing the underdog and, when they finally won the series, relished their reversal of fortune with decidedly unsportsmanlike glee. Of course, baseball was only the subtext of the twins' rivalry. The real issue at stake was which of the two twins, born four minutes apart, was the better man?

"All right, all right," Blaine conceded. "Let's put this aside for a moment."

Billy folded his arms over his chest, attempting to change the subject.

Blaine offered Billy a saccharine smile then, without further fan-fare, launched into his favorite speech. "Let's, for a minute, remem-ber Tug Johnson's history-making at bat. The Yanks are down three runs in the bottom of the ninth. The bases are loaded, they've got two outs, and Tug is at the plate. The Red Sox bring in Cox to close and the stadium goes wild. Cox takes his time at the mound, really stares Johnson down."

Despite Blaine's attempt at a dramatic reenactment, Billy was al-ready bored. He uncrossed his arms then replaced them on his hips at a defiant angle.

"Cox knows what everyone knows about Johnson: this batter will not be rushed. He never swings at the first pitch. He gets a look at the pitcher's stuff, learns all his secrets. So, there we are in the bottom of the ninth, with everything on the line, and what does Johnson do with his first ball? He takes a goddamned strike. Next, he dodges Cox's slider. Now, we've got ball one. Cox throws a splitter. Tug taps it back. Strike two. The crowd explodes. A curveball followed by a slider. There's ball two and three. Now Tug's working a full count. Of course, you know the rule . . ."

Fuming, Billy mustered a nod. Of course, he knew the rule: A Major League batter cannot foul out. In order to get his third strike, he must hit the ball into the field.

"Everyone thinks it's over for the Yanks, but Johnson keeps his cool. He swings and hits eight, nine, ten balls, every one of them a foul. Now Cox is pulling out all the stops: his slider, his knuckleball, his curve. Johnson and Cox are a pair of cowboys and this is their sunset duel. Finally, Cox lets a weak one fly and Tug seizes his chance. He swings and cracks it over the fence, sending players home from every base, winning the game and the play-offs for the best team in the world!"

"So," said Billy. "That was dumb luck. A once-in-a-lifetime event."

"Oh, I beg to differ," said Blaine. "Why do you think he's called Two-Strike Tug?"

"If you need to live in the past," Billy quipped.

"I wouldn't get cocky just yet."

"Your point?" Billy interrupted.

"My point." Blaine exhaled. "My point is even the best players need to use their head. What was Tug doing at the plate?"

"Praying to God," Billy quipped.

"Wrong," said Blaine. He paused dramatically. "He was waiting for the perfect pitch."

Billy stood for a moment, considering Blaine's thesis. He shifted from one foot to the other, then shook his head again. "But I love Bridget," he declared. "We're not playing against each other."

"Until the day we die," said Blaine, "men and women are on opposing teams."

"It's just that kind of thinking that caused your marriage to end in divorce."

"At least I got married," said Blaine. "You may never get to the altar." With this, he turned and marched to the baseline, kicking up a haze of green dust. "Look, I don't care what you do," he yelled. "Just don't take it out on me if you end up striking out."

Billy gazed across the net with new desperation. Without fail, talking to Blaine always made him feel worse. "Fine, then what's your advice?"

Before responding, Blaine tossed and served down the centerline. "Don't be so predictable. Make her work for it."

Billy made a half-hearted attempt to return the serve. He frowned as the ball hit the back fence. "Your love life is a mess," he said. "Why should I trust you?"

"Because somewhere, deep down, you suspect I'm right. And right now, you're batting zero."

"Sometimes I wonder if we're really related."

Blaine smiled mischievously. "Or you could just ask Bell. She's so desperate to get married, she'd say yes to anyone."

"Blaine, you are despicable," said Billy.

"No, just honest," said Blaine.

"When we were younger, you were just a mischievous kid. Now, you're a bad person."

"Strong words from a man who's trying to poach another man's girlfriend."

"They're having problems," said Billy. "Besides, I knew her first." Blaine arched his eyebrows.

"Maybe you're right," Billy said, trying not to cringe. "If Bridget's waiting for the perfect pitch, I'll just keep 'em coming."

"Trust me," said Blaine. He assumed his most pious altar boy smile. "If she loves you, it won't matter how or where you ask as long as it's from the heart."

"Yeah," Billy sighed. "You're probably right." He turned and started toward the bench, but he stopped suddenly, turned back to Blaine, and pounded the net with his fist. "That's it," he cried.

"What's it?" asked Blaine.

"You're absolutely right. If Bridget really loves me, it doesn't matter how I ask."

With new frustration, Blaine waited for Billy to elaborate.

"I'll do what I did ten years ago. No script. No nonsense."

"Billy, that's an awful idea," Blaine said a bit too quickly. "Ten years ago, you offered a baseball cap instead of a diamond ring."

"It's still the most valuable thing I have." Billy smiled and straightened his back.

"You can't afford a second strike," said Blaine. "I really don't recommend it."

"It's the perfect proposal," Billy went on. "Spontaneous and symbolic." At this, Billy lunged across the court, erupting into the most punctilious of victory dances.

As he watched, Blaine did his best impersonation of concern. "I don't know," he said. "I'd definitely sleep on it."

"No," said Billy. "It's been ten years. I've waited long enough. In fact," he pounded the net again, "I'm going to do it tonight."

Blaine smiled weakly at his brother, considering his next move.

"Blaine, I'm sorry I was short before. You've been a huge help."

Blaine managed a muscular smile. "It was my pleasure," he said.

Elated, Billy tossed his racket into the air, caught it gracefully behind his back, then transformed it into a dancing partner, twirling about and smiling as though it had just said something particularly witty.

Blaine stood silently at the net, watching Billy's indulgent display, his horror an equal and opposite expression of Billy's excitement. Of course, he had no one to blame but himself for Billy's latest inspiration. He thought he had some time to spare, but now it was necessary to take radical steps or else watch Billy share the spoils with Bridget when she won her father's contest. And though he felt it unlikely that Bridget would accept Billy's proposal tonight, he spent the rest of the afternoon contemplating a preemptive attack. Nothing would irk him more than to see his brother fall into this fate, winning the loveliest Barnacle girl as well as the Barnacle fortune. In fact, he was so irritated by the thought that he lost the game and set, bringing down his winning average slightly closer to 50 percent.

12

Musical Talent

*L*atrell stood at Columbus Circle just before noon on Saturday, glancing north then south with overwhelming ambivalence. As he stood, he debated the next phase of his search. Uptown and down-town seemed so unlike as to be two distinct cities, two squabbling siblings gradually drifting apart. For no better reason than a red traf-fic light, he decided to turn right, then headed north past the statue of Columbus, the patron saint of all explorers. Anxious to keep a safe distance from Benita's telescope, he hugged the perimeter of the park. As he walked, he hazarded the hope that the afternoon would mark a change in his luck. The first few days of his expedition had been less fruitful than he'd hoped.

Latrell had wasted the morning on yet another bogus lead, sitting through services at Central Synagogue. He had kept on his yarmulke for the duration of the three-hour service, resisting the urge to itch and rip the silk hat from his head. After suffering through this endless borage of chanting, Latrell had hoped God would reward his patience. Instead, the organist stared at him with a blank and vaguely angry look, shooing him off when he approached, apparently offended by the interruption to his prayers. On this one issue, Latrell agreed with Barry; Bella had wasted her money on his religious education. Three years of spotty attendance at Temple Emannuel's Wednesday afternoon Hebrew school had only alienated him from the Jewish faith.

Undeniably, Latrell had begun his search with two disadvantages; very little information and a very bad map. The scant knowledge he had of his father was unreliable at best, perhaps because it had come from Bella, a wholly unreliable source. According to Bella, Latrell's father was a pianist of such staggering charisma and talent that he could cause an entire audience to weep by playing a single note. As the story went, Latrell's birth mother had died in a freak accident; Bella wasn't sure exactly what sort but suspected it had been something glamorous like a plane crash or a boating mishap. At this point, Latrell's father had faced a Gordian choice, forced to choose between his divine gift and his only son. Unfortunately for Latrell, art trumped obligation. Promising to return at his earliest chance, the pianist bid Latrell good-bye to heed the call of Orpheus.

While it was hard to understand how a man could abandon his only child, it was forgivable, Bella argued, due to this musician's unique talent. And, she concluded, all for the best, since it had ultimately allowed her to meet Latrell. Unfortunately, this was the extent of Bella's information on Latrell's father. The man had left no contact numbers at the shelter and she'd never known his name. Still, whenever Latrell pressed Bella for details, she assured him that hope was not lost. She was certain his father was somewhere in New York, making people cry in some great concert hall or church, or, possibly, though this was very unlikely, in some very popular bar.

Lacking memories of his father, Latrell used music in memory's place. He saw his father in the face of every musician he met. He had made a project of it since he was eleven years old, spending hours camped out beyond the gates of outdoor concerts in the park, making countless attempts to sneak into crowded, smoky venues, spending hundreds of dollars in tickets in New York's great concert halls. He had waited outside the stage door at Carnegie Hall after every weekend summer concert; had followed and questioned a concert pianist after his premier at the Metropolitan Opera House; had wandered into every church and synagogue on the Upper East and West Sides. He had even managed to sneak past the bouncers of Birdland only to find his allowance fell short of the cover charge. But, despite this herculean effort, Latrell had consistently struck out. Luckily, he was a uniquely optimistic boy, ostensibly unflappable from an early age.

Certainly, growing up without parents promoted its fair share of loneliness. And yet, the forty other boys in residence at the Bronx Boys Home did their part to fill the void. They provided a warm, if noisy substitute; doubling as a makeshift family, replacing customs like nightly tuck-ins with raucous joviality. As a child, Latrell excelled in school, socialized well, and busied himself with an only slightly above average number of daydreams. But as puberty approached, his restlessness increased, manifesting in the form of a constant vague dissatisfaction, an otherworldly distracted quality that caused Latrell to appear, even when listening, very much tuned out. By ten, this benign airiness evolved into something more worrisome, transmuting into what caretakers feared were the first flares of a temper. So it was with great relief that the director of the Home entertained Bella's request and allowed her to leave her volunteer shift with Latrell in tow.

While hardship had a hand in forming Latrell, it had an unlikely effect, causing him to open himself to the world instead of turning against it. A natural musician from an early age, Latrell heard music where others heard noise, fashioning rhythm out of subway tracks, symphonies out of city traffic. Throughout his time at the Home, Latrell confounded his caretakers with his odd perception; hearing beats where they were inaudible to others, in the hum of a bulb, the rattle of an appliance, or in everyday silence. Gradually, his tastes refined through avid study of the radio. He favored early jazz to hiphop, Romantic composers to Baroque, and complex Indian beats to the eight counts of rock 'n' roll. Soon interest turned into expertise. Piano lessons at the Barnacle house, though enforced with distasteful rigidity, allowed Latrell's nascent skill to flourish from a knack to a talent.

Latrell's new digs provided the perfect finishing school. The one to four male to female ratio at the Barnacles' endowed him with the sense that the world was a burgeoning matriarchy and he its only prince. Having sisters often instills this unique respect for women. But, in Latrell's case, it gave him a unique understanding of men. Being in the minority to such a confident contingent imparted the unshakable sense that men and women were equal contenders, and that women, perhaps, had the advantage in an impromptu wrestling match. The gifts of this new setting were incalculable, giving Latrell an ease with both genders, while instilling the best aspects of femininity. As a result, he was neither stranger to his emotions nor to the scores of most Broadway plays. He was the kind of boy women praise for being sensitive and macho men call "gay."

Though his thoughts were consumed, much of the time, by the usual teenage things, Latrell was preoccupied by loftier concerns. Like all teenage boys, he spent a substantial amount of time considering and critiquing the great comic books, analyzing the big summer movie releases, and defending the hegemony of hip-hop. But he was not content simply to bang balls with bats, nor obsessed with the typical pornographic thoughts. To be sure, he spent a substantial amount of time considering baseballs and bra size, but these thoughts were peppered with other more aesthetic interests. He was blessed with a certain awareness, a sensitivity to sound, color, and feelings that gave him a sweetness usually associated with the female gender.

But the greatest single force on Latrell was a relatively recent acquaintance. His adopted sister Beryl bewitched him from his first day in the house. Closest in age and interests, Latrell and Beryl were fast friends, bonding over their shared love of music and general skepticism of people. Since their schools were close to each other, they traveled together, pooling financial resources for luxuries like taxis and three-pound bags of gummy bears. They spent after-school hours together as well, withstanding Barry's enforced piano regime and a sentry so vigilant that it threatened to rob music of its appeal. But once these duties were complete, the two would linger in the music room, exhausting the Barnacles' extensive archive of pieces for two hands or simply experimenting with free-form improvisation. Soon enough, teenage concerns polluted piano practice, forcing Beryl and Latrell to wince at pastimes they had enjoyed only months previously. Luckily, they quickly found more sophisticated modes of recreation and set out to fill their leisure time with a methodical exploration of the city.

Two things coincided with this trend to fuel their wanderings. The first was the innate and irresistible teenage craving for loud music, a force that pulls adolescents to dark, cacophonous venues much like lemmings to the sea. The second was Latrell's sudden interest in finding his biological father, an obsession that grew in tandem with his interest in loud music and therefore seemed similarly connected to the hormones of puberty. So, it was with great vigor but age-appropriate nonchalance that Latrell and Beryl pursued these two goals simultaneously. Armed with little information on his father, Latrell enlisted Beryl to join him on a combined quest for truth and music and—pooling all disposable cash for concert tickets, using fake IDs borrowed from older siblings, and an impressive assortment of disguises fashioned from borrowed clothing—they managed to wriggle their ways into music venues where they had no business being. For a while, the two searches proceeded at the same pace. But when Latrell turned thirteen, the hunt for his father graduated from a half- to a whole-hearted search.

Throughout, it never occurred to either one that their relationship was particularly intense and when it did, it was only in the innermost quadrants of their hearts. At times, Latrell was completely over-whelmed by Beryl, finding her inexpressibly smart and beautiful, her inscrutable silences confounding, her long dark hair impossibly shiny, even at night. Sometimes, when they played piano together, their knees would accidentally touch and a small electric force would surge from his toes to his ears. Or, while sitting next to each other at the dinner table, her hand would casually brush his knee and he would have to fight the urge to grab and hold her hand. Just the other day, when the two were strolling in Central Park, her blue eyes looked so inexplicably sad he wanted to stop in the middle of the Great Lawn and kiss her closed eyelids. Of course, Latrell sensed there was a stigma attached to such strong feelings. But, having never had sisters before, he prayed these desires were among the correct and natural expressions of fraternal love.

But as puberty persisted, benign dreams gave way to bawdier ones and Latrell began to suspect himself of more serious perver-sions. Was it normal, for example, to find oneself consumed by such yearnings to touch a girl's shoulders? Was it acceptable that even the mildest compliment from her made him blush from ear to ear? Was it odd, that when she was in the next room, he could still see the outlines of her face, that he spent minutes, sometimes hours men-tally tracing the shape of her lips? Was it strange that when she sat in front of him while watching TV, he passed the time by staring at the hairs on her neck? Was it possible, he wondered, that these fascina-tions were, in fact, the first flowers of lust; that he was not only strange but sick and, worse still, condemned to love someone who would be forever off-limits?

And so it was with some effort that Latrell relegated Beryl from friend to nuisance, a demotion that was aided by the banality of do-mestic life. To this end, he focused on such things as Beryl's unfortu-nate yellow flannel nightgown or her retainer, an apparatus whose ugliness was surpassed only by its compromise to dignity. (It at-tached to her braces with rubber bands, made a small clicking sound whenever she spoke, and was prescribed for use during sleep for another six months.) Focusing on such images helped, but it only made a dent. So, despite the pain it caused, Latrell made a conscious effort to treat Beryl with chauvinistic disdain to remind her of their slight age difference, to pull rank regarding their shared skills, and, whenever possible, to exclude her from activities. All of this helped transform lust to anger much like hydrogen to water at very high temperatures. Best of all, it allowed Latrell to mask his awkward and unholy feelings and to soften the blow when he realized he had to leave the house.

Now, as he headed up Central Park West, Latrell forced Beryl from his mind. He did his best to remain positive despite his recent setbacks. At the moment, he reminded himself, there were several things working in his favor: a hastily packed bag of provisions consisting of items from the seder table and a few critical articles of clothing, some much-needed space from his adopted sisters, and all the time in the world. On a whim, he headed out of the park toward Lincoln Center, crossing Broadway despite a red light and sprinting up the steps toward the grand central plaza. He had always loved the sensation of walking across the white granite, slowing down despite Bella's urging that he hurry on those occasions when she brought him to the opera. The matte white stone colluded with the sparkle of the central fountain, amplifying its gurgles and splashes like sand does the ocean's waves.

Careful to avoid making eye contact with anyone in the area, Latrell hurried across, glancing right at the symphony hall and left, at the ballet. Luckily, a previous foray endowed him special knowledge of the practices of Lincoln Center's security guards. Having once joined Beryl in a covert dip in the reflecting pool in front of the Vivian Beaumont Theater, he knew the length of the intervals at which they patrolled the area. He walked up to the pool, threw in a penny, pretending to make a wish, and then managed to slip into the symphony space through the freight entrance. Walking on the tips of his toes, he hurried across the empty foyer and pushed at the doors to the central concert hall. Once inside, he remained at the door and surveyed the awesome space. He stayed this way, undetected, for several moments.

One other person occupied the vast space. A pianist sat at the grand piano in the center of the darkened stage, playing simple fourths and fifths as though leading a monastic chant. A mass of dark hair, not unlike Latrell's, obscured the man's face, filling Latrell with the usual surge of expectation. Frequent visits had endowed him with a detailed knowledge of the hall. Its piano boasted ninety keys as opposed to the traditional eighty-eight, extra pieces of ivory that were not meant to be played but rather to buzz in sympathy with the pianist's notes. But to call these additional keys "extra" was to misunderstand their use. They were two wholly essential parts of the piano, integral facets of the hall's sublime acoustics.

Slowly, Latrell walked down the center aisle and approached the stage.

The pianist, blessed with sensitive hearing, looked up immediately.

Now slightly closer to the stage, Latrell noticed the pianist's light skin and felt the usual tightening in his heart.

"Can I help you?" the pianist asked.

"No, thank you," said Latrell. He already knew. He stood motionless for another moment, stilled by a mixture of disappointment and awe. He apologized for the interruption, turned back up the aisle, and headed out of the divine quiet into the noisy city.

13

Calculated Hair

*L*ong after their morning tennis game, Billy and Blaine were still plagued by a nagging awareness of the other. The boys were cursed with telepathy, both subjected to the other's point of view as though a running commentary of the one's thoughts had been broadcast into the other's head with the explicit purpose of driving him slowly insane. And yet, even despite their differences, love made twins of Billy and Blaine, ostensibly leveling the boys and bringing them to their knees.

So it was at the stroke of twelve on a perfectly lucid Saturday night, both boys, without discussing such a plan, climbed up their neighbors' fire escape with the very same intention. Arguably though, the two were moved by wholly different motives. Billy was fueled by love alone while Blaine was guided by something yet stronger, pure cash incentive. Still, an innocent bystander would never have known from looking since greed and love resemble one another even from a very close distance. In spite of this distinction, both twins forged the exact same route, both of them wholly unaware of the other's intentions. Just like this, they made the treacherous climb to the girls' window, Blaine arriving ten minutes ahead of Billy to attempt the odd and ingenious feat of parroting an event before it happened. And though this rendered both boys hopelessly ill-equipped for the task ahead, neither one had the good sense to put a ring in his pocket.

Luckily, the girls received their guests with a sense of humor, gleefully swearing off sleep for the night and accepting the boys' invitations. Ignoring Barry's certain rebuke and their mother's vigilant eye, they all but leapt from their bedroom window, delighted by the chance to forget their cares and self-consciousnesses. It was nothing short of exhilarating to sneak out at this age. Audacity brought on the feelings of youth, just as youth had once spurred daring. Of course, it was not lost on the girls that sneaking into their house in order to sneak right back out posed some logical questions. But it was understood that these were the types of sacrifices one must make for love. Luckily, the girls were blessed with the giddy ignorance of their youth and so resolved to make the odd pilgrimage. Despite their earlier differences, Bell and Bridget made twins of themselves, tumbling guiltlessly from their window, one ten minutes after the other, both transported to the past as though by some feat of magic.

Outside, the warmth of spring combined with the cold of recent months, causing the air to match body temperature like certain tropical water. As a result, when you moved your arms even slightly to the left or right, the air didn't feel like something separate but an extension of your fingertips. Old familiar sounds were somehow infused with new life. Even the simple act of breathing felt completely miraculous. As they took their first steps down the grates, they were greeted by the city sky and, forced to rethink their stance once again, decided it didn't matter one bit that the light of the city's skyscrapers obscured the light of the stars. But sensory pleasures were the least of the night's offerings. It was as though, by virtue of some strange glitch in time, Bell and Bridget had been released of the full weight of human experience.

Every stage of the descent brought on a new sensation. They may as well have been astronauts encountering their first planet. By the time they reached the tenth-floor landing, sidewalk sounds started up. Green lights signaled the swell of taxis while red made them muffled and soft. On the sixth floor, taxi cabs were joined by sharper city noise. Partygoers tripped down the avenue, their laughter wafting into the air like lost helium balloons. On the fifth, they could hear conversations playing out on the sidewalk below. Mrs. Fullerton, who lived on the seventh floor, was just returning from some benefit and asked Carlos, the night doorman, whether he had yet to receive a delivery of her dry cleaning. As they approached the first floor, the girls thought guiltily of their father. But with every downward step, he lost his grasp on them a little. Why was it so easy, Bell wondered, to repeat the events of one's youth? Why did freedom feel so much freer, thought Bridget, when you had to break some rules? And why, both girls wondered as they leapt into the darkness, why oh why was it so much fun to sneak out of a life you chose?

Blaine began the evening with a typically grand statement, informing Bell that for the duration of the night, they would only bother themselves with places or activities on her list of all-time favorites. First, he demanded that she name her favorite place in the city. Bell was hard-pressed to name any one place; she simply loved too many. But Blaine was not so easily dissuaded from his plan. In a flurry of excessively gallant gestures, he hailed a cab, handed the driver a large bill, and asked him to drive for as long as it took to see all of New York's great landmarks. As they headed down Broadway towards Time Square, Blaine asked Bell to name her favorite drink. At the next red light, he jumped out of the cab, disappeared into the nearest bar and emerged with two glasses of Champagne, a gesture Bell found so irresistibly charming she allowed herself a few sips.

The rest of the night involved all sorts of similar excesses. Blaine asked Bell to name her favorite song and then promptly sang it. He demanded she name her favorite poem then recited it. Next, it was to her favorite bridge, Brooklyn's own cathedral. Then back up Canal Street to be stalled in her favorite traffic and right off Canal onto Sixth Avenue to enjoy Bell's favorite food, two slices of Joe's pizza. They turned on West Fourth and then Christopher to get onto the West Side Highway, all so Bell could drive by the Hudson, her favorite river. Then they cut across Forty-second Street to catch a glimpse of Bell's favorite theater, turning south yet again to reach Thirty-fourth and Lexington for the best view of the Chrysler Building. And finally, when Bell made the mistake of answering in earnest, they rode all the way back up Madison to Central Park; Bell's favorite place in the world.

Oh sure, Bell knew that she and Blaine were not quite the ideal match but a critical shift in her heart made it possible for her to suspend judgment; she had long since given up on the notion of perfect romance. She was way too old and cynical to fall prey to such quaint delusions, had had her heart broken too many times, had slept in too many beds. No, she saw her night with Blaine for exactly what it was. Theirs was a marriage of convenience. She wanted a father for her child and he wanted a quick replacement. Oh God, when she put it like that, it seemed terribly sinister. Perhaps it was better to think of it like this: She was a woman with a full plate and he was a man with an empty stomach. No, that was no good, either, perhaps even worse than the first assessment. But who was she to submit love to unreasonable standards? She was an accomplice to love's degradation, had all but destroyed it herself, joining in its gleeful desecration like a soldier tearing down a statue of a deposed tyrant. So, though she knew the whole charade was something of a farce, she decided to act as she would in Rome and simply hammed it up.

A half hour later, the pair emerged from the cab exactly where they had started and, faced with the sight of their parents' building, contemplated a new direction for their evening. Despite a somewhat heated debate over the best bar in the neighborhood, they opted instead for a stroll and, heading south on Fifth Avenue, enjoyed the slightly colder air that emerged from the trees in the park. They paused at the steps to the Arsenal to examine a clump of tulips, their green buds, still yet to blossom, threatening to burst from excitement. Then, for no particular reason, they ignored their parents' lifetime mandate, and turned down the steps on Sixty-fourth and Fifth to enter the darkened park.

They sat for a while on the long, low bench that faces the Central Park Zoo, straining to hear the sounds of sleeping animals. To their right, the time-weathered Delacorte Clock meandered past one o'clock. And, remembering time for the first time in hours, they simply stared at the aged clock, marveling at the power it had had over them when they were children. Indeed, this clock had figured prominently into their childhoods, its proximity to their apartments rendering it as reliable a fixture as ice cream trucks or church bells. Every hour on the hour, the clock serenaded the neighborhood while a menagerie of stone animals circled the clock tower. And just when it seemed the night's momentum had begun to slow, Blaine issued a new challenge. Due to the surprisingly low height of the fence surrounding the zoo, he simply couldn't think of any good reason to refrain from climbing over.

Bell, despite Blaine's aggressive campaign, resisted his peer pressure. But Blaine was now far too intrigued with the thought to dismiss the notion altogether. After a quick promenade around the perimeter of the fence, he made the decision to risk arrest and hurtle himself over it. He glanced one last time toward Fifth Avenue in a cursory check for parents and cops, rolled his pants legs up to his knees, then managed, with only a small running start, to climb up and over the fence. Once inside, he taunted Bell with overblown "oohs" and "ahs," promising that mere inches separated her from hands-down the coolest thing he'd ever seen in his life. But, refusing to submit, Bell remained seated on the bench. She was finally persuaded if only due to her sudden awareness of the darkness and the fear that if she didn't, Blaine would simply leave her behind. Luckily, her earlier window descent had sufficiently limbered her muscles, providing her with the agility needed to make the leap without undue embarrassment.

Without a word, the two split up to canvass the zoo. They spent the next half hour wandering on their own in a state of awed silence. The polar bear paced its cage restlessly as though it had been awakened from a bad dream. But on sight of a visitor, it assumed a deceptively demure look that caused Bell to feel such remorse that she had to keep walking. The monkeys slept, intertwined in elaborate configurations, exposing their light pink stomachs to Blaine and boasting, it seemed, their eerie resemblance to human beings. The tropical birds presented a welcome burst of color, their bright red heads and neon feathers glowing in the dark. At night, the zoo was perfectly still, a far cry from its daytime frenzy, causing the lucky and still slightly drunk explorers to feel as though they had stumbled into an enchanted forest. The city even upped its meager offering of stars. This night was unlike any other, Bell thought. Everything in the world was at its loveliest.

Finally, just before one thirty, Bell and Blaine converged at the seal tank. Having fully forgotten the surrounding city, they climbed onto the circular steps, and sat, heads tilted toward the sky, shoulder to shoulder.

"Pretend it's a million years from now," Blaine said. "Evolution has been hard at work. Close your eyes and picture it. How do the animals look?"

Bell looked around for inspiration then turned back to Blaine and smiled.

"Go on," said Blaine. "I know you can do it. Use your intuition."

Bell opened her mouth to speak but quickly stopped herself, concerned happiness might compel her to say something overly earnest. She prayed that her eyes hadn't given away the wild feeling in her stomach. It had been so long since she and Blaine had been alone together. She had completely forgotten how he smelled, like warm milk and almonds. Over the years, she had forgotten the details of his complexion, had forgotten he looked like a matinee idol but with lovelier imperfections. She had forgotten the way his light brown hair fell jauntily over his eyes, the way his eyebrows twitched just before he laughed and, when he got very worked up, how his lower lip trembled. She had forgotten the color of his eyes, their warmth and intensity. In fact, she had forgotten most everything about Blaine including how completely overwhelmed she felt in his presence. And yet it was natural, she decided, to have suffered this temporary amnesia. Had she remembered any one of these things, she could never have stood being near him.

Still staring into his eyes, she remembered he'd asked her a question. She reminded herself she had nothing to lose, did her best to filter breathy nervousness out of her voice and answered in earnest. "Polar bears are blue," she began. "Frogs are bigger than whales. Rhinoceros horns are ten feet long and knotted like branches. Monkeys finally got it together and figured out how to talk. Mice are the size of horses and they carry their babies in pouches."

"Fish finally got fed up," Blaine jumped in, "with being waterlogged. Now, they walk for miles on end and split their time between the East and West Coasts."

"Luckily, panda bears haven't changed much. They're every bit as cute. Bats are the size of elephants. And sharks are now mammals."

"The great thing about evolution," Blaine concluded, "is it made everything better. What other force can claim responsibility for such widespread improvement?"

"Except for the unlucky few that are endangered or already extinct."

"And," Blaine looked at Bell pointedly, "those rare perfect specimens that evolution didn't dare mess with."

"What happened to them?" Bell asked. "Did those guys miss the boat?"

"Nope," said Blaine. He gazed at Bell. "They haven't strayed too far from home. They've come full circle."

"Oh," Bell said. Her stomach dropped as she gleaned Blaine's full import.

Blaine brushed a strand of hair off Bell's face. "Yes, it's true," he concluded. "Some creatures were already perfect."

Instinctively, Bell swatted her neck to slow her racing pulse.

"Bell, I have to show you something," Blaine said.

"Oh really. What's that?" Bell whispered.

Blaine fidgeted with his shirtsleeve for a moment, smiled gingerly at Bell, then, without further fanfare, raised his hands to his head and removed his Yankees cap.

"As you know, I first offered you this cap when I was sixteen years old."

"And then, yesterday," Bell interrupted, "you asked me to give it back."

But Blaine was far too determined to be delayed by such a trivial fact and managed, with one winning smile, to render Bell speechless. "Bell," he said, "I've known this since the first day we met . . ."

Bell straightened suddenly and turned to face Blaine head-on. There was something vaguely familiar about his tone, the theatrical lilt in his voice, his absurdly formal verbiage; the sincerity was un-characteristic. All of it carried the unmistakable echo of a familiar ritual. But Bell forced herself to dismiss the thought. The chances were one in a million. Blaine would never. Would he?

"Time stopped for me ten years ago when you rejected my pro-posal," Blaine began.

"But I didn't reject it," Bell interrupted. "Don't you remember what happened?"

Blaine paused and looked to the ground, confounded by this tech-nicality. Then, taking a large gulp of air, he launched into his speech again. "Bell," he said, but suddenly his script raced out of his head. Vowels abandoned consonants. Words merged into a senseless blur. He racked his brain for poetry but found cliché instead. "Since the first day we met," he began. Oh God. What was he thinking? "You see, I've always known," he tried. No, that wouldn't do, either.

"Remember when Tug was signed by the Yanks." Oh God. This was harder than he'd thought. "Oh to hell with it," he said. His eyes widened with genuine terror. "Will you marry me?" he asked.

Certain phrases in the English language possess an almost godlike power, arming the speaker with the ability, at best, to change a person's life and, at worst, to make them choke. Still, despite her shock, Bell found the strength to respond with decorum. Without blinking, she smiled at Blaine and said, "No, not tonight."

Blaine, however, failed to find comfort in Bell's graciousness and poise. He suffered, in the wake of her rejection, a wholly foreign vulnerable feeling. But like most men, he only grew more intrigued after being spurned and spent the next several minutes using every charm and excuse to get Bell to change her mind. Finally, he agreed to walk her back to their building, admitting, he claimed, only temporary defeat, demanding that she forgive his blunder and accept his belated invitation to the first baseball game of the season.

Despite a somewhat heated debate about the best bar in the neighborhood, Billy and Bridget spent a full hour circling their building block, engaged in courtship's odd ritual of talking about nothing. Finally, just after one o'clock, they ventured up Fifth Avenue, lingering for a moment on Seventy-second Street near the entrance to the Boat Pond. Smiling, they paused to recollect the hours they'd wasted there, piloting rented electric boats as children and later, sitting on the benches for hours, pondering Holden's question: where on earth did the ducks go during the winter months? Then, as though exhausted by nostalgia, they started up their stroll again, veering slightly right. For no particular reason, they ignored their parents' lifetime mandate and, precisely ten minutes after Bell and Blaine, headed into the park. Both Billy and Bridget were blissfully unaware of the force that spurred them on. Bridget was merely convinced by Billy while Billy was pulled by nothing less than nature's own magnet. And yet, for all he knew, he was simply following a whim. He needed Bridget's help, he claimed, unraveling a mystery that had bothered him since child-hood.

"You know that clock in Central Park," he said, "the one with the animals?"

"Of course," said Bridget. "The Delacorte Clock. We went there practically every day when we were growing up."

"That's the one," Billy said.

"What about it?" asked Bridget.

"I've been wondering ever since," said Billy, "do you think the an-imals still dance around after it gets dark?"

Bridget regarded Billy with mixed shock and confusion. "Of course they do, silly," she said. "That's a stupid question."

But Billy was not so easily swayed by Bridget's dismissal. He re-quired, he claimed, more compelling evidence of the clock's nightly mechanisms. And though Bridget did her best to resist his various ap-peals, she was finally persuaded to follow him yet farther into the park and to join him in his clock vigil, eyes peeled, standing watch. As Bridget predicted, at the strike of two, the animals sprung to ac-tion, circling the graying clock tower with military precision. Still, despite this definitive proof that the laws of physics remained intact, they soon found a new object for their curiosity. The clock's music, Billy and Bridget agreed, sounded slightly eerie in the dark and therefore, according to Billy, the only sensible recourse was to hop the surprisingly low fence that surrounded the Central Park Zoo so as to compare the live to the stone animals and see if they followed suit.

As it turned out, the live animals looked quite a lot like the stone sculptures except they were, if possible, decidedly more stoic. The mountain lion, a new transplant, prodded and pushed a sleeping cub as though the night permitted him to drop his act of intimidation. A troop of marmots, blessed with a startling re-creation of their natural habitat, huddled secretively under a tree, seeming to finalize the details of their escape route. The seals slept on their island rock, occasionally rousing to stretch their necks like ladies at a beach club. Nearby, the moon made silver ripples on the water's surface.

Everything around them was perfectly still except for the occasional rustle of trees and hushed city traffic. Entranced, the two old friends tripped up the steps that lined the seal tank and sat in silence for several minutes, their knees barely touching. There was simply no denying it, no matter how hard Bridget tried. When she was with Billy, she felt inexplicably happy. Unfortunately, she lacked the words to express the sentiment. And, every so often, this feeling alone caused her to erupt into laughter.

"What?" said Billy.

"Oh, nothing," said Bridget. "I was just thinking about something."

"What about?" he asked.

She paused to consider. "Nothing in particular."

The two fell into silence again but soon Bridget broke it with another laugh, this time breaking into a more extended fit of combined hiccups and chortles. Again, when pressed, she claimed nothing in particular had caused her sudden outburst, at which point Billy became increasingly intent on finding the cause. Still, regardless of his determination, Bridget failed to cite one trigger and only grew more prone to giggling the more Billy pressed her. In response, Billy waged a new campaign, whereby he attempted to cure Bridget's laughter with a series of absurdly serious faces, a tactic that only succeeded in producing the opposite effect of sobriety and finally caused Bridget to erupt into complete hysterics. Enraged by this slow escalation and his utter powerlessness to stop it, Billy finally burst himself, demanding that Bridget explain the joke or else stop laughing at once.

"I'm sorry," she said. "I really am." She forcibly flattened her mouth with her hands as though muscles and mood could be forced to mirror one another.

"Unless you have further comments," Billy said, "there's something I need to tell you."

On sight of his overly serious face, Bridget struggled to stifle a laugh. "Wait," she said. "I'll go first. You have something in your teeth. Looks like spinach."

Humbled, Billy opened his mouth and removed the offending object. He sat in embarrassed silence for a moment and fixed his eyes to the ground. But he forced himself to speak quickly, scared that any further delay could finally cost him his chance. "Bridget, I have to show you something."

"Come on. No more suspense," she said.

Billy nodded and inhaled deeply, wrung his hands out, cracked a knuckle then, without further fanfare, raised his hands to his head and removed his Red Sox cap. "As you know, I gave you this cap once before but you wouldn't accept it."

Bridget straightened suddenly then turned to face Billy head-on. There was something vaguely familiar about his tone, the theatrical lilt in his voice, his absurdly formal verbiage; the sincerity was uncharacteristic. All of it carried the unmistakable echo of a familiar ritual. But she quickly forced herself to dismiss the thought. The chances were one in a million. Billy would never. Would he?

"Time stopped for me ten years ago when you rejected my proposal . . ."

Bridget narrowed her eyes at Billy. Had she heard him correctly? His gaze betrayed too much intent, like a clown at a children's party. He stressed certain syllables oddly as though he had rehearsed this speech in front of a mirror. Of course, it was cruel to treat love as a game, romance as an audition. Still, Bridget couldn't help wishing Billy would relax a little.

"That night ten years ago . . ." Billy went on. He paused, searching for words.

Bridget took the opportunity to make a mental list of his defects. So often, Billy's earnestness denied the world its subtleties and, even worse, his ego conspired with his earnestness. He was like a suitor from another time, his methods embarrassingly outdated. He was worse than a hopeless romantic; he was positively constipated. He was also way too easy on himself, awfully fond of his own voice. He had an incurable weakness for melodrama to the point of being maudlin. How could she ever love someone so oblivious to his shortcomings? Of course, there were a few key facts that Bridget had to concede. Billy was sweet, admirably tenacious, often funny, charming even, and, at the moment, his big green eyes looked completely irresistible. Unfortunately, the power of this sentiment prohibited its translation and, despite her efforts, Bridget burst into giddy laughter once again.

Billy stared at the ground for a moment, completely confounded then, taking a last gulp of air, began his speech again. "Bridget," he said, but suddenly his script raced out of his head. Vowels abandoned consonants. Words merged into a senseless blur. He racked his brain for poetry but found cliché instead. "Since the first day we met," he began. Oh God. What was he thinking? "You see, I've always known," he tried. No, that wouldn't do either. "Remember when Tug was signed by the Yanks." Oh God. This was harder than he'd thought. "Oh to hell with it," he said. His eyes widened with genuine terror. "Will you marry me?" he asked.

Spending ten years avoiding these words had infused them with a certain sacred power. As a result, Bridget had always assumed that she would surely collapse should Billy ever utter them. But now she surprised even herself with her measured response. After waiting a moment to catch her breath, she said, "Oh Billy, not again."

Billy stared at Bridget for a moment, at a loss for words. Of course, on some level, he'd expected her to say no, but now that it had been uttered, he refused to accept it. "Why not?" he demanded.

"Well, for one," Bridget began, "there's no ring in sight. It needn't be big nor impressive. The point of the ring is to prove to the girl that you planned ahead. Second of all, that was one of the worst proposals I've ever heard. Terrible delivery. Weak preface. Where was my charming anecdote? As far as originality, I couldn't even begin to judge. I lost you after the first sentence. Everything else, you mumbled."

Billy stared at Bridget now with new irritation. Who did she think she was anyway? She was acting like Billy was an Olympic skater and she was the Russian judge.

"Regarding the ring," Billy stammered. "I will get one soon. I just thought . . ."

"What did you think?" asked Bridget.

"I just thought I had better rush since I have . . ."

"Yes?" Bridget crossed her arms.

"Since I have . . ."

Bridget raised her eyebrows.

Billy took a deep breath. "Since I have competition."

"Competition," Bridget cried. She stood suddenly from the step. She stared at Billy indignantly as both hands flew to her hips. "Of all the unromantic things . . ." she cried. "Oh, Billy." She shook her head. Suddenly, her voice dropped an octave. "You'd think with all the practice you've had," she said, but she trailed off, still shaking her head as though she had been rendered speechless by sheer disappointment. "Well," she mustered finally, "Billy, you botched it again."

"No," Billy wailed. He fell to his knees. "I'll do it better next time."

Bridget's sigh carried both anger and fatigue. "I won't hold my breath."

Seizing the chance for a dramatic exit, Bridget stormed out of the park, leaving Billy alone with the animals in the zoo to contemplate his second strike. Still, from one perspective, the night had been a success. Billy had added one truly horrific proposal to Bridget's all-time-worst list.

And yet, this very silly night had serious consequences. Bell rose suddenly in Blaine's estimation while Billy sunk in Bridget's. Worst of all, the boys did themselves a terrible disservice, subjecting themselves to unforgivably bad hair and condemning any passersby to utter confusion. As promised, without their caps on, the twins were indistinguishable. Even those who had known them since birth were liable to mistake one for the other.

14

Mean Streak

*S*unday mornings at the Barnacles were always a competitive affair long before the contest wrought its own peculiar havoc. The whole family assembled at the dining room table and, while they raced to inhale the meal, engaged in a daily cutthroat attempt to annoy each other into skipping breakfast. Still, when she woke, Bell was cheered by a positive passing thought: Beth and Belinda were back at school, which reduced the female population from six to four and hopefully, in turn, the volume. But Bell's hopes were dashed the moment she took her seat at the table. Even with Beth and Belinda away, the apartment still veered dangerously close to maximum levels of chaos. The noise produced by Beth and Belinda had been immediately replaced, as though by an interior thermostat whose purpose was to maintain constant unrest as opposed to room temperature. In fact, the current residents, the two eldest and youngest sisters, were a dangerously combustible group, the combined volume of Bridget and Benita alone enough to power a small city. As a result of this slight escalation and the looming presence of the contest, breakfast conversation teetered on the edge of total madness.

"Would you please pass the milk?" Bell demanded.

"Would you like me to pass it clockwise or counterclockwise?" asked Benita.

"Do you think she cares which way you pass it?" asked Bridget.

"How would I know?" asked Benita.

This standoff of meaningless questioning was not any ordinary fight. It was rather a hallowed family game, a favorite mealtime distraction that had evolved long ago in response to Barry's mandate that his daughters question everything. As though to prove the absurdity of their father's request, the girls took him at his word, answering questions with more questions, sometimes spending entire meals without uttering a declarative sentence. Like every other sport at which the girls competed, this was a ferocious game. But today there was a new intensity to the exchange, since all discussion at the table quickly led back to the contest.

"I just thought you should know," Benita announced, "I'm about to win."

"It's not a good idea to brag," said Beryl. "The future abhors planners."

"Benita, I hate to break it to you," said Bell, "but you have as much chance of winning as the Sox have of beating the Yanks again."

Of all the taunting, it was this comment that put Benita over the edge, causing her in mid-spoonful of cereal, to spit her milk across the table. Due to group consensus, Benita was given two options: She could either leave the table immediately or refrain from speaking altogether.

"Don't mind Benita," Beryl declared. "She's obviously just jealous. Everyone knows Bridget's one night away from winning the contest."

"I wouldn't be so sure," said Benita.

"And why not?" asked Bridget.

Benita looked from Bell to Bridget slyly, then puffed out her stomach and patted her belly, intimating she was onto Bell's secret.

Though she wanted more than anything in the world to slaughter her sister in cold blood, Bell did her best to control her homicidal feelings. Instead, she funneled her reproach into a glare and, still eyeing Benita in a threatening way, stood from the table and headed down the hall to her bedroom. Seconds later, Bridget muttered an excuse for why she, too, had to go and hurried down the hall after Bell, anxious to discuss the night's events.

Bridget insisted on recounting first, as was the custom. But her enthusiasm precluded a linear retelling, causing her to speak in an annoying digressive manner that combined endless tangents, dreamy generalizations, and rhetorical questions. Had Bell realized, she wanted to know, how pleasant it was to stroll in Central Park at night, that it wasn't even particularly scary once you got used to the dark? Had Bell ever noticed how spring's first leaves shimmered under the lampposts, causing them to look the same at two in the morning as they did in broad daylight? Had Bell ever known how easy it was to sneak into the Central Park Zoo? Did she have any idea how completely adorable seals looked when they were sleeping, that they all huddled up in a little clump like a pile of dirty laundry? More importantly, did Bell have any idea how much better Billy was looking these days? Had she ever noticed, I mean really noticed, the color and intensity of his eyes? Had Blaine experienced the same transformation? Since the twins were identical in every way, had Bell had just as much fun?

"Yes" had been Bell's slightly irritated response to Bridget's breathy questionnaire, especially as she began to detect the resemblances between their two dates. Still, despite her aggravation, she listened as though she were two people. On the surface, she was the attentive older sister, eager to interpret and offer advice. Underneath, she was a meticulous scientist, scrupulously gathering data. What, exactly, had Billy said? What time did they enter the park? Why did they choose the Central Park Zoo instead of the Boat

Pond? Had he checked his watch a lot? Did he seem distracted? As Bridget rambled, Bell peppered her sister with questions, engaging in a tacit investigation, pressing her sister for specifics. Unfortunately, Bridget didn't offer Bell much help. She'd been very drunk, she claimed, and now could not remember much. Luckily, she did remember one critical excerpt from the night. In fact, she remembered every word of Billy's memorable monologue.

"Bell, you're not going to believe what he said next."

"Oh, you must tell," Bell said dryly. "I can't take the suspense."

Bridget batted her eyes demurely, pausing for effect. "Bell," she said, then paused again, "Billy proposed to me."

"He what?" Bell snapped.

"You heard me," Bridget repeated. She shook her head and widened her eyes as though in reluctant effort to discern between the truth and a perfect dream.

"You're kidding," said Bell.

"Oh, he did it·very badly, but that's hardly the point."

"Bridget, please be serious. Did that really happen?"

"I know," Bridget said. She shook her head again in that same slightly insufferable way then smiled to herself as though enjoying her own private joke. "Isn't that insane? I can hardly believe it myself."

"No," said Bell. "It's terrible." She looked away from Bridget as though to complete complex mental calculations.

"Oh, he'll get it eventually," Bridget went on. She stood and walked to her dresser to stand in front of her mirror. Lifting a hairbrush to her head, she indulged in one luxurious stroke then stopped and addressed her reflection. "Maybe next time you could help him out. You know, coach him a little."

Bell said nothing for a moment, distracted by Bridget's supreme self-absorption, but she did her best to focus again on the evidence. Perhaps she should not bother Bridget with the news until she was sure exactly what had occurred. But glancing at Bridget once again, she found her engaged in the odd ritual of looking in the mirror and singing to herself and, deciding Bridget could handle it, she smiled heartily, and cleared her throat. "Bridge," Bell said, "what I'm about to say will probably upset you."

"Try me," Bridget said and smiled. "Today, I'm immune to stress."

Bell smiled and looked at the ground, inspected the rosebuds in the rug's floral border, and debated, but only for a fleeting second, the selfishness of ruining Bridget's good mood. "Last night," Bell said, "well . . . oddly enough . . ." She paused, searching for the right words. "I'd guess about ten minutes before Billy asked you, Blaine asked me, too."

Bridget squinted and wrinkled her nose. "Ha-ha. Very funny," she said. "Then, let me guess," she said, playing along, "at precisely one thirty-seven, he sneezed three times, then lost his balance and stubbed his third toe."

"Bridget, it's not a joke," said Bell.

"I know," Bridget said, "which explains why I'm not laughing." Bridget offered Bell a frivolous smile as though to flaunt her unflappable good humor.

But Bell held fast, combating Bridget's mirth with her most serious look. "Why would I make this up?" she asked.

Bridget narrowed her eyes skeptically.

Bell nodded for emphasis.

"What do you mean?" Bridget demanded.

"Exactly what I said."

"What did he say? What did you say? Why are you making this up?"

"Bridget," said Bell. She let the word hang in the air.

"You know, Bell," said Bridget. "It's not nice to do this just because you're jealous."

Deciding a calm, neutral gaze was the most efficient way to make her point, Bell said nothing, only sighed and walked toward her sister, then extended her hand and placed it patronizingly on Bridget's back. Bridget shirked Bell's hand away, but the gesture had the intended effect, causing Bridget to look, still in the mirror, from Bell to herself then finally, accepting Bell's authority, to crumple onto the bed. Relieved by Bridget's détente, Bell followed her sister across the room then, doing her best to suppress a satisfied smile, sat next to her on the bed.

"What did you say in response?" Bridget asked.

"I said 'no,' of course," Bell said. "A boy's got to work for these things."

Bridget stared harder at her sister then focused her gaze at the wall, as though awaiting a slide show.

"What did you say?" Bell demanded.

"Obviously, I said 'no,' " Bridget snapped. "He didn't have a ring. Besides, I have a boyfriend."

Though she was tempted to take issue with one of many of the problems with Bridget's statement, Bell forced herself to remain on message. "Bridget," she said. "Don't you think this is a little weird?"

"No," snapped Bridget. "For all we know, it was just a coincidence."

"They took us to the exact same place and said the exact same thing," Bell said, her volume rising noticeably.

"So," said Bridget. "It's not such a shock. There are only so many places to go. They both just chose the most interesting place in the neighborhood."

"Bridget, don't be obtuse," said Bell. "Our nights were identical."

"Of course, they were identical," snapped Bridget. She stood suddenly from the bed. Whatever bond had existed between the sisters a moment before had been broken. "What do you expect?" she went on. She paced the full length of the room. "We went out with identical twins. Ever since they were little boys, they've been doing bizarre things like this. They say the same thing at the same time, they get sick at the same time, their game score in tennis is practically even and, in case you've forgotten, almost ten years ago, they climbed in our window within ten minutes of each other, and . . ." Bridget trailed off suddenly. "Oh God. Do you think?" she asked.

Bell nodded solemnly. Slowly, she recalled the events of a night ten years earlier. Hindsight, she realized, was better than 20/20.

Hindsight was clairvoyant. The double proposal was not a fluke; it was a practical joke.

"At the time," Bell said, thinking aloud, "we credited nature."

"But, over the years," Bridget jumped in, "nurture molded their differences."

"Then why, after spending so much time apart, would they act like they shared the exact same brain unless they had planned it beforehand as some sort of elaborate stunt?"

Still leery of Bell's thesis, Bridget played devil's advocate. "Sometimes, two different roads take you to the same place."

"Why are you making excuses for them? We are the butts of this joke."

Bridget stopped pacing, her route blocked by the bedroom door. She glanced out the window helplessly, as though another person waited just outside with a valuable third perspective. "Oh, Bell," she said, "does it really matter? We had fun either way, right?"

"That is not the point," Bell snapped.

"What is the point?" asked Bridget.

"You should be totally outraged," Bell said. "You should be indignant!"

"Oh Bell, you're such a grouch," Bridget said.

But Bell had made her point. Defeated, Bridget limped across the room and threw herself across the bed.

At Bell's request, the girls retreated to their father's office, locking the door so as to prevent unwanted interruptions. Over the years, Barry had compiled a comprehensive file, charting the twin's every move in scrupulous detail. The files presented a colorful mosaic of the boys' histories: height charts, IQ scores, locks of hair, lost teeth, A papers, blue ribbons. Blaine's fifth-grade science fair project presaged his future obsessions: a test of the durability in soda, water, and acid of nickels, dimes, and quarters. Billy's first poem was penned in the tiny, curling font of a deeply obsessive mind and, incidentally, both girls had to agree, a terrible poem. Growth charts of the boys revealed that Blaine had always been an inch in the lead.

Even Blaine's baby booties exposed the discrepancy; they were a full size bigger than Billy's. The archives, spread out on the floor, presented a compelling case, amounting to nothing less than Billy and Blaine's life stories. And yet, in some way, this evidence revealed more about Barry than the boys. This was not the research of a scientist, but the scrapbook of a doting dad.

It was, of course, very sensitive work to make their analysis. In fact, Bell told Bridget, it was entirely critical to their mission that they block off their hearts from emotion as though staunching the flow of blood with a tourniquet. In order to know the truth, she felt, one must view reality from a distance. In order to know love, she reasoned, one must first fall out of it. To be sure, romance can benefit from such ascetic objectivity, permitting the student to filtrate the elements, to separate lust from passion. But there are also risks involved in taking this tack. Such a clinical approach threatens to corrupt love's natural process. Still, Bell felt completely justified in her investigation, convinced the best way to tell true love from false was to place it under a magnifying glass. Bridget, however, was a reluctant apprentice. She was still not convinced that the boys had conspired and objected, she said, on empirical grounds to Bell's behaviorism. Her argument was based in girlish emotion. She claimed the boys' prank, if it was one at all, was meant with the best intentions.

"We enjoyed ourselves, didn't we?" she asked. "What harm did they really do? Besides, if we confront them now, we'll just look like idiots."

But Bell held firmly to her point. Love was already brutal enough.

Finally, Bell had no choice but to petition her sister, for she knew that their best shot at revenge was to join forces. They must sacrifice themselves for the cause and go on second dates with the boys. But this time, they would be on their guards, armed with chilling awareness and emotional indifference.

"This is the perfect experiment," Bell argued, "to discern the boys' true motives."

"This is the perfect way," Bridget countered, "to rob life of all its romance."

"This is the perfect test," Bell tried, "with which to gauge Billy's manhood."

Here was a game of huge proportions, both girls finally agreed, at once a challenge to nature's might, nurture's malleability, and a battle in the oldest contest in the world, the war between men and women.

"Here's to sugar on the strawberries," Bell said, raising an imaginary glass.

"Here's to sugar on the strawberries," Bridget seconded.

And they laughed so hard that neither one noticed as a wholly unforeseen new variable entered the experiment.

Billy awoke on Sunday morning in a state of complete bafflement. This was not merely the confusion of a hangover. He was at a loss for certain vital statistics, such as how he'd gotten into his bed and the decade in which he lived. Memory graced him in stages as he winced at a patch of sunlight. He was not in his room, but rather in Blaine's. And, if he could glean anything from the creases on his face that formed the perfect shape of shirtsleeves, he had fallen asleep in his clothes and slept quite soundly. Despite this rush of disturbing information, he was greeted with some happy news. By some stroke of luck, he had worn a shade of blue last night that did wonders for his complexion. Another discovery amplified this sense of good fortune. A bright red patch on the upper corner of his neck promoted an obvious deduction.

Unfortunately, something in the image triggered a critical neuron in his brain, causing Billy to regain a patchy recollection of his night, along with the crushing awareness that this spot was not a love bite but rather a climbing scrape. Now, the remainder of his evening flooded his consciousness with cruel specificity. At some point around three o'clock in the morning, he had tripped back to his room from the Barnacle apartment to find his room occupied by Blaine. Still, one remaining missing fact perpetuated his mental fog. Billy blinked as he surveyed his room. What on earth had he been doing?

The boys' living quarters resembled the girls' only in physical lay-out. But due to the size of the Finch family, both boys had enjoyed the privilege of solitary habitation, while the girls across the hall, cursed with overcrowding, had been forced to double up. Both rooms were perfect expressions of the boys' respective personalities. Billy's exhibited the lack of hygiene and order befitting a teenage boy as well as the early, if slightly strained, signs of a young man trying to emerge. The walls were crammed with colorful posters of athletes and lascivious-looking women, the shelves were cluttered with trophies, board games, and toys left over from childhood. The room's remaining surface area was covered with the prerequisite mural of female body parts, advertising beer and ski equipment as though the closet hid a secret stash of items for purchase.

But underneath the typical litter of so many male hormones, there was evidence of a quiet sensitivity, one might even say an artistic sensibility. A black-and-white photograph of his mother developed during a summer photography course; a montage of cartoons torn from the *New Yorker* with scrupulous carelessness; towering stacks of screenplays; and, tacked up to a corkboard, thirty pages of a novel he'd never finished. All of these things could be found in odd corners of Billy's room like bloody fingerprints at a crime scene. Each artifact was evidence of some secret, delicate part of Billy's soul struggling to break through the more mundane aspects of his masculinity.

Blaine's room, on the other hand, was entirely devoid of testosterone. It exhibited the direct influence of his mother's femininity. The room's color scheme was an intricate balance of solid and patterned fabrics, combining a powder blue duvet with darker blue accents and a simple beige-and-white striped wallpaper that elongated the walls while drawing the eye toward the window. If possible, Blaine had managed to surpass even Mrs. Finch's attention to detail. He was not only the recipient of her acute eye but the lucky beneficiary of all the fabric she had amassed over the years. As a result, he had developed a painter's sense of the complementary relationships of colors and had graced the walls with four paintings he had completed himself. The paintings were simple color blocks but quite expert in their contrasts, harmonizing perfectly with the room's palate.

He kept an old-fashioned manual typewriter on his desk purely for aesthetic effect and stowed his laptop underneath in a convenient but well-hidden chamber. In the spring, he removed a small vase from this drawer and placed it on the edge of the desk so as to enjoy one added sliver of color. As though in silent acknowledgment of the room's fastidiousness, he had searched the city for the perfect cohesive detail. Finally, he had found the exact thing at the weekly flea market on Twenty-sixth Street, a large black-and-white photograph of Muhammad Ali, arms raised in flight. The image provided the perfect backdrop for his screenwriting efforts, serving as a reminder that all drama was born in conflict.

As teenagers, the boys had shared a room for one brief and ill-fated month after a misguided attempt to merge their real estate. In the hopes that a single empty room could be devoted to nefarious activities, the boys doubled up in Billy's room, constructing a bunk out of their two beds and converting the spare room into an all-purpose area. In concept, the extra room was meant to serve a variety of needs, acting as a clubhouse, a liquor cabinet, a hi-fi center and ladies' lair. Unfortunately, the plan backfired within a couple of weeks when the twins' notorious single-mindedness compelled them to bring young ladies to the room during the same time slot. As a result, they quickly reclaimed the titles to their original rooms and returned to their original configuration. They resided in these separate bedrooms up until they went away to college, using Central Park and neighborhood bars to serve the same needs as the spare room.

Lately, however, Blaine had taken it upon himself to adjust the living arrangements. Upon returning from his nuptial apartment to his parents', he had found that sleeping in his childhood room was simply too painful a reminder of his adult failures. So, without consulting his parents or Billy, he had taken the liberty of switching rooms, eschewing his own bedroom in favor of Billy's. This move, he felt, threatened no one in particular since the layouts of the two rooms were mirror images. He felt further justified because when he made the switch, Billy had yet to return. When he did, of course, he lacked Blaine's tragic circumstances and the claim on real estate to which they entitled him. Moreover, Blaine felt such brazen acts were the birthright of the firstborn son. Of course, this move had repercussions Blaine could never have foreseen, depriving friends and family of yet one more method with which to tell the twins apart.

Finally, acknowledging the time, Billy fumbled from his room and walked, or rather crept, down the hall in search of some clean clothes. He reached the door to his bedroom and tapped it open with his foot. Immediately, he was forced to squint. The sun struck the window at such an angle as to transform it into a mirror, causing Billy to confront his own reflection. He stared at himself for a moment, taken aback but not altogether displeased. In fact he decided, if he dared say so, he was looking rather handsome. His clothes were smart if a bit rumpled on the side on which he'd slept, but the rumpling did him no great disservice, causing him to look at once rugged and sincere, boyish and yet virile.

His hair looked coifed but not intentionally so. His eyes were younger than the rest of his face. His cheeks, though slightly full for his age, were tinged a charming pink color that made him look quite lovable. It was, of course, more difficult to deny the effects of time on his hairline, but even now, as he ran his hands through his hair, he was not hard-pressed to see how baldness could give a man the mark of distinction. He had certainly put on a couple pounds but you could never call him "fat." Satisfied, he gave his hair a tousle. However, he stopped tousling in his tracks when he realized, to his great confusion, that his reflection was not tousling back.

"What are you doing?" Blaine demanded.

Billy stared at Blaine, perplexed. He checked his brother's face for inconsistencies as though it were entirely plausible that he had just addressed his reflection and his reflection had addressed him back.

"Billy," said Blaine. "Snap out of it. Why do you look so stunned?"

"Oh, it's you," Billy sighed. "Without your baseball cap on, you look . . . well, you look like my reflection."

Blaine scoffed as though Billy had just uttered the most mundane of statements. Had he said "the moon is made of cheddar cheese," he might have earned a better reception.

"I suppose it's only natural," Billy muttered. "It happens to everyone else." Kicking himself, he stared at Blaine, then brought his fingers to his neck to make sure his heart was still beating. Comforted by the beat of his pulse, he scanned the bedroom curiously. Finally, his outrage returned. "Anyway," he said, "this is *my* room. What are *you* doing?"

"Mom said I could stay in here," Blaine snapped. He placed his hands on his hips.

"Did it ever occur to you to check with me first?"

"It's not your room anymore," said Blaine.

"Of course it is," said Billy.

Blaine assumed the impertinent air of a very seasoned attorney. "I have nowhere else to go," he said. "You're here voluntarily."

Failing to find a response for this, Billy looked at the ground, then, still flustered, alternated his gaze between Blaine and his own belongings.

Finally, Blaine took pity on Billy and offered him a chair.

"Sorry to wake you," Billy said.

"No, it's perfect," Blaine said dryly. "I find the best cure for a hangover is not to sleep at all."

"Good," said Billy. He managed, as always, to miss Blaine's sarcasm. He settled into a large stuffed chair whose cushion boasted the additional padding of a heap of dirty laundry.

"So," said Blaine. "What happened last night? Did she fall to Cupid's arrow?"

"No, she did not," Billy sniffed. "As much as I hate to admit it."

"That's terrible," Blaine said, sighing. "Tell me what went wrong."

Billy regarded his brother with appropriate suspicion. Such overt shows of compassion from Blaine were always accompanied with some risk. "Where should I begin?" Billy began, eyeing Blaine cautiously. Then, giving him the benefit of the doubt, he asked, "In short, what didn't?"

Blaine, who was now sitting on the bed, switched into a reclining position, placing his hands behind his head in an exaggerated show of interest.

"It's my fault for proposing without a ring," Billy said. "I should have listened to you."

"What were her objections?" Blaine asked. He tilted his head to one side like a bored therapist.

"Oh God," Billy sighed. "Where to start? The proposal. The ring. The suitor."

"Consider it a blessing," said Blaine. "Now you know what you're dealing with. Who wants to devote his life's work to someone so high-maintenance?"

Billy crossed, then uncrossed his legs, considering Blaine's counsel. His advice was sound but also carried the impersonal ring of words from inside a fortune cookie. "Hopefully, Mom will take pity on me and give me Grandmother's ring."

"Oh no, don't do that," Blaine said, his voice jumping an octave. He quickly qualified his response. "Don't let her think she can push you around. Make her sweat a little."

Startled by his brother's tone, Billy glanced at Blaine then, doubting himself again, he replaced his head in his hands and resumed moaning.

"The last thing you want to do," Blaine went on, "is come across as desperate. If you capitulate too quickly, you set a bad precedent."

"Grandmother was a very tough lady," Billy countered. "And she liked that precedent."

"Fine. Don't listen to me," said Blaine. "Just don't be surprised if you get another rejection."

Billy slumped deeper into the upholstery of his chair, then, tiring of his surroundings, removed a dirty shirt from the pile on his chair and used a soiled oxford shirt to block the sunlight and completely cover his face.

"Can I just say one last thing?" asked Blaine.

Billy muffled his assent through the shirt.

"If I were you, I would take the day off. You can't afford another strike."

Billy began to construct his rebuttal but quickly thought better of it. Perhaps he should heed his brother's warning and take a short hiatus. Lacking the strength to decide either way, he sat paralyzed for a moment and then, in the absence of a better plan, resolved to take a short nap. Without further delay, he emitted one last helpless sigh and thanking his brother for his help, he hoisted himself from the chair without removing the shirt from his head, and stumbled back to Blaine's room. Perhaps the room trade would result in some inadvertent lucky break, blessing Billy with Blaine's luck as though by osmosis.

15

Double Vision

*A*nger and love often make a surprisingly compatible match. The seemingly opposite emotions sometimes come together to form the most graceful of dancing partners. So, with this very pair swirling within her own heart, Bell emerged from her window at midnight. The journey began with a steady ascent up her fire escape and culminated in a challenging chin-up and hoist that required a small feat of gymnastics. The fire escape ended just five feet shy of the building's roof, forcing Bell to reach for the top of the building with one hand while maintaining a firm grasp with the other on the railing below. Then, doing her best to avoid a glance at the distant sidewalk, she faced the final risk; catapulting herself over this short distance to reach the safety of the roof.

Comparatively, the second portion of the journey was much easier than the first. It required crossing the roof with sufficiently light steps, wary, particularly on the Finch side, of Mrs. Finch's light slumber. The only route from the Barnacles' to the Finches' entailed traversing the ceiling directly above the Finches' master bedroom. The third portion of the expedition was essentially a repetition of the first, a short drop down the other side of the building to reach Blaine's bedroom. This segment of the journey, however, was defined by one critical difference. When rappelling down the Finches' side, one's fall was cushioned by a minute speck eighty feet below posing as a trash Dumpster. Still, it was entirely possible to pick up some speed on this side, provided one took a lover's leap of faith, hugging the building for dear life without promise of a returned embrace.

The trip was exactly as Bell remembered; a steady perilous climb peppered with moments of euphoric relief and grave danger. But time had somehow lent the journey added treachery. The metal grates were louder now, despite her cautious steps. The drop seemed not so much higher as closer to death. Even the building itself had aged considerably over the years, its red bricks fading to light brown, its bright copper gutters dulling to green, and black paint peeling off in thick chips on every surface. Bell herself had changed considerably since her maiden voyage. Her steps were less certain, her hamstrings less supple, her confidence shaken. But finishing the climb required maintaining a positive outlook. Luckily, the city offered ample distraction. A taxi door slammed. A bus whistled. A pair of lovers fought. The city felt her excitement, Bell decided. They were in on this together. For a moment, she forgot the dire nature of her mission. How odd, she thought, that love and hatred could produce the same sensation.

Finally, she reached Blaine's room and paused to catch her breath. From the window, it looked exactly as she remembered: completely immaculate. In the darkness, his powder blue duvet appeared an almost ghostly white. The yellow plaid still provided the perfect foil to his beige striped wallpaper. The pillows on the bed remained perfectly ordered despite Blaine's tumultuous sleep. In fact, of everything in the room, it was Blaine who had changed the most. His hair was tossed sweetly over his pillow and his lips parted slightly in a smile, causing him to look uncharacteristically cherubic and docile. Seen through the glass, he seemed softer somehow, younger, more innocent. His chest rose and fell with a disturbing slowness, as though he were not a man but some rare amphibious species that required less oxygen. He murmured things occasionally and changed his expression. It was as though sleep had robbed him of his evil intentions. It was nothing short of torture for Bell to see him in this vulnerable state. For ten years now she had pictured this image instead of counting sheep. But she did her best to detach from emotion. Her aspirations were so much bigger than love: She was after vindication.

She hesitated a moment before moving toward his window. Was it possible that her sister was right, that telepathy alone had twinned the boys' courtships? Was there any chance, she wondered now, that she'd made the wrong judgment, that Blaine had spoken from his heart the night before, that finally, after all these years, he had simply and suddenly seen the light, had woken up and realized he had spent his young life on shallow pursuits and wasteful women—or was it shallow women and wasteful pursuits?—and that the best, nay, the only way, to give his life meaning was to make Bell his wife? Even entertaining these thoughts lifted Bell's spirits, but as she peered more intently through the window, she realized Blaine's smile was more of a sneer and, kicking herself for her gullibility, promptly dismissed the notion.

Without further delay, she reached for the window. Many close shaves with uncooperative doormen had made her as proficient at the art of window entry as window exit. She applied the necessary combination of forward and upward force, managing to lift Blaine's window a whole foot without so much as a squeak. Next, she met the final challenge of the outdoor journey. She shrunk herself to the smallest possible diameter, then wriggled through the window. Duly relieved by the sensation of solid ground once again, she lay prostrate on the rug for several moments, taking in her coordinates. Luckily, Blaine had failed to note even the slightest disturbance.

He'd reached, if possible, a yet deeper state of repose. One arm was stretched casually above his head as though his bed was a sandy beach and a fruity drink was perched on his pillow. Wholly entranced, Bell lingered for a moment, watching Blaine sleep, then, giving into a strange impulse, she surveyed the room to appraise the decor as though she was an honored guest enjoying a guided tour. Finally, Bell braced herself for the last leg of her journey then, taking a lesson from her father, silenced the rustle of her clothes by rolling across the floor.

A long, low moan interrupted Bell's covert approach. Blaine was still sleeping soundly, only now he lay on his side, cradling his head in his hands like a small forest animal. He looked so innocent in this pose that Bell was flummoxed again, finding herself hard-pressed to remember her cynicism. Unfortunately, nine times out of ten, passion trumps reason and so Bell ignored her better judgment, lifting herself from the floor in order to climb into the bed and nestle herself very close to Blaine in a spooning position. In her haste, she failed to notice certain critical environmental details. She had not yet admired the yellow daffodil posed daintily in the vase on Blaine's desk, nor had she noted the simple fact that the man sleeping in Blaine's bed was not Blaine at all.

"Blaine," Bell whispered.

Billy shook his head and wrinkled his face to a dot. He turned onto his back, lifted his arms then clasped them across his chest.

"Blaine," Bell repeated. She turned toward him, rotating into an embrace.

His eyes still closed, Billy turned to face Bell and muttered something unintelligible.

Slightly frazzled by the commotion, Bell took a deep, strengthening breath then, flouting fate and gender roles, she coyly slid her hand from Billy's shoulder to his waist. Billy smiled in response conveying his deep subconscious satisfaction. Then, smiling widely once again, he rolled toward Bell. "Oh, Bridget," he said.

Bell lay perfectly still for a moment, staring at Billy's closed eyes.

His eyelashes were long and thick. His skin was smooth and sweetly scented.

"Blaine," she whispered. She inched her hand lower toward his hip.

Billy said nothing in response, only smiled with deep pleasure and yawned extravagantly.

Bell stared at the sleeping boy, immobilized with yearning then, losing patience, shook him gently and woke him with a kiss on the lips.

Billy puckered his lips for several seconds before he opened his eyes and realized the object of his affection. "Bell," Billy gasped. "What the hell?"

Bell braced every muscle in her body.

"Bell," Billy repeated. "What are you doing?"

Bell said nothing for a moment, weighing her options frantically. As she saw it, she had two choices: attempt to hide under the duvet or make a dash for the door. And yet, after a careful assessment, Bell opted for a third, risky choice, wrapping her arms around Billy's neck and sticking her tongue down his throat.

"Oh," said Billy.

Bell took this as a good sign and clasped the back of his neck with more force.

"No," said Billy.

Bell pulled away suddenly. "Oh," she whispered. "I'm sorry."

On reflex, Bell turned away from Billy to face an impartial wall. She wished she believed what she had as a child, that simply by closing her eyes very tight she could make herself disappear from the world. Without another word or glance, she lunged out of the bed, sprinted down the Finches' hall, and burst into her own apartment like a drowning swimmer reaching the shore. Finding the sight of Bridget simply too much to bear at the moment, she bypassed their bedroom, opting instead to sleep on the living room sofa. The sight of so many familiar objects did its part to transport her somewhat, but the rigidity of the sofa provided its own obstacle. Fortunately, she was graced with sleep within thirty minutes, but even this brought its own form of distress as her dreams were plagued with nightmares in which she single-handedly took on an army of twins, fighting pairs of every shape and size with little success.

At just this moment, Blaine awoke with a terrible start. Yet another dream featuring the Barnacle girls made him feel as though he might unravel. In the dream, the six girls had multiplied into six hundred. Each girl had been possessed by an evil, bloodthirsty demon. Each one wore a more beguiling expression as they marched toward him en masse, with military precision. Frazzled, he wandered into the kitchen to fix himself a snack. As always, salami and swiss beckoned as the sirens did Odysseus. He opened the refrigerator, removed the essentials from the fridge and placed a small pile of cold cuts on a plate, alternating, in his odd fastidious way, one slice of cheese between every slice of meat. But, once he'd finished its assembly, Blaine only stared at the striped sandwich. He stood in a trance for several minutes, contemplating his predicament. If all went well, he would soon be engaged to a young heiress. But if Bell continued to resist his advances, Billy would beat him to it. Nothing would irk him more than to watch Billy lap him at the finish, rendering Bell the second-place winner and Billy, a millionaire's husband. Finding his appetite suddenly diminished, Blaine abandoned his sandwich. He needed to see Bell immediately. Surely, she could be persuaded.

Sadly, the Barnacles' living room was heavily guarded. Having overheard snippets of Bell and Bridget's plan, Benita had set up camp near the front door in order to police traffic. To distract herself during quiet hours, she'd brought a deck of cards and dealt her fifteenth hand of solitaire as the night proceeded into the morning hours. While she played, she devoted dormant parts of her brain to the usual pastimes, reviewing her lines for Monday's talent show audition, settling her dolls' raging custody battles, and otherwise plotting her sisters' destruction. She funnelled all other neurological energy toward her lifelong goal: whichever came first, her marriage to Billy or Billy's seduction.

Of course, Benita knew their union was impossible for the time being. The world of adults was too simple-minded to overlook their age difference. And yet, Benita felt certain the future offered some hope. Though many would oppose their union now, in ten years, they'd have fewer opponents. Taking some comfort in these statistics, she redoubled her card-playing efforts and moved through the dealer's pile, three cards at a time, stopping only occasionally to cheat and check cards for preferable options. Yet again, her mind strayed to her favored topic. By the time she was twenty-five years old, Billy would be forty-three and by then their love would be acceptable in the court of public opinion. Furthermore, time would afford Benita an added selling point. By then, their age gap would turn into an advantage, rendering Benita an appealing alternative to boring middle-aged women.

And while Benita knew it was a lot to ask that Billy wait, she suspected, even at her tender age, that love required sacrifice. Regardless, there was one issue on which she would not relent. If she couldn't have Billy to herself, she would rather he was alone. The thought of Billy and Bridget together turned her purple with rage. With each new card she overturned, she considered a new act of vengeance. Perhaps she could tell Billy about Bridget's past and thereby tarnish her image, or maybe do more serious harm by digging up some damning pictures. Either way, she was determined to find a way to sabotage their romance and found, for the first time since learning about the contest, an equally worthy challenge. Consumed, she continued her game of cards with increasing fervor, seeing, instead of hearts and spades on her cards, the face of her neighbor. As a result, it felt like prophecy when chance brought her a visitor and Benita looked up from her game of cards to find Billy standing at the door. And yet, Benita would soon face an equally astounding shock considering the fact that the boy standing at the door was not Billy at all.

"Billy," said Benita. She pursed her lips and pushed out her chest flirtatiously.

Blaine ran his fingers through his hair then, realizing the reason for Benita's mistake, decided not to make the correction.

"Billy," said Benita. "What are you doing? It's after midnight."

"I was having trouble sleeping," said Blaine, "so I came for a visit."

"Who did you come to see?" Benita asked. She batted her eyes coyly.

"You know I can't go a day without you," said Blaine then, lifting his palm to his forehead, he assumed a melodramatic tone. "Love is all consuming."

Benita blushed and reveled in this compliment for a minute. Then, recognizing sarcasm, stopped smiling and narrowed her eyes. "Bridget's sleeping," she announced. "You'll have to come back later."

"And Bell?" he asked.

Benita regarded him suspiciously. Why did Billy care what Bell was doing? "Bell's with Blaine," she said haughtily. "She left an hour ago."

"I see," said Blaine. And now, a truly insidious thought entered his head. But he felt he could not be blamed; circumstance had conspired with him. It was almost too easy. "If you don't mind then, I might just go and knock on Bridget's door."

"Suit yourself," Benita sneered. "If you don't mind damaged goods."

"Oh come on, Benita." Blaine offered an insincere pout.

"It's your loss anyway," she said. "Bridget's not going to win."

"Win what?" said Blaine.

Benita indulged in a demonic smile. "My father's contest," she said. "But, then again, what would you care?"

"Why is that?" Blaine demanded, his interest finally piqued.

"Sorry," she said. In an instant, she completely transformed her expression, replacing her diabolical look with one that was equally angelic. "I can't tell you. It's too big a secret."

"Now, Benita," Blaine scolded. "I'll take it to the grave."

Benita performed a pantomime with excruciating accuracy, locking her mouth at the corner of her lips and then, opening her mouth again to swallow the invisible key.

"Come on, Benita," Blaine whined, matching her tone inadvertently. "I'm practically your brother. I'm definitely trustworthy."

Benita twirled her hair demurely, considering Blaine's plea. "Oh fine," she said. "But you can't tell a soul." Then she whispered, "Bell's pregnant."

"What?" snapped Blaine.

Benita nodded. "I thought you might want to know. Bridget's not the one to marry. Bell's already won."

Blaine said nothing for a moment, dizzy with questions. Could this little imp be trusted? Was this reliable information? "But what if Bridget accepts Billy's—" Blaine paused, catching his mistake. "But if Bridget accepts my proposal," he went on, "will she and Bell tie for first place?"

Benita looked at Blaine sharply, alarmed by his choice of words. His mastery of the contest's rules was striking, surpassing even her own. But greed overwhelmed her intuition for the moment. More distracted by Blaine's question than his verbiage, she devoted the better part of her brain to considering this outcome. "Yes," she finally admitted, placing her hands on her hips. "But if you don't mind, please don't tell Blaine that part."

Blaine said nothing, only stared at Benita, considering the new data. Then, remembering his previous goal, he said, "Well, thanks for the tip. I'm off to see Bridget."

Benita stared at Blaine for a moment, outraged by his treatment. Had she known, of course, that Blaine was Billy, she might have felt less injured. Unfortunately, she was condemned to curse her miserable luck. She'd intended to sabotage Billy and Bridget's romance, not fan the flames of their passion. Finally, lacking a response, she wrinkled her face into a grimace then, resisting the urge to stick out her tongue, turned on her heel and stormed down the hall, muttering to herself. Surprised by Benita's violent reaction, Blaine watched her angry march. As she disappeared down the hall, Blaine entertained a wicked thought. Without his baseball cap on, the world was at his disposal. He could indulge his every whim under the veil of Billy's good reputation.

Finally, once Benita's footsteps had faded and her door had slammed several times, Blaine proceeded after her down the hall toward his intended destination. The change of scenery presented an unexpected challenge. Blaine stopped short at the door of Bell and Bridget's room, lulled by the sight of Bridget sleeping and the room's overwhelmingly feminine fragrance. The heady scent of rose perfume combined with the warm spring breeze and a faint trace of sweat to give the room an intoxicatingly feminine quality. Forgetting himself, Blaine remained still, as though hypnotized, surveying the contents of the room with new fascination. Solitude and moonlight afforded the room a magical glow and, blessed with the leisure to snoop, Blaine wandered around the perimeter with the entitled curiosity of a museum visitor. Bridget's belongings announced themselves in bold colors. A pink boa and a pair of red heels rested on a wooden chair. An abundance of hanging, frilly things filled the room like windblown feathers. Leather bags poked out from every corner broadcasting every designer label. Countless pails overflowed with nail polish like Thanksgiving cornucopia; all of these artifacts asserted their owner's heavenly girliness.

Bell's possessions, though harder to locate in the fray of ruffles and fringe, painted a more complex portrait. The colorful ribbons and awards of a precocious childhood were patchy in their commitment to a single pursuit. The garbled posters and photographs were an earnest, if clumsy, attempt to try on various points of view. The endless and seemingly haphazard array of books revealed, in patches, particular phases of interest and various abandoned pursuits. The peculiar selection of objects—a collection of tiny glass elephants, a cardboard diarama of the Grand Canyon, a pair of homemade roller skates fashioned from sneakers and skateboard wheels—betrayed a wonderfully eccentric mind, a person unafraid of failure. Here was evidence of a person striving to discover herself, to decide what in the world mattered, what causes merited her devotion. Here was a person trying to wrangle a worthy path from this beautiful abundance.

Unfortunately, Blaine's musings were disturbed by a low, angry growl. Charles lay resting on the bedroom floor, seemingly guarding Bridget while she slept and, from the look on his face, begrudged Blaine the interruption. At the sound of his growl, Bridget rustled slightly but then integrated the noise into her dream. Benita, however, already on alert, darted from her bedroom to her post in the hall, assuming position just in time to watch Blaine enter Bridget's bedroom.

Over the years, Bell and Bridget's room had been host to various neighborhood boys. Even so Bridget was startled by the sight of Blaine and totally disoriented. Fatigue and darkness colluded with Blaine's insidious intent. And lacking the baseball cap as a crutch, Bridget mistook Blaine for Billy for the first time in her life.

"Billy," she whispered.

Blaine stopped short, amazed by Bridget's mistake.

"Billy," she repeated, "I thought I told you to stop coming over uninvited."

Blaine remained perfectly still, considering his options.

"Oh well," said Bridget, "as long as you're here, come over where I can see you. Stop lurking in the shadows."

As he obliged and crossed the room, Blaine's conscience flared up. His opportunity for honesty was running out. If he planned to set her straight, he had exactly one second. But, like all great criminals, he paired spontaneity with cold-blooded intent. It was irresistible to lie. If he could pull this off tonight, the possibilities were endless.

"Tie game, 'eighty-six World Series," Blaine whispered, parroting Billy and Bridget's game.

"Not now," Bridget said, playing along. "Can't you see I'm busy?"

"Sweetheart," Blaine pressed. He took a seat at the edge of Bridget's bed, careful to position himself far from the patches in which the moon lit the room.

"After this inning." Bridget sighed. "I need to see this pitch."

"But darling," Blaine begged, "I know you're busy, but my question is urgent. I need to know right this instant. Which do you love more? Me or baseball?"

Bridget paused for a moment to give the issue serious thought then, offering a reluctant smile, she admitted, "You, I guess."

Blaine took this concession to heart and nodded gratefully. Then, in efforts to keep up the momentum, upped the ante. "Okay, I've got a good one," he announced. "One of the year's ten best. In fact, this one is so good, I'm certain you'll never beat it."

Her interest piqued by the challenge, Bridget propped herself up in the bed, taking the opportunity to place a pillow behind her back.

"Crosstown bus," Blaine began, "the Understatement of the Year. They haven't been dating very long. Too soon to expect the commitment. They're on their way back from the grocery store. Brown paper bags at their feet. The bus stops suddenly at a red light. 'Sweetie,' he says."

"Yes," Bridget replied.

"It doesn't matter what we're doing. Buying groceries, reading the paper, riding the crosstown bus. Life is exciting when you're around. Sweetheart," he said.

"Yes," she whispered.

Then, something unexpected happened. Try as she might, there was no denying the physical sensation. Bridget's stomach turned a full revolution. Her heart thumped madly. Her ears got hot. For one split second, the beating of her heart quite possibly stopped.

"Your turn," Blaine said.

Bridget swallowed and looked away, embarrassed by her reaction. She turned to study the window frame with feigned interest.

Suddenly, long-forgotten emotions flooded her heart. Why had all the weight in her body dropped from her head to her toes? Had Billy alone caused this response? Had he felt the same things himself? Finally, she had no choice but speak or betray herself. "Teenage Romeo," she managed. "Two twins. Two sisters. One night, without discussing such a plan, both boys climb in the same window."

"Ah," Blaine said, nodding knowingly. "The notorious Double Proposal."

"But, they're not teenagers anymore. Now the stakes are much higher."

"Is that right?" Blaine asked.

Bridget nodded solemnly. Suddenly, her instincts understood what her brain had yet to infer. Surely, this was the end of the line, the moment, the question.

But Blaine was so surprised by his success he suddenly lost his gumption. What in God's name had he been thinking? He couldn't propose to Bridget. "So, how about those Sox," he said, changing the subject quickly. "I'm expecting a strong start from Cox. What's your prediction?"

Bridget regarded Blaine strangely, forcing him to meet her gaze. Overwhelmed by the color of her eyes and the odd weight of the moment, Blaine ignored propriety and his conscience and took her hand in his. But this gesture marked a strange and unexpected turn. As she gave her hand, Bridget's heart was suddenly devoid of all sensation. Her pulse did not race. Her palms did not sweat. Her toes did not tingle. Her heart beat as it normally did, no speed, no thrill, no thump. None of the other telltale signs accompanied Blaine's romantic gesture. No flutter in the stomach, no weakness in the knees, nothing resembling excitement. In fact, if pressed, Bridget would have had no choice but admit she felt no more extraordinary than she did after a hearty breakfast. So it's official, Bridget decided with some measure of relief. She was not in love with Billy Finch. If she were in love with Billy, she reasoned, she would have felt something. Charles raised his snout as though to confirm his agreement then glared at Blaine, sniffed the air, and issued a menacing growl. Blaine, who had always been scared of the dog, took this as his cue. He released Bridget's hand, muttered an excuse, and promptly bolted.

16

Persistence

For a person who spends any amount of time doubting, loathing, or in some way engaged in the negative assessment of himself, disapproval from others often has an antithetical effect. Far from its feeling like an attack on the sensitive soul, a cool response from another person, whether an all-out assault or merely a subtle rejection, can provide an unexpected relief, offering a rare confirmation of the doubter's worst fears. He may even experience a sort of detached satisfaction much like a pessimistic meteorologist on sight of a thundercloud. The moment of rejection, much like the forecasted storm, may present a momentary inconvenience but its discomfort is immediately overwhelmed by the thrill of corroboration. This rejection, therefore, while certainly sad, is arguably a happy event for it serves at once to justify and legitimize the preoccupations of the tormented mind.

For this very reason, Trot viewed Billy's recent intrusion as a mixed blessing. Though it cost him the company of his girlfriend, it allowed him to sanction his usual pastime, thorough analysis of his own faults, followed by the faults of everyone else, and therefore avoiding a complete overhaul of his personality. While the absence of Bridget was, to be sure, a nuisance, Trot had not suffered a net loss. His worldview remained completely intact, in fact, it grew only more steadfast. His writing had hopefully found new fuel and his girlfriend, with any luck, would return to the apartment by the end of the week with a renewed appreciation for him. With these arrows in his quiver, Trot awoke rather later on Sunday but nonetheless with a general air of conviction as opposed to the sullen rage and recrimination one might expect. In fact, he was positively buoyant as he opened his eyes at half past four and patted the empty half of his bed in confused recollection of Bridget's exit. Far from mourning her absence or lamenting her treatment, he was grateful for her mistake. He padded across the empty apartment to a patch of floor that was fully saturated with afternoon sunlight and, surveying the space, considered how best to fill his only full day off from the bakery that week.

Of course, Trot's oddly chipper response begged an obvious question: Did his incongruous complacency result from the fact that disappointment fit into his perverse gestalt, or rather from the fact that he did not actually miss Bridget? From the start, Trot had repressed the notion that the two were incompatible, ignoring the abundant evidence that supported this fact. Bridget's friends and family seemed to have the most convincing assessment of their union. Trot could see it in their eyes every time Bridget forced him to socialize. It was as though no matter what question he was asked—"How have you been?", "How's the bakery?", "How's your writing?", or "Isn't the weather unseasonably warm?"—the inquiry was not about the said topic. In fact, these people were asking a far more urgent question; "What on earth is a girl like Bridget doing with a guy like you?" Of course, Trot knew that paranoia made him prone to construe cruelty out of mere inquisitiveness. Still, he felt there was some merit to his suspicions. Perhaps, these objective parties could see something that Trot and Bridget could not.

Still, despite his compulsive pessimism, Trot was blessed with a healthy, even arrogant sense, of himself when he was alone and had no trouble answering the echoing question. It was perfectly clear what he offered Bridget: He provided an ongoing escape, much like an engrossing book, allowing her to uphold the delusion that she had strayed far from her family when in fact she had strayed not at all. By dating someone with such a different background, Bridget could comfort herself with the notion that she was admirably open-minded. She could delude herself into thinking she was the black sheep of the family. She could view their West Village apartment as a den of creativity, crowded by books and cigarette butts, an artist's hovel in which dirty paintbrushes shared space with vats of red wine. Holed up with her bohemian boyfriend, writing poems, singing songs, rehearsing scenes, Bridget could uphold the myth that she was roughing it. She could think of herself as a struggling artist despite the obvious disconnect; her struggle was not to support herself with her art but rather to support the notion that she was an artist.

Precisely what Bridget offered Trot was a far more difficult thing to assess and one that required honest introspection of which Trot was not capable. Perhaps the whispers of friends and family could shed some light on the subject. Every boy of humble origins who dates a girl of such auspicious ones must ask himself to what extent he was seduced by the girl's privilege. But it was not her money that tantalized Trot, nor her family's opulence; it was Bridget's brazen confidence, a direct result of her upbringing, to be sure, but not of money itself. But he felt he could not be blamed for falling for the sparkling confidence privilege affords. It was no different than falling for a girl with a beautiful face. Both girls were recipients of the favoritism of her environment and, as a result, of the sneaking suspicion that most of her wishes in life would inevitably be fulfilled, that her future would closely resemble the one she had dreamed up as a child. Could a boy from the middle of nowhere really be faulted for admiring this? He might as well be faulted for choosing the city over the country, his rural hometown. For Bridget was nothing if not a living personification of New York City; sophisticated yet sweet, daunting yet endearing, constant yet constantly changing.

To be sure, there were aspects of Bridget's personality that made Trot yearn for the girls back home. He hated the way she waltzed through Manhattan with little regard for others, willfully crossing streets in spite of red lights, pushing in front of pedestrians whose pace was too slow, wandering boldly at all hours of the night through even the roughest neighborhoods, as though her movements were policed by a cadre of personal bodyguards. This wild, self-destructive self-absorption, this sense of immunity to hardship, this nearly offensive sense of herself as an all-entitled princess; all of these qualities Trot loved and loathed in equal part. And yet, there was no denying that the two shared a durable bond. The couple did not so much prove the adage that opposites attract but rather that something interesting occurs when two very dissimilar people spend so much time together. They had enjoyed their fair share of happy times, had even fostered some necessary mutual maturation, Trot softening Bridget's rougher edges just as Bridget emboldened Trot. But perhaps, Trot now acknowledged, they had learned all they could from one another and they risked untold psychic damage by staying together any longer.

Amidst this, he thought, fruitful assessment of his relationship with Bridget, Trot had taken a seat at his desk and found himself faced with a new oppressive presence. Now only inches from his blank computer screen, he was accosted by all of his old self-doubt as though by an angry ghost. But rather than reconcile, he forced his imagination onto wayward paths. Surely, recounting Billy's loathsome qualities could distract him for a while. Thus occupied, Trot managed to squander an entire precious hour of his day by mentally listing and then actually typing out Billy's worst qualities. Having pinpointed Billy's personality long before they met, Trot had little discerning to do by the time they were face-to-face. And yet, at the Barnacles' Passover seder, Billy had surpassed all stereotype and suspicion, allowing Trot to find new reserves of venom.

Billy Finch was the living emblem of everything Trot hated. He was, in short, the perfect bull's-eye, his ruddy face an easy target. It was self-proclaimed artists like Billy who made life difficult for Trot, crowding the annals of contemporary culture with mediocrity. They were not technically in direct competition, with Billy striving for legitimacy as a filmmaker while Trot slaved for simple relevance in the world of fiction. Still, the division between the two might as well have been a poet and a plumber. In Trot's mind, categorization was simple enough; Billy was an aspiring screenwriter while Trot was a real writer. But even this simple distinction failed to give Trot comfort. He was plagued with a far more pressing problem. For though film and fiction seemed to exist on parallel, harmonious planes, the two forms were, in fact, engaged in a heated race, the winner of which would survive through the ages while the other died a slow death. In Trot's opinion, real writing and screenwriting fought a frenzied, deadlocked battle, the winner of which would earn the prize of relevance and longevity. Trot feared this match was but a token formality, a means of assuaging the grief felt by writers as they watched their form fade out.

Like all writers, Trot was relieved to find a scapegoat for his own shortcomings and cursed Billy, while he should have thanked him for this valuable service. In addition to this Trot was armed with the unquestioning smugness of an underdog and firmly believed that it was better to produce nothing than something people had seen before. What service did Billy offer the world? At least Trot strove for originality. At least he strove for newness. Billy was one of a generation who failed to see art as the great privilege, who saw art as his birthright as opposed to a chance to contribute to history. In

Trot's opinion, the artist, unlike the doomed dodo or the miserable manatee, had one blessed shot at skirting extinction, the opportunity, though by no means the guarantee, to leave a legend for the next generation and thereby to become, in some way, exempt from evolution.

So, satisfied with both his moral and artistic supremacy, Trot stood up from his computer without having written a word. And without making the conscious decision to leave the house, he found himself walking up Eighth Avenue at a brisk, commanding pace, traversing, in reverse, the exact same route Billy had forged two nights earlier. Having not yet eaten a meal, Trot was somewhat overwhelmed by his consumption of coffee, an excessive amount that was further compounded by the only other substance in his stomach: two-day-old cupcakes. Thus fueled by a healthy dose of caffeine and frosting, Trot walked the fifty odd blocks uptown without pausing to catch his breath. As a result, even he was quite surprised by his rapid progress when he found himself, just before midnight, standing at the window of the Barnacle girls, performing an alarmingly accurate impersonation of Billy.

"Bridget, come down here now!" Trot bellowed.

Sadly, no one noticed.

Still undaunted, Trot stepped backward, veering closer to the curb, then tilted his head farther back to get a better look at the girls' window.

"Bridget, come down here," he said again, this time somewhat more forcefully, drawing the attention of Carlos, who shook his head despairingly, more amused than annoyed.

Now, faced with the added mortification of a spectator, Trot felt a rush of degradation and, acknowledging his sadness for the first time since Billy's stunt, he took a seat on the sidewalk as though he were in a grassy field, preparing for a picnic. Fortunately, Carlos took pity on him soon enough, gesturing for Trot to enter the building and shuttling him to the thirteenth floor.

Trot stood still at the front door for several minutes then, tapping it, he found it open and entered the apartment. Now, alone in the large drafty room, he examined the walls with new interest. Solitude allowed him an attention to detail his tour with Benita had not. Now, the finer points of the room struck him with new precision: the intense color of the walls, the bowl of Jordan almonds on the coffee table, the fine George Washington molding, its dainty serrations cut to resemble the teeth of the esteemed president. Enjoying this moment of respite, he walked to the coffee table and, still unaware of Bell's presence on the sofa, took a seat, indulged in a yawn and popped a few almonds into his mouth.

The Barnacles' apartment looked better, Trot decided, in the middle of the night. What appeared in daylight to be chaotic, now looked almost tidy. The piano no longer hovered in the middle of the room like a benevolent whale, but rather seemed to have been parked for the night like a beloved sports car. Books that had been stuffed haphazardly seemed straighter on the shelves. Jigsaw puzzles had been solved, game pieces returned to their rightful boxes; sneakers, formerly strewn across the floor, now waited patiently in pairs, knotted at their laces. Indeed, nighttime afforded the house a decided air of calm. Without the constant commotion of arrivals and departures, the room seemed positively serene. Lulled by this strange tranquility, Trot let his guard down for a moment, leaned his head back on the sofa and finally dozed off. As a result, he failed to notice Bell who, rousing from sleep on the adjacent sofa, now stared at him head-on.

"Trot," said Bell. "What are you doing?"

"Oh, God. I'm sorry," Trot muttered. He lurched from the sofa toward the door. "I'm . . ." He trailed off, then offered a helpless glance. "I was just going."

"Trot, it's okay," Bell said.

Trot paused.

"But, if you're looking for Bridget." She looked down. "She's out for the night." That is, she was as far as Bell knew.

"Oh," said Trot. He glanced away as he gathered Bell's full

import. Flustered, he turned to face the window. Then, suddenly feeling ridiculous, he turned one-eighty degrees and darted toward the front door as though he might skirt by undiscovered if he moved fast enough.

"Don't go," said Bell.

Trot paused in the doorway and surveyed the living room.

"I've had a bad night, too," she said. "Why don't you stay for a little while and we can commiserate."

Trot regarded Bell dubiously, and glanced at the door again. But the longer he looked at Bell, the more confused he felt. "No, I should go anyway," he mumbled. He moved toward the door.

"Wait," Bell said. "Don't go yet. I need to ask you something."

Trot paused, one hand on the doorknob.

"What do you love about Bridget?" Bell asked.

Trot regarded Bell with genuine curiosity, realizing, for the first time since she'd arrived, that she, too, was in a disheveled state. What a selfish jerk he was for failing to notice. "What do I love about Bridget?" he repeated, as though making doubly sure that this was the question Bell wanted answered.

"Yes," Bell said, nodding curtly. "I really need to know."

Trot paused another moment then took a step toward the center of the room, stationing himself in a slightly less awkward position. He checked Bell's eyes one last time to make sure of her alliance then, going forward on this assumption, he relaxed his stilted pose slightly and considered the question. "Her confidence," he began. "At least, that's what I used to think. There's something irresistible about her conviction. You know that better than anyone." Trot trailed off, suddenly concerned he'd overstepped his bounds.

Bell smiled and nodded, encouraging him to go on.

"But of course, that eventually wears off and you're left with a real person and the question is . . . is that confidence real or is it just hiding something?" Trot paused again to ascertain whether Bell was still listening. Her eyes were sincere in their compassion, wide and unflinching. "Perhaps, it's just plain foolishness," Trot went on, "all this talk of your opposite. Would it not make more sense to find your twin, someone you understand perfectly, someone who understands you?" Trot stopped again. He could only assume that his feelings were apparent, that it was perfectly obvious to Bell that he was having a moment of crisis. Now, faced with the dizzying confusion of an honest conversation, Trot was confronted with new insight on his relationship with Bridget. Suddenly, he was hard-pressed to remember the last time they had felt connected. Suddenly, he was hard-pressed to answer the simple question: How on earth had he fallen for someone so . . . someone so unlike himself?

But Bell was too distracted at the moment with her own preoccupations, busy calculating how she might incorporate Trot's advice to aid her efforts in Blaine's seduction. Then, realizing that Trot had finished his passionate oration, she nodded thoughtfully, thanked him profusely for his advice, and sank further into the sofa.

Trot, now fully mortified, mistook Bell's distance for disdain. And punctuating his statement with a pitiful whimper, he muttered an excuse for why he should go, then hurried out the front door, riding the elevator in silence as though he'd just seen a ghost.

Bridget was sleeping when Bell returned to their bedroom. Having slept very badly in the living room, Bell craved companionship of any kind and willfully ignored Bridget's indifference. Even despite the rampant humiliation of her night, she desperately craved Bridget's company and, as she got into her own bed, made every effort, short of yelling in Bridget's ear, to disturb her sister's slumber.

Bridget responded to Bell's request with characteristic directness. She lifted one graceful arm from her side and extended her middle finger.

"What's the matter with you?" said Bell.

"Nothing at all," Bridget growled. She yanked her blankets over her head as though by yanking hard enough she might obscure Bell altogether.

Accepting Bridget's sentiment, Bell turned to face the window.

"Fine," said Bridget. "I'm up now. Tell me. How did it go?"

"Couldn't have gone better," Bell lied.

"Go on. Tell," said Bridget.

"Let's just say somewhere, very nearby, someone's feeling very rejected."

"Oh Bell, you are a master," Bridget said. "I expected no less from you."

Bell did her best to feign satisfaction then, anxious to avoid more questions, she cursed herself for waking Bridget and buried herself under her blankets.

Bridget, of course, was way too proud to permit Bell even this small lead. "Well," she lied, "for now two nights straight, you and I have been on the same date."

"Oh," Bell said. "I didn't realize . . . did Billy come over here?"

"Obviously," Bridget sniffed. "Unless, the boys duped us again and sent Blaine undercover." Bridget widened her eyes in mock terror to punctuate the absurdity of this notion.

"So it went well," Bell pressed.

"Very." Bridget smiled.

Bell regarded her sister with loveless detachment.

"I wish you had been here," Bridget said, "just to see the look on his face."

"Well, think of it this way," Bell grumbled, "in some strange sense, I did."

"Anyway, it doesn't matter," said Bridget. "I'm not interested in Billy anymore."

"Why not?" asked Bell. "With a few minor changes, I'd say Billy's the perfect guy."

"What minor changes?" Bridget demanded.

"Oh, I don't know." Bell sighed.

"What would you want to change?" Bridget pressed.

"I hadn't given it much thought."

"Oh," said Bridget, "that's a relief." Her voice rose into a sneer. "For a second, I thought you were going to say you wished he looked more like Blaine."

17

Fear of Mondays

*E*arly on Monday morning, another disappearance wrought havoc in the building as Mrs. Finch looked out her bedroom window to find one of the red-tailed hawks missing. The nest outside her window was less one of its new chicks. Having spent substantial time and money lobbying for the birds' safety, she was both heartbroken and irate. As many do when faced with these emotions, she immediately turned paranoid and arrived at a list of possible suspects for the crime of bird-napping. Since noticing the bird's disappearance, she had been entirely frantic, spending the morning patrolling the park with binoculars, papering nearby lampposts with flyers, and subjecting those unfortunate enough to be trapped in the elevator with her to her wide array of snide looks.

Finally, hysteria compelled her to drastic measures, causing Mrs. Finch to call Bella and plainly accuse Benita of kidnapping the bird. Oddly, Benita was not guilty of the crime of which she was suspected. The chick had simply grown curious of its surroundings and, following in the footsteps of so many other residents, flown away unnoticed. Indeed, it seemed the youthful contingent of Seventy-first Street and Fifth were privy to all the same temptations. They heard and heeded the call of spring and rattled their respective cages.

This very sentiment consumed Benita as she woke for school on Monday morning. At breakfast, she stared past her sisters, reciting her lines to herself as though muttering sweet nothings. She was like a samurai warrior, her entire being trained on her goal. Contest. Contest. Talbot. Contest. The words were interchangeable. A half hour before the bus arrived, she was dressed and ready to go, and so made use of the spare time to remove and press her uniform. But even after stiffening the pleats of her skirt to resemble corrugated cardboard, she still had several minutes to spare and so retreated to her room to meditate in private. Chanting, she removed her costume from her backpack to examine it one last time and confirmed with relief that she had made the right decisions. The long brown robe and cotton-ball beard afforded Lear the perfect measures of distinction and disarray. Bridget's miniskirt turned Regan into an appropriately impudent tart. Bell's tank dress made Goneril the ultimate dizzy debutante. And the shimmering green taffeta strapless gown "borrowed" from Belinda elevated Cordelia from honor to sainthood.

The school bus was torture for Benita, the greetings of her friends an unwelcome interruption to her pointed focus. Counting the red awnings on Park Avenue, usually a calming morning ritual, today seemed a futile exercise. She resolved instead to close her eyes and visualize her performance and, when she tired of this image, to imagine Mary Talbot, post-defeat, sobbing in a corner. When she arrived at school, she registered her attendance then took a seat in the back of homeroom. As she sat, she did her best to ignore her forty classmates and the uniquely irritating mayhem of forty ten-year-olds crammed into such an empty space. Finally, the bell rang, bringing the buzz to a muffled hush and allowing the homeroom teacher to begin her list of daily announcements. Yet again, Benita tuned out the din. The school had changed its policy on tardiness; girls would be penalized after only ten instances as opposed to the previous twelve. Uniform bloomers were required for PE class; regular gym shorts would not be tolerated. Due to the date on which Easter fell this year, spring vacation would be one week instead of two. As the list of news items droned on and on, Benita struggled to focus. But the final announcement reached her conscious mind and ratcheted her to attention.

Due to a general concern on the part of parents and teachers, this year's talent show would mark a departure from previous years. It was widely felt that the event promoted an unhealthy sense of competition and an unnecessary awareness of the real world's inequitable distributions. Therefore, this afternoon's auditions would proceed with a slight change of plans. The audition process would not require auditioning per se, but rather writing one's name on a sign-up sheet. Nor would any prizes be awarded for the different categories. This year's talent show would be renamed a "Talent Show and Tell." Every member of the class would be entitled to perform. Every brave performer would be given a commemorative pin and photographed as a group. The photograph would hang in the hall behind the gym next to the athletic teams as a reminder that every Chapin School student was uniquely talented.

Indeed, the homeroom teacher concluded, she hoped this marked a new era for the Chapin School in which students would embrace the multiplicity of talents in the classroom as opposed to engaging in a misguided and dog-eat-dog battle to differentiate themselves. Benita gasped as she registered the full import of the announcement. Not only had she been robbed of the chance to put Mary Talbot in her place, but she now had to find an entirely new way to win the contest. Outraged, she spent the rest of the morning in a silent, angry funk until just after recess, when she could take it no longer, she went to see the school nurse and, feigning a stabbing headache, procured an excuse to go home and commence an emergency change of course.

There is nothing that produces a more distinct feeling of isolation than waking in an empty apartment in which every other tenant has long ago left for work, school, or some equally pressing commitment. Even before Bell fully awoke, she knew it in her subconscious. Long gone was the solace of the weekend. It was officially Monday. The rest of the world had awakened hours ago and now was hard at work, enmeshed in exciting, unfolding plans for which Bell's skills rendered her hopelessly obsolete and in which she was not included. The rest of the world was very busy doing important things. They were phoning, faxing, waiting for phone calls and faxes, or otherwise implicitly involved in the flow of business. They were issuing directives, tweaking mission statements, honing in on the brand. Publishers were deciding to print a book. Newspapers were breaking stories. Studios were signing deals with actors. Cases were being closed. Everywhere in the world, Bell decided—that is, other than where she now stood—people were implicitly involved in, if not personally responsible for, the steady rotation of the earth while she lay, in her bed, wishing it would stop spinning.

Monday brought a whole new set of obstacles, presenting the unsettling reminder that she was the only member of the family with nothing to do that day. She certainly couldn't be seen starting her day now that it was nearing one o'clock. She might as well wear a badge that said PARIAH or stop the first stranger on the street and admit she was unemployed. It would be painfully obvious to the stranger that her life was in a state of hopeless disarray and she simply wasn't up to the task of facing his scathing judgment. Sadly, staying in the apartment was not an option either. The noise of her thoughts was too deafening and the minutes passed too slowly. It was as though the Barnacle apartment inhabited its own pocket of the universe in which laws of physics were suspended and time took a little longer. After spending ten minutes staring at the familiar gap in the ceiling, Bell reconsidered her choice and resolved that, perhaps, it was time to leave the safety of her bedroom.

As she rose, she was accosted by the strong and alarming sensation that accosts many tardy risers: that one has slept through the entire day and missed a vital commitment. This feeling is compounded by the knowledge that there is no credible excuse for your absence, but rather, those to whom you are accountable will know that you overslept simply by looking at you. Unfortunately, Bell's predicament was even more pathetic. It was, of course, impossible to "oversleep" when one had no commitments to miss. Moving very slowly, she stood and approached the bathroom. As she did, she was suddenly overwhelmed by a wave of nausea so violent it propelled her down the hall at the speed of a far more energetic person. She entered the bathroom at a sprint, jabbing the door with her fist then nearly fell onto the toilet, clutching her stomach as though it held a stash of precious jewels. Of course, Bell could not be wholly sure whether pregnancy or anxiety had compelled this implosion. Either way, she felt slightly better afterward and hobbled to the mirror to ensure that her face had remained intact.

In the mirror, Bell addressed her face, depriving it the courtesy of silence. "You're so fat already," she informed her reflection, "pregnancy is redundant." Her face, at this cruel proximity, looked old and wizened. Where was the hallowed pregnancy glow, the promised boost to her image? Her large blue eyes no longer shined as they had in younger years. The area directly underneath was creased by a perimeter of worry and shaded by dark circles that seemed to have been drawn there by a playful cartoonist. Her fair skin, once translucent and pink as though warmed by a nearby hearth, was now an odd, gray-green color that emphasized the wrinkles on her forehead with alarming contrast. Laugh lines, a development Bell had always imagined to be a mark of a long, happy life, appeared on her in extreme detail, suggesting not laughter but a recent crying spell.

The shape of her pleasingly circular face had lengthened in an unattractive way. Her hearty smile had flattened under the weight of her cynicism. What had she done, Bell now wondered, to speed her decline so drastically? Ten years ago she had been the kind of girl that strangers stopped on the street. And, as though this fall from grace were not enough of a hardship, she had become, she realized, one of those strange people doing the staring. Irked at the thought, Bell cursed her mother for condemning her to age so poorly and idly considered asking Bridget to share her beauty secrets. But this concept only infused her with a new wave of resentment, producing the unfortunate and ironic result of twisting her already homely grimace into new kinds of ugliness. Perhaps, Bell hoped, pregnancy took some time to work its aesthetic magic. Perhaps, pregnancy would solve so much. It certainly sanctioned, Bell decided, eating a hearty breakfast.

Cheered by this thought, she headed toward the kitchen for a healthy indulgence but as she passed the living room, she was distracted by a flurry of movement. She could not be wholly certain whether it was a hallucination. But based on a cursory glance in the room, it appeared that Benita was feeding the dog a twenty-dollar bill.

"What are you doing?" Bell demanded. She took another step into the room to aid her perception.

Benita either didn't hear Bell or pretended that she had not. "Go on, Charles, you can do it," she said. "Eat Daddy's money."

Bell stared at Benita for another moment to confirm that her first instinct was correct. When she did, she crossed the room to Charles and attempted to void the transaction, using one hand to pry his mouth open and the other to remove the cash. "Daddy would be so proud of you," she sneered.

Benita chose to interpret Bell's sarcasm as sincerity then, smiling as though she had just received praise for a venerable act, whistled her command over the dog, prompting him to hobble across the room and retrieve another twenty.

"What do you think you're doing?" asked Bell.

"It's not what *I'm* doing," she said. "Daddy's the one who's flushing it down the drain. I just think it's better spent."

"So this is some kind of protest?" Bell asked.

"Compared to Billy and Blaine," said Benita, "I think Charles is very deserving."

Flummoxed again, Bell tried to match words with thoughts. "What do they have to do with this?" she asked.

"I hate to break it to you," said Benita, "but Blaine's not after love."

"Oh, really. What's he after?" asked Bell.

"The same thing as Charles," Benita said. "Someone to play with, pat his head, and occasionally buy him dinner."

Bell stared at her sister now with all-consuming hatred. "Don't you have school or something?" she asked. "It's Monday morning."

"Oh, poor Bell," Benita said. She offered her sister a pitying look. "I have bad news for you. It's Monday afternoon."

Again, Bell heard a chorus of critics echoing in her head. Would she still be this incompetent, she wondered, when she was a mother? Newly determined to leave the house, she dismissed Benita's critique. Without further delay, she opened the front door and rang for the elevator.

"I wouldn't do that," Benita advised.

"I'll take my chances," Bell said.

"Okay, suit yourself," said Benita. "I, for one, would rather take the stairs than face the wrath of Jorge."

Instinctively, Bell touched her head as though to will comprehension. Suddenly, her heart stopped in mid-beat. She'd completely forgotten her promise.

"Apparently, you had some deal," Benita said, effecting both specificity and vagueness at once. "Something about working his shift . . . some sort of birthday present."

"Oh God," Bell said. She took an involuntary step away from the door. "Oh God," she repeated, then, to herself, "I'm a terrible person."

"Yup," said Benita. "Luckily, Mom covered for you. Or you'd be in hot water . . ."

In an instant, all the blood in Bell's head rushed down to her toes.

"If she hadn't," Benita went on, now relishing the look on Bell's face, "Jorge would definitely have been fired. Mr. Finch was not happy about having to use the stairs."

Surprise took its time to work its way through Bell's nervous system. When shock finally turned to comprehension, she moved from the foyer to the living room, locking the front door behind her. Indisputably, guilt is an empty emotion of questionable value, usually designed to comfort the guilty and rarely to help the victim. But now, guilt produced a productive reaction in Bell, spurring her to take incremental steps away from the elevator.

"Anyway," Benita continued, "I won't bother you with the details." Her already proud smile swelled into one of largesse. "Jorge just got to the building so you can talk to him yourself."

Bell stared into space for a moment, digesting her remorse. But, resisting the overwhelming desire to run, she planted her feet to the ground and prepared to own up to her mistake. Benita regarded her sister from a new stationary position, having taken a seat on the sofa to better enjoy her older sister's disintegration. Still, Bell found the inner strength to approach the front door. However, her confidence faltered as soon as it had returned. The sounds of muffled banter and whistling ropes announced the elevator's imminent arrival on her landing. Losing resolve suddenly, she flinched away from the door and hurried back down the hall past her bedroom, shoving the back door open for an emergency evacuation. Taking the stairs two steps at a time, she descended all the way to the sidewalk, then darted onto Fifth Avenue seconds before the elevator returned to the ground floor. Now, at a full sprint, she dodged oncoming traffic and entered Central Park on Sixty-sixth. At the Boat Pond, she finally slowed to a walk. Jorge's shift lasted until eight o' clock. She would take a very long stroll.

Outside, April made itself known with all the telltale signs. Everywhere in the city, people shed their winter clothes, baring limbs too pink to reveal, unveiling parts of their bodies long before they should have been shown. The air presaged the future months with gusts of summer heat, causing men to peel off their jackets, children to run in senseless circles, women to hike up their skirts. A troop of private-school girls paraded past the Alice statue in one neat, single-file line, their blue and white uniforms causing them to look like a flock of exotic birds. It was the kind of weather that confronted you the moment you awoke and filled you with the urgent desire to call someone you barely knew and drag him to a picnic. Whereas Fifth Avenue had seemed, days ago, a street made only for cars, it suddenly teemed with human traffic. Every inch on the horizon was devoted to merriment of some kind. On a day like this, Bell cautioned herself, she was seriously at risk. On a day like this, she was an easy target; she could fall in love with anyone.

It was that magical time that falls on a different week every year. It is the moment just after the first bloom, when the blossoms are at their most luxurious, and the rest of the trees in the park have yet to burst in full force. But even these trees seem close to shedding their winter pallor. The promise of buds casts the faintest shadow over their uppermost branches, tingeing every third tree with a film of light pink. Every single blade of grass demanded consideration. Forsythia hung just above the ground. Tulips burst like tiny trumpets. Daffodils strained to keep up. Tree branches seemed to reach for the ground to caress people's shoulders. One magnolia tree opened in a magnificent array, its flowers hovering on its branches like a hundred roosting doves. A cherry blossom, still weeks from its blushing debut, already flirted with springtime, each bud straining to the sky like clamoring baby birds. As Bell turned west onto the Great Lawn, her furrowed brow melted into a smile. There is simply nothing more glorious than springtime in New York.

Bell took a seat on an empty bench, permitting herself to revel cautiously in a patch of sunlight. She sat still, for a moment, surveying the park then she noticed a familiar presence. Trot sat just three feet away, wholly absorbed in a book, his carriage the picture of wistful defeat and decidedly un-springlike introversion. From his rumpled shirt, creased in intricate patterns, and the slightly wild look in his eyes, Bell wondered, for a moment, if Trot had simply camped out in the park for the night. Still, Bell couldn't help but note a decidedly adorable trait. Trot was so completely engrossed in his book that he unconsciously moved his lips as he read, forming the words, as though chanting a prayer.

"Trot," said Bell. "I forgot you and I have the same boss."

Trot stared at Bell, stalled by surprise. He was accosted by the paranoid notion that Bell could tell, simply by looking, that she had been on his mind. Finally, his face brightened and he remembered his good manners. Playing along with her joke, he added, "Oh well, you know how it is. Failure doesn't check the clock."

Bell affirmed with a sage nod. "Who needs a water cooler," she joked, "when you can have this?"

Trot matched Bell's earnestness with his voice. "Paychecks, insurance, retirement plans. Petty office politics," he scoffed.

Suddenly, Bell was accosted by a loud, mocking inner voice. Who was she kidding anyway? Failure required failing at something and she could not even claim that. Failure at something meant having tried first. She could not even call herself a failure. She was merely unemployed. "So, are you feeling better?" she asked, abruptly changing the subject.

"Much," Trot lied. He forced his frown into a weak smile.

"But spring has sprung," Bell announced. "The season to start over."

Trot mustered a hopeful look but skepticism weighed it down. "I thought spring was the best time to fall in love."

"No. Who told you that?" Bell asked. "It's the best time to be alone."

Trot offered Bell a grateful smile meant to convey two things: to thank her for her valiant effort and to silence her forced optimism. "Oh Bell," he said, finally giving up the ruse of composure, "How could something so simple be so complicated?"

"Do you want my honest opinion?" asked Bell.

"Sure," Trot said, wincing slightly.

Bell spoke before she could censor herself. "I'm just not entirely sure you and Bridget are meant for each other."

Bell regretted the bluntness immediately. But Trot seemed unfazed and appeared to consider it.

"Men and women are incompatible," Trot said. "Two totally different species."

"That much is obvious," Bell agreed. "The better question is which will be the first to face extinction."

"When did you become so cynical?" Trot asked. "At least I have a good reason."

"I'm bad at being in love," Bell sighed.

"Did you ever consider that the problem isn't love but the people you've chosen?"

Bell paused to consider this wholly foreign notion.

Trot stared into space as though mesmerized by something in the distance.

"Wouldn't it be nice," Bell mused, "if we could make requests? If we could petition evolution for a couple of improvements."

"Would they be for this lifetime," Trot asked, "or suggestions for future generations?"

"For the here and now," Bell said.

"What kind of suggestions?" Trot asked.

"Strictly outrageous demands," Bell said. "The ultimate wish list."

"I see," said Trot. "Would these wishes be restricted to changes on yourself? Could you, for example, petition this force—"

"Let's just call it evolution," Bell said.

"Could you, for example, petition evolution to make you handsome and rich?"

Bell adopted the sober, judicial tone of a child explaining the rules to a board game. "You could change yourself in any way that would aid your survival. For example, I wish I had stronger ankles so they wouldn't hurt so much in high heels. And I wish my knees wouldn't ache when it rains. You know, things like that."

"I know what I want," Trot declared as though addressing a store clerk. "I would like to say the right thing at all times, not just twenty minutes later."

"I would like that, too," Bell agreed. "I'd also like a better wardrobe. And while I'm at it thinner thighs, fuller lips, immunity to the common cold, and a better relationship with my father."

"Well," said Trot, "as long as you're not holding back . . . I would like a more muscular frame, more hair on my chest. I would appreciate not going bald and I could use a new pair of pants."

"I want new clothes, too," Bell said, feigning impetuousness. "And while I'm at it, I'll take naturally blond hair, a more magnetic personality, and the ability to draw."

"That will be quite enough," Trot said.

"And why is that?" Bell asked.

"Because, if I had to guess, I'd say this force——"

"Evolution," Bell corrected.

"Evolution, nature, God, whomever . . . I'd say this force works best for those who really need these improvements, who require these changes in order to survive, as opposed to those people who are . . ."

Bell nodded.

"As opposed to those people who are . . ." Trot paused. "Already perfect."

Bell began to contest this claim then realized it had been a joke, or rather a very sweet, backhanded compliment. She sat in silence, blushing slightly, beguiled by Trot's kindness. But suddenly she remembered Bridget and her smile abruptly faded.

"My next day off is Thursday," said Trot. "I have a good idea. We could go to the Museum of Natural History and tell the animals what's wrong with them . . . unless you have a new boss by then."

Still smiling, Bell raised her head and nodded vigorously then, remembering her commitment to Blaine, looked down at a nearby pigeon. "Oh no. Thursday, I can't," she said.

Trot's whole carriage fell. He'd clearly overstepped his bounds. What on earth had he been thinking? Seeking a purpose for his hands, he clasped then unclasped them in his lap then, desperate to find some new use, commenced straightening his shirt with obsessive attention. "Well, I'd better go," he managed. "I have work in an hour."

But Bell was not ready to say good-bye. "I'll walk you some of the way," she said. "If you want company."

Trot smiled and admitted that he would indeed, if Bell didn't mind walking downtown. So, ignoring their better judgment, the two wandered gradually south, strolling through Sheep's Meadow and past the carousel before parting on Fifty-ninth Street and Columbus, at which point Bell took her time walking home, grateful for some time to think and slow her racing pulse.

Billy paced madly in Blaine's room, making and unmaking decisions. His mind, in contrast to his tidy surroundings, was an unruly maze of questions. With a ring or without a ring? At sunset or at seaside? Simple or sophisticated? Daytime or dark? He was beginning to fear he was trapped in a nightmare starring the Barnacle sisters. Perhaps it was foolish, Billy decided, to heed his brother's advice. Blaine did not hold the keys to romance. Blaine's only credentials were a list of angry ex-girlfriends and a failed marriage. Perhaps, Billy thought hopefully, Blaine had overcomplicated the situation. Perhaps, he had only to speak from the heart and Bridget would come to her senses. And yet, within seconds of adopting this new optimistic stance, his mind was flooded with new concerns. The simple approach had already failed. He needed a showstopper.

Once again, poor Billy was accosted by doubt. An elaborate plan was the wrong approach; he and Bridget were beyond these games. Their love transcended petty symbols. He had missed the point, he suddenly realized. They didn't need fireworks or diamonds. They simply needed to talk.

Comforted, Billy hurried to his room for a quick change of clothes. Unfortunately, he was thwarted again. In the span of one day, Blaine had completed his invasion, adding to the existing clutter in Billy's room with several bags of dry-cleaned suits, five cardboard boxes full of books, an impressive collection of DVDs, and various and sundry props delivered from his previous apartment. Irritated, Billy ransacked his room to find a path to his closet, but the route had been blockaded by a large wooden armoire, forcing him to scour the visible parts of the rug for remnants of his wardrobe and to discover that the only accessible items were irreparably filthy. So, despite his brother's stringent policy on lending, Billy indulged in some free shopping with complete conviction.

He returned to Blaine's room and opened the doors to survey Blaine's closet. It displayed an array of oxford shirts, boasting every color of the spectrum, organized by maker and color. Billy took his time selecting, trying on various shades and patterns before finally deciding on a lavender one that, he hoped, emphasized his naturally rosy complexion. Satisfied, he walked to the mirror and assessed the goods. Oh, how cruel the years had been to his once-careless looks. He'd undeniably gained weight. The hair was definitely a problem. Perhaps he should approach weekly tennis with renewed vigor, join Blaine in his trips to the gym, perhaps even take up some daily calisthenics. Why would Bridget ever choose him versus someone who was clearly more handsome? And yet, despite his misgivings, Billy assumed a positive outlook, wetting his fingers and mussing his hair with a couple of violent thrusts. Still glaring at his reflection, he lapsed into his good-luck routine, widening his eyes and striking an effortless look of surprise as though he had just been stopped on the street by a very old acquaintance. Finally, Billy left the mirror and headed down the hall, forcing his face into a smile just in time for his arrival at the Barnacles'. Benita saw him through the viewer and opened the door before he knocked, administering a look that conveyed, in equal parts, loathing and desire.

"Oh, it's you again," she said, pushing the door closed again.

"Hey, kiddo," Billy said. "If you grab your coat quickly, maybe I can ditch your sister and take you out instead."

Benita said nothing, only looked past Billy, refusing to acknowledge his presence.

"Oh Bitty, don't be angry with me," said Billy.

"How can I be angry," she asked, "with someone who doesn't exist?"

"Now, don't be a brat," said Billy. "I know you still love me."

Benita paused to consider this in earnest, cocking her head to one side curiously then, arriving at her decision, said, "I love you less than a chair."

Straightening, Billy peered over her head, surveying the area for Bridget but, failing to find any evidence, he lunged suddenly at Benita, succeeding in lifting her from the ground and turning her upside down.

"Let me down," Benita cried. She flailed wildly at Billy's knees.

"Not until you apologize," said Billy.

"No, I won't," said Benita. "I don't care if you keep me here all day."

"Very well," said Billy. "Then, I guess you give me no choice."

Blood surged into Benita's head, turning it a deep crimson color and, still smiling innocently, she reached down and pinched Billy's shin.

"Hey," Billy shouted, hopping on instinct onto the uninjured leg. "Don't do that again unless you want to be dropped."

"Funny you should use that word," said Benita. She let this statement hang for a moment. "Maybe it would benefit you to take your own advice."

It took Billy a moment to understand Benita's implication. He was torn between interpreting the logic of a child or that of a crazed maniac. When her meaning finally registered, he sped the clarification process by rapidly swinging her right-side up and lowering her to eye level. "What word?" he demanded.

" 'Dropped,' " Benita said.

"What about it?" Billy asked.

Benita said nothing. "I will only tell you," she negotiated, "if you put me back down."

Billy placed her back on the ground with a slightly violent thud and then lengthened himself to his full height. "Now, fess up," he insisted.

"It's no big deal," Benita said. Height difference weakened her confidence slightly, reinforcing Billy's advantage. "I just wouldn't get your hopes up. You've got competition."

At this point, Billy reached his limit on patience and understanding. Bile got the better of him, turning vague annoyance into full-blown anger. "Benita, this is serious," he said, grabbing her by the shoulders. "If Trot came to see Bridget last night, I need to know this instant."

"First of all," Benita said, "don't shoot the messenger. Second of all." She paused for effect. "I never said it was Trot."

"Who was it then?" Billy shouted, abandoning all self-restraint.

Benita said nothing and wrinkled her brow in an impersonation of concern. "I just assumed it was you," she said. "Must have been your dead ringer."

Billy said nothing. He stood very still, immobilized by rage, bile coursing through every vein as though he had been injected. Surely, Benita could not be trusted. Her mission in life was to provoke. Surely, this could be ruled out as a bold-faced fabrication. In all these years, it had never occurred to him to suspect his brother. Blaine would never stoop so low, to such biblical proportions. And yet Billy knew somehow he couldn't rule out the possibility. This would certainly explain Blaine's behavior of late, his odd advice on the tennis court, his attempt to delay the proposal. Was it possible, after all these years, that a woman had come between them? Was it possible that Bridget would be the deciding match in their rivalry? Enraged, Billy left Benita without further discussion and hurried back to his apartment to have a word with his brother.

Unfortunately, anger had no chance to be cooled by time or reason. Billy found Blaine in the living room, languishing on the sofa, alternating his gaze between a magazine and the television.

"Where did you spend the night?" Billy demanded. He walked to the center of the room, deliberately obscuring Blaine's line of vision.

But Blaine simply shifted his gaze from the television to his magazine and completed his current paragraph before looking up. "Isn't it obvious," Blaine lied. "I spent the night with Bell."

"But I . . ." Billy said. "But you . . ." For a moment, clarity came to him but only for a brief moment. Within seconds, he sank back into a vortex of confusion.

"Oh no," said Blaine. "Did something happen? I told you to take a night off."

"Nothing happened," Billy snapped. Then, anxious to save face, he lied, "Bridget and I had a great time."

"Oh, Billy." Blaine smiled condescendingly. "You don't have to pretend with me. I happen to know for a fact that you weren't with Bridget last night."

"How do you know that?" Billy demanded.

Blaine smiled. "Twin's intuition."

Blaine checked Billy's eyes quickly for signs of discovery then, assured of Billy's confusion, turned back to his magazine.

Billy felt ten different emotions before settling into despair.

Finally, Blaine took pity on Billy and offered him his full attention. "How about some tennis?" he suggested. "I'm in the mood to beat you."

"What makes you think that would happen?" asked Billy.

"Statistics," Blaine replied.

"You're not better," Billy insisted. "We just have different strengths."

"All right, I'll give you that," Blaine teased. "Clearly, women like me better."

18

Telepathy

After his conversation with Blaine, Billy felt near madness. His brain did not feel like a solid object, but rather a porous substance. Every thought that entered his head bubbled to the surface for a moment then, before he could make sense of it, sunk back down as though pulled by the force of so much swirling liquid. In the hopes that fresh air would revive his spirits, he left the apartment, walked through Central Park and then hopped on the 1 train at Columbus Circle and rode to the West Village. He emerged from the train at Fourteenth Street, headed south down Eighth to Bleecker, picked up his pace to a confident stride as he passed Jane Street and headed for the Magnolia Bakery. The shop, a beloved powder pink hovel on Bleecker and West Eleventh, was notorious for its luscious and creamy cupcakes and accordingly charged its customers obscene amounts for the delicacy. But the overpriced and, Billy felt, overhyped baked goods only added to the mystique. At all hours, the shop was obscured by a line that circled the block, the patrons even more fabulous than the pastries in the windows. When Billy arrived, the bakery was just closing up. He paused across the street and remained there for a moment, peering through the window at Trot. Indeed, for all his professed hatred, Billy secretly admired Trot. Trot was so seamless, so effortlessly authentic. He was, for all intents and purposes, everything Billy was not.

Trot's height and admirable lankiness made Billy feel portly and stout. Trot, though he was in Billy's estimation insufferably self-righteous, was something Billy was not: a living emblem of an artist, slovenly dressed, tortured by his work, arguably hungry, if not "starving," and actually impoverished. Now, for the first time in his life, Billy acknowledged his entitlement. Money had never factored into his sense of himself. If anything, growing up, his parents' fortune had seemed embarrassingly modest compared to some of the people in their circle. But now Billy glimpsed the full scope and abundance of his privilege and instead of feeling gratitude for his good fortune, he found himself wondering if these gifts had, in some way, cost him.

The bakery was annoyingly picturesque, painted three different shades of pastel and populated by a staff of impossibly hip young adults. Each one was outfitted in expensive jeans and T-shirts made to look like they'd been wrangled from the trash. As they cleaned and closed up, they listened to obsure underground techno music with sporadic precious "oldies" thrown in for good measure. As Billy watched, Trot wiped down the counters and glass cases with almost religious concentration. Billy mussed his hair and untucked his shirt in efforts to distance himself from the Upper East Side. Then, ignoring a CLOSED sign in the window, he crossed the street and entered the bakery.

"Trot, what a pleasure," Billy said, forcing a cheery smile.

Trot stiffened at the sight of Billy but managed a polite nod. Billy should have worn his bow tie, Trot thought. The polka dots would have complimented the cupcakes.

Billy scanned the store, and found it confirmed his earlier assessment. What fun it must be to work, Billy thought. He imagined all the frivolity and laughter, the impromptu dance parties, the spontaneous food fights, the delving literary conversations. Finally, one of the girls on the staff noticed Billy and ushered him out.

Trot stopped her, nodding his consent.

"I need a cake," Billy declared.

Trot returned the smile with the minimum effort.

Billy leaned on the counter, Trot thought, as though it belonged to him.

"That could be tough," Trot said. "Unfortunately, we're sold out."

Billy frowned and nodded toward a shelf just above Trot's head. It was cluttered with a luxurious assortment of cakes, each one decadently smothered with frosting. "What about those?" he demanded.

"Those were special-ordered," Trot said.

Billy assumed his most accommodating look.

"Sorry," Trot said. "Store policy."

Refusing to admit defeat, Billy tried a more aggressive tack. "I'm willing to pay double," he said. "It's for a special occasion."

Again, Trot mustered a pleasant smile and began to shake his head.

Billy preempted his dissent, produced a fifty-dollar bill, and flapped it like a sail.

"Sorry," said Trot. He inhaled deeply in the hopes of suppressing his temper. "I don't know what to tell you. We don't make exceptions."

Refusing to accept defeat, Billy forced a smile. Was it possible that Trot knew the recipient of the cake and wanted to sabotage Billy's chances?

But Trot held fast, crossing his arms with new authority. Unfortunately, not everyone on the staff shared Trot's high standards.

"I'll help you out," someone volunteered.

Trot turned to locate the traitor. A girl on the staff shrugged apologetically, then rushed to accept Billy's cash offer.

"Thank you so much," Billy told the girl. He smiled triumphantly.

"My pleasure," she said. She extended her hand for the bill then hurried to the back of the store to fill Billy's order.

Trot stared at Billy, agape, forgetting his manners for the moment. Then he turned to follow his coworker, concerned he might punch Billy out if he didn't put some distance between them.

Billy rode the subway back uptown, cradling the cake box. He felt positively nauseated as he sat on the train, overwrought with the special havoc that accompanies a very long and drawn-out courtship. It was as though his heart had been removed from his chest while he was sleeping. Fortunately, the movement of the train lulled him back toward lucidity. Tonight, he would try the most traditional proposal, drawing on a time-tested cliché. Tonight, he would pay Trot the ultimate insult, using the very instrument of his torture to win Bridget's heart.

To be sure, it was slightly counterintuitive to obscure his grandmother's impressive rock in a mound of pink frosting. But he felt this brazen act bore the mark of all great proposals; it could be easily condensed to a one-liner and therefore retold endlessly. Energized, he sprinted from the subway station back to his parents' apartment, nearly knocking over his mother's housekeeper as he set off to procure his grandmother's ring. The jewel itself, even without such a presentation, could likely convince the coyest of women because it surpassed in size and lineage every ring in the history of proposing. The diamond was less like a rock and more like an article of clothing and sat in its setting like a queen on a throne, as though to remind viewers of the prestige of the owner's family. The round stone, like all cushion-cut diamonds, was cut like a prism. This gave it the distinct illusion that one was not so much looking at a ring as looking into infinity. The fourteen-carat diamond was graced with absolutely no inclusions and bore, in addition to its inherent weight, the heaviness of its surrounding facets.

The setting was a row of forty round one-carat diamonds that orbited the central diamond. The band continued this same pattern, matching the size and quality of the diamonds on the setting, as though the ring was too perfect to sit atop an orb of mere gold, but rather required a carriage comprised of its own perfect constitution. The gem, like all truly great diamonds, cast an unmistakably white light, and boasted the added luminescence of a sparkling history, its length and detail a precise function of the family's venerable generations. According to legend, Bisbe Finch, the son of a daughter of the Mayflower, had ransacked the globe for this particular stone, trying and failing with six similar specimens before finally flying to Africa himself to supervise its purchase.

Thankfully, Mrs. Finch cooperated with Billy's plan, having decided upon giving birth to her twins that the just beneficiary of her engagement ring would not be decided by merit or age, but rather by circumstance. The first boy who required the ring for a proposal would be granted the privilege of offering it, so long as Mrs. Finch approved of the intended recipient. Blaine, of course, had staked his claim as soon as he met Alice, requesting the rock for his young bride and, due to her auspicious ancestry, procuring it without objection. The ring had quickly resumed residence in the Finch family when Alice, despite her friends' and parents' exhortations, had returned the ring to Blaine, or rather hurled it at him. (Alice, though torn between the desire for erasure and remuneration, was finally convinced by her mother's snide assessment that, despite the ring's formidable size, it was really just cocktail attire.)

Luckily, Mrs. Finch's appraiser was far more objective than the Appleton family and wisely took the opportunity of Blaine's divorce to repossess the diamond. She had it cleaned and then placed it in her jewelry box for safe keeping so that it might have time to regain its shine and polish in time for its second coming. As a result, Billy was granted the ring on slightly more rigorous conditions. Not only did his intended need to receive Mrs. Finch's stringent seal of approval but, in the event of a less than amicable parting, she must resist the urge to throw the heirloom and thus risk depreciation. Should the lucky new owner fail to polish it regularly, Mrs. Finch made Billy swear to her he would take on this duty himself. And though Bridget Barnacle was not exactly Mrs. Finch's ideal candidate, she did offer a suitable dowry of her own and therefore, in some way, an equal and opposite capital contribution to offset the clumsiness of her name.

Once assured of privacy, Billy placed the glittering ring on the cake, adding to its ample frosting a shiny centerpiece. He was filled with a swell of confidence as he sat at the kitchen table, appraising his masterpiece, the glittering gem nearly but not completely obscured in its cushion of sugary paste. The cake was the perfect gift-wrapping, at once an ironic trivialization of the costliness of the gift—in keeping with WASP tradition—and a pointed jab at those meager men who actually had to work for a living. Moreover, it provided the perfect emblem of the cake's recipient. Bridget was the most demanding girl in the world. It made perfect sense that she should require a dinner of diamonds. And, even better, the cake was a jab at her soon-to-be ex-boyfriend.

Armed with this new potent weapon and the fragile cake, Billy left just after midnight, carrying his gift from the Finch kitchen to the Barnacles' apartment. Finding it open as usual, he took the liberty of letting himself in, and crept down the hall toward Bell and Bridget's bedroom, his heart threatening to burst from his chest. Sadly, neither foresight nor prescience were Billy's strong suit. Within seconds, he encountered an unexpected problem; the cake was not easily hidden. In fact, obscuring the cake behind his back as one might a bouquet of flowers, producing it with gallant nonchalance on sight of Bridget, would surely cause the cake to topple to the ground, hurling ring from frosting and frosting from cake, thereby ruining the surprise and botching the whole plan. Kicking himself for his foolishness, Billy scanned the foyer frantically but, failing to find an inconspicuous nook, set the cake box just outside Bridget's door and hoped for the best.

Unfortunately, love conquers all including common sense; Billy was way too anxious to take the necessary precautions. Charles, despite his age and infirmity, was still a pup at heart and perked whenever foodstuff of any sort was within a two-mile radius. As a result, he detected the cake as soon as frosting touched floorboard, and stood from his perch in the living room to follow the scent to its source. Charles, however, was only one of three complications. At the time, Billy was still wearing Blaine's lavender shirt and, because he lacked his baseball cap, looked decidedly foppish. This, paired with an enthusiastic smile that bordered on the edge of dopey, caused Billy, in some ways to his great credit, to look rather unlike himself. And to make the matter exponentially more complex, Billy was sighted by Bunny as he entered Bell and Bridget's room. Glimpsing only his lavender shirt, she incorrectly deduced that Billy was Blaine and, having just run into Bell in the hall, filed away the transgression should she ever need the leverage.

Bridget sat up in bed on sound of her visitor. "Hello," she said. "Is someone there?"

Billy paused at the threshold, seriously considered turning back then, inhaling deeply, he entered the room, taking tentative steps. "Hi, Bridget. It's me," he said.

Bridget deflated noticeably. "Oh," she said, then remembering her manners, "You missed her by a second."

Billy offered Bridget a pleading smile and took another step toward her bed. "Come on," he said. "Can't I still come in? Don't tell me you're still upset."

"I suppose," said Bridget. She pulled up her sheets to achieve a more modest pose. "But I really don't see the point. Bell will probably be out all night and I was just falling asleep."

Billy looked up suddenly as though he'd caught a whiff of a strange scent. Could Bridget possibly think he was Blaine? If she did, what did that say about the strength of her affection? And yet, despite his misgivings, Billy suddenly heartened. In an instant, he glimpsed a new side of himself, a new world of possibilities. Would it make him just as insidious as Blaine if he let her go on thinking it? Would it tarnish their romance in any way if he played along for a minute, just long enough for a reconnaissance mission? Deciding his good intentions excused the betrayal in advance, he silenced his conscience for the moment and perpetuated the deception.

"That's all right," Billy replied, curling his lips into Blaine's smirk. "You and I haven't caught up in a while. Mind if I stay for a bit?"

Bridget shrugged and nodded with a half-hearted smile then, satisfied that she'd communicated indifference, she said, "No, Blaine. Suit yourself."

On instinct, Billy fought the reflex culled over years of being addressed incorrectly, biting his tongue to prevent himself from uttering the familiar phrase, "Oh no, I'm afraid you've confused me with my brother. That's Blaine; I'm Billy." Instead, he took the chance to hone his latent acting skills and, ignoring his better judgment, launched into his best Blaine impersonation. "So, how's life in the trenches?" he said, simulating Blaine's easy good cheer.

"Fine, I guess," sighed Bridget. "A little confusing of late."

Then, without asking Bridget's permission, Billy took a seat on her bed. Surprised by this familiar move, Bridget's cheeks flushed to pink. She shifted her position slightly so as to put more inches between them.

Concerned he'd just betrayed himself, Billy stood up suddenly. As a cover, he made an unintelligible excuse about the unseasonable heat and sat down on Bell's bed. He sat in silence for a moment, pretending to look out the window. But he bolstered himself and attempted to up the ante. "Bridget," he said. "I have a confession. There's something I need to tell you."

Bridget displayed the palm of her hand with patronizing ennui. "Blaine, don't say another word. That's between you and Bell. I'm sure it's none of my business."

Billy paused but persevered. "No, Bridget," he tried again.

"Seriously," said Bridget. "I don't want to know."

Billy closed his mouth, defeated.

Bridget joined Billy in his pretense of staring out the window then, as though suddenly moved by the stars above, she allowed one note on the subject. "I will say this: If you break her heart again, all six of us will come after you."

Billy nodded solemnly. "I understand why you feel that way. But, in his defense, I want you to know Blaine has changed a lot over the years."

Now it was Bridget's turn to question her perception. Why had Blaine just referred to himself in the third person?

"But that's not why I'm here," Billy said, changing the subject quickly.

"Oh," said Bridget. "Why are you, then?"

Billy gripped the floral comforter and inhaled deeply. "Well, as a matter of fact, I wanted to talk about Billy."

Bridget sighed in a way intended to convey wizened fatigue, like a mother who has spent the entire day trying to convince her child not to eat his socks.

Sighing is a good sign, Billy thought and forged ahead, encouraged. "I realize Billy's done some stupid things over the years."

"A lot of stupid things," Bridget interrupted.

"A lot of stupid things," Billy conceded. "And sure, he's got some flaws—"

Bridget nodded vigorously.

"But, of course, he's only human. What I'm getting at and I am getting at something." Billy paused again, flustered. Then, impulse and desperation seized. "What I need to know is have you given up on him already or are you just waiting for . . ."

"Yes?" said Bridget.

Billy inhaled. "Waiting for the perfect pitch?"

Bridget tensed up and turned away but her interest was finally piqued. She shifted her gaze from the window to her fingernails then looked Billy in the eye and tried for directness. "Blaine, if you don't mind my asking, what are you talking about?"

Now, it was Billy's turn to avoid eye contact. Searching for some, any new object on which to fix his gaze, he examined a large hydrangea on Bell's comforter as though he were a botanist researching the shape of the petals. "I hope you'll forgive the imposition," he began sheepishly, "but I am his brother and his best friend and . . . well, I'm worried about him."

Wholly unsatisfied with this response, Bridget shook her head angrily and then, refusing to accept this as an answer, she widened her eyes and stuck out her neck, willing Billy to speak.

Billy had no choice, he realized, but to elaborate. It was his fault anyway for being so bold as to choose this mode of indirection. So, accepting the fate he had so boldly carved out for himself, he squeezed the quilted hydrangea into a tiny dot and, without further delay, launched into an extemporaneous monologue. "I think he's finally ready to be the man you want him to be. See, he honestly thinks that you two are counterparts, not just good for each other, but two halves of the same creature. For the first time in his life, he knows he needs to be with you. And he's scared . . ." Suddenly, fear grabbed Billy's chest but he forced himself to continue. "He's scared that his life won't make sense unless you're in it."

Billy stopped to catch his breath and steal a glance at Bridget. But a cautious look revealed she was captivated and so, gaining momentum, he took some poetic license. "Of course, he knows he's been a fool, at times, a total jerk, but he knows he's nothing without you, Bridget. And he wants to evolve with you, for you. He wants to grow old together. What do you think?" Billy asked, finally making eye contact. He realized, for the first time since he'd started speaking, that sheer emotion had pulled him down from the bed, that he was now on the floor of the bedroom, kneeling in front of Bridget. "What do you think?" he whispered. "Will you or won't you?"

Bridget opened her mouth to respond but stopped, reconsidering. The intimacy of their conversation was palpable, not to mention fraught with Billy's odd, symbolic position. "Blaine," she said, recoiling slightly. "This is awfully strange."

"What?"

"You know what . . ." She scanned the room nervously. "Talking about Billy with you . . ."

"Of course, I realize," said Billy. "But humor me anyway."

Bridget shook her head despairingly and looked down at the floor, and though she had had no intention of confiding, she suddenly found herself overwhelmed by her own confusion. "To be honest," she said, "I don't know if I'm ready to commit to anyone. Sometimes, I think there's something wrong with me, that there's no one in the world who would make me happy. Trot is a wonderful boy." She paused. "He's going to be a great man. Still, there's no denying that we're not quite right for each other and this is all the more obvious whenever I'm with Billy. When I'm with Billy, the world makes sense. I feel calm and happy. I'm constantly torn between which I prefer, talking to him or kissing him. When I'm with Billy . . ." She trailed off. "When I'm with Billy . . ." She paused. "Well, I am a barnacle and he is a finch. It's as though we're members of two symbiotic species. When Billy and I are together, I feel like no matter what happens to the world—big bangs, droughts, ice age, war—as long as he and I are together, we'd be just fine."

Billy couldn't help himself. He took Bridget's hand in his own.

Immediately, Bridget was accosted by all the usual sensations: tingling fingers, burning ears, dry throat, swerving stomach. "This is going to sound strange," she confessed. "Perhaps more to you than anyone, but when I'm with Billy, I feel . . ."

Billy nodded.

"When I'm with Billy, I feel . . ." She paused.

"Yes," Billy whispered, leaning closer.

"When I'm with Billy, I feel as though . . . I feel as though I've found my twin."

Billy leaned yet closer as though pulled by a magnetic force.

Bridget too edged toward Billy. Then, without warning, she flinched. She was suddenly struck by a familiar scent, a certain familiar eye shimmer. Suddenly, she felt so many sensations she thought she might faint. The protective layer surrounding her heart mysteriously evaporated and, in the process, seemed to expose raw nerve endings. She had never felt this way around Blaine, never considered him anything but a pest. Now she felt so different in his presence, it was as though he was . . . someone different.

An epiphany has the curious power to make time slow down. And yet awareness came on quickly as Bridget felt the unmistakable thrill. She needed no dog nor baseball cap to discern the identity of her suitor. She only felt this specific sensation around one particular person. Unfortunately, this excitement produced one unexpected problem. Billy was so overwhelmed by love that he failed to hear the commotion in the hall as Charles devoured his proposal cake, hook, line, and diamond.

Bell had been pacing the apartment in a state of helpless rage, making herself conveniently scarce on sight of Billy's entrance. Despite her lovely afternoon, her brain was a maze of conflicting thoughts, a pinball machine of opposing desires. The previous evening haunted her with aching precision, reminding her at every turn of her humiliating error and Bridget's maddening embarrassment of riches. And though she was loath to admit it, she was needled by one other distraction, consumed by an unhealthy preoccupation with her father's contest. Though she hated to play into his warped notion of a meritocracy, she was even more scandalized by the thought of someone else winning. She was caught in a cycle of vengeance and self-recrimination, as repulsed by her father's strange scheme as she was by her susceptibility to it.

For somewhere deep beneath the surface of Bell's hopes and dreams for her life was the cliché notion that by this age, she would be married. And though she cursed herself for indulging such an unoriginal thought, when she was honest with herself, and she rarely was, she was deeply terrified by the prospect of having a child on her own and sincerely regretted her lapse in judgment, or rather the excessive amounts of vodka and fruit punch that had caused the lapse in memory that had caused the lapse in judgment that had permitted the string of irresponsible behavior that had technically caused the conception. It didn't matter how many times she played out the scene in her head, informing her parents with a rueful smile that she had gotten pregnant and then married and that this was finally, irrefutable proof that she was dyslexic. It was perfectly obvious even to Bell how this flippancy would come across. And yet, despite the tangled state of the neurons in her brain, Bell finally found clarity just after midnight. For the first time since arriving at home, she knew her course of action. She no longer had delusions about romance. She would accept Blaine's proposal even if she had to say it for him.

Blaine was sitting on his fire escape when Bell arrived in his room. He had assembled an absurdly romantic vignette replete with Champagne, a checkered picnic blanket, and an impressive array of starlight. Indeed, in this particular contest, Blaine outranked his brother. There was no denying that Blaine was superior to Billy in the realm of courtship. His gaze betrayed just the right amount of care and detachment. The angle at which he leaned toward Bell was at once indifferent and possessive. Words fell easily off his tongue even before the Champagne. And his scent, even the slightest whiff of his musk, was enough to send Bell into seizures. Of course, it is folly to consider love a performance, to turn romance into an audition. Still, Bell couldn't shake the sense that she was in the hands of an expert.

Blaine toasted their history and Bell pretended to sip. But she might as well have been drunk. Even without taking a sip, she felt giddy and light-headed. Finally, she spoke if only to jar herself from a trance. "Oh, Blaine," she said. "It would never work. I far prefer the daylight to this corny starlight stuff."

Luckily, the two neighbors shared identical goals so neither one noticed the clumsiness of the other's tactics. Indeed, the intentions of the one colluded with the other's, blessing the night with the odd and unlikely coincidence of a mutual seduction.

"Pretend it's a million years from now," Bell said. She laced her legs through the grates of the fire escape to dangle underneath. "Evolution has been hard at work. Romance has completely changed. Men don't bring flowers anymore. Now, women are responsible for courtship."

Blaine clasped his hands behind his neck to form a pillow for his head. "That sounds very nice," he said. "I'll take a one-way ticket."

"Girls have to do everything," Bell went on. "Chocolates, wine, roses. They routinely make the first move. Even the proposals."

"Shocking," Blaine said, feigning horror. "What a state of affairs."

"Oh, but it's so much better," Bell said. "No more Sadie Hawkins dances."

Blaine played along with Bell's ruse, adopting the mock seriousness of a professor. "How very curious," he said. "In this place, this time in the future, are these women large and muscular?"

"Oh no, on the contrary," Bell said. "They're gorgeous creatures."

Blaine lifted his head from its "pillow" to rest his chin in his hands. "If you don't mind my asking," he said, "how do these creatures propose?"

"The same way boys do now," Bell said. "Lots of pomp and circumstance. Endless digressions, overly ornate anecdotes, stammering, hemming, hawing."

"So, all the traditions remain," Blaine said, "in this future place. A girl, for example, might get on her knees."

"Yes, she might," Bell confirmed.

Blaine emitted a sharp little laugh, surprised by Bell's forwardness.

Bell offered a mischievous smile. They were finally playing tennis. "Luckily," she said, "all the rules have changed."

"For example?" Blaine asked.

"For example," Bell said, "it's no longer frowned upon to propose without a ring or at a baseball game. And, though you may find this shocking, there's no negative connotation whatsoever associated with proposing after sex."

"Is that right?" Blaine asked.

Bell nodded soberly. "As I said," she confirmed, "things are very different. Evolution changes everything."

"And how do I get to this place," asked Blaine, "this time in the future?"

"You have to be very good," said Bell.

"But when?" Blaine demanded.

Bell smiled coyly and took her time answering the question, determined to enjoy ten years of delayed gratification. Finally, once she was sure that Blaine was sufficiently unnerved, she said, "You'll have to be patient. Someday very soon."

19

Wanderlust

*J*ust when it seemed the Barnacle girls had begun to reunite, a new rift arose, sprinkling them like confetti at a surprise party. Having spent the entirety of the night tormented by restless dreams, Beryl awoke early on Tuesday morning with such a bad headache that she felt exempt from going to school. In truth, she hoped to accomplish something higher on her list of priorities. Despite the frequency of Latrell's expeditions and the inevitability of his return, she was horrified by her family's response. Her mother's ineptitude was startling, her father's coldness was chilling, the indignity of their reactions surpassed only by her sisters' indifference. It was now the fourth consecutive day of Latrell's absence. She had no choice, she now realized, but launch her own search.

For days now, Beryl had been battling a very uncomfortable feeling but, with every day of Latrell's absence, it was harder to deny. What else could explain the vague feeling of sadness she had felt since he'd left? What else could explain the angry knot stiffening her stomach? Latrell incited feelings she was ashamed to admit. Even the rosebud-lined pages of her diary were too dainty for such indelicate thoughts. Sometimes, when she looked at him, she felt the same wet prickle she experienced while watching certain very salacious soap operas, the same guilty delight she had felt last summer, when she walked into her mother's apartment unannounced and, catching the construction workers unawares, had seen a man's naked chest. But for now, she had to confine herself to a safer realm and so replaced her feelings of love with those of irritation.

Latrell had certainly done his best to fall out of her good graces. The last few times she'd accompanied him on expeditions, he'd been decidedly ungrateful, mean-spirited even, blaming her for the slightest misstep, using her as the scapegoat for his disappointment. And yet, for some unknown reason, she continued to forgive him. He had only to pay her the smallest heed for her to forget the last affront, had only to smile in the right way to earn back her adoration. Though she kicked herself for the weakness, she was hopelessly vulnerable to him. He was simply better than any of the other boys she knew. His dark eyes always appeared to be plotting something wonderfully exciting. And his body; she couldn't help notice his recent growth spurt. His shoulders were now visible through his school shirt, his torso long but still lined by a thin layer of baby fat, his legs already coated by the finest manly fur.

As a woman, Beryl was blessed with self-knowledge, if not self-awareness. She comforted herself with the reminder that she and Latrell were not technically related. Prophecy also assuaged her fears. She was certain that Latrell would find his real father sooner or later and therefore felt justified in entertaining her crush. Soon enough, she predicted, Latrell would move out and her feelings would be less scandalous. Even so, it was all she could do to keep from bursting into tears over her breakfast cereal, from settling into a grumpy slouch, from jumping every time the phone rang, lurching when the front door opened. So it was with great relief that Beryl resolved to launch her own search. If Latrell wouldn't come back of his own accord, she would simply find him herself.

Reaching underneath her bed, Beryl produced the folded blue-prints: a detailed, encrypted map of the entire city of New York. Long ago, she and Latrell had collaborated to make this guide. "X"s marked the city's bars, schools, churches, synagogues, hotel lounges, and any other places one might find a piano. Places of worship were also marked with stars because they sometimes allowed wayward children to stay for the night. Beryl was not surprised that Latrell had skipped out, had even been warned in a sense by his recent insistence that he was close to finding his father. And yet despite the reliability of La-trell's flights and returns, Beryl sensed that this time her adopted brother had strayed dangerously far and that he needed her help.

Luckily, Beryl was armed with the telepathy of a twin. For the past few years, the two best friends had privileged each other with their every passing thought and, therefore, sensed it immediately whenever the other was in trouble. Beryl began with a quick review of Latrell's historic forays. Over the years, he had taken shelter in the most unexpected venues, among them the scaffolding behind Lincoln Center, the indoor birds section of the Central Park Zoo, the basement of the public library, and the gift shop of the Guggen-heim Museum. This last venue was his favorite, not only because of the pieces it contained but because it offered the added bonus of lovely midnight strolls down the spiral ramp.

Of all these spots, Lincoln Center offered the most luxurious ac-commodations, since nearby restaurants had generous leftover policies and in the summer, weather permitting, there were free outdoor con-certs. The Central Park Zoo also provided undeniable benefits. The birds' nocturnal coos and gurgles made for a pleasant slumber. The public library was the best deal if you could bear the hard sleeping sur-face. Simply by purchasing a library card, you could enter the library around five, find a forgotten stack, and settle in for the night. But of all these places, Latrell's favorite was Central Park. It offered an endless variety of sleeping nooks, among them the children's carousel, the

tunnel at the Bethesda Fountain, and the space underneath the mush-
room at the statue of Alice. And, as though these lovely vistas failed to
offer enough temptation, you were always within a sprint of a covered
bridge during rain or inclement weather.

The most difficult aspect of sneaking out was, of course, avert-
ing piano practice. After Beryl's boycott the week of Passover,
Barry had been enforcing the daily regimen with new and oppressive rigor. By way of punishment and as a practical measure, he demanded that Beryl play for ten extra minutes a day to make up for
the time she'd lost. He supervised this regimen at a distance, monitoring her practice from his office at the other end of the hall.
Even from there he made his presence felt throughout the hour-
long session, adding to Beryl's discomfort by sporadically bellowing comments.

"So pocht das shicksel on die forte," he shouted. And then, just in
case she'd missed the joke, "This is how heredity knocks on the
door."

As a result, Barry and the symphony conspired to shatter Beryl's
nerves, lulling her with its pastoral refrains only to shake her from
sanity with the next explosion. Beethoven's intent, Beryl decided,
was to write the musical equivalent of a car crash. The symphony
was neither a dirge nor a dance, nor even a military march. In Beryl's
mind, the piece was written to double as a torture device.

Barry saw no problem with this disciplinary mode. He loved
Beethoven's eccentric symphony not only because he himself tended
toward the madcap and melodramatic, but because the music told a
story with which he identified: the battle between fate and the human will, the war between nature and nurture. Beryl appreciated
the piece for different reasons. She loved how it divorced rhythm
from melody, how its strange structure served and still obscured its
narrative as though four movements alone could not satisfy its epic
proportions. She didn't find it madcap, nor melodramatic. She found
it, in turns, serious, like a church with broken windows, light-
hearted, like Benita singing in the shower and strangely somber, like

Central Park in the winter. Mostly, she loved how it made her feel when her father didn't mar it with interruptions. Her heart swelled in the modulating bridge. Her ears twitched during the second movement. Her spirit soared when the brass section surged. She felt the fourth movement's fermata as though her own heart had stopped. And by the last note of the finale, her soul was over-wrought.

Leaving the house would be a feat due to Barry's close monitoring of piano practice. Acknowledging the necessity for an accomplice, Beryl roused Benita before she woke for school to make an arrange-ment.

"Benita," she said, very matter-of-fact. "I'm going to need your help." She refused to adopt her sisters' approach to dealing with Benita, sweetening their voices condescendingly then submitting to her extortion.

Benita rolled over to show her face, matted by heavy sleep, then responded to Beryl with characteristic utilitarianism. "It's going to cost you," she said.

On reflex, Beryl turned away but she knew she had no choice. The urgency of the present circumstances ostensibly put her over a barrel. Deciding the situation forgave such a shameful act of capitu-lation, she regarded her sister with new loathing, and entered nego-tiations. "One night of piano practice," she said. "I'll call if the situation changes."

"Hmm," said Benita, relishing her advantage, "that's a tall order."

"You know the opening of Beethoven's Fifth," Beryl went on.

"Of course I do," said Benita. "But that second movement's a killer."

"What's it going to take?" Beryl asked, refusing further indulgence.

And then, Benita surprised Beryl. "I'll do it as a freebie for now," she said. "You'll get me back when I need it."

Despite the horror of owing a debt to Benita, Beryl accepted. Benita would stand in for Beryl later that evening, dutifully adjourn-ing to the music room at five o'clock sharp to play the piano part for

Beethoven's Fifth symphony as Barry monitored from down the hall, yelling like a sergeant. Benita would continue with this regime until the sooner of two events: Beryl's return with Latrell in tow or the discovery of her absence. With this in mind, Beryl dressed quickly in her school uniform and then left the house with Benita as though meeting the morning bus. She waited anxiously for its approach, tugging at her uniform and peering down the avenue like a late commuter cursing the empty tracks. Finally, the bus arrived and Beryl made her escape. As Benita boarded, Beryl ducked behind the bus, sprinting across Fifth Avenue, and slipping into the park, unnoticed.

It was Beryl's plan to search every inch of Central Park. She would make her way to the inner depths, trekking north up the lower loop into Harlem, stopping to rest and recharge in Strawberry Fields and the Shakespeare Garden. As an added precaution, she would spend every night in a different section lest the nighttime inhabitants of the park remember her face and give her away when questioned by the police. She would spend night one on the first tier of the outdoor theater, night two at the reservoir entrance, and night three camped out on the Great Lawn, adjourning to the tunnel near the Bethesda Fountain in the event of rain. Unfortunately, Beryl had never been terribly fond of camping and therefore found the prospect of three days in the wilderness more than slightly daunting. Central Park might as well have been the Amazon, its inner depths thick with forest, roamed by wild animals, and ostensibly out of the city's earshot.

For the sake of thoroughness, she began her hunt at the very bottom of the park, heading south from the Arsenal to the Sixtieth Street entrance only to turn north again on sight of the Plaza Hotel. She did, however, stop at a vendor to stock up on some provisions, buying an orange soda and a pretzel with extra mustard for added nutrition. No trace of Latrell in the grand courtyard in front of the Plaza. No sign of Latrell on the leafy promenade lined with caricature artists. No Latrell sitting in the lush grass field where the old pony ride used to be. No Latrell on the steps of the Central

Park Zoo, watching the seals sunbathing. Beryl stopped to consult her map and took a seat on the bench facing the zoo. Perhaps Latrell didn't want to be found. The search would be harder than she'd thought. At this moment, the Delacorte Clock struck noon, jarring Beryl from her despair. Despite the growing urge to turn back, she watched the stone animals dance around and waited for the song to end before heading west into the midday heat toward the carousel.

Despite her stated antipathy to Beryl, Benita forged a similar path as though the pain of separation from her sister was simply too much to bear. By lunchtime, Benita was certain she had developed a full-blown allergy to school. She had less than zero interest in the cafeteria meal of Tater Tots and breaded pork—its skin emitted an acrid odor that was vaguely reminiscent of Bunny's seder meal. As she picked at her food, she ignored the giddy ruckus of the lunchtime rush. Her time, she felt, was better spent at home focusing on her new course of action. Throughout her afternoon classes, she ignored her friends and teachers, instead staring sullenly past them, her eyelids heavy with ennui. Mary Talbot, of course, was the recipient of most of Benita's venom, which she expelled through a series of homicidal looks, unapologetic staring, frenzied notebook-scribbling and, when other students could be used as props, blatant whispering and pointing. But even vengeance failed to offer the usual pick-me-up. Benita marveled that she had ever found this life satisfying. Now, she saw school for what it was: a terrible waste of time.

By the end of the school day, Benita had heartened a bit. She spent the duration of her bus ride home considering the positive aspects of her temporary impediment. Perhaps it was a blessing that the talent show had not worked out. The venue, she now realized, was lacking in sufficient worldliness. Suddenly, all previous accomplishments seemed cruelly insignificant. Track meets, spelling bees, science fairs, and living room plays all shrunk from their former stature to seem small and paltry. Perhaps she should set her sights on a more universal forum, a starring role in a Broadway play, a front-page story in the *New York Times,* an invitation to train at NASA, a gold medal at the Olympics. Of course, she feared she lacked the time to attain these lofty goals. At this rate, one of her sisters could win. She needed to do something drastic.

So it was with some excitement that Benita considered a new ploy. She started by recalling the ten instances in her childhood when her father had been most angry. He had certainly bristled over the years at Belinda's gripes, taking on his combative daughter with a certain sporting delight. He had matched the volume of the girls' most violent squabbles, either in efforts to settle their disputes or simply to subject them to the same insufferable treatment. And once, though he didn't know Benita had overheard, Barry had uttered during a fight with Bella, a string of curse words so profane even Belinda had been hard-pressed to translate them later that night. But there was one moment when Barry's distress clearly exceeded all others. The loss of Barry's pet monkey, Harry, combined with the mysterious and likely gruesome circumstances of his disappearance to crush Barry so completely he nearly lost his grip.

Living with a monkey, though seemingly odd, had instilled order in the Barnacle apartment. Every day after work, Barry entered the house and launched into his typical regimen, calling out the name of every daughter in residence, followed by the name of whichever woman was the current matron. This enthusiastic if loud entry had a certain galvanizing effect, causing daughter, wife, and pets alike to rise to a higher level of attention much like a concert musician at the sound of the conductor's stick. One by one, each party made their way from the solace of her bedroom to greet him and submit to a tacit inspection. Greetings were exchanged, moans were uttered, and days were discussed in brief snippets, each daughter offering, according to her age and hormonal level, the appropriate amount of disdain for school, a summary of tests, races, or contests in which she had participated that day, along with a pithy diatribe on the cumulative effects of the mental oppression of being judged on external symbols as opposed to inner merit.

Then, as though mocking both the girls' resistance and their father's demands, Harry would click his heels in a parody of military attention, standing erect to the greatest possible extent given his species' typical posture. Point taken, Barry would smile and silently concede his excesses, at which point defenses would be dropped and the group would devolve into something more like a normal, happy family. Having successfully diffused tension, Harry would launch himself onto Barry's shoulder and administer a series of loving kisses that Barry, despite his fear of germs, was hard-pressed to resist. This was but one of the many tricks in Harry's repertoire. He could also paint excellent self-portraits using Cray-pas and fingerpaint. He could read, or at least, flip the pages of books. He could mimic a song perfectly after hearing it played a single time. And when a family member was feeling sad or had simply had a frustrating day, he could intuit this melancholy from the other end of the apartment and would join the sad sack to cheer her with a smile or to place a hand on her back. Everyone in the house was unanimous about Harry's high level of evolution. The monkey was not merely intelligent. He was graced with empathy, the hallmark of human consciousness.

The most compelling proof of Harry's mental state occurred at a more somber time, during one of Latrell's longest and most alarming disappearances. After searches of local hospitals and numerous calls to the police, the Barnacle house began to approach a state of emergency. That night, while Bella lay awake in bed, praying for Latrell's return, she was roused by a loud, screeching sound coming from the apartment below, in the direction of the indoor jungle. Hopeful of finding Latrell attempting a covert reentry, she rushed downstairs in her nightgown, running down the steps of her spiral staircase like a child on Christmas morning. Downstairs, Barry's apartment was

quiet but for a low, almost indiscernible hiss, which Bella followed
down the hall, creeping past her daughters' bedrooms.

She finally found the noise after a thorough search of perennial
blooms. Harry crouched between a yucca and a rubber plant, staring
mournfully out the window like a sailor at the horizon. At the sound
of rustling leaves, he looked up to meet Bella's gaze, his eyes revealing
sincere and entirely human sadness. But the most peculiar thing of all
was his odd position. His head was bowed toward the ground in an
expression of humble desperation and his hands were clasped in the
middle of his chest as though he were deep in prayer. Of course, the
family debated the exact meaning of Harry's posture, arguing that
clasped hands could signify so many things other than prayer and furthermore, even the most devoted disciple could clasp his hands in the
shape of piety without thinking of anything religious. Still, from that
moment on, Bella was unflinching in her belief in nature. In her mind,
this was indisputable proof that beyond feeling the full range of
human emotion, Harry was graced with an awareness of distinct
perspectives. Indeed, she argued, Harry was endowed with such sophisticated sensitivity as to be compelled by love and compassion to
imagine God in the home of an atheist.

Benita was certain that losing Harry marked the low point in her
father's life. In fact, as far as she could tell the event was more upsetting than his divorce. Bella agreed that the moment constituted a
traumatic event because she claimed it was a reenactment of Barry's
greatest regret, never having a son. It was this conjecture that caused
Bella to react insensitively to Barry's grief and Bella's reaction, in
turn, that caused Barry to suspect Bella had played more than a pas-
sive part in Harry's disappearance. Either way, the details of the
crime scene would haunt Barry for years. The empty stairway, the
severed rope, the desperate scratches on the wall and finally, the indelible image of a noose hanging from the banister, its loop just slack
enough to support two opposing notions: Either someone had untied
the knot and aided Harry's escape or Harry had untied it himself and

was therefore the only ape in the history of the world blessed with opposable thumbs.

Every piece of evidence supported a different explanation: murder, suicide, abduction, or the work of an insider. Throughout, Barry held fast to his theory that the crime was cold-blooded murder or, more specifically, a sinister cover-up perpetrated by a family member. Bella never flinched on her account, deferring blame to Mr. Finch. Bridget believed Harry had learned Bell's escape route and simply followed suit. Bell was positive he had taken his life to spare himself from the chatter of Bella's current dinner party. Some of the girls thought he had been kidnapped by Jorge. Others were more optimistic, assuming Harry had tired of his cramped quarters and simply skipped out. Benita, however, was certain Harry had remained in the neighborhood. Seeking the company of his biological father, he'd relocated to the Central Park Zoo and managed to keep his old zip code.

Regardless of the speculation, Benita was sure of one thing. When her father stared wistfully into space, he was thinking of Harry. Therefore it was not a large logical leap to devise this new radical plan, something that would earn her father's eternal gratitude, as well as the attention of the greater metropolitan area. Energized, Benita alighted the school bus with a new thrill in her step and, instead of turning right toward her own building's lobby, she continued across Fifth Avenue toward the park's Sixty-fourth Street entrance. The promise of rain gave the day the faintest hint of foreboding, but Benita was only spurred on by the tumultuous weather and quickened her pace down the Arsenal steps, heading swiftly toward the Central Park Zoo.

After subsisting for three days on matzoh, parsley, and hard-boiled eggs, Latrell felt he deserved a treat. In the past three days, he had canvassed every corner of the city, interviewing piano players at thirty churches and synagogues, fourteen concert halls, three college gymnasiums, a rec center, and an old age home. Deciding that his diligent work merited dipping into his savings, he turned off Central Park West into the park and stopped at the Bethesda Fountain to buy a lunch of a Coke and a pretzel with extra mustard. Exhaustion made him more brazen, causing him to eat his meal on the steps of the fountain in plain view of pursuers. He sat like this for a while, deeply enmeshed in his thoughts, oblivious to spring's first flowers, noting instead how many trees were still bare and brown.

Finally, he exited the park at the Metropolitan Museum of Art and ducked into the subway station on Eighty-sixth Street. Despite the length of the journey, Latrell had an ironclad plan. He intended to go to Brooklyn to check out a hotel bar on a tip from a friend in the know. According to the bartender at Bemelmans, he bore a striking resemblance to the piano player at a bar in Coney Island. Just before eight o'clock, he hopped a downtown express, jumped to a local train at Union Square, and then managed to transfer almost immediately to an incoming D train at Bleecker Street. Latrell had always been fond of this trip, though until now he had only made it with Barry when he accompanied him on his trysts or, on those rare occasions when Barry took the whole family on a pilgrimage to Coney Island.

The D train was hands down Latrell's favorite line in the city. It was like a roller coaster except better, equally thrilling and rickety but you could ride it an unlimited amount of times for the bargain price of two dollars. He had discovered this wonderful secret the first time he went downtown as a child and had found any excuse to take it since, even when he had no destination. First, it rumbled down the East River, making its way to the bottom of Manhattan. Then, suddenly you had to hold on to your seat as the train swooped up and over the Manhattan Bridge, forcing all the weight in your body to surge from your toes. Turning right, if you squinted at Brooklyn, you could see tiny people waving their arms, cautioning you to close your eyes before the sudden drop. Turning left, there was the sturdy skyline, promising to keep watch no matter how far you strayed from home.

Latrell emerged from the train and headed to Surf Avenue. Brooklyn's brighter light accosted him but he picked up his pace and forced a smile if only for morale. He stopped at a door whose neon marquis spelled out the words MERMAID HOTEL, or tried to, despite a malfunction in the "A" and "E" letters. The word "hotel" was a misnomer considering the building had made the decided de-evolution to motel. Still, it revealed its historical luster in its grand structure and gilded font, betraying, like so much of Coney Island, the distinct presence of the past. Due to its coupled shine and grime, it also carried a quiet admission of defeat. The Mermaid Hotel was one of many similar structures on the strip, once-luxurious summer resorts whose rooms had been quartered long ago to house a less privileged population. For all intents and purposes a welfare hotel, the place combined pomp and ruin in a disturbing ratio. The ground floor contained the remnants of a formerly grand lobby and, in its corner, a small dungeon that doubled as a bar.

The bar's dark interior and smoky air gave it the quality, even during the day, of the middle of the night. Its few inhabitants, and "inhabitant" was the appropriate term because these people appeared to live here, seemed to have occupied their positions at the bar for days if not several months. The pianist was an elderly black man, his short hair salted with patches of white, his height and stature saddled by years spent hunched over piano keys. His playing bore the unmistakable mark of boredom and yet revealed his expertise. His eyes, though obscured by the thick hair of a much younger man, betrayed a certain familiar distance. Despite the audience in the bar, he seemed to be playing for himself. Immediately, Latrell felt the familiar rush. He was finally standing before his father. This time, he was sure.

Latrell stood suddenly and crossed the room, anxious to circumvent his nerves. He stopped a few feet away from the piano, extended a hand to the man, and launched into his prepared speech.

"My name is Latrell," he began.

The piano player looked up from the keys, offering a fraction of his full attention.

Latrell stood very still as though submitting to inspection.

Finally, the piano player registered an emotion. He lifted his hands from the keys, stiffened his back like an angry cat, and stared at Latrell as though he had just paid him an insult. "Who are you?" he barked.

Deflated, Latrell cleared his throat, and took a deep breath. "Latrell," he repeated, then more softly, "Your son."

"Are you Brandy's son?" the man demanded.

Latrell regarded the piano player with mixed despair and confusion. "I don't know my mother's name, but I'm sure we're related."

The piano player said nothing, only continued to stare.

Refusing to accept defeat, Latrell held his gaze.

The two men remained at an impasse for several moments. Finally, the piano player took pity on Latrell, producing his hand to reveal, not the familiar birthmark but rather a scar that he claimed, with some pride, to have earned in a bar brawl.

Latrell did his best to remain stoic as he hurried out of the bar. For the hundredth time, he considered giving up his search. His family was surely worried by now and he missed Beryl an embarrassing amount. Still, as he headed up Neptune Avenue, he knew he could not turn back. Something told him he'd come very close this time. Indeed, he was only off by one generation.

20

Brittle Bones

$\mathscr{D}$iscouraged by a fruitless morning search, Bella returned to the apartment just after ten o'clock. Luckily, her hangover provided a certain advantage, a vague confused quality to her exchanges and minor feats of delusion. It also conspired to give her hope that Latrell might return on his own, that he would simply tire of wandering and, finally missing his mother too much, slip back into the building unnoticed to greet her when she opened the door. As Bella turned onto Fifth Avenue she harbored this very hope and elaborated on a fantasy in which Latrell was waiting in her apartment, completing the finishing touches on a "WELCOME" banner to weave through the banister of her spiral staircase by the time she reached the fourteenth floor. Sadly, Bella's hopes were dashed as she entered the lobby. Bunny was on her way out, nearly obscured by an array of yellow pads and other miscellaneous, suspiciously litigious paraphernalia.

"Any luck?" Bunny asked. She furrowed her brow in an infuriating pantomime of concern.

"No, but he'll come back," Bella said. "He always does sooner or later."

Bunny managed somehow to deepen her grimace from one of concern to pity. "It's sad," she said. "I suppose some kids are simply beyond parenting." Her remark paired feigned empathy with an inappropriate amount of good cheer.

"He's just being a boy," Bella said, taking offense at Bunny's implicit accusation.

"Yes," said Bunny, "this is true. Men do love to wander."

Finally, Bella's temper surfaced, robbing her of composure. "At least he's getting it out of his system. Better now than when he's married."

Satisfied with her retort, Bella pushed past into the elevator, comforting herself that it was only a matter of time before Barry cheated on Bunny. Sadly, Bella was so distracted by this delightful thought that it usurped her concentration and, already prone to sudden losses of balance, took two steps down her hall and, forgetting her renovations, fell into a two-foot hole in the floor, wresting the ligament from her knee, twisting her calf muscle into a braid, and breaking her ankle.

When Bell awoke late on Tuesday afternoon, she was cursed with a nocturnal animal's sensitivity to light. She also suffered such oppressive nausea that she forgot she was pregnant for a moment and, remembering a comparable sensation, wrongly assumed that she had consumed an inordinate amount of vodka. As she stirred to consciousness, her surroundings pulsed as though to a musical beat, sporadically bursting into patches of darkness and blinding color. Desperate for refuge from this maddening disco-ball effect, she tried covering her head with a pillow but this taxed whole muscle groups she didn't know she had and, deciding against a more radical move, she rolled from her right to her left side with the grace of a large sea mammal.

Unfortunately, this too proved an unwise decision. It only served to shift the pulsing light from her right to her left eye and somehow to bisect the bedroom into patches of neon colors. One such blurry patch of pink jogged her back to reality. She had spent the night with Blaine, she realized. Slowly, other fields of color transformed to reveal that they were articles of clothing: a navy blue square was her favorite pair of jeans, a lavender dot was the camisole she had chosen for its delicate straps, a brown circle was a leather clutch borrowed from Bridget, and a pink clump was the bra and underwear she had chosen specially for the occasion.

Bell's vision gradually returned as she surveyed the room. The area resembled a crime scene, personal belongings scattered across the floor as though they had been ripped off during a terrible struggle. Once again, she made the mistake of rotating too quickly, causing the room to lurch yet again and realizing, for the first time since waking, that Blaine was inches away from her face, staring expectantly at her as though waiting for the answer to a question.

"Bell," said Blaine. "Bell, wake up."

Bell opened one eye cautiously.

"Your sister just called," Blaine announced. "Your mother's in the hospital."

Finally, Bell sprung from the bed and rushed to collect her clothes, shoving herself into the nearest, largest garment in a desperate and nonsensical attempt to prevent Blaine from seeing her naked.

The sight of a woman rushing out of his room filled Blaine with uncharacteristic confusion, weakening him to courtship's most powerful force whereby a man gains interest for a woman simply because he is being ignored. Bell's hurried flight from the room was such a new experience for Blaine it managed somehow to twin itself with the sensation of longing, causing Blaine to demand another kiss and to secure Bell's confirmation of their upcoming date to attend a Yankees game.

Bell returned to her apartment to find it uncharacteristically calm. Deducing that her sisters had already left for the hospital, she indulged in a quick detour to the kitchen to enjoy unlimited breakfast options. Unfortunately, the kitchen proved to be another hazardous zone. Benita sat in her usual spot, huddled over a project with such pointed focus that Bell could only assume Benita was trying to camouflage her presence. Benita had long since abandoned the construction of the cotton-ball beard. She was now huddled over a mixing bowl whose ingredients were strewn around the room, their peril a precise function of their ability to be confused for food. In one bowl, there appeared to be several mashed bananas, in another, an entire jar of sunflower seeds, and in the third, a mysterious substance that looked like tomatoes but smelled vaguely like hamburger meat. A lesser sister, Bell decided, would attempt to confiscate Benita's project. A more paranoid person would conclude that Benita was trying to poison the family and thus eliminate the competition.

"I forget," Benita said, assuming a contemplative look. "Do monkeys prefer their food mashed or all chopped up?"

Bell stared at Benita for a moment then continued toward the refrigerator, deciding again on apathy as a tactic. "Aren't you going to visit Mom?" she asked.

"Nope, too busy," Benita said. "Want to know what I'm doing?"

"No," said Bell. Even Benita's questions sounded like demands.

Benita answered anyway. "Making breakfast," she said.

Bell relented and glanced at Benita's mixing bowl, attempting for a brief, misguided moment to determine its contents.

"I just hope he likes it," Benita continued. In one stroke, she mashed a banana with her hand.

Finally, Bell turned to Benita, offering her the attention she craved. Perhaps, Benita would evacuate soon for her weekly trip to the zoo. "Are you going to visit Harry today?"

"Nope. Don't have to," Benita said. "He's already in my room."

"Sure he is," Bell sighed. She turned back to the refrigerator to examine a carton of Chinese food.

"It's true," Benita said, smiling. "Right back in his rightful home after all these years."

For a split second, Bell considered the plausibility of her sister's claim. But she was quickly distracted as she detected an alarming brown film on the top of the carton that brought its date of origin into question. So, dismissing Benita's claim and her raid of the refrigerator, Bell closed the door and moved on to a thorough search of the cupboard.

"Want to see him?" Benita asked.

"No thanks," Bell said. She strained to remove an inconveniently placed box of cereal from the top shelf.

Suddenly, Benita stopped stirring and assumed a grave look. "Promise not to tell Daddy. I want it to be a surprise."

Bell nodded with mock seriousness. "My lips are sealed," she said.

"Thanks," said Benita. She resumed stirring. "Want to know how I'm going to win?"

"Not really," said Bell. She managed finally to nudge the cereal box from its shelf, succeeding not in dislodging it but toppling it to the floor.

"As soon as they realize he's missing, there will be a citywide search." She shook her head with giddy wonder. "There'll be news cameras and policemen everywhere. I bet it's already started. Then, as soon as the whole city is really good and worked up, Harry and I will come out of hiding and it'll be front-page news."

"That won't work," Bell snapped, engaging in spite of herself.

"Why not?" asked Benita.

"Because," said Bell. "You'll be treated as a criminal."

Benita paused to give this a moment of consideration. "Nah," she said. "Not when I prove Harry was ours to begin with."

"And how are you going to do that?" Bell demanded.

Benita rolled her eyes. "Because," she sighed, "there's no other monkey in the world who knows how to pray."

"First of all," Bell began, "any monkey can clasp his hands. That's what monkeys do when they're resting; it's not some special trick. Second of all, there's no way to prove what's going through his head. It doesn't matter whether you're a monkey or a priest, when you're praying, you're usually thinking about what to have for dinner."

Benita offered Bell a look of newfound compassion. "That's just what you think," she said, "because you have no spiritual center."

Again, Bell paused, confused as to which of Benita's errors she should correct first but, realizing it was already well after noon, she decided against wasting her breath and abandoned her search for breakfast food, resolving instead to grab something on the way to the hospital. Now doubly more unnerved than she was ten minutes ago, Bell hurried to her bedroom to change into clean clothes, bracing herself for what was sure to be a family gathering that matched Passover in chaos and volume.

As expected, Bella's hospital room was a bizarre tableau. The whole scene was, in fact, so peculiar that Bell wondered, for a split second, if she had stumbled into the wrong room. The room was filled with a ludicrous amount of colorful flowers and balloons, transforming it into the perfect venue for a two-year-old's birthday party. Bella appeared to be heavily medicated (at least, more so than usual) and was smiling at invisible things in the air. Barry and Bunny stood on either side of Bella's bed like a pair of proud parents. Bell stood in the doorway for several moments, deciding whether to enter or slip away unnoticed.

For some reason, the sight of all three parents—if Bunny could be counted on that list—produced a strange effect in Bell, causing a noxious bubble to apply pressure on her eyes and throat. It was as though the eccentricity of these three people and their odd customs and rituals were suddenly apparent when viewed away from the apartment, as though the outside world had stripped off their clothes and now revealed them, shivering and naked. In an instant, Bell felt like a teenager, her nerve endings dangerously close to the surface. Suddenly, she was

accosted by twenty-nine years of confusion. Of course, the relationship between parent and child is fraught with humiliation. Shame accompanies detachment just as anger facilitates separation. But in Bell's
case she felt the feeling was justified. Compared to the rest of the parents she knew, hers were objectively bizarre.

It had always been a struggle to know her place in between these
two realms; the world of other parents and her own seemed aptly
categorized as normalcy and madness. In some way, she had always
been taught that normalcy was a compromise, that eccentricity was
only individuality painted in a negative light by close-minded con-
formists. And so, she had tried to strike a balance, to find herself in
the midst of this mess, the result of which had been a strange mixture of confidence and self-hatred. Either way, the pairing proved an
unsettling state. And, finding the struggle suddenly too confusing,
Bell burst into tears. She left the room without excusing herself and
hurried down the hall, anxious to expel twenty-nine years of repressed emotion.

Thus overwhelmed, Bell was graced by an odd glimpse of clarity.
It occurred to her that she'd made a mistake, that she had been living
under a fallacy for several years of her life. For so long, she had be-
stowed her anger on her father and her pity on her mother, deeming
anger too vital an emotion for Bella's resignation, too respectful a response. But now Bell questioned whether she'd made a miscalcula-
tion, depriving her mother the emotion she was due. Was it possible
the pity she felt for Bella was simply the most manageable response, a
cover-up for her sense that her mother's failures were a betrayal.

According to family lore, Bella had once been unstoppable. When
faced with unacceptable delay, whether a red traffic light or Barry's
belated proposal, she simply charged ahead with her plans. According
to the demands of the situation, she had either marched across a busy
street or, in the case of Barry, presented him with a ring and forced his
hand in marriage. Her grandmother's ring, though far less formidable
than the Finch heirloom, was beautiful in an endearing way, a small
but fine diamond whose shine and color belied its modest setting.

Considering the showy jewels Bella had amassed during her marriage
to Barry, the engagement ring was a quaint reminder of a more humble time and a symbol of the prudence of her long-term investment.
But in some sense, the ring itself was irrelevant. She would have been
equally proud of a piece of tin, so long as it sealed her fate with the
man she loved and secured his long-awaited commitment.

Bell did her best to imagine her parents objectively. She had only
known her parents when they were at odds, had nearly forgotten
that they had been young, not to mention in love. But she couldn't
help but wonder if the circumstances had been similar to hers. Had
Bella forced the question because she was impatient to start her family or rather because, like Bell, her family was already in the works?
Of course, her mother would never confess such intimate details.
But Bell preferred one interpretation to the other. Despite her lack
of information, she decided on her favorite one: Bella had not been
pregnant, but simply impatient, so desperately in love with Barry at
the time that she had taken him off the market.

It had been years since Bell considered her mother as a person, let
alone a young woman. Bella was an emblem of authority, power, and
discipline for a time and, more recently, despair and loneliness. But
now, Bella seemed somehow separate from all of these concerns. She
seemed a strong, arguably even formidable, woman who had once
been an adorable, whimsical girl. Bella could be accused of many
things; she was indulgent, grandiose, bullheaded. But it could never
be said that she was complacent. Finally, Bell was graced with the
gratitude her mother merited. Bella had been weakened by disappointment, finally crippled by mistreatment, and yet managed somehow to maintain throughout her pluck and compassion. Regardless of
her shortcomings, Bella was an admirable fighter, the moral backbone
of her six daughters, a lifeline to her adopted son and, in every way,
the moral superior of her ex-husband. There was simply no disputing
the fact that she had traded her own happiness for her children's.

Of course, she had not always provided the perfect example of
strength and independence, nor had she been done any favors by

depression and alcoholism. But still, she had fought ferociously with every disadvantage, losing her husband to natural selection and maintaining her femininity in the face of so much sexism. Mothers and daughters fight a war of attrition that always ends in a draw, but by the time Bell reached the spiral staircase, the draw had resolved to a truce. Perhaps, Bell hoped, time would eventually restore her mother's strength. She and Bella were alike in this way, both of them under scaffolding, hopeful for transformations.

In her mind, moving home had always been a temporary fix. But it had only created more problems, causing her to feel even more displaced than she had to begin with. Of course, spending the night with Blaine had been enjoyable, but the pleasure was less like rapture and more like vindication. And, even more troubling than her ambivalence toward Blaine was the fact that another, rather inappropriate boy had occupied her thoughts for most of the night. Now, thinking of Bridget, sadness turned to rage. How could someone so fortunate be so ungrateful? Of course, Bell loved her family. That wasn't in question. It's just that love had trouble thriving in such close quarters. Finally, though the thought terrified her, Bell knew the solution. She would move out by the end of the week. After the last seven days, loneliness would be a relief.

Calming slightly at the thought, Bell started back to her mother's room but found that her distress had propelled her to a different part of the hospital. A sign for the maternity ward invited her to enter. It was an omen, Bell assumed, thinking back to her horoscope, from nature itself. Once inside, she couldn't help but slow her pace to a worshipper's gait and clasp her hands in deference for the abundance of so much brand-new life. Finally, she reached the glass window of the visitors' center. Each newborn, nestled in its crib, seemed to lie in an altar of sorts, draped with ceremonial fabric and seemingly lit from above. Now, for the first time since she'd discovered then promptly tried to forget her pregnancy, Bell considered the activity in her own body with newfound respect. Until now, it had seemed completely surreal, detached from the beginning of life, more like a vague, fuzzy concept that would remain that way so long as she avoided thinking about it too much.

Suddenly, Bell glimpsed the full irony of her current state. While she had been lying motionless in bed, her body had been its most active. In her very body, at this very minute, cells were growing, molecules were dividing, genders were being decided. It almost seemed impossible that she had had anything to do with such impressive productivity. How shocking to think she had accomplished all of this simply by having sex. Of course, at this particular moment, Bell failed to glimpse the full enormity of her new responsibility. But perhaps she did begin to see enormity's tip. For the first time in months, at least since the onset of her recent slump, Bell was graced with wonder, gratitude, and hope for her future. And though she knew it was unrealistic to expect to find inner peace, true love, a new apartment, a stable relationship with her parents, and a good job with benefits overnight, maybe, she decided, she could work toward these things over the next eight months.

Heartened, Bell rushed out of the ward and back to her mother's room. When she returned, the population of the room had changed. Bella was lying in the center of a small crowd, surrounded by three tall, muscular men all of whom, due to the fit of their scrubs, Bell could quite easily picture naked. Barry stood just behind the men, beaming foolishly.

"Bell, good news," Bella announced. "It's only a sprain." She smiled flirtatiously at the largest man in the group. "Have you met my doctor?" she asked.

"I don't believe so," Bell said. She managed an awkward smile.

"Doctor, have you met my daughter?" asked Bella.

The doctor shook his head and smiled, revealing annoyingly perfect white teeth.

Bell made the mistake of glancing at her father. He smiled back, winked conspicuously, and began to mouth something. But realizing his oafish intention, she averted his gaze, accidentally shifting it back to the doctor.

The doctor squinted back at Bell. "Bell," he said. "Is that you?"

Bell rushed to perform the traditional calculus required in such fits of amnesia, multiplying the passage of time with a variety of different haircuts. Finally, a name merged with the familiar face. Good God, she finally realized. The doctor was Duncan Schoenfeld. "Duncan," she stuttered, "what a surprise. How nice of you to stop by."

Duncan regarded Bell with genuine confusion. "No," he said, shaking his head. "I'm your mother's doctor."

Quickly, Bell forced her gaping mouth into a delighted smile.

"Are you around all day?" Duncan asked.

"Actually, I was just leaving," Bell said. Duncan's bedside manner, she decided, combined the worst qualities of a game show host and a politician.

Bella, craving her previous position as the center of attention, interrupted the reunion. "Isn't this room lovely?" she demanded. "It's the most expensive part of the hotel."

"*Hospital,* Mom," Bell said.

Everyone in the room laughed except for Bell, compounding her sense that life was a joke and she was the butt of it.

Now it was Barry's turn to change the subject and he did so with characteristic tact. "Dr. Shoenfeld," he began. He paused in search of the most concise phrasing. "My daughter Bell is still single. You two should go out on a date."

Mortification feels the same no matter what your age. It races to the head at half the speed at which it moves to the heart. All at once, Bell lost her breath and her ability to speak. She was endowed however with the momentary wisdom emergency affords and somehow knew to evacuate. Refusing to acknowledge her father's cloddish attempt at matchmaking, she bid her family a proud farewell and hurried out of the room, stopping only to kiss her mother good-bye and to muster a frazzled grunt when Duncan asked for her number.

Even a full hour later, Bell was still shaken by the encounter. She turned onto Fifth in a bemused daze, barely noticing her location as she entered the lobby of the building. As a result, she was unprepared for yet another confrontation. Forgetting her self-imposed quarantine, she found herself in the elevator, inches from Jorge. "Jorge!" she began. "I'm so sorry. How can I make it up to you?" Cringing, Bell backed into the corner.

Finally, Jorge spoke. "I could have been fired," he whispered.

"I know," Bell said. "I'm a terrible person. I don't know what I was thinking."

Jorge said nothing. He only sniffed and stared more intently at the wall.

"If it makes any difference, I didn't forget," Bell tried.

Jorge cocked his head, curious to hear the excuse.

"I overslept," Bell whispered. She regretted saying it immediately. Even without seeing Jorge's face, she could discern a small shudder.

The elevator ride to the thirteenth floor took twice as long that day, as Bell fidgeted first with the buttons on her shirt and then with change in her pocket. Jorge said nothing. He only stood, silent and condemning. When they reached the landing, the two parted with the coldness of strangers.

Bell lingered in the foyer for another moment, her heart heavy with remorse, debating an appropriate response to her unforgiveable error. Perhaps she could win back Jorge's trust with a delicious homemade baked good. Perhaps she could fashion an olive branch from Benita's crown of thorns. She suspected any meaningful apology would require the passage of time. Still, she yearned from the depths of her soul to make something up to someone. Overwhelmed by this urge, she turned her attention to her mother. Renewed, she rushed down the hall and sprinted up the spiral staircase, determined to sweep Bella's apartment for its store of lost forks.

Bell's tour of Bella's apartment was, in essence, a tour of her childhood, a series of memories relived through forgotten artifacts. A thorough scour of the space under the sofa reaped an army of pens and pencils and a folded program from a Broadway show. A scour of the area behind the stove yielded miniature cakes from her first dollhouse, a pair of scissors, and a crazy straw. In the drawers of an end table in the living room, she found a sixth-grade math notebook, a screwdriver, and a tower of Post-it notes. A thorough search of a filing cabinet yielded six identical birth announcements mounted with pink grosgrain ribbon. She found a pair of ballet slippers tucked behind a bookshelf. But best of all, in all of these places—as well as behind the refrigerator, underneath the dining room radiator, and in a coffee cup used to store pens—Bell recovered a complete set of sterling silver Christofle forks, every single one of the utensils her mother had misplaced over the years.

Satisfied with her scour, Bell amassed her findings then searched the house for one last item with which to complete her gift. She ducked into the storage room and traversed the treacherous path to the sewing box, removed two feet of red ribbon, then tied a bow under the forks' prongs. She stalled for a moment, debating whether the gesture was too frivolous then, satisfied with her effort, left the bizarre gift at the door of her mother's bedroom. As she left, she contemplated leaving a letter along with the gift but, uncertain as to whether the letter should be one of explanation, thanks, or apology, she finally resolved to let the forks speak for themselves. Mere words seemed an insignificant means with which to convey her gratitude and regret, to acknowledge her desire to mend their relationship.

Satisfied with her gesture, Bell descended toward her apartment and hurried down the hall, anxious to spend the rest of the day in the privacy of her bedroom. Sadly, she was deprived of this small measure of relief. Bridget sat in the middle of the floor, looking suitably helpless, seemingly marooned by luggage. She appeared to have two opposing goals: refilling her squadron of bags with clothes and muttering to herself.

"What are you doing?" Bell demanded.

Bridget stared at her bags as though at a funeral pyre. "What does it look like?" she barked. "I'm getting the hell out of here."

Bell said nothing. She only stared at Bridget, trying to decide whether she felt sadness or elation.

"How could I ever love someone who would deceive me like that?" Bridget whispered. "And to think, I was even considering . . ." Then, in closing, "The little bastard."

Bell simply nodded and tried to assume an appropriately commiserative look.

"I've made a terrible mistake," Bridget said. And then, in conclusion, "Will you help me pack? I'm going back to Trot." At this, she buried her face in her hands, resumed quietly moaning, then looked up suddenly and shook her head in response to an inaudible question.

Bell stood still for several moments, taking in Bridget's last announcement. Yet again, she was overwhelmed by conflicting emotions. Dropping slowly to the floor, she sat down beside Bridget and tried to examine how she felt. But now she was accosted by a new sensation that—if she didn't know any better—she would identify as a dull ache in her heart.

As Bunny had told Barry countless times, she was impossible to deceive. She would know, she claimed, within a matter of hours if he ever cheated on her. His recent behavior had been suspicious enough of late as to cause her to meet privately with her lawyer and to consult her prenuptial agreement. In matters of the heart, Bunny claimed, she was as sensitive to clues as a cook was to spice, capable of smelling even the most mild of deceptions, even before they happened. Usually, when a woman makes this claim, she means it literally; she smells another woman's perfume or detects smoke on her husband's clothes. But for Bunny, the scent of betrayal was subtle. She smelled peppermint on Barry's tongue and, noting the disparity between the fresh scent and his typically terrible breath, she immediately deduced the reason for the change in his oral hygiene. She quickly found confirmation of her suspicions when she ransacked his pants for other evidence and found a matchbook in his pocket from what was clearly the site of untold debauchery, the Mermaid Hotel.

Convinced of her hypothesis, she stared at the matchbook for a moment then paced purposefully down the hall and climbed Bella's spiral staircase. Unfortunately, by the time she made it to the fourteenth floor, she ran out of resolve and collapsed in a sniveling heap. Bella searched her apartment for several minutes before locating the source of the noise. Finally, she found Bunny at the top of her stairs, huddled in the fetal position.

"Oh Bella," wailed Bunny, "I'm so ashamed. I should have listened to you." Grabbing hold of the banister, Bunny lifted herself from the floor and then looked at Bella, her nose glistening and her eyes streaked with mascara.

Bella was conflicted for a moment: Should a first wife feel compassion for a second wife, particularly when the second wife was the one for whom she had been ditched? Of course, it was entirely within her rights to turn Bunny away. But Bella was blessed with a big kind heart and, of course, there was something deliciously satisfying about seeing Bunny so contrite and desperate.

"I can't believe it," Bunny sniffled, tipping toward Bella.

Instinctively, Bella opened her arms.

Bunny burrowed herself into Bella's shoulder and began sobbing uncontrollably. "Bella," she whimpered, "I don't know what to do. I never thought it would be me."

"There, there," Bella said, patting Bunny's back, "none of us ever do."

"I'm one of them now," Bunny whispered, "those women who think they're immune. Except I have no right to complain because I'm guilty, too." Bunny stopped talking in order to exhale for the first time since entering the apartment.

Bella was forced to concede Bunny's point. Her previous role as a home-wrecker earned her only measured sympathy. "Hush," Bella said, "it's going to be fine. He's just going through a phase."

Bunny sniffled then raised her volume. "And an entire generation of women."

"What can I do to help?" Bella asked. Once again, indignation surfaced. There was a name for Bunny's situation. It was called "just desserts."

"Nothing," Bunny whimpered. "You've already done too much." She turned again to face the stairs and bolstered herself for her return trip but she broke down again before she could take her first step. When she turned back to face Bella, she was in a pitiful state. "Oh Bella," she said, "I hate to ask, but do you mind if I stay a few nights?"

It was decided, despite the odd circumstance of the arrangement, that Bunny would stay with Bella until the sooner of two things: either she figured out her next move or served Barry with papers. In truth, Bella was happy to have a new houseguest, relieved by the companionship and the distraction from Latrell's absence. The two women spent the remainder of the afternoon trading stories over tea, creating a voodoo doll of sorts whereby they listed Barry's worst traits and his most valuable assets.

Of course, for all her criticisms of Barry, Bunny was far from blameless herself. And because she was far from bad looking, arguably even quite sexy to younger or foreign men, she had had no trouble, over the years, enacting various, she felt, compensatory seductions. During her short marriage to Barry she had sought such revenge several times, indulging in a series of crushes on members of the extended Barnacle family. She felt this was justified not only due to the laws of quid pro quo but because every one of her paramours, each one boasting a different trade, had taught her a different skill. Bella's carpenter, Dennis, educated her about the physics of furniture, imparting useful information, like which household objects held more weight, chairs or tables. Her kabbalah teacher shared various tricks on an enhanced experience in prayer, providing Bunny with firsthand tips on achieving ecstasy. Her masseuse taught her the five basic tenets of inner body relaxation. And once in a brief, if thwarted encounter, Billy Finch gave her a private tennis lesson, allowing Bunny, over the course of one very informative session, to bring her service and return from the level of novice to expert.

Because these various teachers had proven so edifying over the years, Bunny had no qualms seeking further instruction during this time of need. So, desperate for a quick refresher course on flirtation, she employed her most alluring vibrato and called Billy to schedule a second lesson. Billy declined but was ultimately persuaded to be a good sport, joining Bunny for a quick drink at Bemelmans.

She arrived before Billy and chose a private corner booth.

"Oh, Billy," Bunny began, stirring her drink with overzealous attention. "Enjoy your youth while it lasts. Old age just kind of happens."

"Please," scoffed Billy. "Last time I checked, you were only two years older than me."

"Still," sighed Bunny, "when a man treats you badly it puts years on your life. But let's not talk about boring things. Give me some good gossip. Bridget never tells me anything. Fill me in on your romance."

"Well." Billy swirled the ice in his drink and then held the glass up to his face as though to examine a fleck of dirt. Finally, he replaced the glass on the table. "I'm planning on proposing."

"When?" asked Bunny.

"Don't get too excited. I've already done it twice."

"And what happened," Bunny demanded.

He sighed. "I've got two strikes."

Suddenly, Bunny sat upright and leaned very close to Billy. "Are you going to try again?" she asked.

Billy nodded emphatically.

"When?" Bunny asked.

Billy grinned proudly. "Literally any minute."

"No," gasped Bunny. "What are you waiting for?"

"I'm waiting for the perfect moment."

Bunny wrinkled her brow and stared at Billy for a long moment. "Oh no," she said and looked guiltily at the floor, as if to imply that she was cursed with a terrible secret.

"What is it?" asked Billy.

"It's nothing," Bunny said. She shifted awkwardly in her seat and looked back at Billy, pairing innocence with obvious omniscience then, though Billy had not posed another question, repeated, "It's nothing. Really."

"Bunny," said Billy. He widened his eyes, entreating her to confess.

Bunny gestured frantically for the waiter and waited for him to return to their table. Finally, after issuing overly detailed instructions for the correct ingredients for her drink, she squared her shoulders and offered Billy a look of condolence. "Two nights ago," she said, "I saw Blaine go into Bridget's room."

"What?" Billy snapped. "That's ludicrous. Why would he do that?"

"I'm sorry," Bunny said. "But it's the truth. I thought you'd want to know."

Billy said nothing for a moment, considering Bunny's claim. "Oh, sure," he said. "That makes perfect sense. He was probably visiting Bell."

Bunny gave her head a tiny, almost indiscernible shake. "Bell was out of the house," she said.

"But that's impossible," Billy said, regarding Bunny with new suspicion. "Blaine would never . . . Bridget would never . . . That night, I was . . ."

Bunny nodded gently as though humoring a child. "You have no idea how much it pains me to tell you this," she said.

"There's simply no way," Billy insisted. He looked up at Bunny helplessly as though imploring her to change her mind. "I'm sure it's a misunderstanding," he snipped. "I'll just talk to her myself."

Bunny placed her hand on Billy's and offered a pitying look. "I'm so sorry," she whispered. "This must really smart."

Billy opened his mouth to respond, but quickly stopped himself, resolving that further protest would only be construed as poor sportsmanship. Instead, he sank deeper into his chair so that he was eye level with his drink, then signaled the waiter to order one, perhaps two more drinks.

21

High IQ

In Beth's opinion, it was so absurd as to exceed the realm of truth. She had not even thought it possible to be suspended from college for doing too much work. And yet, she had been asked to take a short "period of reflection" in order to gain the appropriate remorse and write a short essay to the disciplinary committee explaining why she had thought herself exempt from the science lab's regular hours of operation, despite her three years in the department, the lenient stance of her professor, and the clearly written schedule printed on the door. Of course, the blow was worsened by Beth's sense of her research. She felt she was at a precipice, finally nearing the sparkling conclusion she had sought for years. Still, as she rode the train from Boston back to New York, she did her best to find the benefits of her unexpected dismissal. Perhaps, it would be a welcome change to be home with her sisters. At the very least, she could further investigate the second area of her scientific interest: the effect of too many co-habitating females on homicidal tendencies.

Beth returned to the apartment just before dinner on Tuesday night. Within minutes, she experienced an attack of claustrophobia that caused her to feel as though she were trapped in a rapidly shrinking elevator. Breathing deeply, she muttered a greeting to the family then, after expressing her deep ambivalence about being home, hurried down the hall to her bedroom to mutter in private. Immediately, she found a new outlet for her anxiety. How was it possible, she wondered, for her bedroom to smell even worse than when she'd left? Why did Belinda feel there was an inverse relationship between having good hygiene and having a good time? Indignant, Beth dropped her bags on the floor and commenced a cleaning tour of the room. But even after a heartfelt scour, the room still reeked of scented candles, dried beer, and stale smoke. Irritated, she opened the window and waved air into the room. As she peered outside, her foul mood corrupted her surroundings. The usually picturesque park looked tiny and theatrical, not grand and dignified as it did in daylight. The budding trees seemed to have been placed there by set designers, the clumps of flowers painted on by sentimental sketch artists. Closing the window, Beth faced her room and contemplated a new pastime, wondering idly what it would be like to live alone.

But, despite the ample books on the shelves and the abundant distractions of the apartment, less than an hour after returning, Beth was excruciatingly bored. She had read everything in the library. She had examined every item in the collections. She had no interest in television. Her mind, she feared, would turn to mush without the stimulation of her work. Her sisters did little to help the situation. Bell had evacuated her bedroom to allow Bridget the space in which to pack in private, turning the living room into her own private clubhouse. She was now lying in front of the television as though held there by a magnetic force. Thinking ahead as to ways to avoid running into her sisters, Beth made a quick foray into the kitchen and stocked up on enough provisions to last her several days. Thus equipped, she hurried back to her bedroom and remained there in a self-imposed quarantine, scanning her shelves for distraction before finally settling on a plan. She would classify and label every item in the apartment's poorly organized collections beginning with the shells, since they were closest to her bedroom and her heart. Relieved, she entered the shell collection with the intention of passing several quiet hours dismantling the shelves and organizing them by color and alphabetization.

But even before a cursory scan of the cowries and the conchs, Bell sensed something was amiss. She was now a full three inches taller than the last time she had been in the room and, as a result, viewed her father's prized prehistoric barnacle from a very different perspective. Before, she had stood at a slight tilt from the beloved specimens and was forced to crane her neck to see their details or tiptoe to remove them from the shelves. Now, she stood at eye level with the odd, ridged creature and was therefore endowed with a far more intimate knowledge of its parts. Careful not to upset the other shells on the shelves, she removed the prized barnacle, the first recorded specimen on record, dislodging it from its place on the shelf to examine its lovely purple shell and its odd, extended organ. On an impulse, she pulled at the sliver of pink that protruded from inside the shell as though she was pulling chewing gum from her sister's mouth. Immediately, revelation slackened her muscles, causing her to nearly drop the shell. In an instant, she glimpsed the clue that had eluded her for so long. Darwin's calling was so much stronger than science: It was an affair of the heart.

Since entering college three years ago, Beth had made good on her promise to investigate her father's long-time obsession, looking into Darwin's famous delay with the intensity of a criminal detective. Her eyes, her posture, her social life all attested to this fact. Hours were spent sequestered in the undergraduate lab, huddled between dissections and drawings, her notebooks piled dangerously close to flaming Bunsen burners. Initially, barnacles had been something of a disappointment. In fact, Beth would have gone so far as to say barnacles were boring. Their shriveled purple bodies were indistinguishable from one another but for the most minor details or their numbered tags. Every barnacle was as homely and straightforward as the next. When pulled, prodded, and pinned across a dissection plate, they all bore a vague and unfortunate resemblance to a pink worm.

Gradually though, Beth gained the refined perception of an expert and learned to discern the species' more subtle identifying traits. Every barnacle, regardless of its subclassification, had the same wormlike trunk, the same fine, fluttering feet, a rigid shell covering in shades of lavender to blue. Every barnacle had a tiny opening at the top of the trunk, the portal for the binding glue with which the barnacle attached itself to rocks, ship hulls, or the bellies of whales, according to geographical demands. Every barnacle observed the same mating rituals—or rather the lack thereof—reproducing like its cellular predecessors by virtue of an immaculate conception, splitting on itself as though the presence of another creature was simply too great a burden. As a member of the crustacean kingdom, every barnacle boasted the same dubious skill as the crab, capable, much like the worst houseguest, of taking comfort almost anywhere.

By her sophomore year, Beth could fairly be called a specialist. She could tell apart the different subclasses after only a brief examination and, on a very good day, by holding them in different hands with her eyes shut tight. She knew the difference between the ridge length of the Mediterranean and Morroccan subclass. She could tell a throned from a thorny barnacle without counting the serrations on the trunk. She knew an Atlantic from a Gulf Stream specimen by the color of its shell; one was a very deep purple while the other was a distinct shade of mauve. Still, as far as she was concerned, barnacles were a naturalist's nightmare, adapting relatively little over the history of the world. Even after three years of such scintillating study, barnacles still seemed so banal to Beth that she was forced to question her father's theory. It no longer seemed a shocking decision that Darwin had favored the finch. The finch provided a vibrant, colorful illustration of evolution, while the barnacle was nothing more than a shriveled little wimp. Indeed, Beth was hard-pressed to believe that the barnacle had ever obsessed anyone, let alone been cited as a possible contender for the origin of life.

But now she entertained a radical new thought. As she stood at the shelf, examining her father's rare prehistoric specimen, curiosity turned to wonder and wonder turned to astonishment. Overwhelmed, she dropped to the floor to examine the creature more closely, running through a potential chain of events like a detective solving a crime. The animal she held in her hands at the moment was a hermaphrodite; in other words, a creature decidedly blessed with the power to reproduce without the bother of courtship. But, in all Beth's time studying the minute parasite, she had never before encountered such a strange specimen; modern Barnacles uniformly appeared in the two traditional genders. Stumped, she stared at the freak of nature with new curiosity. If this was the first incarnation of the barnacle, after several generations in nature, she now realized, the barnacle must have changed its identity. Inspired, she ran through a potential sequence by which such a miracle could occur.

First, the hermaphroditic creature developed a parasite pocket that in turn attached itself to the shell. Over time, this pocket accumulated a supply of reproductive material, expanding into a large gelatinous sac like a slowly inflating balloon. Finally, this inflating sac grew too large for its host, detaching from the shell like a crisp autumn leaf. And yet, this sudden fall from grace marked a new beginning. Once liberated, the parasite pocket grew gradually more self-sufficient until it could eat, see, and move independently. Finally, the new creature achieved the coveted status of its host. Endowed with distinct reproductive material it, too, could "give birth."

But now, as Beth stared at the wrinkled tip of this aged barnacle, she considered a new and scandalous twist on its evolutionary sequence. What if when the humble hermaphrodite finally spread its proverbial legs, it did not descend into the male form but rather evolved into an adorable baby girl? What if the female gender of the species evolved before the male? What would that mean to Darwin's famous theory of evolution? What would it mean, Beth suddenly considered, to the history of the world? In an instant, Beth was struck with the full implications of such a question. What if Eve never sprang from Adam's rib? What if, in the history of life, Eve came decidedly first?

Now, as she sat on the floor of the shell collection, Beth grew suddenly alarmed. She was accosted with an overwhelming desire to distance herself from her work. The author of such a theory could only live out one of two fates: her name would be written in history books or she would be tarred and feathered. Suddenly, Beth saw Darwin in a very different light. His famous delay now seemed perfectly plausible. She, too, could envision spending twenty years, testing and retesting such a theory and ultimately censoring its publication. Better this than spend the rest of her life mocked by her community. Now, she knew for certain that her father's assumption was false. The real question was not why Darwin abandoned barnacles but why he had not done so sooner. Still, amidst the upheaval of her revelation, Beth conceded one undeniable perk: The author of such a radical theory would surely win her father's contest, if not his heart.

While Beth was safely ensconced in the privacy of her bedroom lab, Beryl confronted science up close, completing her trek through the depths of Central Park. A morning tour of the bramble had left her decidedly empty-handed but for the telephone numbers of a handful of friendly bird-watchers who insisted that she join them for their weekly gatherings. The upper quadrant of the park had been a total disappointment. Latrell was not to be found in any of his usual haunts and none of the acquaintances he'd made over the years had any idea of his whereabouts. Still, despite the dismal rewards of the first day of her search, Beryl refused to be discouraged and focused instead on a strange prescient feeling that currently flooded her head.

Beryl had suspected she was psychic since she was four years old. Though her sisters refused to acknowledge this talent, she was comforted by the fact that she had ample evidence to prove her claim regardless. Indeed, Beryl perceived time and space in a different manner than most. She saw the future quite literally, as though it were a sign just ahead on the highway or a distant shape on the horizon. Of course, the first time a premonition occurred, she didn't recognize it as such. At the time, she was building a sandcastle on a family holiday. While her sisters toiled happily on an elaborate mote surrounding the central turret, Beryl saw an apparition of a rolling wave that appeared with such perfect clarity that she actually felt its moisture on her bare shoulders. Distressed by the prospect of losing the fruit of several hours' labor, Beryl urged her sisters to relocate farther up from the shore. But the others ignored Beryl and continued to shovel happily, teasing their sister about her penchant for needless worry. Accepting her lack of influence, Beryl gave up her campaign only to watch the castle ravaged seconds later by a sudden thunderstorm.

Over the years, Beryl's premonitions varied in accuracy. She grew to understand that the images she perceived were not always literal warnings but rather metaphorical suggestions. For example, when Bridget and Billy first began dating, Beryl had a distinct vision of the number seventy-six and understandably assumed she had glimpsed a hint at the duration of the romance. The number, she later realized, did not denote the span of the affair but rather the position of the quarterback who would eventually tear them apart. At the beginning of Beth's senior year in high school, Beryl had a vision of an ivy leaf and made the reasonable assumption that it foretold the poisonous rash. For weeks, she campaigned her older sister to avoid forays into the woods. Three months later, Beth was accepted into Harvard.

In truth, in almost every case, Beryl's predictions were slightly askew, requiring an extra act of associative thinking as well as a feat of the imagination. And yet, her family attributed her predictions to mere coincidence, noting the frequency of her miscalculations as opposed to her successes and, when she was correct, writing it off as a lucky guess. Still, despite this lack of support from her family, Beryl was sure she was on the brink, close to cracking the code with which she might reliably know the future. Indeed, minutes before Bell had returned to the apartment a week earlier, Beryl had seen the image of a ringing bell and made the mistaken deduction that she was late for something. So, even despite her erratic track record, Beryl paid special heed to the premonition filling her head at the moment: the image of a red feather. She erroneously assumed the image pertained to her sister Benita. Momentarily blinded by her literality, Beryl abandoned her current project of feeding the ducks at the Boat Pond and stood from her bench to head south again, toward the Central Park Zoo.

It was now nearing eight o'clock, the hour at which the park transformed from a place for children to adults. The music of street performers, before a cheerful backdrop, grew suddenly more pro-nounced, the high notes somehow more menacing without the treble of children's shouts. As if on cue, flowers on the ground shifted from daytime's warmer tones to more somber pastel shades like a photo-graph drained of color. Even the sun itself submitted to this sudden shift, weaving gray and silver shadows into the last rays of daylight. Finding the area empty but for a few stragglers, Beryl hurried past the Bandshell, picking up her pace as she hurried south. As a result, she failed to notice the approach of a speeding runner and collided with him head-on. Shaken, she muttered a rushed apology, stopped to regain her bearings, and hazarded a quick ambivalent glance to-ward the safety of her parents' apartment.

By the time she reached Sheep Meadow, the park had completely transformed. This was not the New York she knew, but an entirely dif-ferent planet. The area seemed to inhabit its own particular season, not yet touched by the warmth of spring and yet too full of buds for winter. The darkening sky only brightened the sparse but striking col-ors within. Bursts of nearly neon green dotted the first trees. Patches of white and gold poked up where daffodils began their stints. Hazy pink in three different shades forecast magnolia, dogwood, and cherry blossoms. As she walked, Beryl did her best to ignore whole chunks of

her imagination, dispelling countless urban myths and years of warnings from her parents about danger in the park after nightfall. Despite
her racing pulse, she pushed deeper into the park, veering west where
she should have turned east in order to get back home.

The promenade, always a place for peaceful contemplation, now
seemed a haunted entryway. Its canopy of grand elm trees no longer
traced an arch in the sky, but tilted and swayed downward as though to
shroud people underneath. Gradually, darkness worked its magic on
her eyes and imagination, turning tree branches to tentacles, tiny buds
to peering eyes, and a light spring breeze into an ominous whispered
threat. Accordingly, Beryl was quite surprised and more than slightly
relieved to find Sheep Meadow crowded with people who appeared far
too busy to be bothered with nefarious deeds. Teenagers huddled in
small circles, passing around glowing twigs. An older group played
music on a boom box, lowering the volume every several seconds as
though this simple act might enable them to escape detection. With
every step, Beryl discovered a new, unique population, each one using
the park to a different and more wonderful end.

Suddenly, Beryl was overwhelmed with the sense that she'd been
duped. This was not the Central Park she'd been told about. Where
were the trolls and convicts, the roving bands of boys on bikes, the
murderers and the drugs? None of the dangers of which she'd been
warned seemed possible in this enchanted place. Her parents had led
her astray, she now realized, in order to keep her in check. Central
Park was no more dangerous at night than the apartment in which
she'd grown up. In fact, it was safer, she now concluded, for various
reasons. In the park, for example, there was no risk of being be-
sieged by Benita. Comforted, she continued south with a new, if
somewhat unjustified sense of her safety, heading deeper into the
park even though it was fast approaching nine o'clock.

By the time Beryl reached the zoo, the world was entirely dark.
The sounds of the animals seemed louder somehow as though nighttime had adjusted the volume of New York, amplifying the noise
inside the park and silencing everything farther out. Humbled, she

took a seat on the long low bench facing the zoo. Glancing up at the Delacorte Clock, she was reminded of her childhood, afternoons spent listening to the clock's melodies and tracking the dancing animals. As her eyes adjusted to the dark, her perception improved, causing her to note nearby details with heightened awareness. A clump of white tulips beside the gates of the zoo strained their necks like a school of swans. The rush of traffic on Fifth Avenue bore an amazing resemblance to the ebb and flow of the ocean. For the first time ever, Beryl noted the surprisingly low height of the fence around the zoo. It was a wonder, she decided, that more people didn't climb over to enjoy a midnight promenade without the distraction of tourists.

But before she could spend another moment contemplating such a crime, something inordinately strange occurred, ostensibly turning nature upside down and bringing the animals to her. As she sat in front of the old Arsenal, staring at the gates of the zoo, she became aware of a faint chirping coming from the shrubbery. It took Beryl several moments to locate the source of the noise and, once she had, to congratulate herself on another apt, if muddled premonition. Mrs. Finch's fledgling red-tailed hawk teetered in the dirt, either indulging in nocturnal predation or trying to find its way home.

While Beryl combated the wilderness in nearby Central Park, Belinda confronted her own savagery on Manhattan's Lower East Side. Poor Belinda shared her sisters' wildness but none of their savvy, lending credence to the notion that genes skip over siblings like stones over water. Despite the initial excitement she had felt about her scheme, Belinda was having second thoughts. By the third day of her engagement, Belinda wanted to break it off. She had been sustained for several days by the thrill of bad behavior and a short but enjoyable honeymoon in Coney Island. The two had spent two blissful days in the amusement park, indulging in such liberal consumption of the Cyclone and Nathan's famous franks that they promptly ran out of money. As a result, the young lovers were forced to abandon their vacation prematurely, forgoing their plans to travel across country and formalize what was currently only a symbolic union in Las Vegas, the official domain of moronic romance. Lacking the funds, driver's license, and red convertible to do it in style, they had no choice, they realized, but opt for a more modest holiday. Though both had been tempted to admit defeat and return to their parents' apartments, they had kept the sentiment to themselves and spent the last two nights camping out at a construction site in the East Village.

By now the particular joy of upsetting her parents had been replaced by an overwhelming urge to enjoy their food and shelter. This sensation combined with the new glare of longer springtime days to offer Belinda a more complete sense of her companion. She kicked herself for failing to detect his defects earlier. The boy's shaved head pointed to a raging temper, his piercings revealed masochistic tendencies, and his maniacal obsession with Belinda belied deeper mental glitches. The fluorescent light of the train had obscured his facial acne, a problem that, Belinda now realized, had plagued him for many years. His unfortunate reddish brown hair precluded the possibility of her ever taking him seriously. His nose was slightly too large for his face. His clothes were filthy and smelled horribly and buried far beneath their grime was an absurdly spindly frame. Still, Belinda did her best to think positive thoughts. She took some pleasure in imagining the look on her father's face when she finally worked up the nerve to bring her new husband back to the apartment.

Arm in arm, Belinda and the boy wandered through the East Village, stopping first at a vintage record store to pretend to browse for music. After bothering the clerk to help them find obscure records they couldn't afford, they commenced a more pressing hunt, seeking a skilled tattoo artist capable of penning one's name on the other's earlobe in commemoration of their impulsive act. After some searching, they located such an artisan in a dank parlor on St. Mark's Place. But at the last minute, Belinda suggested a switch to piercings instead of tattoos. Tattoos were cliché, she insisted, and prone to fading over the years. Matching lip rings were a far more potent symbol. Unfortunately, Belinda and the boy's plans were foiled once again. Their combined finances only allowed for one of the two to be pierced.

The boy quickly offered an equally compelling alternative. He knew of a restaurant in Chinatown, a favorite of underage delinquents that looked the other way when serving minors and also worked within their budgets, offering an eight-person scorpion bowl for under five dollars. Unfortunately, Belinda had little firsthand experience with the substance and so had no idea that two of these drinks would put her under the table. Within half an hour, Belinda had lost track of her previous concerns, released, by virtue of rum and fruit juice, of both memory and conscience. All thoughts of her family blurred to a vague, nagging sensation. Even her odd companion transformed from a mongrel into a prince. Inside an hour, she was already feeling the first prickle of nausea. Her balance was bad enough to bring her to the floor, her judgment poor enough for her to order a third drink, her vision distorted enough for her to see similarities between this boy and certain rock stars. Her better angel was absent enough for her to find herself pinned up against the wall in the restaurant bathroom, lips locked, head thrown back, pants dangling, her sense of space shifting with the slightest movement.

Bell and Bridget had warned her about the dangers of getting "blitzed." When one was blitzed, one was vulnerable to bad boys, subject to one's whims and disorientation. When one was blitzed, one lost one's inhibitions, good judgment, self-respect, and sometimes a very good pair of shoes. But her sisters had not mentioned the various benefits, that getting blitzed permitted you to break laws of physics, that one could actually lose track of both time and space, that the phrase "to tear off one's clothes" was not merely a euphemism but actually how clothes came off, that one could lose one's cares, self-consciousness, and several hours of one's life and then somehow find oneself in a strange place with an even stranger boy and have absolutely no recollection of how one got there not to mention that one had yelled "I'm wild" while flashing all of Canal Street.

As a result, Belinda was all too susceptible to stupid, impulsive ideas and was halfway across the Brooklyn Bridge when she realized her mistake. The boy knew of a judge-turned-shaman who lived in a basement apartment across the river and was certified to perform legal marriages for a very reasonable bargain. Now, looking back at Manhattan from the bridge, Belinda admired the sparkle of the city, awed not only by its wondrous electric output but by a desperate desire for it to stop spinning. Unfortunately, horizontal and vertical lines soon merged into one, causing the skyscrapers of downtown Manhattan to tumble into the East River. But, for the moment, she was too drunk to realize her precarious state and gladly accepted when the boy offered to carry her the rest of the way. Being carted across the Brooklyn Bridge provided other consolations, among them a moment to nurse her headache, a renewed appreciation for her fiancé, and a second shot, however slim, at winning her father's contest.

22

Endurance

$\mathcal{B}$ell awoke on Thursday morning to the sound of a family gathering. It had been exactly one week since she returned; an appropriate amount of time, she now concluded, for a resurrection. Once again, she made the trek to the front of the apartment, finding her bedroom strangely lonely without Bridget's constant prattle. The rest of the Barnacle apartment reflected this same emptiness, much like a baseball team who had lost its best player to injuries. Aside from Bell, Beth and Benita were the only two Barnacle sisters in residence. Bridget had returned to her apartment to reconcile with Trot. Beryl was still roaming the city, looking for Latrell, and Belinda, though everyone naturally assumed she was still at school, was nursing a hangover on the banks of the East River.

But, despite the two recent departures, the house maintained a constant volume. Beth's return did its part to replace the previous noise, supplying Benita with a new and vocal sparring partner. At the moment, the third and sixth sister were assembled in the living room, both busied by the same goal, trying to simulate the noise of all six sisters with their yelling. This chaos was the girls' response to Barry's latest announcement. He had issued another invitation, a seder to celebrate the last day of Passover or, more accurately, to celebrate the fact that Passover was over. It would be an evening of announcements and denouncements, he explained. Every member of the family would be given the floor to argue why she was entitled to the prize and to heap slander upon anyone else who dared make the same claim. Barry would make his decision immediately after the meal, rendering one of the Barnacle girls an heiress by the time dessert was served.

Spurred by the noise, Barry rushed from his office to the living room. He stood at the door, observing the mayhem with impartial amusement as though he'd merely happened upon the scene, and not set it in motion.

"I have bad news," Benita announced.

"What's that?" Barry asked.

"Bell, Beth, and I are the only ones here. I guess that means the others are not eligible anymore."

"Nonsense," said Barry. "Where's everyone else?" He scanned the room impatiently, noting the diminished population.

Benita frowned with transparent delight. "Bridget went home, Belinda's at school, and Beryl, well, Beryl's not around."

Barry scowled at Benita as though searching for a flaw in her logic.

"I'm afraid I can't make it, either," Bell said, shooting her father a defiant look.

"Why not?" Barry demanded.

Bell shrugged innocently. "I've got a date tonight."

Barry offered Bell a sharp look, acknowledging her successful manipulation. A date was the one thing he could not overrule since he himself had made it an urgent mandate. Lacking the energy to issue the traditional reprimand, he simply sighed and closed his eyes as though eclipsing the world better enabled him to shut out his profound disappointment.

"I'm sorry, Daddy," Bell said. "I'm sure I won't be missed." And, having heard Benita's monologue recently enough to remember it verbatim, she recited Cordelia's famous words. "Unhappy that I am, I cannot heave my heart into my mouth. I love your majesty according to my bond, nor more nor less."

Yet again, the noise in the apartment spiked to a dangerous level, every sister doing her best to deafen the others with her point of view. Refusing to submit to hysteria, Bell settled into the sofa and opened the newspaper. According to her ritual, she refused the front page even a perfunctory scan, eschewing more pressing news in favor of the obituary section. It was, indeed, an odd compulsion but it comforted her to see the lives of other New Yorkers summarized in fifty words or less. First, she read the notice for a ninety-year-old man. He had died of natural causes, leaving behind a sprawling family. Then, she read one for an elderly lady who had died rather suddenly. She had lived with several cats and a bird but had little family to speak of. Saddened, Bell searched the page for a more hopeful story. Unfortunately, the next obituary was even more maudlin than the last, a freak accident involving a very young girl; the tragedy as sad as the odd, hurried prose in which it was written. The deceased girl was the same age as one of her sisters. Suddenly, Bell thrust the newspaper down. The obituary described Beryl.

Benita laid low while the house was ransacked, terrified to confess her knowledge of the crime. She was unwilling to relinquish Beryl's whereabouts lest she forfeit her side of their trade. Within minutes, every member of the family had concocted her own theory. Barry was not concerned at all, convinced Beryl had lost track of time in pursuit of a contest prize. Bunny was sure she had fallen in love and was holed up at some boy's apartment, the greatest threat to her safety second-hand smoke and bad music. Beth suspected she'd joined a band of roving gypsies, preferring their company to her family and seeking their tutelage in the art of crystal-ball reading. Benita did her part to throw her family off the scent, suggesting Beryl had been unhappy for years and was probably gone for good. But Bella was blessed with a mother's sixth sense and guessed the reason for Beryl's flight; deducing correctly that her daughter was ransacking the city for her adopted brother. Unfortunately, this knowledge failed to offer Bella much comfort. Now, two of her beloved children roamed the city as opposed to one.

Deeming all of these theories unduly melodramatic, Bell returned to the solace of her bedroom. She had reached the penultimate round of her own competition and needed to focus. Of course, she knew perfectly well that she had resorted to foul play, securing Blaine's affection with less than honorable tactics and stooping to new levels in desperate behavior. But circumstance had foreclosed her options. She could no longer afford the luxury of immaculate standards, and so she did her best to find the positives in her situation. Though Blaine was perhaps not the man most likely to provide her with unconditional love, he would at least join her in the task of providing for her child. Or, at the very least, he would permit her to approximate her father's expectations while she found a way to provide for herself. Of course, Bell knew that marrying Blaine was a compromise of sorts. But reality required such acknowledgments. "Compromise" was just another word for "getting what you want."

Renewed, Bell focused on the current task, selecting the perfect uniform for her date that evening. Finding an outfit that was both alluring and casual was one of life's great challenges. One could always couple jean shorts with a snug black camisole but there was something about this particular ensemble that betrayed a certain desperation to showcase one's attributes. Jean shorts always ended up causing so many unforeseen problems. The exact length and extent of the fringe often required last minute alterations and, even worse, caused shedding at the most inopportune moments. Cotton pants were certainly another viable option, but unless they were cut in the latest style, they risked making one look as though one was heading off on a camping trip.

Skirts were always a welcome possibility after the endless New York winter, allowing a girl to enjoy added freedom of movement or, when necessary, to speed the negotiations of a first date. But skirts and baseball stadiums made for such an awkward match, subjecting the wearer to mysterious surfaces and, when one was not vigilant, the odd, unwelcome itch. Jeans then, perhaps, were the best option, sensible and still sexy, permitting a girl to maintain the illusion of nonchalance, even when she had put hours into her appearance. Her anxiety allayed by this careful analysis, Bell redirected her energy to the next decision: Which of the shoes Bridget had left behind provided the adequate lift for her silhouette without seeming overly dressy? Finally, a full hour later, Bell reached a satisfactory decision. She wore dark blue jeans, a white camisole, a pair of black kitten heels with green polka dots, and Blaine's beloved Yankees cap to complete the ensemble.

Appraising herself in the mirror, Bell took in the full significance of the upcoming moment, and then proceeded cautiously to the living room to await Blaine's arrival. Unfortunately, her confidence faltered in the presence of her sisters. Beth and Benita had joined forces to combine the collective power of their disapproval. It was unspeakable, Beth explained, for Bell to go to the game while Beryl was still at large. More to the point, it was moronic for Bell to spend time with a boy with such transparent motives. Benita simply grinned and claimed that Bell was headed for disaster. But Bell did her best to ignore her sisters; she had worked too hard to give up now. If life were a baseball game, this would be the ninth inning.

One faces, at certain junctures in a romance, a choice between desire and dignity. And though he was torn, Billy had no choice. The only graceful thing to do was to break things off with Bridget. At noon on Thursday, he sat on his bed, paralyzed with anger, debating, for the twelfth straight hour, whether Bridget's or Blaine's betrayal was more wicked. Bridget's was worse, he decided. He expected such treachery from Blaine. No, he changed his mind again. Blaine had sinned against his own blood. Blaine was the real bastard. Fuming,

Billy comforted himself with a new resolve, plotting an elaborate and mortifying revenge for both parties. Luckily, Blaine's revenge was already in the works. Since finding out, Billy had assaulted his brother with an aggressive silent treatment. Unfortunately, Blaine had been in such a good mood that he had not yet noticed Billy's boycott and had left the apartment for a jog before Billy could inform him of it. Bridget's revenge was slightly harder to implement than Blaine's due to the fact that her feelings about Billy were already somewhat ambivalent. And yet, Billy realized, there was one perfect solution. His sudden and violent disappearance from her life could put an end to that.

Billy tore out of his bedroom and headed for the Barnacles'. His speech, he decided on his way down the hall, would be merciless and pithy, causing permanent emotional scars without requiring too many words. His stance, he decided in the foyer, would be humble but self-assured. He would swear his eternal wrath at Bridget, vow never to speak to her again, and itemize his plans for revenge all inside thirty seconds. Furthermore, he decided as he waited for his knock to be answered, he would demand repayment for his grandmother's ring. Bridget had likely reached in and recovered it from the dog's belly, and then hidden it in some dark, cushioned drawer to appraise and later pawn. But as he stood at the Barnacles' door, Billy's confidence faltered somewhat. He acknowledged the great challenge of such kiss-offs, conveying complete and utter apathy while going to so much trouble. Either way, he was spared the burden of a performance. By the time he reached Bridget's room, Bridget was already gone.

Defeated, Billy lingered at the bedroom door for a moment. As he stood, he fell into a small trance and, as a result, was quite shocked to find Bell standing inches from his face.

"Billy," said Bell. "Are you okay?"

"Oh yes," he lied. "Very."

Bell smiled lovingly and raised an eyebrow, as though to suggest she was immune to such transparent displays of bravado.

"Oh fine," Billy sighed. "What's the use in pretending?"

Bell followed him into the room, closing the door behind them.

"You think you know someone," Billy began. He took a seat in the girls' stuffed chair then changed his mind and stood up. He walked to the bookshelf, removed a book, flipped through the pages for a moment, and replaced it on the shelf. Then, in a final admission of defeat, he walked back to the chair and fell into it, looking up at Bell pitifully like a tortured poet.

Bell offered Billy a consoling smile then took a seat facing him on the edge of her bed. "Knowing," she said, "is not the problem. The problem is that sometimes people you know do not behave like themselves."

"It's just not fair," Billy said.

"You're telling me," said Bell. "Try living next door to a pair of twins." She invoked Blaine's favorite line. "It ain't all it's cracked up to be."

Billy accepted Bell's point with a begrudging smile then, remembering his miserable state, contorted his face back into a scowl. "I expect this from him," he moaned. "But how could she do this to me? But the thing that really hurts . . . the thing that really gets me . . ." He stopped to clear his throat. "If Bridget really, truly loved me, she'd have no trouble telling us apart. She'd feel it in her bones."

"Come on, Billy," Bell said sharply. "It's a very easy mistake. Let's not forget that you and Blaine have spent the last thirty years perfecting this very deception."

Billy considered this earnestly and appeared to be somewhat consoled. Then, picturing his brother and Bridget together, he resumed moaning and cursing.

"Besides," said Bell. "I can assure you, nothing happened that night."

"How do you know?" Billy sighed.

"Because," said Bell. "Bridget does know the difference and she's only in love with one of you."

Billy searched Bell's eyes imploringly as though the very answer he sought was buried beneath her gaze.

"So, if I were you," Bell concluded, "I'd hurry up and remind her that she has a very valuable pair of tickets in her possession."

Billy looked up suddenly as though Bell had just said something very controversial. "Oh come on. Bridget would never. Everyone knows there's nothing worse than proposing at a . . ." He trailed off suddenly. "That's it!" he shouted.

"What's 'it'?" Bell said.

"I can't believe it took me so long. In Bridget's mind, the best proposal would be the all-time worst."

Bell smiled, amused by Billy's incurable histrionics.

"I'm still in the game," Billy declared, then, thanking Bell, he turned to go and headed home at a sprint.

Bridget arrived at her old apartment without calling Trot in advance. Lacking the energy for a more thorough move-in, she walked up the stairs of their fifth-floor walk-up, heaved her luggage to the top, then left it on the landing with the intention of retrieving it later or, better yet, convincing Trot to do it for her. When she arrived, Trot barely acknowledged her entrance, busied by what seemed a very pressing commitment, sitting at his desk, intermittently staring into space and doodling in a notebook. Undaunted, Bridget marched into the apartment, dropped her accoutrements, and commenced a cleaning tour of the kitchen designed less to clean than to broadcast the number of dirty dishes in the sink. Finally, realizing she lacked the expertise to complete such a task, she abandoned the pretense of washing dishes, marched across the apartment, threw herself onto her bed and said, "Fine. You win. I'm ready."

Trot was, of course, more than slightly offended by Bridget's brazen entrance. The gall of assuming he would take her back, let alone without an apology. Did she think she could treat him however she pleased and he would simply tolerate her abuse? Did she think that under the circumstances, his proposal was still on the table? Bridget waited for a response. Trot stared at the page of his notebook then, without acknowledging the presence of so much as a new breeze in the room, he raised his hand and placed pen to paper as though he had finally found the perfect verbiage for a line of fiction. Bridget watched with shocked outrage as Trot scribbled contentedly. She lifted herself from the bed with an overwhelming grunt, crossed the room to Trot's desk, snatched the pen out of his hand, and took a seat on the desk atop Trot's current project.

"Excuse me," said Trot. "I'm doing something."

"Did you hear what I said?" Bridget demanded.

"Yes," said Trot. "Very clearly. Did you hear my answer?"

"No," sniffed Bridget. "You didn't say anything."

"Exactly," said Trot. "Know why?" He took the liberty of answering his own question. "Because there's nothing left to say."

And with that, Trot stood up, walked to his closet and commenced a long-overdue project: packing his clothes to move out.

At this very same moment, Billy geared up for his performance. Though Bridget had not yet responded to his message, he was sure she would cave at the reminder of the tickets. In all his life, he'd never known her to pass up a chance to see the Sox play, let alone a chance to witness such a symbolic and significant match. It was true the seats he'd managed to secure were less impressive than Blaine's, but it was a feat that he'd snagged them at all and, besides, it didn't really matter where they sat as long as they could see the field. At least, this is what Billy told himself as he waited for Bridget to return his call. Even if she was not swayed by the opportunity to spend time with him, surely she would be convinced by the momentous occasion in baseball. Dizzy with nerves, Billy regarded himself one last time in the mirror and attempted to quell his anxiety by rehearsing sotto voce his third and, necessarily most successful, proposal. Unfortunately, a knock on the door interrupted this private moment. Blaine entered without Billy's permission. Billy stood, stoic and silent at the mirror, vowing not to be dissuaded.

"I just came to wish you good luck," Blaine said, "on this, your last chance in hell." Blaine crossed the room with all the good cheer of a talk show host, and then paused to stand behind Billy, making eye contact in the mirror, that most eerie of fifth dimensions.

Billy met Blaine's pointed gaze and returned serve with an unflappable smile.

"So, you're oh for two," Blaine said, assuming the deep and over-enunciated delivery of a sportscaster. He held up an invisible microphone. "How does that feel going into this game? It must be a crippling burden."

Billy managed to strengthen his smile without releasing Blaine's gaze. "Actually, I feel confident that today's the day. I've got a fail-proof plan."

"I sure hope so for your sake," Blaine said, "considering that the day holds so many other disappointments."

"How do you figure?" Billy asked. He focused on his own reflection.

"Well, for one, I'm proposing to Bell and I can't imagine that will help your cause. Second, and you know how much it pains me to beat you but—and of course, I'm no psychic—the Sox are about to go down."

"Oh, you think so?" Billy asked.

"I'd bet my life on it," Blaine said. Then, he had the nerve to wink.

Finally, Billy disengaged from Blaine's gaze and turned to regard his brother head-on. Now, as he stood mere inches away from his identical twin, Billy noted his brother's defects as though seeing him for the first time. Blaine's lips were thinner than his, causing him to seem as though he was constantly judging and making him look much older than his twenty-eight years. His eyes were small and permanently squinty which made him look mean-spirited. In fact, Billy noted, there was some truth to all their jovial teasing. Despite their superficial similarities, he and Blaine looked nothing alike at the level of their souls. As he stared into Blaine's eyes, something snapped in

Billy and, before he could think better of it, he extended his hand, smiled broadly, and said, "Okay, you're on."

"Pardon me?" asked Blaine.

"You heard me," Billy said. "I accept your bet. But I want to raise the stakes."

Thrown, Blaine shifted his weight as though to station himself better to the ground then folded his arms, cocked his head, and waited for Billy to elaborate.

"If the Yankees win," Billy explained, "you go ahead with your plans and propose to Bell. If they lose, you walk away and accept defeat like a man."

"And you?" asked Blaine.

"Same goes for me. If the Sox win, I propose to Bridget."

"And, if they lose?" Blaine demanded.

"If they lose, I give up for good."

Blaine stared at his brother for a moment as though to make sure he was indeed looking at flesh as opposed to a reflection. Then, regaining his previous composure, he smiled as though to coax Billy back into the realm of laughter.

"What's the matter?" asked Billy. "Have you lost faith in your team? Are you scared they might crack under the pressure?"

"Absolutely not," said Blaine.

"So, do we have a bet?" asked Billy.

Blaine said nothing. He only smiled and extended his hand to shake.

And, for the umpteenth time in as many years, the twins sacrificed their good judgment to a history of wagers, challenges, and dares.

Bridget waited until five o'clock to leave her apartment. She had spent the better part of the afternoon writing hateful letters to Trot, assembling his left-behind clothes in piles, and calculating his outstanding debt. But her willpower faltered after computing his portion of the telephone bill. Perhaps, Bridget decided, Billy could be granted temporary amnesty due to this highly anticipated event in the history of baseball. Comforted by this new resolve, she scrutinized piles of half-packed clothing to select the perfect uniform for her date that evening. Finding an outfit that was both alluring and casual was one of life's great challenges. One could always couple jean shorts with a snug black camisole, but there was something about this particular ensemble that betrayed a certain desperation to showcase one's attributes. Jean shorts always ended up causing so many unforeseen problems. The exact length and extent of the fringe often required last minute alterations and, even worse, caused shedding at the most inopportune moments. Cotton pants were certainly another viable option, but unless they were cut in the latest style, they risked making one look as though one was heading off on a camping trip.

Skirts were always a welcome possibility after the endless New York winter, allowing a girl to enjoy added freedom of movement or, when necessary, to speed the negotiations of a first date. But skirts and baseball stadiums made for such an awkward match, subjecting the wearer to mysterious surfaces and, when one was not vigilant, the odd, unwelcome itch. Jeans then, perhaps, were the best option; sensible and still sexy, permitting a girl to maintain the illusion of nonchalance when she had put hours into her appearance. Her anxiety allayed by this careful analysis, Bell redirected her energy to the next decision: Which of the fifty-odd pair of shoes strewn about her floor provided the adequate lift for her silhouette without seeming overly dressy? Finally, a full hour later, Bridget reached a satisfactory decision. She wore dark blue jeans, a white camisole, a pair of black kitten heels with green polka dots, and Billy's beloved Sox cap to complete the ensemble.

Billy and Blaine arrived at the Barnacles' within seconds of one another. This forced the two estranged twins first to stand in the foyer between the two apartments in complete and utter silence and then, once they'd made the unanimous decision to open the front door, to stand in the Barnacles' living room and make awkward banter. Both boys chose against sitting. Billy opted to pace aimlessly, while Blaine chose to stand and examine a painting on the wall. Finally, tiring of these two activities, Blaine picked up a magazine and pretended to read, and Billy took a seat on the living room sofa and fidgeted with his shoelaces. Finally, a third party to their rescue. Barry entered, this time not rolling, but practically running into the room.

"Boys, what a pleasure," Barry declared. "So glad you decided to come."

Blaine regarded Barry quizzically, unsure of the event to which he was referring. Wary of offending his potential patriarch, he clarified the reason for his presence. "I'm here to pick up your daughter. We're going to the game tonight."

"As am I," Billy added.

"If his date accepts," Blaine corrected.

Barry said nothing, just stared at the boys as though he'd forgotten their identity for a moment. "Very well, then," he said finally. "Please take off your shoes while you wait."

Both boys smiled an apology and fumbled to remove their shoes. Then, as though moved by the very same emotion, both boys shifted their weight nervously, both boys sat awkwardly on the sofa, then suddenly stood back up, both boys cleared their throats and mumbled something unintelligible and both boys, without discussing such a plan, opened their mouths to ask Barry for the privilege of marrying his daughter.

"Mr. Barnacle," Billy and Blaine said in unison.

Billy paused to glare at Blaine.

Blaine paused to glare at Billy.

Suddenly, prescient of their twin goal, they turned simultaneously to one another, issued the same bullying look and then attempted to monopolize Barry's attention.

"Mr. Barnacle," said Billy.

"Sir," Blaine said louder.

Then, in perfect unison, both boys said, "There's something I need to ask you."

Barry understood their intention immediately and preempted their next question. "Boys," he said, "I truly thought this day would never come."

Finally, the twins' responses varied. Billy smiled and Blaine winced.

"So, you approve?" Billy asked.

"Of course, I don't approve," Barry scoffed. "It's more a case of the devil you don't know versus the devil you do."

Once again, the three men stood in awkward silence. Barry broke the pause with a volcanic chuckle. He stopped laughing just as suddenly as he'd begun, indulged in a wicked smile, and gestured for the twins to join him in a huddle. "Can you keep a secret?" he asked.

The twins nodded solemnly.

"Now that you're going to be members of the family, I think I can trust you with this. And, I could use your support later on in the case of a mutiny."

Though both were now terribly confused, Blaine and Billy did their best to smile encouragingly.

"But, even in the worst case," Barry went on, "I've accomplished what I set out to do."

Billy widened his eyes.

Blaine tightened his stomach.

"There is no contest prize," Barry whispered. "Or at least, not the one they think." He rubbed his hands with glee. "Oh, the girls are going to be shocked," he said, "when they realize there's no money."

"What?" Blaine said sharply.

"Excuse me?" said Billy.

"But you said——" Blaine blurted.

"Oh, I never said a thing," Barry smiled. "They jumped to their own conclusions. Or rather, their stepmother did."

Both twins remained speechless for several moments. Billy crossed his arms playfully. Blaine stood still with shock, scanning the room as though for modes of escape.

As Barry beamed at the boys, it was hard to tell which pleased him more: the plans he harbored for the contest or the effect of this announcement.

Billy recovered first and offered Barry congratulations. "You old devil," he said, punching him on the arm. "You really had me going."

Blaine attempted his own playful punch but found his arm inexplicably paralyzed. Luckily, the front door opened at this moment, drawing attention away from Blaine. Bridget and Bell arrived to meet their dates in perfect tandem, dressed so similarly as to be confused for one another. Somehow, the last ten minutes had resulted in a dramatic turn of events, transforming two dissimilar sisters into twins and turning two identical twins into polar opposites. Everything Blaine held dear flew rapidly out the window as, for the first time in his life, he headed to Yankee Stadium, praying for the Red Sox to win.

23

A Good Arm

$\mathscr{D}$espite the dwindling headcount in the apartment, Barry called the family together. Benita was eager to commence before any unexpected arrivals, thrilled by the implications of congregating with so few of her competitors present. She had dressed up in honor of the occasion, taking advantage of Belinda's absence to wear the controversial dress she had "borrowed" days earlier. The dress, however, required some alterations. She had hemmed the skirt and cinched up the back, causing the ensemble to look like a last-minute Halloween costume. But blinded as usual by her competitive designs, she deemed the outfit impossibly glamorous. As a finishing touch, she pulled her hair into a tight ponytail. She congratulated herself in the mirror. The dress, she felt, provided the perfect context for her upcoming win. It was fitting that she wore the clothes meant for Cordelia since she was, in her opinion, the only deserving sister.

With four of the six Barnacle sisters in absentia, the table felt unusually bare. Still, those in attendance made up for the missing with a surplus of nerves and anticipation. Finally, just before six o'clock, Barry yelled up the spiral staircase, threatening to start without Bella and Bunny if they weren't downstairs within thirty seconds. Never one to make idle threats, Barry commenced counting backward, adding emphasis to urgency by bellowing through the apartment and clinking an empty glass with a spoon. Bunny leapt over the last step as Barry reached "ten."

Bella appeared at the last possible moment, impressively mobile on her crutches, her hair so perfectly windblown that she appeared to have slid down the banister.

Barry settled into his seat and banged his fists on the table. "Let's skip formalities tonight. Shall we? Who wants to go first?"

Benita waved her hand with frantic spastic movements as though she might slip into a seizure if she was not called upon. "I do. I do," she clamored.

"That's fine," Barry said. "We'll go youngest to oldest. If that's all right with everyone else?" He searched the table for dissenters but finding only Beth, nodded at Benita.

Benita smiled smugly, scanning the table like a seasoned politician. Finally, she stood from her seat, clasped her hands, and pursed her lips as though she were delivering a book report. "As many of you know, I was favored to win the Chapin School talent show," she said. "But it turns out the school's meritocracy has fallen to the tyranny of political correctness, besides which Mary Talbot would have won anyway due to the rampant anti-Semitism in my class." She paused here to take a breath. "Luckily, that was a fallback plan. I thought of something much better, something sure to bring honor to the Barnacle name and fill our home with love. Daddy," she paused, "I know how much you've missed him over the years, so I went to the Central Park Zoo and got Harry back for you."

Benita clapped her hands and whistled, cuing a stampede of tiny footsteps and the appearance, seconds later, of a medium-sized macaque. The monkey had the exact same features as Barry's beloved pet, the same gray and black speckled fur, the same wide, deeply inset eyes, the same stumped tail, the same pink toes, the same resemblance to a little old man.

The family regarded the monkey in silence as he bounded into the room. Finally, Beth broke the silence with a derisive snarl.

"That isn't Harry," she sneered.

"I thought you would say that," Benita said. She smiled with unflinching confidence then clapped again in two short rhythmic beats, spurring the monkey to leap to the sofa and assume the familiar position. Indeed, as they watched, he perfectly replicated the behavior Bella had witnessed years ago, clasping his hands in front of his chest and bowing his head in prayer.

Benita curtsied for the table.

"First of all," Beth began, "any monkey can clasp his hands. Besides . . ." here, she invoked her mother's argument, "everyone knows when people pray, they're not really thinking about God. They're thinking about what they're going to have for dinner."

Finally, Benita began to weaken. Excessive blinking and sniffles hearkened an imminent temper tantrum.

Bella lowered her voice to a soothing tone. "Sweetheart," she said, "I have a confession. Harry doesn't live in New York anymore. I sent him to Florida ten years ago. He's in a better place."

Benita tightened imperceptibly. Everyone at the table braced for the explosion. But instead of erupting, she only shuddered slightly, offered Bella a look of betrayal, then stood from the table and ran down the hall, sobbing. The entire table listened as her shrieking receded. Barry took the opportunity to pet the controversial guest, but he soon submitted to the general consensus that the monkey should be given back to the zoo before the day was over.

With the matter settled, Barry surveyed the group with a look of unflappable cheer. He leaned back in his chair to a ninety-degree tilt, scanned the table for the next speaker, then cleared his throat and attempted to reclaim his audience. "Beth, you're up," he announced. "What do you got for me?"

Beth eyed her father tentatively. It was unlike her to engage in such a blatant act of bragging. But acknowledging the benefit of the prize, she swallowed hard, met her father's gaze, and presented her findings. "I believe I've figured out why Darwin gave up on barnacles," she announced.

Cautiously, she detailed her new theory, laying out her evidence. She and Darwin, she claimed, had stumbled down twin paths. Both had journeyed across the world to find their greatest resources in their backyard. Both had realized, after tireless searches, that the thing for which they searched had always been close to home. And yet, myopia had delayed both scientists' discoveries. Darwin's barnacles were fixed to his shore long before the *Beagle* set sail, just as Beth's lay on her father's shelves years before she left for college. Of course, she knew that rushing to publish could prove a grave mistake, but she faced the scientist's greatest dilemma: prudence versus priority.

Indeed, the story of Darwin offered a cautionary tale. Alfred Wallace, the barnacle to Darwin's finch, arrived at a twin theory to Darwin's exactly six months prior. In fact, the two scientists drew identical conclusions. But Wallace had dallied while Darwin rushed to publicize his theory. Wallace, of course, remained obscure while Darwin became unspeakably famous. And though the destinies of the two men could be attributed to timing, their story begged certain difficult questions. Was it possible, Beth asked the group, that luck shortchanged Wallace? Or was fate's neglect a more sinister act? Either way, Beth felt it was irresponsible to avoid the more disturbing question: Might the famous contest have ended differently if Wallace had not been a Jew?

"Don't waste your time," Bunny scoffed.

"What do you mean?" asked Beth.

"People will laugh in your face," said Bunny.

"But I've done the research," said Beth.

"Trust me," said Bunny. "It's a fool's errand." She smiled imperiously. "Darwin had to fight the Church of England. You're taking on every man in the free world."

"Pfft," Beth scoffed. Then, she added under her breath, "I guess you know all about that . . ."

While cattiness overtook dinner conversation, more weighty debates raged in Benita's room. Benita lay facedown on her bed, attempting to block out her family and to discern whether pillows could be used to fashion a soundproof wall. But, finding a stack of six failed even to muffle their sound, she abandoned her bed to scope out more remote places with her telescope. Luckily, the view of Central Park comforted her somewhat, providing the illusion that the world was a green sphere and she, at its center. All hope was not lost for the contest, she decided. She was poised for a ninth inning comeback. This very night she could locate an undetected star and earn the right to name it. Encouraged, she tilted the telescope to survey the evening sky. But she quickly tired of this pastime and resorted to spying on passers-by.

Central Park provided abundant victims. A couple strolled around the Pond, arm in arm. Another pair embraced and then parted ways. A young woman struggled to pitch a tent in Sheep Meadow. Intrigued, Benita allowed her lens to rest on the stubborn girl. The girl seemed oblivious to nearby picnics and dogs, completely engrossed in her task. Sadly, she was either too small or too inexperienced for such a strenuous job. Finally, admitting defeat, she fell to the grass and lay motionless on her back. Benita lingered on this vignette, comforted by the girl's failure and, somehow, encouraged to demand more of herself. As she stared at this distant girl, she felt suddenly very close to her. Startled, Benita stepped away from the telescope. Consciousness caught up with perception. The girl on the grass was not a girl, but rather her sister Beryl.

Yankee Stadium was at full capacity when the couples arrived, each section projecting its own personality like a family of squabbling siblings. As in any other environment, the park's hierarchy was a delicate and complicated balance, each level indicating a different status and affording the spectator with unique prerogatives. The field-side seats offered a fan the honor of stature and proximity. The middle bleachers surpassed the volume of the lower levels, offering the best acoustics for cheering and banner waving. But even despite the obvious totem of the baseball park, the bleachers offered a unique advantage. In Billy's opinion, the highest seats were unfairly stigmatized, since they provided the most magnificent view of the park and, despite their distance from the action, afforded the fan his best weapons: perspective and omniscience.

As usual, Blaine and Billy's seating reflected the dynamic of their rivalry. Blaine and Bell had coveted field-side seats, while Billy and Bridget were condemned to watch from the nosebleeds. But both pairs were too nervous to be bothered with such trivialities, all four of them engrossed in the status of the game and their part in the competition. So it was with high spirits and even higher expectations that the four old friends made their way into the mobbed stadium. Just before seven o'clock, Bell stole a nervous glance at Blaine and settled into their field-side seats, taking in the pregame crowd's unique electricity. Much farther up, Bridget and Billy climbed the stadium steps, fighting the tide of drunken fans and hot dog vendors. Luckily, both were elated by the other's presence and so didn't mind as they narrowly avoided collisions with oncoming traffic.

Suddenly, action on the field united all points of view as the Red Sox starting pitcher, David Wells, threw his first pitch of the night. The match-up between pitcher and batter made the moment all the more fraught. None other than Tug Johnson, the Yankees darling and lethal weapon, stood at the plate, waving his bat to warm up his arms like a samurai wielding a sword. Wells's first throw sailed through the air with less than typical bite. Johnson seized his chance and cracked the ball down the first-base line, sending in a run that made exactly half of the stadium go wild. Blaine watched the play with rapt attention, pumping his fists in the air then, catching Bell's gaze, managed a carefree smile and tried to appear nonchalant. Billy was too busy

negotiating with an usher to notice this turn of the tide, having managed, after much pleading and several dollars, to secure fifteen seconds
of the camera's attention. Depending on the fate of the Red Sox, his
proposal would be broadcast on the stadium screen when they
reached the bottom of the ninth inning. The scoreboard changed to
reflect the incoming run just as Billy returned to his seat. Realizing
the news, he threw up his arms and cheered ferociously.

Back at home, Barry persevered despite rising tension at the table.
Sadly, his guests denied him the attention he craved. Beth and Bunny
exchanged muffled barbs while Bella looked on with ennui. The others
gave into their hunger and began helping themselves to food. Finally, a
knock on the door usurped everyone's attention. Benita entered the
apartment, smug and triumphant. Beryl loitered in the doorway just
behind Benita.

"Beryl!" shouted Beth.

Bella stood from her seat, overcome with relief.

Everyone rushed at Beryl at once, surrounding her in an embrace.
Beth was the most overjoyed of the group since she'd silently assumed responsibility for her sister's disappearance. Accordingly, she
allowed herself to be moved and, when no one was listening, to admit that the apartment had been insufferably quiet in Beryl's absence.

In the excitement, Beryl forgot the tiny bird cupped in her hands
and, loosening her grip for a moment, allowed it to drop to the
floor.

"Mrs. Finch will be so happy," said Bella.

Beryl regarded Bella with sincere confusion.

But clarification was delayed as the front door opened once again.
Belinda entered, trailed by a dirty-looking boy, her soiled clothes
contrasting sharply with her neon green hair, which was the perfect
complement to her tattered white veil. The Barnacles stared at the
pair for several moments, as though to make absolutely sure they
were not hallucinating. Finally, accepting the reality of Belinda's

rebellious act, they focused their attention on the new member of the family. Formal introductions were delayed, however, due to more pressing needs. The boy crossed the room and began greedily filling a plate from the dining room table. Belinda simply stared at her family then, though it pained her to express such kindness, confessed, "Believe it or not, I actually missed you idiots."

This outpouring of affection was quickly cut short as Belinda greeted Benita and, much to her horror and outrage, recognized her green strapless dress.

"Take it off right now!" she screeched, lunging at Benita.

Barry reacted quickly, grabbing both girls by the elbows and guiding them toward their chairs. Finally, tiring of the chaos, he removed a fork from the table and banged it against the nearest glass. "If I could have your attention," he bellowed, "I've made my decision."

The announcement functioned as a ceasefire, muffling all bickering and fidgeting. Everyone settled into a chair, forgetting her grievances for the moment. Everyone, that is, except for Beryl, who crept to the television, muted the volume, and turned on the baseball game.

"So," said Belinda. "Who's the lucky girl?"

"Yes, do tell," said Beth.

Benita indulged in a boastful grin, certain victory was imminent.

Barry scanned the room leisurely.

The girls waited, silent and expectant. And for one brief, uncharacteristic moment, the Barnacle apartment was so quiet one could have heard a teenager sneaking out the window.

"Thanks to my hard work," Barry began, "you've led a comfortable life, wanting for nothing and blessed with every opportunity and privilege." He paused to ensure everyone was listening. "But, abundance itself has a cost. In the wild, excess turns to waste. In the home, it detracts from the hunger that molds greatness." Here, he paused to assess the impact of his last statement then continued, making the conscious choice to speak even more indirectly. "The civilized world is not wholly unlike the wilderness. The exact same forces are at work. Shortage breeds aspiration. Excess breeds complacence." Another pause during which he attempted in vain to dislodge something from his teeth. "But complacence," he went on, "is a terrible trait, one that will surely be left behind by evolution."

Finally, the girls registered alarm and glanced nervously at one another.

Barry sighed and increased his volume like a teacher forced to resort to a simpler explanation. "Recently, I'd seen this very trait in you, my own daughters. Which is why I took it upon myself to cultivate a new one in its place. I am your father and therefore entitled to take such liberties." Here, he took one last excruciating pause, during which he appeared to make some headway on the thing lodged in his teeth, first with exclusive use of his tongue and finally, his forefinger.

By this point, Barry's audience had realized the severity of his oration. The girls braced themselves for bad news. Beryl finally abandoned the game and took a seat at the table.

"As you know, it has always been my opinion that behavior can be altered by environment. And I have essentially spent a lifetime pursuing evidence. The contest was an experiment designed to test this theory, that man is merely a well-taught monkey, or, put another way, that nature is nurture's fool."

Barry looked quickly to the group but they refused him the smile he craved. Everyone was too consumed with anticipation.

"My hope was that you would find a way to immortalize the Barnacle name. Notoriety, however, has a short half-life. True renown can only come from hard work, ferocious perseverance. Yes, it's true that infamy has a certain longevity, but this was not the brand I had in mind when I conceived of the contest. So, it is with much regret that I must inform you of my findings. To my great disappointment, nature has won another round."

A collective gasp arose from the group. Each girl looked to another.

Barry smiled with satisfaction.

"So, what does this mean?" Beryl asked.

One last insufferable pause. "Due to dishonorable tactics," Barry announced, "every one of you is disqualified."

No one spoke for several moments.

"This is bull," Belinda said finally.

"Complete," said Beth.

Benita stomped her foot. "You said you didn't care how we did it, so long as we did."

Barry flinched imperceptibly, acknowledging the truth of this statement. But he dismissed Benita with a flick of the wrist. "There's nothing you can say to change my mind. You've done more to disgrace the Barnacle name than to perpetuate it." At this, he lifted a napkin to his mouth for the first time maybe ever, then stood from the table as though he'd finally tired of his companions.

Indeed, Barry had left out one critical detail when he issued his curious mandate; he never specified any rules or parameters, never mentioned the words "honor" or "merit." And yet, good intentions had paved Barry's path from the start. He was conflicted about the life he'd provided for his girls, seeing their privilege as both the fruit of his success and the foil to their perseverance. He had hatched the plan, as fathers do, with his daughters' best interest at heart, as a concerted ploy to motivate them, to instill a stronger work ethic. He could not be faulted, he felt, for this purely altruistic endeavor. The contest was the culmination of his lifework, an attempt to outsmart evolution.

But the girls were too enraged at the moment to appreciate their father's logic and instead reacted to Barry's announcement with a full-scale mutiny. As if on cue, the girls assumed position around their father, each one poised at the perfect angle to obstruct any attempts to flee their charge and to hurl pointed questions. Barry's response to this uprising was calm and disaffected. He ignored their questions like a criminal does the press after indictment, then inched slowly out of the dining room, forcibly removing his daughters from his path. Throughout, Bella observed the scene with a mixture of affection and boredom. But suddenly she took a new interest in the proceedings.

"Barry," she said, gazing pointedly. "We've all done shameful things. Barry," she said, this time louder, "we all have our secrets . . ."

Barry acknowledged Bella's threat without blinking or flinching. Even after spending ten years apart, the two still enjoyed telepathy. Accepting her tacit challenge, he surveyed the raucous crowd. But, as he did, his resolve weakened. All at once, he was stilled by the presence of his daughters. All at once, he was struck by the force of their youth, the enormity of their aspirations, the weight of their hope for his approval, the burden of all this yearning. Shaken, he took a long, deep breath and shuddered ever so slightly. Then, much to his own surprise, he accepted Bella's challenge. "Girls," he began, "there are things you can only learn by making mistakes." He managed a smile then furrowed his brow once again. "But oh, how I wish I could write them all down for you to keep in your pockets. It would spare you so much time." He paused. "So much heartbreak."

Bella moved quickly from her chair and took the seat next to Barry. She covered his hand with her own and nodded encouragingly.

"While you have spent the last seven days attempting to build your futures, I've been taking apart my past, remembering . . . reliving. Thirteen years ago," he said. He trailed off, unable to speak.

Bella smiled lovingly and patted Barry's hand.

"Thirteen years ago," Barry repeated, "I made a grievous error. At the time, I thought it was necessary. At the time, I thought it was helpful." Finally, emotion overwhelmed him. He closed his eyes and bowed his head.

For a moment, the room was completely still, devoid of movement and breathing.

"Latrell is my son," Barry blurted out. He forced himself to look at his daughters. "Latrell is my son," he whispered and then, simply, "I'm Latrell's father."

Indeed, Barry's recent trip to Coney Island was not the senseless detour it seemed, but rather an attempt to quell his conscience by finding its tormentor. Though he had failed to locate it in any of the likely places, he had eventually found his way to remorse like a blind man to music.

Beryl barely batted an eye in response to the latest announcement. She had played Beethoven's Fifth enough to expect a sudden turn in the last movement.

Bella, who had guarded the secret for years, smiled proudly at her ex-husband.

Beth and Belinda remained speechless.

Bunny squinted and muttered.

Benita recovered first to point out a pressing new technicality. "Wait," she gasped. "According to your rules, that means Latrell automatically wins the contest."

Benita's announcement sent a new ripple into the fractured crowd.

"I suppose you're right," Barry said, newly confounded. But he quickly regained composure. "Consider yourself lucky." He shrugged. "There's no faster way than inheriting money to ensure it gets squandered."

"It's no fair," Benita wailed. "I win for finding Beryl. What could be more important than bringing the family back together?"

"Benita, would you please shut up," said Belinda.

Once again, Benita lunged at Belinda, this time grazing her cheek with her nails and obstructing Beryl's view of the television in the process.

"All of you, please be quiet!" Beryl yelled, surpassing the crowd's volume. "They're tied in the top of the ninth. I need to see this."

Finally, Bella took command and issued the leveling blow. "Benita," she said, "you can't win the contest."

"Why not?" Benita stomped her foot.

"Because Barry's not your father."

At this, Bella cleared her throat to make her own confession. Soon after discovering Barry's tryst with Brandy, the governess, Bella was confronted with more unfortunate news when Mrs. Brown, Brandy's irate mother, called to inform her that her eighteen-year-old daughter was pregnant. Horrified, Bella begged Mrs. Brown to keep Barry's betrayal to herself, promising anything to keep the scandal a secret. The two women arrived at a settlement. Bella would send Brandy a monthly sum and Brandy would put the child up for adoption. Both women felt comfortable enough with this agreement; Mrs. Brown because it enabled Brandy to move past her mistake, Bella because it allowed her to bury her anger in monthly installments.

But, as every woman knows, resentment digs a shallow grave and it did not take long before Bella's reached the surface. It was not so much that she resented Barry for having the affair, but rather for the more egregious crime of conceiving a son with another woman. Sadly, this forced her to question herself instead of her husband. Tormented, she arrived at the perfect revenge. She signed up as a volunteer for the Bronx Boys Home and ostensibly inherited a family of forty sons. In fact, the choice to adopt Latrell was not the coincidence it seemed, but rather an elaborate plan, a calculated decision. As soon as she met Latrell, her motivation changed, her mission evolving from one of revenge to one of renewal.

But Bella was not without blame. She had made certain choices earlier in her marriage that contributed to its deterioration. After daughter number five, she began to question the underlying science. And after careful study of current research, she began to consider that the problem was not her x chromosome, but rather Barry's y shortage. In the hopes of solving this mystery, she took matters into her own hands. She conducted her own experiment: when attempting to conceive child number six, she made a "constant" of herself and a "variable" of her partner. To this day, neither Barry nor Benita's biological father knew the culprit. One could only infer from Benita's traits: x or y, Barnacle or Finch, Barry or Peter?

"So, I'm related to Billy?" asked Benita.

"I'm afraid so," Bella confirmed.

Benita's face registered fifteen different emotions. But she skipped the trembling that typically preceded tears and advanced to the bellowing part.

"Take heart, Benita," Barry chirped. A devilish look replaced his somber expression. "If you're very nice to Latrell, maybe he'll share his inheritance."

Yet again, the room devolved into abject chaos. Bunny rose quickly to quell the crowd. "Don't worry, Benita," she said, "Latrell won't get your money. When your father and I got married, we signed an iron-clad prenup. Most of the contract is a blur. My lawyers just told me where to sign. But there's one clause in particular I remember: If Barry cheats on me at any time, I'm entitled to every penny."

Guests and family barely flinched, now completely immune to surprise.

"Oh my God," Beryl gasped.

"I don't believe it," Beth seconded.

"No," Beryl said. She pointed at the television. "In the box . . . next to the announcers." She grinned. "Latrell's at Yankee Stadium."

Five miles north, the stadium boasted its own particular brand of madness as the game headed into the ninth inning with the underdog in the lead. With the Red Sox a staggering four runs ahead, Blaine and Billy stared at their futures: Blaine, a complete and total nervous wreck, intermittently switching his gaze from the scoreboard to the dugout and Billy, several rows higher, indulging in a preemptive sigh of relief, stretching his arms above his head and extending his feet. As the ninth inning commenced, Blaine and Billy exchanged their usual telepathy. But though their prayers were exactly the same, their fears were very different. Billy was more determined than ever to propose to Bridget and, regretting the bet he'd made, frantically cheered for the Sox. Blaine, however, due to Barry's disconcerting confession, now second-guessed his plans to propose and, for the first time in thirty years, prayed for the Yanks to lose.

Every species of Red Sox pitcher boasted a unique specialty, adding its own specific hierarchy to the pecking order of the stadium. The starting pitcher launched the game, pitching the first hundred-odd throws with the same obvious intent, to give up a couple of hits and runs with the expectation that the closer would prevent further scoring. The middle-reliever entered the game in the fifth or the sixth inning with the unglamorous goal of continuing the starter's efforts and maintaining the status quo. The closer occupied the highest position on the totem pole. He arrived on the scene for one reason alone, to lead his team to victory. Bred for this precise purpose, the closer had one mission alone, to throw the lights out of the ball for one straight inning and then go home. Closers were always colorful types, and often intimidating figures. The rock stars of baseball, they were widely known for their tempers and reckless behavior. Cox had a unique advantage even among this wild species, having mastered a crushing fastball, a slider, a curve, a splitter, and a knuckle ball so lethal that it had earned him the nickname "Cox the Killer."

Suddenly, the loudspeaker crackled and buzzed, demanding everyone's attention. The entire stadium stood in an ovation as Johnson strode from the dugout to take his place at home plate. At six foot five, he didn't appear to walk like most human beings, but seemed to sail just above the grass like some sort of futuristic machine propelled by hydrogen. Due to his 20/10 eyesight, Johnson boasted another decisive asset. It was said that he could read the label on the ball as it left the pitcher's hand. At once a natural and obsessive student of the game, he was rumored to require his lovers to share the bed with his bat. Even from eighty feet above, one could tell how handsome he was. As he walked, he tipped his hat to the crowd and puffed his chest proudly, inviting hollers from every Sox fan from New York to Boston.

Blaine noted Tug's confident entrance with mounting concern and did his best to diffuse it from his seat with an outpouring of negative energy. "Tug's really on the ropes," he said.

"No he's not," Bell snapped. "Last season, he hit three-twenty with a hundred thirty RBIs and forty home runs."

"Watch it," said Blaine. "Hubris is the Yankees' fatal flaw. Look what happened last year. They can't afford to get overconfident."

Bell turned to Blaine and regarded him strangely, confused by his ambivalence. In the thirty years she'd known him, she'd never heard him utter even the most minor critique of his team. "Still," she said, "let's not forget the legendary series-winning run when Johnson hit Cox's tenth pitch out of the park with a full count on his shoulders."

"Please," Blaine scoffed. He racked his brain for a suitable rebuttal. The hypocrisy of his next comment appalled even him. "What happened that year was a total fluke. A once-in-a-lifetime event."

On the field, Johnson adjusted his cap, causing more wild applause in the crowd.

"What do you think the odds are?" Bell asked.

"Slim to none," Blaine said.

At this same moment, Cox sidled up to his place on the pitcher's mound, sending a second shock through the stadium, turning excitement to mayhem. Up in the bleachers, Billy and Bridget strained to get a better view of Cox, both praying for different teams to win but, unbeknownst to Bridget, rooting for the same outcome.

Down on the field, Cox accepted Johnson's challenge, striking a formidable pose, making up for what he lacked in height in his ample girth. He leered at the crowd through his facial hair as he walked to the mound. His compact, muscular frame gave him a heft that Johnson lacked, endowing him with the same density and threat as a military tank. Cox's signature tactics were well known throughout the league, his windmill windup designed as much to instill fear in the batter as to amplify the speed of his pitch.

"Cox, don't let me down!" Billy shouted, standing from his seat.

Bridget bristled at the noise. "Billy, if you're going to cheer that loud, could you please try not to do it so close to my ear?"

But Billy was now lost to Bridget, completely possessed by the game. "With forty-five consecutive saves," he chanted by way of comforting himself, "Cox pitched eighty scoreless innings last year. No one would dispute he's got the fastest fastball in baseball."

Billy fumbled for his pulse as he squinted at the scoreboard. He dared not take a breath of relief. As the game headed into the bottom of the ninth, the Yanks were down by four runs.

Suddenly, the stadium went silent. All noise faded into a point. Johnson took his stance at the plate. Cox remained frozen for several moments, relishing the charge in the air. Then, without further fanfare, Cox commenced his windmill windup, emitting, with each rotation of his arm, an even louder grunt. But this sound was soon overpowered by something even more powerful, as Cox's hurtling, shoulder-high curve ball skimmed Johnson's kneecaps and seemed to approach a sonic boom.

"Low and outside. Ball one," yelled the announcer.

The stadium erupted.

Billy raised his arm and pumped his fist. "All right, here we go, Sox."

"Don't get too worked up," said Bridget. "It's not over yet. It could always happen again. Full count and then . . . pow."

"No, don't say it!" Billy yelled, grabbing Bridget's shoulders forcefully.

Bridget shoved Billy away, indignant. "God, what's gotten into you?" she sniffed. "It's just a game, Billy."

Humbled, Billy loosened his grasp and shrugged an apology. "Sorry," he said, then by way of explanation, "I've got a lot riding on it."

The crowd's volume swelled and receded as the scoreboard switched to reflect the first ball. Gradually, all attention drew back to the field. Johnson stepped coolly to the plate while Cox took his sweet time getting into position.

"Cox in the stretch," said the announcer.

Pure silence for another moment. Cox repeated his bizarre windup and released the ball with celestial speed, causing Johnson to swing and miss so completely that he checked his bat for defects.

"Strike one."

The stadium exploded in a million angry sounds, a perfectly awful symphony of hollers, hoots, and yelps.

Down by the field, Blaine rejoiced in this progress for the Sox. Though he was now barely breathing, he turned to Bell with renewed hope. "There we go. Keep it up," he cheered. "That's what I'm talking about."

Up in the bleachers, Billy closed his eyes and muttered a heartfelt prayer. But he made this appeal in vain; when he opened his eyes, the ball was halfway across the field, whizzing past Johnson's nose.

"Ball two," yelled the announcer.

The audience booed and hissed.

Cox took advantage of the noise and tried a follow-up punch, sending a ball, at lightning speed, into Johnson's stomach.

"Ball three," yelled the announcer.

Finally, the crowd lost control, conscious of the possibility of a repeat performance. Each section made a dissonant sound like an orchestra of confused musicians.

"And so Johnson works the count full," Bell taunted, mimicking a sportscaster.

Overwhelmed by mixed emotions, Blaine could feel his heart beat through his chest. And, just sixty feet away, Billy experienced the very same sensation. Yet again, the two were cursed with matching meditations. Perhaps nurture gets the last laugh, Blaine decided. Not so fast, Billy thought. Slow and steady wins the race.

What followed was a series of pitches so bizarre no psychic could have made the prediction. The fourth and final movement of the ninth inning ended with a hair-raising, if slightly expected eleventh-hour modulation. Unfortunately, the rest of the Barnacle family was stuck in traffic on the FDR Drive so they missed the major-to-minor shift and the rollicking trumpets of the triumphant finale. But they managed to catch the cab radio's sportscast and they were, of course, equipped with Beryl's nearly 99 percent accurate crystal ball.

"Cox in the stretch," the announcer yelled over the cab radio. "He fires. It breaks. Johnson can't get a piece of it. Cox in the stretch. He fires. It flies. Johnson hits it down the left field line. It curves, but he fouls! Cox in the stretch. He fires. Johnson hits it way out to the right. That ball looked like it had legs, but the wind had its way with it. Foul! Now, Johnson calls for time. He paces and smiles at the crowd. Cox stares him down. Johnson takes his time coming back to the box. The home plate umpire gives a warning. He nods, apologizes. Cox in the stretch. He fires. It pops. And Johnson . . . no, it can't be. Lightning, my friends, just struck twice as Johnson hits his first grand slam of the season. My friends, this one's out of the park."

By the time the cab reached Yankee Stadium, fans were already streaming out. But, ever unflappable, the Barnacle family fought the tide of the crowd, converging on the baseball field like cops on a drug bust. Newly accredited by the win, Beryl led the group across the field, climbing the stairs to the announcer's box, and ending at the organist's booth. As predicted, Latrell sat on the bench, slumped over the organ, exhausted from his time on the lam and still reeling from another failed attempt. And yet, his search had paid off in one unexpected way. The organist's booth boasted the best view of the park and the most immediate jolt of the game's exhilaration. Luckily, Latrell's odyssey had finally come to an end. Barry swallowed hard and looked him in the eye. "Latrell, I'm your father," he said.

And so it was that the Yankees won their opening game against the Red Sox with Johnson making another historical comeback, sending in all three bases off a ball and dancing into home plate. Of course, this had another equally momentous implication. Blaine had technically won his bet with Billy despite the fact that, for the first time in his life, he badly wanted to lose. Still, he felt he had no choice but accept the fate he'd chosen. He inhaled deeply as though taking his last breath, knelt down on the stadium floor, and prepared to end his free life.

"Bell, will you marry me?" he asked.

Bell said nothing for a moment, just stared at Blaine curiously. Suddenly, she was graced with clarity and, seeing through Blaine's confusing facade, she realized she would rather be alone than settle for him. "No," she answered.

"No?" asked Blaine.

"No," Bell repeated.

And with that, Bell kissed Blaine on the cheek and hurried out of the stadium, determined to make good on a promise to spend an afternoon at the Museum of Natural History in the company of more benevolent creatures.

Much higher up, evolution itself orchestrated the symphony's coda as Billy proposed to Bridget for the third time, now without having to utter a single word. Indeed, like all great lovers, the two were blessed with the telepathy of twins. As a result, Bridget understood Billy's intent before he said it and simply smiled and nodded. For the next half hour, the two old friends kissed as though they'd just won the World Series, stopping only occasionally to laugh and reminisce.

A baseball stadium, during a game, is a testament to man's potential. But when a stadium is completely empty, it produces the strangest sensation. The space holds too much hope and yearning for one man alone, much like an empty concert hall without any musicians. Now, removed from the sounds of the game, Billy and Bridget adjusted to the quiet. All at once, they felt the urge to kneel. The stadium had become a cathedral. And somewhere, higher even than the nosebleeds, nature and nurture shook hands.

And so it seemed that Barry's favorite sport was not a race, but rather a ham-handed fistfight. Luckily, his daughters were able to perceive such subtleties. For the girls, in addition to all their attributes, were blessed with the giddy omniscience of youth, so they knew that if you look from high up enough, you can see the city with dizzying perspective and this is precisely when its vast gray grid reveals a glorious fractal of colors which, if you squint, seems to be a huge crowd, huddled, elbow to sweaty elbow, tiny feet crushing other tiny feet, but if you let your eyes relax, refines to reveal that New York is truly an arc, swarming with people estranged from their pair, each one fighting his way across the city, looking for her lost twin.